The
CAPTAIN'S
DAUGHTER

The
CAPTAIN'S
DAUGHTER

JENNIFER DELAMERE

BETHANYHOUSE

a division of Baker Publishing Group
Minneapolis, Minnesota

Published by Bethany House Publishers
11400 Hampshire Avenue South
Bloomington, Minnesota 55438
www.bethanyhouse.com

Bethany House Publishers is a division of
Baker Publishing Group, Grand Rapids, Michigan

Printed in the United States of America

Library of Congress Cataloging-in-Publication Data
Names: Delamere, Jennifer, author.
Title: The captain's daughter / Jennifer Delamere.
Description: Minneapolis, Minnesota : Bethany House, a division of Baker
    Publishing Group, [2017] | Series: London beginnings
Identifiers: LCCN 2016049172| ISBN 9780764230387 (cloth) | ISBN
    9780764219207 (trade paper)
Subjects: | GSAFD: Love stories. | Christian fiction.
Classification: LCC PS3604.E4225 C37 2017 | DDC 813/.6—dc23
LC record available at https://lccn.loc.gov/2016049172

Scripture quotations are from the King James Version of the Bible.

This is a work of fiction. Names, characters, incidents, and dialogues are products
of the author's imagination and are not to be construed as real. Any resemblance
to actual persons or events, living or dead, is entirely coincidental.

Cover design by Koechel Peterson & Associates, Inc., Minneapolis, Minnesota

Author is represented by the BookEnds Literary Agency

17 18 19 20 21 22 23   7 6 5 4 3 2 1

For Elaine Luddy Klonicki,
with heartfelt thanks
for your insight and friendship

"A man's heart deviseth his way: but the Lord directeth his steps."

—PROVERBS 16:9

"His compassions fail not. They are new every morning: great is thy faithfulness."

—LAMENTATIONS 3:22–23

Prologue

DARTMOOR COAST, ENGLAND, 1873

I'M NOT SURPRISED to find you here," Rosalyn Bernay said, wrapping an arm around her sister's waist.

Cara leaned into her, acknowledging the gesture, but her eyes never stopped scanning the crashing waves on the rocky coastline beneath them. The wind whipped at their dresses and at Cara's bonnet, which was dangling, as usual, down her back. After a few moments Cara murmured, "Will you sing to me?"

Rosalyn didn't have to ask which song. Lately Cara had taken to requesting the lullaby their mother used to sing to them. Now, when they were on the verge of parting, Rosalyn couldn't fault her sister for it. She began to sing, soft and low. Somehow it didn't seem strange to be singing a lullaby on a bright afternoon. They had always taken comfort in it.

The breeze gently carried away the final notes as Rosalyn reached the end of the last verse. Cara remained silent but stayed close. Behind them, they could hear the shouts of a hundred other girls—fellow residents of George Müller's orphanage—playing on the wide meadow that led down to the cliffs.

"Penny for your thoughts," Rosalyn prompted, although she could well guess what was on her baby sister's mind. Cara was thirteen—at the brink of womanhood—but to Rosalyn, she would always be the curly-headed toddler who clung to her so relentlessly the day the three sisters had been brought to the orphanage.

Cara gave a long sigh. "How I will miss hearing that song when you go away." She tore her gaze from the sea, her wide, blue eyes searching Rosalyn's face. "I wish you weren't leaving. Not just yet."

Rosalyn tried to give her a reassuring smile. "I'm seventeen now. It's time for me to make my own way in the world. The Müllers are kind and generous, but not even they can support us forever."

Cara took Rosalyn's hand in an impulsive gesture. "Can I come with you, then?"

Rosalyn laughed. "I don't think Mrs. Williams will be pleased if her new maid arrives with a young sister in tow."

"But I could work too. I already know how to wash, iron, and clean. Besides, lots of girls go into service at my age."

With her free hand, Rosalyn tucked a golden curl behind Cara's ear. "Somehow, I don't think this is about your keenness to become a housemaid."

Cara's grip tightened. "I just hate that we'll be broken up. After all, we promised Mama—"

"I'm sure Mama knew that one day we would grow up and begin separate lives. Besides, aren't you forgetting about Julia? Are you so willing to abandon her?"

Cara frowned. "Jules has no problem looking after herself. And once you're gone, she's bound to take on the role of *eldest* and start ordering me around." Her face scrunched tighter. "More than she does already."

"Don't make that face!" Rosalyn admonished. "You'll get wrinkles."

Cara opened her mouth to reply but was cut off by the sound of their sister's voice calling out, "Caroline and Rosalyn Bernay! What are you doing so close to the cliff?"

"You see?" Cara said pointedly. "It's already started."

Julia approached them with long, purposeful strides, looking every inch a school matron. There was no bonnet falling down her back—it was firmly on her head, her dark brown hair neatly in place under it. "You know Mrs. McHugh told us to keep away from the cliffs," she said as soon as she reached them. "It's dangerous here. You could get hurt." Her dark eyes flashed as she pointed an accusing finger at Cara. "Especially you, with your penchant for daydreaming. You're likely to fall right over the edge."

"I was not aware that daydreaming was a sin," Cara returned with a sniff. "As opposed to, say, anger or hubris."

"Please don't fight today," Rosalyn pleaded, taking both girls by the arm. "It's our last day together. Let's enjoy it." She led them over to a bench that, while far enough from the precipitous drop to appease Julia, still had a stunning view of the wide ocean stretching toward a hazy horizon.

The three of them settled on the bench with Rosalyn in the middle. She was always in the middle, Rosalyn reflected. It seemed her daily task to act as peacemaker between the impulsive Cara, whose head was indeed always in the clouds, and Julia, who found comfort in rules, routine, and clearly defined boundaries. Rosalyn loved them both *because* of their unique temperaments rather than in spite of them. The only thing that troubled her was their tendency to bait one another. Once she was gone, the two of them would have to learn to resolve their differences.

The silence between them stretched although the air was alive with sound. A stiff breeze rustled the grass and played along the hems of their skirts. Below them the waves crashed, and behind them the joyful screeches of the younger children being "caught" as they played tag were as shrill as the sea gulls crying overhead.

Cara's gaze had returned to the sea.

"You can watch all day, but it won't help." Julia's voice was flat and unyielding. "He's not coming back."

Pain flickered across Cara's features. "You don't know that for sure."

"He's gone, Cara! Just like our mother. You need to accept that."

Both girls stiffened as they turned to face one another, tempers rising.

"There's no point arguing over it," Rosalyn interposed hastily. "Cara wishes to believe differently than you, Julia. And so long as we don't know exactly what happened to Papa, I'm not going to fault her for it."

Julia's face twisted in a frown, but for once she said nothing.

"Nor do I think *you* should continue to hold these unyielding explanations for Papa's disappearance," Rosalyn went on. "Anything might have happened. His ship might have sunk, or he might have succumbed to some tropical disease once he reached the West Indies."

Cara shook her head impatiently. "You think he's dead, and Julia thinks he's abandoned us. Why am I the only one who believes he's still alive?"

"Because your brain can store nothing but nonsense," Julia replied.

"None of us knows for sure what happened!" Rosalyn broke in before Cara could retort. "But here's one thing I do know: We cannot keep dwelling on the past. We must look ahead. Remember Mr. Müller's admonition that God will always meet our needs."

"But that's just it!" Cara jumped on Rosalyn's words. "Don't you see? I *need* to know what happened to Papa!" She stood up, lifting her face toward the cloudless sky as she raised her arms heavenward in a beseeching gesture. "I need to know!" She turned back to her sisters, her eyes bright with tears. "Sometimes I feel like this uncertainty is crushing my heart."

Her expression was so forlorn that she looked exactly as she had all those years ago when the three of them had stared helplessly at the bed where their mother lay dying. That day was sealed in Rosalyn's memory forever.

Even Julia appeared moved by this display of sorrow. She stood up and threw her arms around Cara, squeezing her tightly. "Don't cry," she soothed, stroking Cara's hair. "I'm sorry if I was too harsh. I forget sometimes how much this means to you."

Cara said nothing, but she made no move to pull away. Her breathing steadied, and some of the tension seemed to leave her as she remained in Julia's arms.

After a moment, Julia murmured, "It says in Psalms that when we commit our ways unto the Lord, he will grant us the desires of our heart."

Disengaging herself from Julia's hold, Cara straightened and wiped her eyes. "I should have known you'd quote the Bible at me." But her voice was more teasing than disparaging, and her lips wavered as she attempted a smile. "However, so long as you pick verses like that, I suppose I don't mind."

Julia gave a little smirk, and the two girls hugged each other again. Rosalyn wiped away her own tears as she watched them comforting one another. They would be just fine, the two of them. On some level they understood that each had something vital to impart to the other—something each would be incomplete without.

And Rosalyn? What did she have?

At the moment, she wished only for strength to face the unknown challenges that awaited her.

Reaching into the pocket of her frock, she pulled out the fine gold watch that had been a gift from their father to their mother. That, along with a faded photograph, were the only mementos they had of him. It seemed fitting, she thought, as she fingered the fine lettering: *To Marie. Oceans can never separate us. Love always, Paul.* They had marked eight years' worth of hours with this watch. Eight years since their mother had died and they had come to Bristol. And, she thought with a touch of bitterness, oceans *had* separated them.

But she was determined not to allow melancholy thoughts to dwell in her soul. She was beginning a new chapter in her life. Wherever she went, she knew that the memories of her parents and the love she shared with her sisters would remain as tangible to her as the watch in her hand.

CHAPTER

1

Six Years Later
October 1879

ROSALYN CROUCHED as low as her sturdy walking gown would allow, hiding behind the hedgerow. When she'd left the orphanage to begin her life as an adult, she'd anticipated some hard times. But never could she have imagined herself in the predicament she faced now.

She held her breath, although she knew it was impossible for him to hear her. The thunder of his approaching carriage, its wheels rattling through the ruts frozen into the road after a week of rain followed by frost, was deafening.

No, it was the sight of her that would bring the carriage to a stop. What would happen if he took her back to Russet Hall to face wrongful accusations of theft—or worse, what she would have to do to buy his silence—she could not allow herself to imagine. Not if she wanted to keep her courage.

Overhead a crow screamed. Startling at the sound, she nearly fell over into the prickly hedgerow. Worried that any nearby sound would draw attention in her direction, she crouched even lower. The crow flew away, the noise of its call replaced by the blood rushing to her ears as her heart rate increased with every turn of those swiftly approaching carriage wheels.

In seconds the carriage would pass her hiding spot. Shivering from cold and fear, Rosalyn reminded herself that despite how it might look, she now had an advantage of sorts. Mr. Huffman had assumed she was headed for Bainshaw, which had the closest and busiest railway station. However, once his carriage had passed out of sight, she could backtrack to the crossroads and head south toward Linden.

She'd fled the house in the dark gloom just before dawn. It had taken her four hours to reach this point, carrying all she owned in a carpetbag that had grown heavier with each step she'd taken. She'd counted on putting in a good distance before she was discovered missing, thinking no one would look for her before breakfast, but it appeared she'd miscalculated.

With unrelenting speed, the carriage approached. The pounding of hooves and the rattle of the wheels drowned out every other sound. Somehow Rosalyn was able to scrunch down even lower, squeezing her eyes shut—as though by some childish logic he would not see her if she couldn't see him.

The carriage rolled past, not even slowing down. Rosalyn cried out with relief, then clapped a hand over her mouth. She stayed crouched behind the hedgerow for several long, agonizing minutes, listening as the sounds of the carriage gradually receded.

Again she closed her eyes, this time because her heart was flooded with thanksgiving that Mr. Huffman had caught up with her here, when she had only to backtrack a quarter mile or so. In Linden the trains were less frequent, but she decided to take the first one, wherever it led. Once she had broken free of Mr.

Huffman's grasp, she could work her way back to Bristol and the loving safety of her sister Julia, who now worked as a nurse and lived in a respectable boardinghouse.

Julia would know what to do. Julia *always* knew what to do. When they were children, this character trait had manifested time and again as irritating bossiness. But now that they were adults, Rosalyn was glad for her sister's unwavering faith and her uncanny ability to find an answer to even the thorniest problems. And Rosalyn could not think of a worse problem than this.

After a last, wary look in both directions, Rosalyn stood and stretched. One large hurdle seemed to be overcome. But she knew this ordeal was far from over. It had only just begun.

No, that wasn't true, she thought as she took hold of her carpetbag's well-worn handle and began to walk back in the direction she'd come. It had begun the moment her employer, Mrs. Williams, allowed herself to be courted by Mr. Huffman. Still reasonably young at forty, she had fallen in love the moment she'd met the self-confident man who'd made his own fortune in imports and exports. She'd been blind to the darker aspects of his brash nature—things that had become glaringly apparent to everyone else in the household from the day he'd come to live at Russet Hall.

A gentle breeze blew over Rosalyn's face, and the sun eked out a hint of warmth. With no traffic on the roads, the countryside was peaceful again. Birds flew and swooped with gentle calls. Several feet from the road's edge, the dry brown grass rustled as some creature—probably a field mouse—scurried to an unknown destination.

The sun was higher now, although still stingy with its warmth. Even so, Rosalyn found herself wiping sweat from her brow—whether from the exertion of walking or as a reaction to the fear

15

she'd experienced, she did not know. She only knew that, like the mouse, she was headed for destinations unknown. Unlike the mouse, it was probably going to take a miracle or two to get her there.

⚜

Nate Moran jumped nimbly from the open carriage as the driver brought the horses to a stop at the station yard in Winchester. He paused to slap road dust from his red army coat as the other man in the carriage, Colonel Gwynn, stepped down after him. The greying head of Nate's former commander once seemed to contradict his fit and vigorous body, but it was clear the colonel was beginning to feel his age. He stifled a groan as his feet hit the ground and he straightened, perhaps a tad slowly, to his usual ramrod-stiff posture.

Nate eyed him with concern. "Are you really returning to India with the regiment in the spring, sir?"

His question only caused the old colonel to stand even straighter. "Don't you worry. I'm fit as a fiddle. The damp weather gets to my bones, that's all. It will be good to get back to India." He gave Nate a slap on the back. "It will be good to have you with us, too."

Nate nodded, appreciating this vote of confidence. He'd spent the past year in the reserves after an injury had coincided with the end of his seven-year enlistment. But now he was determined to rejoin his regiment and return with them to India. Today he'd taken a real step toward his goal: The colonel had promised to spend a day observing Nate in his reserve company's winter drills at Aldershot in three months' time, shortly after the new year. Nate needed only to prove that his hand had regained the dexterity needed to qualify him for active duty.

Discreetly, he flexed the muscles of his right hand. It was still stiff at times, and certain movements could cause pain. But Nate

16

was not going to allow these facts to deter him. "I appreciate all you've done for me, sir."

The colonel waved away his thanks. "Purely self-serving. I haven't been able to find a supply sergeant worth his salt since you left."

Nate smiled, knowing this gruff remark was in fact high praise.

"There is one more thing, I believe, that we might need to discuss before you go," the colonel said.

Nate looked at him expectantly. "Yes, sir?"

"Since you've already served a term of seven years, and now that you have—quite rightly—risen to the rank of a non-commissioned officer . . ."

His voice drifted off. Nate could not remember seeing the colonel hesitate like this before.

Gwynn cleared his throat. "In the army, as you know, we are not entirely unaware of matters of the heart, such as they might affect our men."

Nate's gut clenched. Now he knew where this was going.

"There was, I believe, mention of a sweetheart? If you wish to marry and bring your bride with you to India, I will not refuse my permission."

He paused, looking to Nate for a response. Most likely he expected gratitude. Having his commander's permission meant that Nate could be married "on the strength." The army would provide services for his wife and extra pay for him to support her. It was a privilege not granted to everyone. Nate knew, however, that the colonel would not be offering it to him if he knew the truth about how Nate's former "sweetheart" had already affected the regiment.

Nate set his face to an impassive mask, hiding the anger that still filled him at the thought of her. He said evenly, "I thank you, sir, but there is no one." Seeing the colonel's eyebrows lift in surprise, Nate amended, "What I mean to say is, there is no one *now*."

Gwynn's lined face softened with sympathy. "Was there some calamity—?"

"Nothing like that, sir."

No, the woman in question was alive and well. It was Nate's dream of a future with her that was dead.

Understanding dawned in the older man's eyes. "The ladies can be fickle. But you are young, and there will be time enough for those things. May I offer you a word of advice?"

"Sir?"

"As you are unencumbered, use this opportunity to focus on your career. Given the speed with which you advanced to sergeant, and given your leadership capabilities and the way the other men look up to you . . ." He seemed to be pausing for effect. Nate was trying to follow the man's line of thought, but he was still wrapped up in thoughts of *her*. "Not many enlisted men obtain commissions, but I believe you can join that group of honored few. Once we are established in India again, I think it not unlikely that the rank of second lieutenant might be offered to you."

For a man from the rank and file to become an officer was a rare thing indeed. When Nate had first enlisted, he'd had just such a lofty goal in mind. Things had changed quite a bit since those optimistic early days.

Nate shook his head. "With all due respect, sir, I don't see how you can consider me fit for such an honor."

"Because of what happened in Peshawar? Nonsense. All men make mistakes. It's what they do afterward that shows their true mettle. You fought back the attackers and saved Sergeant Danvers' life. Those are actions befitting an officer."

Gwynn's assessment of the incident—which became the army's official record—placed far more emphasis on Nate's heroism than on his mistakes. Given Nate's good record and the army's desperate need for men, this decision was understandable. The colonel knew that while Nate had been on guard duty that night, he'd missed critical signs of an enemy attack. But he didn't know that Nate's lapse of attention had been caused by his distress over being jilted via a letter. Fortunately for Nate, the colonel hadn't pressed for details. It had been easier to ascribe the error to the usual causes: fatigue or boredom.

But Nate knew the truth, even if he'd not admitted it to anyone. In his own estimation, he had a long way to go to be worthy of a commission. "Thank you for your good opinion of me, sir."

The sharp old colonel easily recognized Nate's equivocation. "Don't shrug off the idea so quickly," he advised. "Give it more thought. You may see things differently in time. You're a conscientious and loyal soldier, just as your father and grandfather were before you. Think of the honor you would do to their memory, as well as the higher service you could extend to your queen and country."

His commander was perceptive. He knew his reference to the Moran family history would have a special appeal. Nate thought of his grandfather, who had fought Napoleon's army as a mere lad of sixteen. Nate's father, too, had been a soldier, serving honorably in the Crimea. Both men would have been proud to see Nate's rise to a commission. That was something they'd never done, even though each had received honors for bravery. When Nate was a young recruit, he dreamed of becoming an officer. But that was before he learned for himself all the things about life in the army that his father and grandfather had never told him.

Nevertheless, Nate was honor-bound to return and prove himself a worthy soldier. He gave the colonel a curt nod. It was the best he could do.

"Very good. I will say no more for the present."

19

A train whistle sounded in the distance, signaling the approach of Nate's train.

Gwynn extended a hand. "Good-bye, Moran. We'll see you in January."

The colonel's strong handshake sent a burst of pain up Nate's arm. But Nate held the grip. *The hand is healing,* he told himself. *It's nearly there.*

Ten minutes later, Nate leaned back in his seat as the train pulled out of the station. He let out a tired sigh as he watched the landscape speed by. The day had already been full, but Nate's work wasn't over yet. He'd risen well before dawn in order to complete the most vital of his duties at Jamieson's stable, make this trip, and still be back in London by nightfall. Working at the ostler's—a stable of horses for hire—was enough to fill a man's day, but now Nate was working nights, too. He'd taken his brother's job backstage at a theater to hold the position until his brother's broken leg healed. He could not afford to be late. Not with his family depending on him.

It had been good to see his family again after nearly seven years. Nate was glad, too, that he'd been here to help in their hour of need. Even so, he ached to be away again. It was time to finish what he'd begun in the army and to right the mistakes he'd made.

It was time to leave London, too. He supposed he shouldn't be surprised that Ada chose to marry a prosperous merchant instead of facing an uncertain future with a mere soldier. That didn't mean he wanted to spend week after week seeing her happily ensconced on the arm of another man. Nor could he forgive her for the manner in which she had jilted him, and for her letter's disastrous consequences. She had come through the experience unscathed, but Nate's life would never be the same.

He crossed his arms and tried to settle into the most comfortable position he could find. The train ride would give him time for a nap, and he knew he'd better take it if he wanted to keep his wits about him tonight. The last thing he needed was to injure himself because he'd wasted good sleep in agitation over the past. Nate was pretty sure he'd get more sleep if—no, *when*—he returned to the army.

⁓⧫⁓

The town clock was tolling four when Rosalyn walked into Linden. She sent furtive glances toward the people around her as she made her way up the main street to the railway station. She had not been a frequent visitor to this town, so she had no real reason to worry she'd be recognized. Even so, every one of her senses remained on high alert.

The railway station was busy. Sidestepping a young boy trying unsuccessfully to lead a very large dog, Rosalyn made her way to the ticket booth. The clerk sitting behind the iron grill was an older gentleman. His gaze skimmed past her, perhaps looking for her male escort. Realizing she was alone, his eyes returned to settle on her. "Where to, miss?"

"When is the next train to Bristol?"

He checked the schedule on the wall next to him. "Seven o'clock."

Rosalyn looked toward the station gate as she considered the potential hazards of waiting here for three hours. Down the road she saw a puff of dust rising. There was no reason to suppose it was Mr. Huffman, of course, and yet she kept staring, straining her eyes as she waited for the vehicle to crest the rise.

Moments later, Mr. Huffman's carriage came into view. She also—thankfully—heard the whistle of an approaching train.

"What train is that?" she asked the clerk.

He frowned. "You don't want that one if you're going north. It's going south—bound for London."

21

"I'll take it," she said, pulling money from her reticule.

This would work. It *had* to work. Surely she had not gone through all this for nothing.

She took the ticket and turned away from the booth. As she set off for the crowded platform, Rosalyn kept her back to the station entrance. She sidled up to a group of two men and three women standing together, chatting excitedly about the things they were going to see when they got to London. Rosalyn did her best to blend in, to appear as though she were traveling with them.

The train came to a stop, its brakes squealing, smoke and steam pouring out in all directions.

"Miss Bernay! MISS BERNAY!" The imperious voice of her former employer carried across the crowded platform. Rosalyn did not turn, hoping he would think himself mistaken.

"MISS BERNAY! Come here!"

Why was he not advancing toward her? She risked a glance in his direction. He had been stopped by a burly gate attendant. Mr. Huffman gestured, pointing at her, but the guard held his ground. He directed Mr. Huffman toward the ticket counter, clearly telling him he must buy his own ticket before he could access the platform.

Rosalyn waited impatiently as a large family with several toddlers and seemingly endless baskets and bundles exited the railway car before she could enter it. When the carriage door was clear, Rosalyn ran up the two steps and inside.

She took a seat by a window facing the train platform, unable to look away. Surely Mr. Huffman would not attempt to drag her off the train? Did he have the authority to do so? Would anyone here listen to him?

She waited anxiously as seconds ticked away. It seemed as though time itself was suspended, the large hand on the station clock refusing to move. Yet inexplicably, he did not reappear at the gate. Had he given up that easily?

In a moment, she was able to guess the reason for his delay. An elderly couple, moving very slowly, hobbled through the gate. Perhaps they'd been at the ticket counter, holding up Mr. Huffman's ability to buy a ticket. The train whistle blew. It was about to leave. Rosalyn's heart leapt with joy at the sound.

The platform guard hurried forward to help the elderly couple onto the train, closing the door sharply behind them just as the train began to pull forward. Rosalyn craned her neck as the train gathered speed to keep the platform in view for as long as she could. She had just enough time to see a frustrated Mr. Huffman race onto the platform before the train left him and the station far behind.

As the countryside became a blur, Rosalyn pulled her gaze away and looked down, surprised to see that her hands were trembling. She took several slow, deep breaths, trying to get her heart rate and her breathing back to normal. After hours of walking a knife's edge, relief washed through her. For better or worse, she was on her way to London.

CHAPTER

2

Rosalyn woke from a dreamy doze. She noticed her
fellow passengers collecting their things and ladies re-
adjusting their hats. She had no idea how they knew the
train was approaching London. The windows might just as well
have been made of lead, for all the view they afforded. Dense fog
blocked out the last of the waning sunlight.

But then the high brick walls of Paddington station rose up
out of the gloom, and soon the train squealed to a stop. Rosalyn
stood and stretched. Taking hold of her carpetbag, she followed
the other passengers off the railway carriage. Once on the platform, she tried to get her bearings—it was hard to do, given the
murky light and the bustle of people all around her.

"Would you be needin' help, miss?"

Rosalyn turned at the sound of a man's voice, expecting to see
one of the porters. Instead, she saw a lean man in faded corduroy
trousers and a heavily patched coat, a worn cloth cap pushed
back on his head. He must have been around thirty years of age.

His smile was pleasant enough, although one of his eyeteeth was badly chipped.

Surprised at being addressed by a stranger but not wanting to turn away help, she replied, "I'm looking for the ticket booth."

"But you've just arrived!" He moved closer. "Where else would ye be needin' to go?"

The man spoke with a soft lilt that Rosalyn recognized as Irish. Although there was nothing overtly threatening about him, his nearness made her uncomfortable. He smelled of hair tonic and some other odor that she suspected was whisky.

She took a step back. "I believe I see what I need over there." She gestured vaguely in the direction everyone else seemed to be heading and began to walk, praying the man would take the hint and stay behind.

Instead, he fell smoothly into step with her. "Now don't go takin' offense. I meant what I said about helpin' you. For example, if you were needin' a place to stay—"

"I am only passing through," Rosalyn replied curtly.

She picked up her pace, relieved to see there was no line at the ticket counter, and marched up to the clerk. Her self-appointed "helper" was not rude enough to join her there, but neither did he leave. He stood a few feet away, making no effort to hide his interest in what Rosalyn was doing.

In a low voice, Rosalyn said, "Please tell me when the next train leaves for Bristol."

"Bristol?" The clerk did not pick up on Rosalyn's desire for confidentiality. He spoke loudly, perhaps to make himself heard above the din around them. Rosalyn flinched. From the corner of her eye, she saw the Irishman frown and scratch his head. No doubt he was confused at her odd actions.

"That'll be the mail train. It leaves at 11:45." Mistaking her look of disappointment for misunderstanding, the clerk clarified, "Just before midnight."

Midnight. Rosalyn looked at the large clock on the wall. That was nearly six hours from now. What would she do in the meantime? Her growling stomach gave its vote. She had eaten nothing all day, but she did not dare leave the station, and the food for sale here was bound to be costly. She took a deep breath, considering. "Have you a ladies' waiting room here?"

"Why, naturally, miss. We have every comfort here at Paddington."

"So you have a place to take tea, as well?"

"Yes, miss. We also offer service for the ladies in their waiting area."

Rosalyn made up her mind. Waiting here would have to do. Men were not allowed in the ladies' waiting area, so she would presumably be able to shake off the attentions of the fellow behind her. "How much is a ticket, please?"

The clerk rattled off the range of prices. Even a third-class ticket seemed an outrageously large portion of the money Rosalyn had left.

The Irishman joined her then, using his bulk to force her away from the ticket window before she could pay the clerk. "Surely you're not wantin' to spend six hours alone in an uncomfortable waiting area?"

Rosalyn said frostily, "Were you eavesdropping on my business, sir?"

He merely grinned. "Let me buy you a meal. There's a friendly place not five minutes from here."

Taken aback by the man's forwardness, Rosalyn began to refuse.

He took hold of her arm. "Don't say no out of hand. Let me warn you: traveling at night is dangerous for an unescorted young lady."

At his touch, Rosalyn felt a surge of real fear. How was she to get rid of this man? She looked toward the ticket booth, but the clerk was now busy with other customers.

The Irishman's grip tightened. "You'd be wise to take an offer of help when it's given."

Quite suddenly, a soldier stepped between them, forcing the Irishman to relinquish his hold on Rosalyn. "I don't believe the lady is interested in your particular brand of help."

The soldier was impressive—tall and broad-shouldered, his well-polished boots and bright red coat providing a stark contrast to the other man's shabby appearance. In normal circumstances Rosalyn might have thought him handsome, although at the moment his face was marred with a scowl.

"And what business is it of yours?" the Irishman shot back. He seemed undaunted even though his opponent stood half a head taller. "No one asked you to come buttin' in."

The soldier didn't even spare him a glance. He was studying Rosalyn, taking her in from top to toe, from the dirt on the hem of her gown to her dusty carpetbag. "Are you new to London? Just arrived?"

The Irishman gave him a shove. "The lady is with me. Leave us be, or I'll call the police."

The soldier grabbed the other man's coat and pulled him up sharply. Rosalyn noticed a long scar running down the back of his right hand. "The police!" the soldier said acridly. "Yes, why don't you go ahead and do that."

"Please stop!" Rosalyn exclaimed. She was grateful for his intervention, but the scene was rapidly turning ugly. "I will thank you *both* to leave me alone."

The soldier looked stung by her words. "You don't understand. I'm trying to help—"

He was cut off by a shrill female voice. "Oh, my dear, *there* you are! I've been looking all over for you!"

Rosalyn froze in astonishment as an elderly lady, moving swiftly despite the use of a cane, came up and enveloped her in a hug. Over the woman's shoulder, Rosalyn saw the soldier's grip on the Irishman slacken. The look of confusion on both men's faces mirrored what she felt. Why did this woman think she knew Rosalyn?

"I'll bet you thought your old Aunt Mollie had forgotten about you. But it was the fog! Oh my, it is nearly impossible to see in front of one's face." Still holding her close, the woman rasped in Rosalyn's ear, "Pretend you know me, dearie. It's your best hope of ridding yourself of these troublemakers."

Rosalyn understood. "Oh, hello . . . Aunt . . . Auntie," Rosalyn stuttered. She awkwardly returned the woman's hug as she sent a sideways glance at the men.

The Irishman acquiesced surprisingly easily. He extricated himself from the soldier's hold and tipped his cap toward Rosalyn. "Well then, since you've been delivered into the loving arms of your family, I see you have no need of my help after all." He had the temerity to give her a wink. "Do have a pleasant evening, lass."

After shooting a brief, malevolent glare at the soldier, he turned and sauntered away. Rosalyn imagined he was headed back to the train platform to scout out another victim.

Her would-be protector, on the other hand, did not move. He said skeptically, "This is your aunt?"

"Yes." Rosalyn felt a blush rising from the shame of having to lie, but she plunged on. "So you see, I'm quite fine." She added, with genuine sincerity, "Thank you for your help."

He nodded, accepting her thanks, but still looked doubtful.

The old lady patted Rosalyn's arm. "Now then, dearie, let's get going. I've procured a cab with a good lantern on it, and there's a warm dinner waiting for us when we get home."

She began shepherding Rosalyn toward the main entrance. Rosalyn went along willingly, intending to make her way back to the ladies' waiting area as soon as she had lost sight of both men. To the older woman she said, "Thank you, Mrs. . . . ?"

"My name is Mollie Hurdle. And it was no trouble. I certainly couldn't let those two men bully you."

They had gone perhaps twenty yards when Rosalyn heard the soldier shout, "Wait!"

He ran up and stepped in front of Rosalyn, stopping both women in their tracks. "Do you *really* know this woman?"

His brown eyes searched her face so intently that Rosalyn found it impossible to answer. She hated to lie again.

It was Mrs. Hurdle who responded. "Sir, you are quite overstepping propriety. I must ask that you let us be."

But the soldier had gleaned the correct answer to his question from Rosalyn's silence. He said fervently, "I know a safe place where you can stay. I'm heading in that direction right now—you can ride with me."

"What effrontery!" Mrs. Hurdle exclaimed. "Do you really expect a nice young lady to go off into the night with a soldier?"

"I'm speaking the truth," he insisted, still directing his words to Rosalyn. He took hold of her arm. "I don't think you know what you're getting into—"

She didn't give him time to finish. She'd been roughly handled by far too many men that day. Earlier she'd thought the soldier intended to help her, but now she wasn't so sure. Angrily, she shook herself free. "I am perfectly capable of taking care of myself. Let me pass."

He stared at her in disbelief. "Are you going willingly with this woman?"

Rosalyn lifted her chin. "More so than I would ever go with you."

Mrs. Hurdle pointed an angry finger at him. "You heard her, soldier. Now be off with you."

He shook his head. "I was trying to help you, but it appears I am too late."

Still, he did not move. The women were forced to step around him in order to continue on their way.

"Thank you," Rosalyn said to Mrs. Hurdle once they were out of earshot. "I think you must be an answer to prayer."

The older woman's thin lips parted in a smile. "It ain't often someone tells me that, I can tell you. Call me Aunt Mollie. Everyone does. I run a boardinghouse close by. Would you be needing a place to stay?"

"Well, I . . ." Rosalyn paused, considering. She ought to remain here. Yet she'd already been accosted by two men. For all she knew, the station was filled with base fellows waiting to prey on unescorted women.

They stepped outside, and immediately Rosalyn's senses were assaulted by the foul-smelling fog that nearly enveloped them. Added to this was the odor of horseflesh and dung, for the area was packed with dozens of cabs, from sleek, two-seater hansom cabs to larger, old-fashioned vehicles with proper doors and windows.

Uneasiness settled over Rosalyn as Mrs. Hurdle led the way toward one of the larger cabs. She could not shake the feeling that, despite its perils, remaining at the station was the better choice. She came to an abrupt halt. "In fact, I plan to take the 11:45 for Bristol."

Mrs. Hurdle looked at her quizzically. "But I thought you just arrived."

"I have. But I need to leave as soon as possible."

Mrs. Hurdle nodded. "I see. You have perhaps left your home suddenly, and now you are beginning to regret the decision?"

"Yes! That is . . . well . . . not exactly." She sighed. "It's a rather long story."

The old woman patted her arm in a friendly, comforting gesture. "You have no one here in London? No friends or family?"

"No."

"Come home with me," Mrs. Hurdle urged.

"You are very kind, but I cannot afford to pay for lodging."

The woman waved a hand. "Then I shall offer this as a favor to a young woman in need."

Rosalyn marveled at this stranger's generosity. "Is it far from here? The cab fare . . ."

"It is walkable. However, I am not as sturdy on my pins as I used to be. Let's take a cab. You can always board a train to Bristol tomorrow. It will be much safer for you to travel by day."

She couldn't deny that sounded logical. "Thank you for helping me shake off those men."

Mrs. Hurdle frowned. "I shouldn't be surprised if the two of them were in on it together."

"How could that be!" Rosalyn exclaimed. "Each was trying to chase the other away."

"I've seen it before," the older woman said with a knowing nod. "The first man makes you uncomfortable, and then a second one comes in like a chivalrous rescuer."

"Surely not," Rosalyn protested. After all, the taller man's military uniform had seemed real enough. But as she thought back on the encounter, an odd realization struck her. The soldier had had an Irish accent, as well. It was far less pronounced, as though he'd been living in England for a long time, but it was unmistakable nonetheless. She would never distrust a person simply for being Irish, yet it might point to a connection between the two men.

Rosalyn turned to look back. The soldier had come outside. He stood next to another cab with his hand on the carriage door, but was making no move to get in. Instead, he continued to watch Rosalyn with an intensity that only increased her discomfort.

She was dismayed to see the Irishman come through the doors, too. He leaned against a pillar, hands in his pockets, casually observing the activity in the station yard.

Was Mrs. Hurdle right about the men and their intentions? How could Rosalyn know for sure? Her thoughts swirled in confusion.

Mrs. Hurdle waved a hand to regain Rosalyn's attention. "Help me in, will you, dear?"

Instinctively, Rosalyn reached out to help the old woman into the cab. Mrs. Hurdle stumbled while still gripping Rosalyn's arm tightly, and somehow Rosalyn found herself landing right next to her on the seat.

The driver quickly tossed in Rosalyn's carpetbag and shut the door. He wasted no time putting the carriage in motion. Through the window, Rosalyn could see the soldier still watching as the carriage moved out of the station yard. His shoulders sagged a little, as if in disappointment. That gesture, coming from such a forceful man, unexpectedly troubled her.

His eyes met hers, and he straightened. He called out to her, but whatever he said was lost in the clatter of wheels and horses' hooves as the carriage entered the wide, bustling thoroughfare.

CHAPTER

3

The cab made its way down increasingly narrow and dark streets. It was, in fact, a greater distance from the station than Mrs. Hurdle had implied. When they finally stopped, they were behind a house in the carriage lane. Mrs. Hurdle paid the cabbie and ushered Rosalyn up a few rickety wooden steps.

The heavy door opened onto a kitchen. A plump, middle-aged woman turned away from the stove and greeted them heartily as they came in. Wiping sweat from her brow, she smiled as she looked Rosalyn up and down. "Looks like you've brought home some company, Mrs. Hurdle."

"I found this young lady at the train station. She'll be spendin' the night with us. Go and make sure the small room is clean and ready."

"Right away, madam," the other woman replied and quickly departed.

"It's too small for a regular lodger, but I think you'll find it comfortable enough," Mrs. Hurdle explained.

Rosalyn gave her a grateful smile. "You really have been most kind."

"Would you like a cup of tea?"

"That would be heavenly."

Lifting a kettle from the stove, Mrs. Hurdle filled a teapot.

Piano music and laughter drifted in from another part of the house. Seeing Rosalyn start in surprise at a particularly boisterous round of laughter, Mrs. Hurdle said, "Don't be alarmed. That's just my boarders enjoying a few parlor games."

She set a cup of steaming tea in front of Rosalyn. Lifting it to her lips, Rosalyn tasted her first hot beverage since the day before, and for several seconds nothing else mattered.

After Rosalyn had consumed a second cup of tea and a generous helping of beef and bread, Mrs. Hurdle led her to a room where she could sleep. It was tiny, with no windows, and contained only a narrow bed, a simple wooden chair, and a washstand. But to Rosalyn, it was as good as a palace. Tears stung her eyes. "Mrs. Hurdle, I can't thank you enough."

The old woman patted her hand. "Your gratitude will be payment enough for me." She closed the door, leaving Rosalyn alone in the room.

Rosalyn quickly took off her dusty coat and walking skirt and changed into the nightdress she'd packed in her carpet bag. She knelt by the bed and prayed, thanking God for His protection and asking for His guidance. Mr. Müller, the founder of the orphanage, had taught them that God would provide for their needs if they prayed and believed.

Her prayers complete, Rosalyn crawled into the narrow bed. She lay there in the darkness, listening to the other sounds in the house. The laughter was downright raucous now. Mrs. Hurdle's boarders must have had some unusually energetic parlor games. For the moment Rosalyn seemed safe; and yet the soldier's words, *I am too late*, returned to her memory, bringing a whisper of doubt. It also occurred to her that she'd never asked why Mrs. Hurdle was at the station. She tried to set these discomforting thoughts aside and eventually fell into a fitful slumber.

Sometime later—with no windows, Rosalyn had no way of gauging the time—the sound of voices coming from the kitchen startled her awake. A groggy tiredness still enveloped her, but given her uneasy sleep, that was no surprise. She rose from the bed and carefully made her way to the door. The rough wooden floor felt scratchy on her bare feet. She opened the door a crack, just in time to hear a man's voice say, "Now don't you go tryin' to cheat me, Mrs. Hurdle. I found her for you, so you owe me."

Rosalyn recognized that voice. It belonged to the Irishman who'd accosted her at the station.

"You nearly chased her away!" Mrs. Hurdle accused. "If I hadn't stepped in when I did—"

"That's the beauty of it! She went straight into your arms—even though that red-coated pest tried to interfere. We're a team, that's all."

"Well, here's half a crown," the old woman said grudgingly. Over his protests, she added, "Don't argue, Mick. If she works out, we'll see about raising the amount."

"But wait—I ain't told you everything I did tonight. When I do, you'll say it was far more valuable that I stayed at the station."

"Oh?" Mrs. Hurdle sounded unconvinced.

Rosalyn's hand gripped the doorknob as she waited for Mick to say more.

"I watched four, maybe five more trains come in, looking for potential girls for your fine establishment."

"And yet it looks to me like you came here alone," Mrs. Hurdle rejoined. "If you think I'm paying you for wasted time—"

"It wasn't a waste!" Mick insisted. "There was a man got off one train who caught my attention. A fine-dressed bloke he was, and yet he weren't carrying no valise or carpetbag. Not attended by any servant, neither. So of course I immediately wonder what's what. I follow him—all casual-like, you know—just to see if maybe his money is in a convenient location."

"Pickpocketing again, Mick?"

"Well a man's got to earn a living, don't he? I ain't gonna do it on those half crowns you dole out."

Mrs. Hurdle only snorted. "Go on."

"So like I said, I followed him. And I see him go straight up to the platform attendant and ask whether he'd noticed a young, unchaperoned lady gettin' off the train from Linden."

"Oh, ho!" said Mrs. Hurdle, her irritation now replaced by interest. "Did the man describe the girl he was looking for?"

"He did. Brown hair, medium height, russet-red walking gown and matching jacket."

Mick spoke with relish, and Rosalyn could picture the two of them nodding together in agreement that he'd just described her.

"But that's not all I heard," Mick went on. "It seems your new little boarder is wanted for stealing! But it can't have been much. She wasn't acting like she had any money."

"Ah, you're growing daft now, Mick. Don't you see—she took *property*, not cash. Something valuable but portable. Jewelry, most like. Now she needs to pawn it, which is why she's come to London."

Rosalyn's stomach turned at hearing herself described like a common thief. But given how devious Mrs. Hurdle was showing herself to be, it wasn't surprising that she'd see the actions of others through the lens of her own deeds.

"We'll have to take a careful look through her bag tomorrow," Mrs. Hurdle said, and Rosalyn could hear greedy excitement in her voice.

"Would you pawn stolen goods?" Mick asked in surprise. "Don't you worry about the police trackin' you down?"

"Not a chance," Mrs. Hurdle answered confidently. "I'll take it to Simon. He can make anything disappear without a trace." After a pause, she added, "So long as you didn't say anything to the toff about her whereabouts."

Rosalyn imagined the woman giving Mick a hard stare or perhaps a poke in the chest.

"Now I ain't so daft as that," Mick protested. "I didn't say nothin'. But I did stick close—long enough to hear the man give his name and the hotel where he could be found. So if we should discover the reward for her capture is worth more than what she stole—"

There was another pause, presumably as Mrs. Hurdle assimilated this information. Rosalyn waited on pins and needles, fully expecting her to ask Mick for more details.

But Mrs. Hurdle only said, "Mick, you're smarter than I thought. Here's another half crown. For that kind of money, I expect you not to tell anyone else about this."

"You drive a hard bargain, Mrs. Hurdle," Mick answered cheerfully. "But you can trust me."

"No, I can't," Mrs. Hurdle contradicted. "I'll be watching you. Now, be off. If you plan to spend that money on Brenda, go around to the front entrance like the rest of 'em."

Heart pounding, Rosalyn gently closed the bedroom door. She had been tricked by both of them! How had she not seen? Why had she been so determined to ignore the warnings of that soldier? She wanted to curse herself for her own stupidity.

One thing was certain—she had to get out of this house as

soon as possible. She decided against lighting a lamp for fear of drawing Mrs. Hurdle's attention. Groping in the darkness, she made her way to the chair where she'd draped her gown. Her fingers fumbled as she blindly did up the buttons.

She heard steps—a light tread accompanied by the tap of a cane—retreating down the hallway. Taking hold of her carpetbag, Rosalyn opened the door, beginning with the tiniest crack, to ascertain if anyone else was about. Hearing and seeing nothing, she stepped into the hallway and cautiously made her way to the kitchen. In the light of the banked fire, she pulled out her pocket watch and saw that it was four in the morning. Could she risk roaming this neighborhood in the predawn hours? She would have to.

The kitchen door was secured by a heavy bolt. As Rosalyn reached for it, she could hear noises outside, including loud arguing and the wail of a cat. A pistol shot rang out, followed immediately by a fury of sound—more arguing, women crying, a dog barking. Rosalyn drew back from the door as tremors moved through her.

Suddenly the sound of footsteps came from her right, and she realized that the far corner opened onto a set of narrow stairs leading to the upper floors. Before Rosalyn could retreat, a woman bounded down the last few steps and into the kitchen.

Rosalyn guessed her to be somewhere above thirty years old. She wore a light cotton shift and wrapper, and her feet were bare. Although dressed for bed, her hair was pinned up, and her face was heavily painted with rouge and charcoal. Seeing Rosalyn, she immediately began peppering her with questions, speaking with unnatural energy. "Hello, I'm Penny. Who are you? Are you one of the new ones? Where are you from?"

The last question was delivered with a playful poke at Rosalyn's ribs, as though goading her to speak. Rosalyn raised her hands to fend her off. "I'm from Bristol, and I'm going back there today."

Penny laughed, but to Rosalyn it sounded closer to hysteria than amusement. "You sure about that? I'll bet you're here because you heard the men like the fresh ones." She glared at Rosalyn. "Well, they don't. They prefer someone with experience." Her mouth widened into a salacious smile. "Someone who can stoke their passions and drive them wild with ecstasy, so that they forget their own names. That's when they reward you most handsomely—"

Her words confirmed Rosalyn's worst fears about what this place was. "Come away with me," she interjected swiftly. "You don't have to stay here."

Penny placed her hands on her hips and looked at Rosalyn skeptically. "Go with you? To Bristol?" Her nose scrunched in distaste.

"Surely anyplace is better than here."

From somewhere outside, another gunshot exploded, followed by more screaming. Rosalyn flinched, and Penny instantly picked up on her alarm. "What do you know about it, Miss I'm-from-Bristol? As you can see, London's no town for a woman without protection. Mrs. Hurdle takes good care of us."

"When she's not bringing in competition." Rosalyn surprised herself with this caustic remark, but she was determined not to cower.

Narrowing her eyes, Penny sidled up to her. "You will never be my competition. I am the best, and the men what comes here knows it."

Despite her proud words, there was only emptiness in her large brown eyes. Rosalyn held her tongue, reminding herself that plenty of unfortunates had been living in darkness for so long that they could not even envision a better life, much less strive for it.

Outside, the confusion increased. Footsteps pounded, doors slammed, and people shouted and cursed out of open windows. But in Rosalyn's soul, an odd kind of peace blossomed and she knew with certainty that this was the moment to move. She took hold of the heavy bolt with both hands and shoved it aside. "You're right," she said to Penny. "I am not your competition. Because I am getting out of here."

"You are either mad or stupid," Penny replied flatly. "You'll be back—if you survive."

Clutching her reticule close to her side, Rosalyn opened the door and slipped out. As she paused on the steps, her vision adjusting to the gloom, she realized her carpetbag was still on the floor of the kitchen. Before she could turn back to the door, she heard the bolt being slid into place. Penny was making her point as surely as Rosalyn had. There was no turning back now. She would have to leave her belongings behind.

As soon as she reached the bottom of the stairs, Rosalyn heard more footsteps approaching. She pressed herself into a gap between the wall and a large bin filled with refuse. The bin smelled unspeakably foul, but its bulk kept her hidden as two men hurried past.

Deciding which direction to go next was easy enough. With a crowd collecting at the far end of the alley to her left, Rosalyn would turn right. A larger, busier street was about fifty yards off. Rosalyn could see people walking past the entrance to the alley, along with the occasional hansom cab and some ramshackle carriages.

Another sound broke into the night, this time from just over her head. "What do you mean, 'she's gone'?" It was Mrs. Hurdle's voice, shrill with anger. Rosalyn stood below the kitchen window. Although it was closed, the sound of the ensuing argument reached her clearly enough.

"She said she was too good for us," Penny returned petulantly.

Rosalyn bristled at this clear lie. "She said she was going to be better than mere whores, and that you was an evil and greedy old woman."

There was the sickening sound of flesh hitting flesh.

"Ow! What'd you slap me for?" Penny protested. "You can't do that and damage the merchandise."

"Your time is passing, girl," Mrs. Hurdle said, her voice hard. "No one is interested in you anymore. You bore them."

Rosalyn shivered. Despite Penny's harsh words to her earlier, she still felt bad for the woman. The world had ill-used her, and Rosalyn could not imagine what kind of future lay in store for her. For a moment, she wished Penny had accepted her offer to come along.

"When did she leave?" Mrs. Hurdle demanded.

"Must have been twenty minutes or more. She's long gone by now. Ain't no way you can catch her."

Again, this was a complete lie, but Rosalyn prayed fervently that the old woman would believe it. If she were to come out in the alley now . . .

Mrs. Hurdle must have made some indication that she was planning to, because Penny said, "Oh, she didn't go that way. She went up through the receiving room, shouting all manner of obscenities at us."

Rosalyn was stunned by the string of lies that came so effortlessly out of Penny's mouth. It seemed she was doing all she could to help Rosalyn get away, but why? Rosalyn was tempted to be grateful even though she knew Penny's actions must be entirely self-serving.

Apparently, Mrs. Hurdle knew Penny too well to accept her words at face value. She said brusquely, "Out of my way, girl."

Once more, Rosalyn heard the bolt sliding. She had to move, and quickly. She turned and fled down the alley.

As she ran, something caught at her right hand. She felt a sharp pain as her wrist was wrenched backward, forcing her hand to open, her fingers straightening of their own accord, and the reticule slipped from her grasp. There was a blur of movement, no higher than Rosalyn's waist, and the sound of bare feet slapping in the mud. A small boy must also have been hiding in the alley. Now he was running off with the only money she had left in the world.

Afraid to cry out lest she advertise her presence to Mrs. Hurdle, Rosalyn raced silently after the boy. She nearly caught up to him, but he deftly took a leap to the left, avoiding a puddle he must have known was there. Rosalyn slipped and staggered in the wet slime, barely managing to stay on her feet.

The boy turned a blind corner into the street. Rosalyn regained her balance and ran after him. When she reached the street, her eyes were temporarily blinded by a glaring street lamp. People jostled past her. She saw the boy, darting in and out of the people and carriages. "Stop!" she cried out after him. "For the love of God, stop!"

Now she didn't care if Mrs. Hurdle was on her heels or not. Her mind was focused on the small, ragged boy slipping away through the traffic. She ran into someone and nearly stumbled again but murmured a quick apology and kept after the boy.

"Ho there! What's going on?" Broad hands and a wall of a chest stopped Rosalyn in her tracks.

It was a policeman. Thank God, it was a policeman. "That boy!" she shouted breathlessly. "He's made off with my money!"

The man turned his gaze to follow where she was pointing, but the boy had disappeared. In those few seconds, he had melted away—probably into one of the side streets. Rosalyn gasped, trying to catch her breath, tears blurring her vision.

"I don't see no boy," said the policeman. "Can you describe him?"

"He was small, maybe five or six years old. Dressed in rags. Barefoot."

"That describes half the boys in London. Did you see his face?"

Rosalyn felt her shoulders sag. "No."

"Did you see which way he went? Sometimes we can find 'em by the warren they're living in."

"No." Desperation began to settle in. Now she had nothing left but the clothes on her back.

"There she is!" Mrs. Hurdle's voice rang out. "Thief!"

The policeman instantly grabbed Rosalyn's arm. "What's this, then?" he asked Mrs. Hurdle. "You speaking of this young lady?"

"Lady," Mrs. Hurdle repeated with a scoff. "She took advantage of a kindness, that's what she did. I gave her a cab ride, a meal, and a room for the night. But here she is, trying to sneak out without paying."

The policeman's gaze leveled hard on Rosalyn. "Is this true?"

Rosalyn's mouth fell open. Shock and fear kept her throat bound and her mind blank. It was true Mrs. Hurdle had spent money on her, even if she'd had underhanded reasons for doing so.

Mrs. Hurdle took advantage of Rosalyn's silence. "You see? She doesn't deny it." She held out a hand. "You owe me."

"But I . . . but she . . ." Rosalyn drew another breath, desperate to speak. "She wants to turn me into a prostitute!"

"What?" Mrs. Hurdle looked genuinely shocked. "I've never heard such slander. I run a respectable boardinghouse."

The policeman's grip tightened on Rosalyn. "Will you pay this woman what you owe her, or do I have to take you down to the station house?"

"But I have no money!" Rosalyn protested. "That boy just ran off with it!"

"Is that what she told you?" Mrs. Hurdle interjected. "That's exactly what she told me when she approached me outside the railway station. Gave me a story about being robbed. Just trying to garner sympathy, I'll wager. A good way to take advantage of a trusting old woman."

This lie was so preposterous that Rosalyn was tempted to snort, despite the fear coursing through her.

The policeman's skeptical gaze rested on Rosalyn, taking in her soiled gown and muddy boots. "Come to think of it, I didn't see any boy, and your description of him was awfully vague." He turned to several people who had clustered around them on the sidewalk. "Did anyone else see a boy running through here?"

The people standing around them shrugged. A few slunk away, bored with the lack of drama.

"We're taking a walk to the station," the policeman announced.

"Wait," Rosalyn pleaded, resisting his tug on her arm. Turning to Mrs. Hurdle, she said, "My bag is still in your kitchen. Surely my belongings are worth whatever I owe you."

The old woman's brows furrowed in calculation. Most likely she was remembering the conversation with Mick and her suspicion that Rosalyn had stolen goods. Would that be enough to appease the old woman?

"So you admit you skulked away from my house!" Mrs. Hurdle said triumphantly. "Constable, I insist that you arrest her!"

Too late, Rosalyn realized she'd miscalculated. If Mrs. Hurdle thought something valuable was in that bag, she was going to ensure Rosalyn couldn't come back for it.

Rosalyn knew she could not go down to the station. If she told the authorities who she was and where she'd come from, they might send her back to Russet House. Already she could see the smirk on Mr. Huffman's face and imagine what he would do after he "forgave" her. No, whatever she did, she could not allow that to happen. Surely there was some way out of this.

When the answer came to her, it threatened to tear her heart in two. It would leave her worse than destitute, for she would be losing her most precious connection to her parents. But as the policeman began once more to tug on her arm, she made her decision.

"Wait." Rosalyn planted her feet firmly. She could not have stopped the policeman if he'd been determined to drag her away, but something in her demeanor caused him to pause.

With her free arm, she reached into the pocket of her gown and extracted her mother's gold pocket watch. Slowly, fighting every instinct to withdraw, she held it out. "This will cover what I owe you, surely."

Mrs. Hurdle's eyes gleamed as her gaze landed on the watch. She snatched it from Rosalyn's hand. She opened it and read the inscription. Her eyes lifted to Rosalyn, and Rosalyn could see what she was about to ask—or rather, the accusation she was about to make, that Rosalyn had stolen it.

"It was my mother's watch," Rosalyn said. "A gift from my father. Accept it and let me be. Or give it back this instant."

Rosalyn knew it was risky to offer this woman an ultimatum. But she had been stretched far enough.

She could see Mrs. Hurdle weighing the options in her mind: whatever might or might not be in Rosalyn's bag, there was no doubting the value of the watch in her hand. After a long moment, she gave a crisp nod. "I suppose this will do." She waggled a threatening finger at Rosalyn. "But I'd better not see you around this neighborhood again. It can be a *dangerous* place for people who don't know their way around."

The implied threat was perfectly clear to Rosalyn. Refusing to cower, she drew herself up and said acridly, "I thank you for your concern, but you need have no worries on that account."

She met Mrs. Hurdle's cold stare and knew the two of them had made a bargain.

Mrs. Hurdle said, "Constable, I don't believe there's any need to press charges. Thank you for your help." She turned and walked away. In a moment, she'd turned into the alley leading to her home and was out of sight.

"London has strict laws against vagabonds," the policeman said as he released Rosalyn's arm. "You'd best be off quickly, or I'll still take you in for vagrancy."

Rosalyn could not believe the injustice of this. He'd just seen her parted from everything she owned! But she was learning that in the big city, you had better act like you knew what you were doing, even if it was a lie.

"I am not a vagrant. I am on my way to . . ." She paused, giving a little cough to buy herself a few more seconds. As she did so, an address came to mind. One she had not thought of for several years, but which had—thank God—remained in her memory. "I'm going to 385 Ryder Street, St. James Square. The home of Miles Tunbridge, esquire."

She spoke with calm authority, and it was clearly a proper address, for the policeman seemed to recognize it. "And how would you be knowing someone who lives in St. James Square?"

"Mr. Tunbridge is my . . . my uncle."

Rosalyn told herself it was not so terribly untrue, for Mr. Tunbridge was, in a sense, a spiritual uncle—or a benefactor, at least. He was a frequent contributor to the orphanage and had visited the place at least half a dozen times. One of Rosalyn's tasks during her final year at the orphanage had been to help Mr. Müller address envelopes for the thank-you letters he wrote to donors. Mr. Tunbridge's address had thus been imprinted on Rosalyn's mind.

The policeman looked unconvinced. "What are you doing in this neighborhood if you have an uncle in the better parts of London?"

It was a question Rosalyn could not answer. But she was spared from further temptation to lie, as their conversation was cut short by alarm bells clanging and the rush of horses' hooves on the brick street.

"Fire!" someone yelled. "There's a fire on Clark Street!"

Another policeman rushed up to them, shouting over the increasing din. "We've got to get over there!"

This decided the constable. He gave her a little shove. "On your way. We've got more important things to attend to."

The two of them raced off. Others were running in that direction too, and Rosalyn stepped into the recessed doorway of a tobacconist's shop to keep from being swept up in the crowd. She stood alone, her back pressed against the damp brick wall. In the distance, she could see black smoke rising through the fog, lit by the city's street lamps in the flat darkness before dawn.

But at least she had a destination. She would go to Ryder Street. She would walk the entire way there, no matter how far it was. Surely Mr. Tunbridge would remember her and would help her.

CHAPTER

4

N ATE WAS WOKEN by a soft touch on his arm. "It's nearly time," a gentle voice said.

He opened his eyes, taking a moment to regain his bearings. After rising at four in the morning and putting in eight hours of work at the ostler's, he'd come home and fallen asleep in a chair by the fire. He sighed and rubbed his aching neck, looking up into the soft green eyes of the woman standing at his elbow. "I'm sorry, Ma. I've done it again, haven't I?"

"It's nothing to apologize for. You've been driving yourself pretty hard, my boy." Even though they'd been living in England for over a decade, her speech had lost none of its Irish accent.

She handed him a cup of hot coffee, which he gratefully accepted. "What time is it?"

"Nearly three."

"*What?*" This news wiped away the last vestiges of his drowsiness. He realized how quiet the house was. Normally his family members kept it bustling with activity. He downed the coffee quickly. "Where is everyone? Why did you allow me to sleep so long?"

"They went out," his mother answered simply. "We all agreed you needed the rest."

Nate was already on his feet, setting the coffee cup aside. Hastily he tucked a loose shirttail into his trousers. "There's no point in my trying to keep Patrick's job for him if I'm just going to get the sack for being late."

"Don't fret yourself so. You've got time."

"You don't understand. I've got to be there early today. We're changing out a new flat."

"You're not leavin' this house until you've had a bite to eat," his mother insisted. She picked up a plate holding a slice of buttered bread and a generous chunk of cheese and thrust it into his hands.

Despite his worries, his mother's imperiousness brought a tiny smile to Nate's lips. "You're a good woman, Ma. Always lookin' out for me."

His mother's expression said *Don't I know it* even as she refilled his cup from a small coffeepot she'd brought into the room with her. "I've been takin' care of you for twenty-six years, and I'm not about to stop now."

Nate might have pointed out that for seven of those years he'd been in the army—and out of the country. But he didn't bother to argue. He was too busy eating his food as quickly as he could without wolfing it down.

His mother studied him. "I can't say you looked as though you were sleeping well."

Nate turned his gaze toward his cup as he took a long swallow. "Of course I wasn't sleepin' well, Ma. I was upright in that chair."

She shook her head. "It's more than that. You were mumbling, and you shook your head several times as though you were havin' a bad dream. What's troubling you?"

Nate finished the cheese, knowing his full mouth would give him a brief excuse not to answer. His mother waited patiently until he swallowed the last bite of food. "You know I'm worried about losing Patrick's job—or mine. Mr. Jamieson doesn't like the fact that I can no longer work my usual twelve hours."

His mother took his empty plate and cup and set them aside. "And?" she said, the inflection in her voice telling him she knew there was more.

Nate sighed. There was no point trying to put her off. Not if he wanted to get to the theater on time. "Yesterday, I noticed a young lady at Paddington station. She'd been accosted by one of those unsavory fellows who always hang around the station. I tried to run him off for her."

"That's noble of you, son."

He shook his head. "It might have been, if I'd succeeded. But an old lady came up, claiming to be the girl's aunt. The girl said this was true, but something didn't seem quite right to me. It was only as they were walking away that I realized what it was. The older woman had called herself Aunt Mollie."

"Oh no," his mother said. Like Nate, she was familiar with the name of one of London's more infamous brothel owners. Their church helped dozens of women out of such places.

"I can't be sure, of course," Nate added hurriedly. "The name might only be a coincidence. But what if it wasn't? What if, no longer content to pick up homeless women off the streets, Mollie Hurdle is now trawling the railway stations, as well?" The very idea that he might somehow have caused an innocent young lady to walk into the arms of a brothel owner enveloped him with guilt. "I offered to bring her here, but she rebuffed me. And who knows what may have happened to her by now? If only I'd tried harder—or taken some other approach—"

"There now." His mother held one of his clenched fists, caressing it until it relaxed. "I've no doubt you did the best you could."

"No. I should have done more." He spoke bitterly, weighed down by disappointment. At the last minute, he'd tried to call out to her the name of their church's charity house and the street it was located on, hoping she might be able to remember it as a place of refuge. But it had been too late, and he doubted she'd heard.

His mother gave him a tiny, sympathetic smile. "You mustn't beat yourself up so. As you said, you may be worrying over nothing. And if not—" She paused, letting out a sigh. "We've seen many an unfortunate girl in this city since we arrived. There simply is no way to help them all. It's a hard truth, but we must accept it."

"I know that, Ma. But it's more troubling to actually see it happening, to be in a position to help—and yet not be able to."

He saw tears glisten in her eyes. "I'm so proud of you, son. You may have spent years as a soldier, but you haven't lost your tender heart."

"It's conscience, that's all." If she was in trouble, Nate couldn't shake the idea that somehow he was to blame. He should not have tried to physically take hold of her. It was then that he'd lost her. It had been a rash, stupid thing to do.

Nate cleared his throat and blinked to be sure his own eyes were dry. This was no time for morose thoughts. He had work to do, people who were depending on him.

He strode into the front hall and grabbed his coat from a rack near the door.

His mother followed him. "There's one more thing I want to tell you, son."

Nate paused but did not turn around. "I must be on my way, Ma."

"You know the Lord has brought us through some pretty dark times." Her voice was firm, unwavering.

His hands tightened on his coat. It was true that his family had suffered many deprivations after the sudden loss of his father when Nate was still a child. But even in their most desperate days, Nate and his siblings had been able to rely on their mother's tenacious strength and wisdom. The woman at the station had been alone. How could his mother think the two situations were alike? But he respected her too much to try to argue the point. He said quietly, "Yes, Ma. I know."

"None of us knows the future. If that woman is in trouble, there may yet be hope for her. Remember that."

Her words were meant to reassure him, but they only rang hollow in Nate's heart. The woman at the station had been so striking—not only beautiful but filled with contrasts that continued to tease at his thoughts. She'd projected an air of confidence, joining right in with "Aunt Mollie" at giving him a stern rebuke. And yet the last moment he'd seen her, she'd had such a look of vulnerability. A touch of fear, even. It haunted him, leaving him confused, sad, and even angry—at her, as well as at the unfortunate circumstances.

But there was no time to explain all this now. So he turned and gave his mother a soft peck on the cheek. "Thank you, Ma. I will remember."

✦

It took Rosalyn the better part of the day to make her way to Ryder Street. She kept getting lost and having to ask for directions from shopkeepers or street vendors. The city was an overwhelming confusion of movement and noise. On the broader avenues, carriages, carts, and omnibuses fought their way through jams or sped up dangerously to claim a rare stretch of open space. Rosalyn soon discovered that simply crossing the street could put a person's life in danger, as drivers gave not the slightest leeway to pedestrians. Smells both foul and pleasant mingled in the air, competing for dominance. One of the more appealing scents came from hot meat pies a man was selling from a cart. But even this two-penny luxury was beyond her means. Realizing she still had a clean linen handkerchief in her pocket, Rosalyn was able to barter with an old woman selling apples from a frayed wicker basket. The large, tangy apple helped assuage the hunger gnawing at her, but she was still thirsty. She hesitated to drink at the public wells, though. She'd heard grim tales of the ways people could die from the bad water in London.

By the time she found the imposing white townhouse that matched the address from her memory, Rosalyn was lightheaded from thirst. She stood, leaning against the black iron railing in front of the house, trying to regain her steadiness before going up to knock at the door.

In the end, she did not have to move at all. A woman came out of the lower servants' entrance and hurried up the steps that led to the street, intent on some errand. Was she the cook? The housekeeper? She stopped short when she saw Rosalyn. "What's your business, girl?"

Rosalyn was taken aback by the woman's harsh tone, but she pressed on. "I'm here to see Mr. Tunbridge. Is he in?"

The woman eyed Rosalyn's wrinkled and mud-splattered clothing. "And what would you want with him? I ain't heard that we was hiring any more servants."

Rosalyn stood straighter, striving to affect the air of someone higher up the social scale than this woman. "My business is of a private nature. Please just tell me, is he in? It's important."

"Mr. Tunbridge is not in town," the woman answered curtly. "He and Mrs. Tunbridge have gone up to York, and we don't expect them back until after Christmas." Her eyes narrowed. "If you are a *particular* friend of Mr. Tunbridge, you'd know that."

Rosalyn felt her face grow hot. "I'm an acquaintance only. Someone who knows Mr. Tunbridge through mission work."

"Oh, I see." But she looked unconvinced. "Well then, if you have business with Mr. Tunbridge, I can fetch the butler, and you can leave a message with him."

The woman said this as a challenge, clearly expecting Rosalyn to withdraw. Rosalyn was tempted to speak to the butler simply to prove her wrong, but there was no point. Mr. Tunbridge was not here, and based on this encounter, she doubted there'd be anyone in the house who'd be willing or able to help her.

Still striving for dignity, Rosalyn said, "That won't be necessary. I shall come back another time."

She turned and strode purposefully away. She fancied the other woman's eyes were on her until she turned the corner at the next intersection.

Earlier in the day, Rosalyn had passed a house with a sign declaring it was a refuge for destitute women, but she'd pressed on, wanting only to reach Mr. Tunbridge. Now she desperately wished she could remember where it was. She began to walk in the direction she thought she'd come, trying to remember which streets she had taken, but nothing looked familiar. After a while she knew her attempt was useless. There was no way she'd be able to retrace her steps.

A sign on a nearby building informed Rosalyn that this busy street was called the Strand. She paused and leaned heavily against a lamppost as people hurried past her in both directions. After several minutes, she decided to find the nearest public pump and drink from it, preferring to face the possibility of illness over the certainty of fainting dead away on the street and leaving herself vulnerable to any kind of wrongdoers.

Among the many people moving along the street was a man wearing a sandwich board. The advertising on it read, *Don't miss*

HMS Pinafore *at the Opera Comique! Wholesome opera! Unparalleled wit and music!*

Rosalyn felt a tiny smile lift her parched lips. Although she'd never seen the show, she knew the music. Mrs. Williams had purchased the sheet music and libretto, and they'd passed many happy hours singing those songs together.

She stepped away from the lamppost and into the man's path. He paused and tipped his bowler hat, looking at her with an inquiring smile. Rosalyn took heart that he, at least, seemed friendly. "Excuse me. Do you know of someplace where I could find water?"

He waved his arm in a broad gesture to his left and said, "The River Thames is just three blocks over. Plenty of water there."

"I mean drinkable water. A fountain or well."

He shook his head. "There ain't no drinkable water in this city. Far better off with something healthier, like beer. In fact, if you can wait until I get off work, I'll take you someplace myself."

"Please," she croaked. Her head was swimming.

The man sobered. "I'm sorry, miss. I didn't mean no harm." He turned and pointed in the direction he'd come. "Turn left at that street up there. There's an alleyway leading off it that has a pump." He reached into his pocket and pulled out a coin. "Here's a ha'penny for you. Maybe get yourself some bread."

"I'm not here to beg," Rosalyn protested, humiliated that he would perceive her as destitute—even if it was the truth.

"Just take it." He pressed the coin into her hand.

Rosalyn accepted it gratefully. "Thank you."

"Take care of yourself, miss."

With one more tip of his hat, the man continued on.

Rosalyn followed his directions and soon found the well. It was in a small courtyard of houses that, while decidedly down-at-heel, were not nearly as decrepit as the buildings where the brothel had been located. The pump worked, quickly bringing up water. She splashed her face and hands and drank deeply. It was amazing the difference the water made. It put her in mind of a proverb: *As cool waters to a thirsty soul, so is good news from a far country.*

At the moment, Bristol felt as distant as a far country. But somehow she would find a way to get there.

She dried her hands on her skirt and surveyed her surroundings. Everything seemed in sharper focus now. On her right stood a building four stories high. Music drifted from a second-floor window. When a woman with a sweet soprano voice began to sing, Rosalyn was drawn irresistibly toward the sound. She sank down on an empty crate, listening.

> Poor wandering one,
> Though thou hast surely strayed,
> Take heart of grace, thy steps retrace,
> Poor wandering one!

Rosalyn sighed. It was as though the woman were singing directly to her.

"Take heart, fair days will shine . . ."

She closed her eyes, drinking in the music.

"Take heart! Take heart!"

Rosalyn felt her heart being soothed by the high, lovely notes. She breathed in deeply and repeated the words: *"Take heart of grace, thy steps retrace—"*

"Ho there! What are you doing down below?"

The shout—sharp, threatening, and suspicious—came from above, startling Rosalyn off the crate. Stumbling to her feet, she looked up to see a man of about forty with prodigious whiskers glaring down at her. In her confusion, Rosalyn could only stare at him dumbly.

"What's the trouble, Gilbert?" This query came from a gentler male voice. A second head popped out the window. This man had a round face, hair that was thinning on top, and side whiskers that were pronounced, if not so bushy as the other man's. His expression was one of mere curiosity. "Who's this?"

"A spy, I'll wager. I saw her trying to memorize the lyrics. Sullivan, those blasted pirates are determined to steal our new work before it's even halfway written!"

Sullivan responded with a wry smile of amusement, which only seemed to annoy Gilbert more.

Rosalyn recognized their names. Mr. Gilbert had written the libretto to *HMS Pinafore*, and Mr. Sullivan—one of England's best-known composers—had written the score. It was impossible to believe she was actually looking at these two famous men! She still couldn't speak, dismayed as she was by Mr. Gilbert's bizarre accusation.

"Aha!" Mr. Gilbert shouted in triumph. "You can see I'm right. There is guilt written all over her face."

Rosalyn swallowed, trying to find her voice. Mr. Gilbert looked as though he wanted to throttle her.

A third head appeared at the window. This one belonged to a woman—a pretty brunette who looked about Rosalyn's age. Upon seeing Rosalyn, her brows instantly drew together, her lips making an O as she looked down with compassion. "With all due respect, Mr. Gilbert, this woman looks more famished than piratical."

Gilbert gave an unconvinced grunt. He pointed a finger at Rosalyn. "Don't leave that spot. I'm coming right down. Miss Bond, you stay here and watch her."

"We'll *all* be right down," Miss Bond amended, her cheery tone softening her contradiction of Mr. Gilbert's orders. "I'm sure Blanche can watch her while we go down."

"Certainly" came another female voice from inside the room. The two men disappeared, and Miss Bond was joined by an exquisite blonde. She peered down at Rosalyn with the same mild curiosity that Mr. Sullivan had shown.

Still dumbfounded, Rosalyn stood rooted to the spot, heartily wishing she'd taken one more drink of water before having to face this unexpected inquisition.

Miss Bond turned away from the window. In no time, Rosalyn heard their voices discussing the situation as they came out the door to the courtyard.

"Gilbert, I really do feel you are jumping to conclusions."

"It's fine for you, Sullivan, if you don't want to worry about pirates stealing the very food out of your mouth. But I've got bills to pay."

At the same time, Rosalyn saw an older woman in a brown, well-worn coat turn into the narrow lane and come their direction. When she reached Rosalyn, the woman said, "Are you the new cleaning woman that Miss Lenoir was to have hired?"

"Well, I . . ."

"Of course she is," Miss Bond said. "That's why I told you that you needn't worry, Mr. Gilbert. I met this woman myself when she came to be interviewed by Miss Lenoir."

Once more, Rosalyn marveled at the ease with which city people could speak bold untruths. But this time she was grateful for it. She had no idea why this Miss Bond would come to her aid, but she would not refuse any offer of help.

Miss Bond looked at Rosalyn expectantly. "Go on. Tell them your name."

The directive was accompanied by an encouraging smile, and Rosalyn took heart. "Miss Rosalyn Bernay."

Even as she spoke, she realized it sounded outlandish for a prospective charwoman to give her name in this manner.

Sullivan picked up on this, too. "Miss Rosalyn Bernay!" he

echoed playfully. "A very French name. Tell us, Miss Bernay, do you also do a bit of opera-pirating on the side?"

"Certainly not! I love your work! I've purchased both the libretto and the sheet music."

It came out with such horrified sincerity that even the crotchety Mr. Gilbert barked out a laugh. "Is that so? Well, clearly you have good taste. I suppose that is the main requirement for a charwoman these days?"

Miss Bond crossed her arms and looked at him askance. "Mr. Gilbert, you are an incorrigible old curmudgeon. Please tell me you do not intend to have this poor woman drawn and quartered for piracy."

"Not today, at any rate." His voice was still gruff, but it was clear he was no longer angry. With a nod toward the older woman, he said, "She's all yours, Mrs. Hill." He turned back toward the door, evidently dismissing the matter from his thoughts. "Speaking of pirates . . . Come on then, Sullivan. We've only got Miss Rosavella for the afternoon, and I want to test her out on a few more songs."

Mr. Sullivan gave Rosalyn a smile and a wink. "I wish you much success in your new position, Miss Bernay."

"Thank you, sir." In the presence of Britain's most revered composer of sacred choral music and opera—who, it was rumored, was being considered for knighthood—it was all Rosalyn could do to keep herself from dropping a curtsy. "If I can listen to more of your marvelous music, I will happily work my fingers to the bone."

He chuckled. "Well, let's hope that won't be necessary." He turned to Miss Bond. "Coming, Jessie?"

She shook her head. "I'll just be another minute, if you please."

"Well, don't dawdle too long, or you'll raise Mr. Grouch's hackles again."

They both smiled, and Jessie Bond nodded her acquiescence.

"Come on, then," Mrs. Hill said briskly to Rosalyn. "We've a lot to do before the house opens tonight."

She started toward the entrance, but Rosalyn hesitated. Here was a chance to earn some money, but she could not go on pretending she was someone she was not. "Mrs. Hill, I'm not the woman who was hired for this job by"—she struggled to remember the name she'd heard—"by, er, Miss Lenoir."

Mrs. Hill shrugged. "The way I see it, you're here, and that other girl ain't. Would you be looking for work?"

"I'm afraid I haven't any references."

"No matter. I'll know in two hours whether you'll work out." She studied Rosalyn. "I can tell by your manners you've been raised properly. Plenty of people fall on hard times for reasons that ain't their fault."

"Thank you," Rosalyn said, meaning it with all her heart.

"I think she could use a bit of food first," Miss Bond observed. "Poor soul looks like she hasn't eaten in days."

"Only one day."

"How terrible," Jessie murmured sympathetically. "Has some man put you in this predicament?"

The question took Rosalyn by surprise. "How did you know?"

"A hunch. And let me tell you that I understand what you're going through."

Rosalyn sensed depth behind the simple words. Perhaps this lighthearted woman had known true sorrow, as well.

"MISS BOND!" Mr. Gilbert's voice boomed once more from the window. "If you would prefer to work *backstage* rather than *upon* it, I can ensure that happens."

"Coming, Mr. Gilbert!" But Jessie didn't sound at all chastened. It seemed her breezy charm enabled her to tease him and get away with it. She took Rosalyn's hands and gave them a quick squeeze. "Good-bye for now. Remember, take heart!"

Take heart.

Jessie hurried through the door to the theater and out of sight.

"Come with me," Mrs. Hill directed. "I'll find you something to eat while I show you around."

They went inside and began walking down a dimly lit hallway. "Those are the offices," Mrs. Hill said, pointing off to the left. "And up those stairs is the practice room. The backstage area is straight ahead."

The sound of men's voices came from the direction Mrs. Hill had indicated.

"That'll be the stagehands preparing for this evening's performance," Mrs. Hill explained.

"Nate!" one of the men shouted. "Where's the backing for this flat?"

"Coming!"

A man carrying a large wooden frame suddenly emerged from the shadows. He started to brush past them but stopped as soon as his eyes fell on Rosalyn.

Their gazes locked, and Rosalyn's mouth fell open in surprise.

She was staring into the intense brown eyes of the soldier from Paddington station.

CHAPTER
5

THE BRIGHT RED COAT and polished boots were gone. Today the man standing before her looked altogether different. He wore faded trousers and an old shirt covered with splotches of paint and grease, and there was a smudge of dirt on one cheek.

"You!" he exclaimed. "You're all right? You're not . . . harmed?" Setting down the object he was holding, he took a step back, falling into a brighter pool of light near the lamp on the wall. Rosalyn took an unconscious step forward, following him into the light. His gaze continued to take her in with a kind of wondering disbelief.

She offered him a tentative smile. "It was a rough night, I admit, but no harm came to me."

His eyes closed for a brief moment. When they opened again, the anxiety he'd shown was erased by relief. "Thank God."

Hearing this, she saw how wrong she'd been at the station to presume he had malicious intentions toward her. "Yes, His divine hand helped me." It came out with a slight stammer. "I should apologize for my rude words to you last night."

He shook his head. "I blame myself for the way I barged into the situation. You already had one man harassing you. I must have looked like one more scoundrel trying to take advantage of you."

"It did seem that way," Rosalyn admitted.

"You two know each other?" Mrs. Hill's surprised voice interrupted them.

"Not really, but perhaps we should remedy that." He tipped his head in a crisp bow that would have been perfectly suited for when he was in uniform. "My name is Nate Moran."

"Rosalyn Bernay."

"I am happy to make your acquaintance."

He extended a hand. His shirt sleeves were rolled up to his elbows, revealing the full length of the scar Rosalyn had noticed at the station. It was seven or eight inches long, running well above his wrist. She hesitated, then reached out to accept the handshake. His grasp was firm but gentle, and she found her reaction was completely different than when he'd taken hold of her yesterday. Warmth traveled all the way up her arm. His smiled widened, lightening his eyes. The heat from his touch continued to diffuse throughout her body.

After a moment, she recollected herself and withdrew her hand.

Nate said, "Tell me, how did you wind up here, of all places?"

"I believe it was Providence. Mrs. Hill has offered me work."

He blinked in surprise. "You're going to work here? So you have a place to live, then. You went to the charity house after all?"

"Charity house?" Rosalyn repeated, mystified.

"I wasn't sure if you heard me calling out the name and address to you at the station yard. The carriages were making so much racket."

"Well, I . . . that is . . . ," Rosalyn stammered, flummoxed.

Another yell echoed down the hallway. "Nate! Hurry it up, lad, or Mr. Gilbert will have all our hides!"

"Coming!" Nate called over his shoulder. But his gaze held hers for a moment longer, and she could see he was brimming with as many questions as she was.

"Perhaps we might talk more later?" Rosalyn suggested.

"Aye," he said, looking pleased at her request. "I will look for you." He picked up the wooden frame he'd been carrying and gave her a brief smile before turning to hurry down the hallway.

Rosalyn watched him walk away. She could hardly believe the change in him from last night. Or perhaps the change was simply in her perception of him.

"All right, then," Mrs. Hill said. "To work we go."

They walked down a narrow hallway to a small, windowless room packed with mops, brooms, and buckets. Mrs. Hill hung her coat on a peg and reached for an apron. She motioned Rosalyn toward a stool next to a battered sink. "Have a seat."

Exhausted from the harrowing day, Rosalyn happily complied.

Mrs. Hill took a tin of biscuits from a small cupboard and handed them to Rosalyn. "It ain't much, but it's something."

While Mrs. Hill busied herself filling a bucket with water, Rosalyn pulled a biscuit out of the tin and bit into it. It was dry, but it was food, and she was thankful. As she ate, her mind kept returning to the soldier-turned-stagehand and the odd circumstances that had brought them together not once, but twice. "Mrs. Hill, how long has Mr. Moran worked here?"

"About a month. But he's only here temporarily."

"When I first saw him yesterday, he was wearing an army uniform. Why do you suppose that was?"

Mrs. Hill set the full bucket aside and reached for another. "I believe he's still in the reserves. I know he was in active duty—or 'the colors,' as they say—until a few months ago. Got wounded in some kind of skirmish in India. Of course, Patrick idolizes him. That's Nate's brother." She paused to emit a warm smile. "Patrick's a good 'un, he is. Been working here for years. A few weeks ago he slipped off the narrow ladder that leads to the fly gallery. His leg punched right through a bit of scenery and got broke in the process. Nate's been taking his place so Patrick will have a job to come back to after he heals up."

"You mean Patrick would lose his job, even though he was injured while working?"

"Well, the shows got to keep running, don't they? If you're not here to do your job, there's three others in line to take your place. It's a sad fact, but it's true. Things is tough all over."

Rosalyn believed the truth of this statement. She'd seen more than a glimpse of the harsh realities of city life since her arrival. But she said nothing, merely chewed another biscuit as she thought over this new information about Nate Moran. How wrong she'd been to fall for Mrs. Hurdle's insinuations about him at the station.

After setting the second bucket next to the first, Mrs. Hill dried her hands on her apron. "Now, then," she said briskly, "ready to work?"

"Indeed I am." Rosalyn stood up, reluctant to leave the comfort of sitting down but telling herself she had to keep moving. She prayed that the prospect of earning money would make her strong enough to accomplish whatever was asked of her. Already this theater felt like a safe harbor, and she was determined to do everything she could to be allowed to stay.

Mrs. Hill grabbed an apron that had been draped over a mop handle. "Put this on. It ain't the cleanest, but it'll keep the worst of it off your frock." Once Rosalyn had donned the apron, Mrs. Hill handed her a stack of towels. "Let's start by getting these to the dressing rooms. We'll come back for those buckets later."

They retraced their steps down the hallway. "There's one set of stairs backstage that leads to the ladies' dressing rooms, and another on the opposite end of the stage that leads to the men's," Mrs. Hill explained. "Some people see the theater as a wicked place, but Mr. Gilbert is adamant that everything in *this* theater stays proper and aboveboard."

Rosalyn didn't say that she was one of those people raised to regard the theater in a bad light. Even singing opera songs with Mrs. Williams for amusement had felt at times like a guilty pleasure. She'd never considered the fact that theaters provided work for decent, hardworking people like Mrs. Hill.

Smoke from the feeble oil lamps might have lent an oppressive air to the place, yet to Rosalyn it only added an enticing air of mystery. Rounding a corner, they came into a wider area that Rosalyn saw immediately was just to the side of the stage.

"Are you familiar with theaters?" Mrs. Hill asked. "This area here is called the 'wings.'"

Four portable gas lamps, set on T-shaped poles about eight feet high, were placed around the stage, bathing it in light. The startling brightness stung her eyes after the gloom of the hallway.

"Those is just working lights," Mrs. Hill explained. "They're taken away during the performance."

Half a dozen men knelt around a massive square of wood-framed, painted canvas, carefully attaching it to sturdy ropes. They must have been trained exactly how to do this, for each man seemed to be securing his rope with the same elaborate knot. One by one, as they completed their task, each man stood up.

When everyone had finished and stepped back, one of the men called up toward the rafters. "Ready, Nate?"

"Ready!"

Rosalyn looked up. Through the glare of the lights and a cloud of dust, she saw a railed platform high above them. This must be the "fly gallery" Mrs. Hill had spoken of. She could see Nate, his back and arms straining as he and another man turned cranks that pulled ropes wound around huge pulleys. Slowly the canvas lifted from the floor, and the men onstage guided it into place.

Rosalyn gasped in delight. What was essentially a giant painting now covered the rear of the stage. It depicted a seaside harbor and the bright blue sky of a sunny day, the flags on several ships' masts flying saucily in the breeze.

It brought back the memory of her early childhood in Plymouth, before her mother had died. Rosalyn and Julia would take long walks together, clambering up the cliffs and standing breathless and joyful as they looked down over the harbor. Although she'd left Plymouth when she was just nine years old, Rosalyn vividly remembered the sight of those masts and the colorful flags in the stiff wind. She and Julia would gaze out at the ocean, trying to imagine where their father was at that moment. Those daydreams turned to sad longing when the years passed and their father never came home. But right now, standing on this stage, the painting evoked happy memories of the sea breeze on her face and the warmth of the sun shining down on her head. She breathed deep, almost smelling the tang of salt in the air.

"Do you like it?"

It was Nate's voice. Once more, Rosalyn looked up toward the fly gallery. It must have been at least two stories above the stage, but he was leaning casually against the railing as though on solid ground, not giving his precarious position a second thought.

He'd been watching her as she stared at the canvas and grinned like a fool. Feeling mildly abashed, she answered, "It looks exactly like Plymouth."

"Are you from Plymouth, then?"

"I lived there as a child. I still remember it well."

A stagehand standing nearby said, "Our scene painter really outdid himself, I think. That's my son, you know. I raised him in Plymouth, but we moved here five years ago. Life in the theater is much nicer than working on one of those ships, I can tell you. Being separated from one's family for months at a time—not to mention the dangers of the sea."

"Yes, I know," Rosalyn said with a sigh. She looked up again to see that Nate was still watching her. Not wanting to reveal the range of emotions flooding through her, she cleared her throat and brought her gaze back to stage level. Several of the men were wiping their brows. They must have put in a hard day's work already, but they were smiling.

"Will that do, Mr. Turner?" said one of the men.

Mr. Turner, a tall, balding man of about forty who was evidently the foreman of this group, eyed the canvas with a satisfied air. "Aye, that'll do just fine." Peering up at Nate, he added, "Perhaps we ought to thank your brother for damaging that other flat on his way down. This one is far superior. I believe the audience will be right pleased."

Nate matched the man's grin. "Does that mean Patrick will get a pay rise when he returns?"

Mr. Turner gave a gruff laugh. "You'll have to take that up with Mr. Carte. Or worse, with Mr. Gilbert!"

"Best be careful with your jesting," Mrs. Hill teased. "Mr. Gilbert is in the building."

Upon hearing this, some of the men quickly looked around with expressions of mock worry, followed by exaggerated expressions of relief when Mr. Gilbert did not suddenly appear and berate them.

"All right, let's get this stage *shipshape*," Mr. Turner ordered, drawing a few chuckles with his joke. "There's less than an hour until curtain."

From the fly gallery, Nate watched the men scatter to their assigned pre-show tasks. He had work to do, too, and a short amount of time to do it in, but he lingered at the railing, his attention still on Rosalyn. From his vantage point, he could hear as well as see everything on the stage. Mrs. Hill began giving Rosalyn instructions, and she nodded, listening intently. Nate couldn't help but think how resourceful she was, to have come this far in just twenty-four hours. He wanted very much to know more about her and what had brought her to London.

He noticed Jessie Bond scurrying through the wings, tugging a bedraggled young woman behind her.

"Here's your missing charwoman," Jessie said, pushing the girl forward to stand in front of Mrs. Hill. "She came in the wrong door. I found her wandering around in that warren of hallways."

The girl wore a faded cotton frock, patched many times over, and battered boots that looked too large for her feet. Everything about her signaled her poverty. She looked at Mrs. Hill, utterly contrite. "Please forgive me, ma'am. It won't 'appen again." She mumbled the words so low that Nate had to strain to hear them.

"I'm sorry, my girl, but you're too late," Mrs. Hill replied. "We've already found someone else." Her words, though direct, were spoken with kind regret.

"Please let her stay," Rosalyn begged.

Mrs. Hill shook her head. "I can't take on two people. Much as I'd like to."

"Then give the job to her."

Nate thought he heard a slight tremor in Rosalyn's voice, but she evidently meant what she said. She removed her apron and handed it to the girl, whose face lit up with amazed joy. "To be honest, I won't be in London for long. Perhaps it's better if I go now." She turned to Mrs. Hill and said, "I do thank you for your kindness today."

Jessie held out a hand to stop her. "Wait. I have an idea. Mrs. Hill, you know we're having a bit of a crisis up in the dressing rooms. Lilly hasn't shown up again. I'm afraid there will be a mutiny among the ladies if we don't get a new dresser soon. Perhaps Rosalyn could help us."

Mrs. Hill looked doubtful. "I think you'd need to ask Miss Lenoir about that first. Cleaning's one thing, but working as a dresser is quite another."

"Miss Lenoir's out of town until Monday," Jessie said. "We have a show to put on tonight."

"I worked as a lady's companion for five years," Rosalyn interjected eagerly. "Does that qualify?"

"It will do for now. Don't worry, Mrs. Hill, I'll settle it with Miss Lenoir." Jessie took Rosalyn's hand. "Let's go. There's no time to waste."

Marveling over this turn of events, Nate watched them hurry toward the dressing rooms. He was impressed that Rosalyn had been willing to give up her own livelihood in order to help a person in need. It was a selflessness he didn't see every day. Certainly not inside the theater.

The grizzled face of Sam, one of the other lighting men, appeared at the top of the ladder. "Ready to set the lights?"

Nate nodded, clearing his mind to focus on the task at hand. It was time to collect the containers of gas that fueled the limelights. Because they were volatile, they were kept in a special storage closet until needed. But even as Nate turned away from the railing and followed Sam back down the ladder, he found his thoughts returning to the woman who'd arrived in London in such odd circumstances and kept landing on her feet. Surely it was only natural to be intrigued by such a person. Who wouldn't be?

Still, as he and the other men prepared the lights, he would have preferred not having to work quite so hard to keep his mind on his job.

⁂

"Thank you so much," Rosalyn said to Jessie as the two made their way up a narrow flight of steps.

"Well, we couldn't very well throw you out," Jessie answered breezily. "Not after we'd already rescued you once. I had you pegged as a governess, but a lady's companion is even better. That means you have some experience with fine clothes, yes?"

"Yes," Rosalyn said, too breathless from the climb to say more.

In truth, she wasn't sure what qualified as adequate experience. Mrs. Huffman had a lady's maid to help her dress and attend to the daily tasks of maintaining the wardrobe. Rosalyn's experience had been primarily in accompanying Mrs. Huffman on shopping trips and dress fittings. But this had exposed Rosalyn to a wide variety of dress materials and styles. Surely that would be useful for something.

They reached the top of the steps, and Jessie led her down a long hallway. Pushing open a door, she said, "Here's the dressing room for the ladies' chorus."

The large room was lined on one wall with vanity tables and mirrors. Along another wall stood racks of gowns. Women milled around in various stages of dress. Some were seated at the tables, applying makeup. Without hesitation, Jessie steered Rosalyn to the nearest chair. "Why don't you sit here for a moment and catch your breath?"

Rosalyn sank into the chair and immediately found herself staring into the eyes of the woman seated next to her.

"Hullo, who's this?" the woman asked.

"Helen, this is our new dresser," Jessie said.

71

"Well, saints be praised!" Helen spoke enthusiastically, if somewhat sarcastically. "How on earth did you get Miss Lenoir to agree to a new hire?"

"Just be happy she's here. But I think she needs to rest a bit before she gets started." Seeing Helen about to protest, Jessie held up a hand. "There's plenty of time. *Cups* hasn't even started yet." She turned to Rosalyn and explained, "Tonight's curtain raiser is a one-act operetta called *Cups and Saucers*. That has just three people in it. We go on with *Pinafore* once that's over."

"The poor thing does look a bit peaked," one of the other ladies observed. She extended a small bottle toward Rosalyn. "Need a little nudge?"

Jessie took the bottle and sniffed, then frowned at the woman. "Elsie, no wonder you never have money for the cab ride home if you're spending your hard-earned salary on brandy."

"Aha, so you recognize the smell of brandy, do you?" Elsie shot back in an accusatory tone, bringing snickers from the others. She snatched the bottle back from Jessie. "A nice gentleman from last night's audience gave it to me. You know, if you weren't so determined to turn away suitors, you might have some fine things yourself."

"Oh no," Jessie replied with feeling. "That's too dear a price to pay for a little brandy."

Elsie pressed the bottle into Rosalyn's hand. "Go ahead—take a sip. It'll revitalize you."

Rosalyn had never drunk spirits before. She held the bottle gingerly and gave Jessie a questioning glance.

Jessie sighed. "You might as well take a little. It is medicinal." With a pointed look at Elsie, she added, "In small quantities." But Elsie only smirked.

Rosalyn took a hesitant sip. The liquid burned her throat, stinging as it went down, then sent a surge of heat through her entire body. She gasped and gave a little cough, her eyes opening round.

"Bracing, isn't it?" Elsie said proudly, taking back the bottle. "But, as Jessie said, a small amount is enough."

"Besides," added Helen, "novices shouldn't overdo it the first time—right, Elsie? Or is it just that you want to save more for yourself?"

Elsie gave her a sarcastic grimace as she capped the bottle.

"Does anyone have food, by any chance?" Jessie asked. "I think Rosalyn could use a bit of sustenance."

"I've got a small meat pie." Helen pulled a paper-wrapped object from the satchel on the table next to her. "You may have it." She extended the pie but then pulled back just as Rosalyn was stretching out her hand. "*If* you promise to help me dress before the others."

"I would say something about self-sacrifice being out of fashion . . ." Jessie began.

"It's been replaced by obstinate practicality," Helen insisted. "You know I always have a devil of a time getting that infernal sash tied correctly."

"I'll be glad to help you," Rosalyn said. Her voice came out as a rasp, her throat still stinging from the liquid fire.

"I can tell we're going to get on just fine," Helen said with a smile.

Rosalyn unwrapped the pie. It was warm, its fragrance waking a powerful hunger in her. She took a bite, and as the warm gravy and tender crust melted in her mouth, she nearly moaned with happiness.

One of the other ladies stood with her arms crossed, studying Rosalyn critically. "You *do* have experience as a dresser, don't you? We haven't time for someone who doesn't know what they're about."

"Sarah, let her eat before you start peppering her with questions," Jessie admonished.

Sarah gave Rosalyn another skeptical look and returned to her dressing table.

Rosalyn was just finishing the pie when the door flew open and a beautiful brunette strode in, looking harried. "Jessie, my hem was torn during the matinee. What shall I do? I haven't time to mend it and still prepare for tonight's show." She gave a dramatic, exasperated sigh. "How are we supposed to manage without a dresser?"

"Don't fret yourself, Emma," Jessie soothed. "We've got a dresser." Turning to Rosalyn, she said, "You *are* handy with a needle, I hope?"

"Oh, yes, I've mended many a frock. Hundreds, perhaps."

"Hundreds!" Helen repeated in amused surprise.

"I grew up in a very large orphanage."

"In that case, would you care to mend my stockings, too?" Helen asked with a wink. "I can bring them from home tomorrow."

Rosalyn found herself smiling at Helen's constant quips. Or perhaps it was the bracing effect of the meat pie and Elsie's brandy. Whatever the reason, Rosalyn felt at ease here. The camaraderie of women was something she knew well after growing up in a dormitory filled with girls. She stood up. "Why don't you show me the gown? I'm sure we can get it fixed straightaway."

"Wonderful!" Emma took Rosalyn's hand and began to pull her toward the door.

"Wait!" Elsie called after them. "I thought she was going to help us!"

"You don't come on until well into act one," Jessie called over her shoulder. "She'll be back."

Emma and Jessie ushered Rosalyn down the hall, passing several doors but not stopping until they reached one with two signs reading "Miss Howson" and "Miss Bond." Emma flung open the door, and they went inside. This room was much smaller than the wide room for the ladies' chorus. There was just enough space for two dressing tables, crammed side by side against a wall, a dressing screen, and an open wardrobe stuffed with gowns. The three of them together left room for very little else.

"Emma and I are sharing a dressing room for the time being," Jessie explained. "Mine is next door, but it fell victim to a leak in the roof and is not usable until they get it repaired. I think this whole building might fall down around our ears at any moment. There's a reason these buildings are called 'the rickety twins.'"

"Rickety twins!" Rosalyn repeated, bemused.

"Yes. The theater next door is the mirror image of this one. They even share the same backstage wall." Jessie giggled. "Sometimes when the show there is particularly boisterous, you can hear it on our side."

"That's enough idle chatter," Emma directed, picking up a gown that had been tossed over a chair. "I need you to see if you can mend this."

She set it down on the table, and Rosalyn immediately saw the tear.

"Oh dear," Jessie said. "When did that happen?"

"Right at the end of act two. Mr. Grossmith stepped on it when we were singing the encore of 'Never mind the why or wherefore.' He never does pay attention to what he's doing."

"He does get rather exuberant sometimes," Jessie agreed with a smile.

Rosalyn inspected the tear. "This is easily mended. Shouldn't take long at all. With the way these ruffles fall around the hem, I don't think it will even show."

"You are worth your weight in gold already," Emma declared.

"I'll show you where the costume room is," Jessie said. "We can find sewing supplies there."

The next hour passed like a whirlwind. Rosalyn mended the gown while Emma and Jessie put on their stage makeup. She might have saved a minute or two if she hadn't been watching them out of the corner of her eye, fascinated at the layers of paint they applied to their faces. After she helped them into their gowns, Rosalyn went back across the hallway to the chorus room. There were twenty ladies in there now, all chattering nonstop as they put on their makeup and fussed with the ribbons and folds of their gowns. Rosalyn found plenty to do.

The talk ceased abruptly at a knock on the door, and a girl's voice said, "Ten minutes!"

"Who was that?" Rosalyn asked.

"That's Millie," Helen said. "She keeps us informed of our entrances, since Mr. Gilbert allows no men up here."

"She sounds very young."

"Her father is the prompter. But I think she gets a few coins for her work, too. After all, even the tykes have to earn a living, don't they?"

Rosalyn thought of the many children she'd seen on the streets of London that day. Some were begging, a few were earning pennies as crossing sweepers. Others drooped languidly against buildings, watching the passersby with a dejected air. One was being hauled off to the police station for pickpocketing, struggling and shouting words no child should know. She realized just how blessed and protected she'd been in Mr. Müller's orphanage. She had not always been thankful for it when she was younger. Today's walk through London had made her painfully aware that even an orphanage that housed two thousand was but a small drop in a very large sea of need.

The ladies quickly filed out of the dressing room. When the last one had gone, the room fell quiet, like the stillness after a storm. Rosalyn took a deep breath, still marveling at her presence here.

After a few moments, she wandered into the hall. Even without checking, she could feel from the way the silence had settled that all the other rooms were empty, too.

What should she do? Should she remain up here? She might easily take a nap in one of the chairs, but she was too intensely curious to see what was going on downstairs. She moved to the edge of the stairway and peered down. A little girl sat, chin in hand, on the bottom step.

Hearing Rosalyn's tread on the stairs, the girl stood up and watched her come down.

"Are you Millie?" Rosalyn asked.

She nodded. "Who are you?"

"I'm the new dresser." It felt good to say it—as though Rosalyn had a place to be and a reason for being there. Even if it might only be for tonight.

Millie looked her over, and Rosalyn could tell the girl must be thinking that she didn't *look* like the dresser.

"I suppose you could say I got this job on the spur of the moment," Rosalyn said. "And to be honest, there hasn't been time for anyone to fully explain my duties to me. Do you know if I am supposed to remain upstairs during the show?"

Millie took a moment to think this over. "I don't think so. Lilly used to come down a lot. There's only one costume change for the ladies, and that's Miss Howson during intermission."

She sounded very grown-up and knowledgeable. Rosalyn was astonished at her self-possession. "How long have you been working here?"

Millie shrugged. "Forever. My da is the prompter."

"Oh, I see. Do you like working here?"

"Most of the time the show changes after a few weeks, but this one has been going on for *years* and *years*." Millie gave a dramatic sigh. "I wish we could get something new."

Rosalyn smiled at Millie's exaggeration. Now she sounded exactly like the ten-year-old she appeared to be.

The girl brightened. "But we're to have a new show in the spring. That's what Da says. I'm glad."

"I imagine you've seen this one hundreds of times."

"Thousands!"

Rosalyn swallowed another smile. "Well, I've never seen it."

"Never?" Millie's eyes widened in surprise. "I thought *everyone* had seen it!"

"I'm probably the very last person who hasn't," Rosalyn agreed. "Do you suppose it would be all right if I were to stand backstage and watch?"

"Sure. That's what Lilly used to do. You just have to be careful not to block the actors' entrances and exits. You can ask my da. His name is Mr. Giles. He'll tell you what to do."

"Thank you!" With a smile and a wave, Rosalyn left Millie and walked toward the music.

CHAPTER

6

R OSALYN PICKED her way along a corridor cluttered with tables, boxes, and odds and ends of furniture. She slowed as she neared the wings, uncertain whether she was straying into forbidden territory.

A man hurried past her and placed several items on a long table before continuing on. He didn't seem the least bit concerned about her presence. Rosalyn paused to look over the objects on the table. Next to a dozen silk bouquets and two parasols sat two very different items: a pistol and a whip. The whip was a cat-o-nine-tails, to be exact. Rosalyn knew from having read the libretto that the captain of the *Pinafore* never uses it on anybody, he merely threatens. But this particular cat-o-nine-tails looked extremely realistic. Perhaps it *was* real and not merely a prop. But surely the pistol must be fake, thought Rosalyn. Otherwise it would not have been placed out here so casually. She tentatively reached out to touch it.

Immediately something grey, striped, and furry leaped upon the table, startling Rosalyn. She stepped back with a yelp.

"Quiet!" a voice hissed.

Rosalyn turned to see a short, wiry man staring at her. Even in the dim light, she could make out wide-set hazel eyes similar to Millie's. This must be Mr. Giles.

"I beg your pardon," she said, her voice just above a whisper. "The cat startled me."

He nodded in acceptance of her quiet tone. "That's Miss Bella. She guards the props table. She won't hurt you, though. Most likely she's looking for you to pet her." He stepped forward to get a better look at her. "But who are *you*? Mr. Gilbert and Mr. Barker don't allow *unauthorized persons* backstage."

Something in the way he said "unauthorized persons" made Rosalyn sure he was directly quoting Mr. Gilbert. Even as he spoke, she could tell he was keeping an ear cocked toward the stage. She had no doubt he was carefully following the business on it.

"I . . . I am the new dresser." She held her breath, awaiting his reaction, hoping the title of "dresser" qualified her as an "authorized person." Just twenty feet away, out on the stage, Emma Howson was singing a lovely aria. As she moved, her gown flowed smoothly behind her, showing no sign of the mended tear.

Mr. Giles seemed to accept Rosalyn's words. His eye followed her hand, and she realized she'd begun scratching the little cat behind the ears. It had been an automatic gesture. Rosalyn quite liked cats—probably because Mrs. Huffman's cat, Penelope, had been a beloved and constant companion in the Huffmans' home. She could feel, rather than hear, Miss Bella purring beneath her touch. Judging from his expression, Mr. Giles appreciated Rosalyn's affection toward Miss Bella.

Still speaking softly, he said, "No doubt you are wanting to see this famous show for yourself."

"Yes," Rosalyn admitted. "I've never seen it, although I am familiar with the score."

He gave a wry sort of grimace. "So is everyone in England. Can't go anywhere without hearing someone whistling a tune from it. Although it's the organ grinders on street corners who are the most insufferable."

Onstage, Miss Howson was coming to the end of her sad ballad. Her character, Josephine, was the daughter of the ship's captain. Alas, she was in love with Ralph Rackstraw, a mere sailor, who was considered beneath her station, and their union could never be allowed. Not too far from where Rosalyn stood, the ladies' chorus was assembling with quiet deliberation. In the opposite wings, Rosalyn could see the men's chorus, all dressed as sailors, standing at the ready for their next entrance.

Clearly it was time for Mr. Giles to go to work. "Just be careful to keep out of the way," he told Rosalyn. "If anyone in the chorus trips over you, there will be a terrible row, and you'll find your employment ending quicker than it started."

"I'll be careful," Rosalyn assured him. But he had already turned away and begun to oversee the movement of the women into position—still in the wings, but very close to the front of the stage.

Rosalyn squeezed between the props table and the wall. She watched in surprise as the ladies began singing right there in the wings. They were following hand signals given by one of the chorus ladies who could see the conductor. Even though she'd read the libretto, Rosalyn had not pictured the scene unfolding this way.

"Over the bright blue sea comes Sir Joseph Porter, K.C.B. . . ."

As the women sang, the sailors filtered onto the stage, listening with pleased expressions. After several verses, the ladies filed past Rosalyn, joining the sailors onstage in a lively song of meeting.

"*Gaily tripping, lightly skipping, flock the maidens to the shipping . . .*"

From her vantage point, Rosalyn had a good view of the action—especially when the actors were standing downstage, closest to the audience. She could see the heads of the musicians in the orchestra pit and the energetic conductor.

She didn't see Jessie anywhere onstage, but a few minutes later Jessie and one of the other actors approached her from somewhere in the wings. The man was thin and of moderate height, although he stood several inches taller than Jessie. He wore a red admiral's coat festooned with elaborate braiding, white knee-breeches, and an enormous bicorn hat topped with white feathers.

When they reached Rosalyn, the man peered at her through a monocle. "I say, who's this?" Although he spoke in a quiet backstage voice, his exaggerated upper-class accent was easy to discern.

"This is Rosalyn Bernay, the lady I was telling you about," Jessie whispered.

"Ah, the stray. Just like Miss Bella there." He pointed toward the cat, who stretched and yawned disinterestedly.

Jessie said, "Rosalyn, this is Mr. George Grossmith. He plays Sir Joseph Porter."

"Among other things," Mr. Grossmith corrected her. "I am an actor and bon vivant extraordinaire."

"He's also incredibly humble," Jessie teased.

Rosalyn playfully gave him a smart little curtsy. Careful to keep her voice low to match theirs, she said, "Pleased to meet you, sir."

"A very polite and pleasing young lady," Mr. Grossmith declared. "Did you see the curtain opener, by any chance?"

"I'm afraid not."

"She was upstairs. She is now our dresser," Jessie reminded him.

"Ah yes, so you said. Poor Lilly seems gone forever. Deserted the regiment." He pointed toward the men onstage.

Jessie poked him in the ribs. "Those are sailors, not soldiers. You are mixing your metaphors."

Grossmith disregarded Jessie's chiding. "It's too bad you missed *Cups and Saucers*," he whispered to Rosalyn. "It's so good that *Pinafore* actually pales in comparison."

Jessie rolled her eyes. "He's only saying that because he wrote it."

"Did you?" Rosalyn said. "I must be sure to find a way to see it."

Grossmith smirked in approval. "Miss Bond, I can see you have brought in a stray who is astute as well as useful. We really must keep her."

From the orchestra came a very loud *rat-a-tat* of drums, played several times in succession. Jessie tugged on Mr. Grossmith's arm. "There's our cue!"

From the stage, the captain sang, *"Now give three cheers; I'll lead the way!"*

"Hurray! Hurray! Hurray!" sang the chorus.

In a moment, Jessie's and Mr. Grossmith's entire bearing changed. They had been relaxed and casual as they'd chatted with Rosalyn, but now Mr. Grossmith stood ramrod straight, and Jessie's chin lifted. She positively radiated self-satisfied pride as she and Mr. Grossmith walked regally out onto the stage. Rosalyn was awestruck at the sudden transformation.

Mr. Grossmith, as Sir Joseph, launched into a wildly improbable song about how he came to be the First Lord of the Admiralty. Jessie and the ladies' chorus chimed in at various moments. Rosalyn found herself smiling broadly at his comical facial expressions and actions. The reality was even better than she had ever imagined. It was astounding to her that such a pretty and appealing person as Jessie could convincingly play the part of a lovesick cousin whom Sir Joseph wanted nothing to do with. In fact, Jessie became so clingy and overbearing, despite her small stature, that Sir Joseph's dislike of her was entirely understandable. And the audience was eating it up, roaring with laughter.

This is the theater, Rosalyn thought. *People do this for a living, transforming themselves for the delight of others.* She had been schooled that the theater was a wicked place, wasteful of precious time and unedifying to the soul. But as she watched, she considered the idea that perhaps there could be a place in life for *enriching* amusements. She tried to imagine what it would be like to be out there onstage, bathed in bright lights, looking up at the smiling faces of the people in the upper galleries. She felt guilty for even imagining such a thing—until her attention centered once more on Jessie and the laughter she was drawing from the audience. Jessie seemed like a good person; perhaps a life in the theater didn't have to lead inevitably to ruin.

A few minutes later, Mr. Grossmith and Jessie left the stage. "Are you enjoying it?" Jessie whispered when they reached Rosalyn.

"Yes!" Rosalyn answered without hesitation. "You were wonderful!"

"Ahem," murmured Mr. Grossmith.

Rosalyn was equally happy to give him the compliment he was fishing for. "You were a delight, as well, Mr. Grossmith! My side hurts from laughing."

"Yes, we must definitely keep her," Grossmith said. "Or better yet, get her a job as a reviewer for *The Times*."

Mr. Giles motioned to Jessie. "You're nearly on."

"Here we are, my last entrance before intermission. There are so many entrances and exits for this act! Wait for me here, and we'll go up to the dressing rooms together."

"Of course," Rosalyn replied. In truth, nothing would tear her away from watching the show. She wanted to savor this new pleasure. She watched, breathless, as Jessie and the entire chorus raced onstage as Ralph Rackstraw stood with that prop gun to his head, threatening to kill himself unless Josephine admitted her love for him. It was a tense and dramatic moment. Soon Josephine gave in and confessed that she did indeed love him. It was a joyous, thrilling ending to the first half, full of the promise of love winning despite all odds—or at least, ready to face the obstacles that were bound to come.

Rosalyn reached out to pet Miss Bella. The buoyant music lifted her spirits. After the harrowing events of the past few days, this amazing reprieve was revitalizing her strength and her senses. As the curtain came down to thunderous applause, Rosalyn's eyes brimmed with tears of thankfulness for this sudden—if somewhat bizarre—escape from the terrible fate that had threatened to befall her.

⌒◌⌒

Nate leaned against the railing, watching the action below. After five weeks at this, he knew every one of the actors' lines and gestures by heart. It was always the same; not because the actors lacked imagination, but because Mr. Gilbert allowed no room for improvisation. In fact, he had given instructions to Mr. Barker, his assistant stage director, to fine the actors a half crown if they did not follow their blocking exactly. Mr. Barker seemed only too willing to carry out this directive. Nate had seen him do it a number of times.

About halfway through the first act, his gaze strayed to the wings, and he noticed Rosalyn standing by the props table. She was speaking with Jessie Bond. Grossmith was there, too, doing his usual mugging and playing up to other people. Rosalyn seemed to be enjoying it, however.

Sam joined him at the railing and looked down, following his gaze. "That Grossmith has an eye for the ladies, don't he? Especially the pretty ones."

Nate shifted uncomfortably. "Indeed."

"Of course, he has a wife and four children," Sam added. "So it's all just playacting."

"Does he?" Nate said in surprise. The way Grossmith carried on, Nate had no idea the man was married.

"Not that that ever stops *some* people," Sam went on. "Least of all an actor."

Given what he'd seen over the past few weeks, Nate could readily concur. He felt a twinge of apprehension for Rosalyn. She had shown herself last night to be somewhat gullible. "Would Grossmith really be unfaithful to his wife?"

"Nah, I don't think so," Sam answered. "At least, I've never heard of any scandal attached to him."

Nate reminded himself that Rosalyn had shown she could protect herself, or else she wouldn't even be here.

The drums signaled the cue for Jessie and Grossmith's entrance. As they walked out onstage, Rosalyn remained where she was, watching everything with rapt attention. Nate wasn't surprised; who wouldn't want to see the most popular show in London? By the time Grossmith was halfway through his song, Rosalyn's face was radiating amusement and joy.

As the show progressed, Nate found his gaze returning to her, intrigued by the play of delight on her features. He could easily guess that she was seeing it for the first time. He'd grown accustomed to this show and all of its spectacle and music; he'd even begun to grow bored with it. But Rosalyn's enthusiasm caused him to see everything afresh. And he found he was rather enjoying it.

 ✦

Rosalyn watched, exhilarated, as the company took yet another bow. The audience was exuberant with applause and shouts, and

Rosalyn could easily understand why. She had missed some portions of the show due to her other tasks, but what she had seen, including the rousing finale, had produced a joy so intense that it pushed all her other worries into the background.

As the actors continued their bows, a bouquet of roses landed at Jessie Bond's feet. Jessie smiled, picking up the flowers and waving toward the audience in the general direction the flowers had come from. Then she turned and beckoned toward the wings where Rosalyn was standing.

Rosalyn froze in surprise. Did Jessie expect her to go out on the stage?

Behind her she heard a deep guffaw from Mr. Giles. "Mrs. Hill!" he called into the shadows behind them. "Yer wanted."

"Coming!"

Mrs. Hill strolled past Rosalyn and out onto the stage, still in her dirty apron and holding a well-worn mop. Friendly catcalls from the audience greeted her. Jessie held the flowers out to Mrs. Hill with a gesture that said, *I believe these are for you*. The cleaning lady accepted them with a broad grin and threw a big kiss toward the audience, provoking a fresh round of laughter and applause. She then ambled off the stage, and the cast continued their bows.

Mrs. Hill handed the flowers to Rosalyn. "There you go, dearie. An extra tip for you tonight. That was a kind thing you did earlier."

"Thank you. I couldn't have lived with myself otherwise."

Mrs. Hill nodded in appreciation and understanding.

Rosalyn brought the bouquet to her nose and inhaled deeply, savoring the unexpected pleasure of holding red roses and white orchids in the winter. "What was your charade all about?"

"It's something Miss Bond and I cooked up together. It's her way of being gracious but also letting the would-be suitor know that she ain't that kind of gal."

"Oh, I see. She accepts the compliment but doesn't want to encourage the man."

"Precisely," Mrs. Hill replied with a grin. "Works every time."

"You were charming out there. You should be an actress yourself!"

Mr. Giles gave a snort. "Mrs. Hill on the stage! Fancy that!"

Mrs. Hill swatted at him. "Don't say you haven't thought of it yourself, Fred."

"Why, sure! You and I could sing a duet. Along with Miss Bella here."

As if on cue, the cat gave a meow.

"Don't be daft," Mrs. Hill said. "If Miss Bella sings, too, then it wouldn't be a *duet*!"

Rosalyn joined in their laughter. Onstage, the curtain came down once more—for the last time, it seemed.

Earlier, one of the chorus ladies had pointed out Mr. Barker, the assistant stage director, to Rosalyn. He'd come backstage several times but had spent much of the night watching the show from the house. A good way to ensure the actors hit all their marks.

Now that the curtain was down, Mr. Barker came out on the stage and announced, "Very good. No notes tonight. Everyone is dismissed."

A collective sigh of relief rippled through the whole company. As they began to disperse, Rosalyn heard one of the men say dryly, "I can't believe Mr. Barker let us go. With only three curtain calls tonight, I was sure he'd give us another lecture about keeping up the energy in our performances."

"Personally, I think he ought to have called out the ladies," a second man said. "They were definitely flat tonight."

This comment came from a chorus member Rosalyn had noticed several times during the show. He was handsome, with sandy brown hair and blue eyes, but what had set him apart for Rosalyn was his expressive acting and his strong tenor voice. She was startled to hear his negative assessment of the ladies' chorus, especially since she had thought they sounded very fine. To her further surprise, she realized the remark was aimed at Elsie, who was passing by.

Elsie glared at him but said nothing and continued on her way.

"At least we had Mrs. Hill's antics to liven things up," another man said. "Her bit with the flowers is always good for a laugh."

The tenor's gaze rested on Rosalyn. "Look here—the sweets have landed in sweeter hands than old Mrs. H's."

He smiled at her, showing teeth that were straight and white. Rosalyn could barely believe his attitude had been so caustic a moment ago. Now he exuded charm, and she felt it working on her and blushed under his scrutiny.

"Come, come, don't tell me Miss Bella's got your tongue. I won't bite." His eyes gleamed. "Then again, maybe I will, but I promise you'll like it, Miss, er—?"

"Bernay. Rosalyn Bernay."

He gave her a formal bow. "Mr. Anthony Hollingsworth Hayes, at your service. But you can call me Tony. Did you enjoy our little performance?"

"I did—very much," Rosalyn stammered, still unsure what to make of him.

Jessie came over and said briskly, "Rosalyn, you are needed upstairs."

"Don't tell me you are the new dresser!" Tony exclaimed. "And here I thought you were one of our new singers. You certainly are beautiful enough to be onstage."

"Don't pay attention to Tony—he's an inveterate flirt." Jessie spoke lightly, but she tossed him a cool glance.

Tony held up his hands in a gesture of innocence. "You say

2222

22

'inveterate' as though it were a bad thing. I say, if one is going to do something, one ought to give it their all. Isn't that right, Miss Bernay?"

Before she could answer, Jessie tugged on her arm. "Come on."

"Until the next time!" Tony's cheery voice called after them.

Nate and Sam were coiling ropes and resetting the backstage area when Nate happened to overhear a conversation between two of the actors as they made their way toward the dressing rooms.

"That new dresser is a beauty, isn't she?" said one. "Far prettier than Lilly."

Nate recognized the voice of Tony Hayes, a man whose crass attitude toward the ladies had frequently galled him.

"But I thought you rather fancied Lilly," said the other man with a chuckle.

"Seeking new horizons, my friend," Hayes answered. "It's what keeps a man going. And in any case, Lilly was a bit of a bore once I got to know her."

"And you got to know her *very* well," the other man rejoined.

Hayes laughed. He lowered his voice and made some comment, but by then they were out of Nate's hearing.

Nate gripped the rope so tightly that its rough strands bit into his palms. It was not his duty to guard Rosalyn, but he kept picturing her as a lamb among wolves.

Later, when they'd finished their tasks, Sam looked surprised to see Nate lingering at the theater instead of hurrying off. He said, "Joinin' us at the pub tonight, Nate?"

On Saturday nights, Sam and several of the others went to a little pub across from the stage door to enjoy a round or two before going home. Once or twice they'd invited Nate, although he had yet to accept.

"Thanks, Sam, but I'll be heading home soon."

He didn't bother to explain that he'd decided to wait for Rosalyn to come down from the dressing rooms. The salacious conversation he'd overheard was still worrying him.

Sam looked at him quizzically but merely shrugged and said good-night.

※

It took nearly an hour to help everyone out of their costumes and to get all the frocks, hats, scarves, and ribbons properly put away. By the end of it, Rosalyn felt like an old hand. Even Sarah, the unofficial leader of the group who had initially doubted her, complimented her on her good work.

Gradually the ladies filtered out, and soon Rosalyn was alone in the big room. She sat down at the long dressing table. With a tired sigh, she leaned an elbow on the table and contemplated what to do next. She had chosen, perhaps foolishly, to stay here when she might have been better off seeking safe shelter before nightfall. She'd kept pushing the worry to the back of her mind, telling herself that somehow things would work out. She'd been embarrassed to admit her true circumstances to anyone. And to be honest, no one had asked. They'd simply accepted her presence as a new member of the theater staff. They wouldn't think twice about what her living situation might be.

Next to her on the table stood the roses she'd been given by Mrs. Hill. One of the ladies had found a vase to put them in. Rosalyn drew them close, shut her eyes, and inhaled the sweet scent of summer. She sang a comforting little child's hymn she'd been taught at the orphanage. As always, singing it soothed her. *He is my song in the night.*

It was so tempting to stay here, to remain in this moment. But slowly, reluctantly, Rosalyn forced herself to stand up. After one last look around, she took a deep breath and went out the door.

When she reached the bottom of the stairs, she saw no one, not even Miss Bella the cat. She considered spending the night in the theater. Was it trespassing to remain if she'd had a reason for being here in the first place?

Still contemplating this idea, Rosalyn inspected the enormous set, designed to look like the deck of a ship. She opened the doors to the "captain's quarters," where Jessie and others had made several entrances and exits. The area behind the doors was empty, of course, but it could provide her with a good hiding place to stretch out and rest.

Now that she was on the stage, Rosalyn couldn't resist taking a moment to walk out to the center. She paused just where Emma Howson had stood when she'd sung her aria. Looking out over the rows of empty seats, Rosalyn saw again the beaming faces of the audience and heard their enthusiastic applause. She peered down into the orchestra pit, imagining what it would be like to follow the conductor's baton. Surely there could be nothing more wonderful than to sing accompanied by an orchestra. She imagined it would feel like being gently buoyed on a friendly sea. At the orphanage, there had been plenty of singing but no musical instruments—not even a piano.

Opening her arms wide, she breathed deeply, aching to sing at full voice just to see what it would sound like from this spot. She settled for listening to the music in her head, reliving the happiest melodies in her imagination.

O joy, O rapture unforeseen, the clouded sky is now serene . . .

Suddenly, she heard a noise from her left. Turning sharply, she realized it was the sound of boots on metal ladder rungs. Dropping her arms guiltily, she hurried offstage toward the sound. Nate Moran was making his way down the ladder that led to the lighting platforms. He was still here! A surprising rush of relief flooded through her. How amazing that he should now feel to her like a friend. She found herself watching his broad shoulders and solid legs as he moved confidently down the narrow rungs. Was this the ladder his brother had fallen off of? Nate took it with ease and confidence.

She stood, waiting, wondering sheepishly if he'd seen her actions on the stage. Even so, she was heartily glad to see him.

❧

"I thought everyone was gone," Rosalyn said, looking at Nate with a curious mixture of pleasure and embarrassment.

He imagined her flustered expression was due to what he'd witnessed on the stage just now. He'd decided to wait in an area out of the way—so as to avoid questions about why he was still there—that had a view of the stairs to the ladies' dressing rooms. He hadn't counted on seeing Rosalyn's little display. One night in the theater, and already she was stagestruck. He'd been tempted to wait and see what else she might do but decided he'd do neither of them a favor by spying on her.

"I'm just about to leave, actually." This was basically true, but for some reason Nate didn't want to admit he'd been waiting for her. "Where are you going? Can I escort you there?"

She gave him a grateful smile. "The thing is . . ." She paused, and the blush already tinging her cheeks grew deeper. "I'd like to go to that charity house, if you think they'll have me."

Nate stared at her in surprise. "You mean you haven't been there yet?"

"No. I never heard the information you called out to me at the station. I didn't know what to do, or where to go. They stole everything from me."

She spoke simply, but a constriction in her voice and a flash of pain in her eyes signaled a deeper horror behind her matter-of-fact description. It brought back all the emotions he'd felt after the events at the station—his guilt only barely lessened by the evidence that no real harm had come to her.

"I was still wandering the streets when, through a miracle, I was offered a chance to work here," Rosalyn continued. "Naturally, I accepted. But now . . . well . . . do you think it's too late for me to go to that charity house you spoke of?"

"I don't think they'd be prepared to accept a new arrival at such a late hour," Nate said truthfully. He ran a hand through his hair, considering what to do. There was really only one alternative. It would mean pulling his mother and sisters out of bed, but Nate had no doubt they would agree with his decision. "Would you like to come home with me?"

Rosalyn's eyes grew wide.

Nate realized how forward his offer must have sounded. "My mother and two sisters live there, too, so you have nothing to fear." He made a wry face. "Granted, my sisters can be frighteningly overbearing at times. But at heart they are good souls." He was encouraged to see her smile at this feeble attempt at humor.

"I see now why you were trying so hard to get me to go with you at the station. You knew what that woman was. And yet I was abominable to you."

"No. I blame myself for not having the presence of mind to explain things more clearly. And also, from your words, I thought . . ." The way she looked at him caused his words to falter.

"I thought you knew what you were doing. But I should have known better, because anyone can see that you are not the type of woman who would fall in with people like that. I sincerely apologize to you for thinking, even for a moment, that you were."

She straightened, as though some burden had eased off her shoulders. "Thank you for that."

"So will you allow me . . . ?"

He let the question hang, unfinished.

After a few moments, she seemed to make up her mind. "Thank you," she said with a nod. "I honestly thought I might have to sleep behind the scenery tonight."

Nate's breath caught in disbelief. She tried to make it sound like a lark, but that only revealed even more what an intrepid woman she was. He cleared his throat. "Let's go, then."

As they walked down the corridor that led to the stage door, Nate was surprised to hear Jessie calling out from behind them. They paused, waiting for her to catch up.

"Where are you going?" Jessie threw a suspicious glance at Nate, which he didn't appreciate. Did she think he was planning to abduct Rosalyn?

"Nate has kindly invited me to stay with his family tonight," Rosalyn answered.

Jessie's brows drew together as she regarded Rosalyn. Nate saw the realization dawn on her, as it had for him, that Rosalyn was adrift in London. It would appear she hadn't told anyone the particulars of her situation.

Recovering from her apparent surprise, Jessie said smoothly, "Oh, but you're coming home with me. Don't you remember?"

"I am?" Rosalyn said in astonishment.

"Yes, it's all settled."

She smiled sweetly at Nate as she spoke. It was a smile calculated to win over any male. Time and again he'd seen how it worked on other men, although Nate found it was powerless on him. He could easily guess why Jessie had suddenly made up this tale. Aside from Grossmith and a few others, she seemed to have a deep distrust of men.

"I asked a cabman to come 'round for us at two," Jessie said. She opened the stage door. "There he is now."

A hansom cab was indeed waiting at the curb.

Rosalyn's gaze shifted from Jessie to Nate and then back again. It was easy to read the bewilderment on her face. Suddenly she had *two* offers of a place to stay. Given that one of those invitations came from a woman whom Rosalyn had been watching all evening with undisguised admiration, Nate was pretty sure which way she would go.

Sure enough, she turned to Nate and said, "I don't want to seem ungrateful to you, but . . ."

"I understand."

Nate was surprised that his words came out harshly, as though he were disappointed. He ought to be relieved, really. It was probably the easiest solution for tonight, and he could offer no real objection. By all accounts, Jessie lived respectably. She seemed determined to avoid the scandalous behavior that most people expected from actresses. Rosalyn would be safe—and hadn't that been his goal?

Jessie bounded up into the carriage and looked back at Rosalyn expectantly. Rosalyn moved to follow her but paused, seemingly uncertain about where to place her foot.

"Hansom cabs can be odd to navigate at first," Nate said. He offered his hand and helped her into the carriage.

"Thank you," she said with a smile. Unlike with Jessie, Nate could see no guile. Her smile was appealing precisely because it tried not to be. He reluctantly stepped back to make room for the cabman to close the little half-doors that shielded the women from the waist down.

Jessie took the blanket proffered by the cabman and put it over both their laps. "Yes, many thanks," she said breezily. "*A bientôt!*"

Nate knew the phrase loosely meant "see you soon." But as he watched the carriage drive away, he remembered that tomorrow was Sunday. There were no performances on Sundays. And where would Rosalyn be by Monday? He could not imagine Jessie meant to house her indefinitely.

He told himself it was not a question he was responsible to answer. The fact that he felt compelled to help her was undoubtedly just a lingering consequence of their first meeting, when she was so clearly in trouble. But she had shown herself adept at surmounting her problems, and now she had Jessie and others in the theater to help her. If she did not require Nate's assistance, that was a good thing, right? There were enough women complicating his life already—his mother and sisters among them. *And Ada.* Surely the last thing he needed was one more woman added to his list of concerns.

Unfortunately, taking this rational view did nothing to assuage his curiosity about the woman who had entered his life in such a remarkable way. As he walked home, he found himself reviewing each of the brief interactions he'd had with her, like repeatedly watching the same scenes from a play. Every detail was vivid in his mind, but none provided real clues as to what had brought her to London or how she had wound up at the theater.

And why was it so important to him to know the story of a virtual stranger whom he might not even see again? That was one question he wasn't so willing to ponder.

CHAPTER

7

R OSALYN DREW the blanket around her to ward off the
chilly night air as the carriage moved briskly down the
near-empty streets. "Jessie, I can't thank you enough for
this. You don't even know me, and yet you take me into your
home."

"You must think me completely dense," Jessie answered apolo-
getically. "I could see you were facing severe hardship, of course—
so many people in the city are in desperate need of work and food.
But I didn't realize . . ." She turned to scrutinize Rosalyn. "Are
you completely alone in London? With not even a place to live?"

"I'm afraid so. I only arrived yesterday, and I don't know anyone—outside of the theater, I mean."

"And yet you went straight to work and did such a good job."
Jessie shook her head in astonishment. "What a good thing I
stayed late at the theater tonight. I would hate to think you were
compelled to go home with one of the stagehands."

"I truly believe he was only trying to help," Rosalyn insisted.

Jessie looked doubtful but did not contradict her. "I generally go home straightaway, but tonight I was trying to avoid a certain gentleman who has been lurking at the stage door."

"The man who threw flowers to you?"

"Exactly. I've done everything I can to discourage him, but so far to no avail. Tonight I not only stayed late, I asked Sarah to tell him I'd already gone home by another door."

"It's a shame the gentleman won't take you at your word."

"People think all actresses are loose women, but I assure you it isn't so. I guard my reputation very carefully. Of course, I have more reason to do so than most. . . ." Her voice trailed off, and she sighed.

Rosalyn wanted to ask why but thought it might be pressing for more information than Jessie was willing to divulge. So she stayed silent and watched the city as it rolled past.

The air was thick with frosty mist. Street lamps glowed on every corner, illuminating damp sidewalks and buildings that were largely dark. Only the pubs seemed open at this hour; periodically they passed glowing windows showing plenty of people within. Over the pub doors, painted signs displayed their unique and sometimes curious names, such as The Queen's Head or The Three Horseshoes.

"Ah, well, water under the bridge, as they say," murmured Jessie, apparently still thinking of her previous statement. "Of course, my parents were horrified when I accepted Mr. Sullivan's offer to perform in this opera. I'm a trained concert singer, which is far more respectable. But I told my parents they needn't be concerned. *Pinafore* has nothing risqué or objectionable in it, and Mr. Gilbert sets up so many rules of conduct for the cast that you'd think we were at a convent school."

Rosalyn could hear the smile return to Jessie's voice as she said this.

The cab drew to a halt in front of a tall townhouse. Once the cabman had been paid, Jessie led the way up half a dozen steps to the front door. She produced a key and swiftly unlocked the door. Inside it was pitch black, but Jessie must have known exactly where everything was. Within seconds she'd lit a match and touched it to a waiting candle. Rosalyn could see they stood near the foot of a flight of stairs. A hallway stretched beyond the stairs, shrouded in darkness.

Touching a finger to her lips, Jessie whispered, "We must be very quiet. My landlady knows I come home late because of my work, but she's not particularly happy about it. And she doesn't like even the slightest disturbance at this hour."

They tread softly up the stairs to the third landing. Jessie took another key and unlocked the door to her lodgings, motioning Rosalyn inside.

Once she had secured the door behind them, Jessie lit a small oil lamp and extinguished the candle. The lamp sent a warm, comforting glow over the living area, which consisted of little more than a small sofa, a low table, and two chairs. Off to the right was another door, presumably to Jessie's bedchamber.

"Please sit," Jessie said, motioning to the sofa.

Rosalyn eased gratefully onto the well-worn but comfortable cushions.

Jessie knelt by the fireplace and quickly brought the banked fire to a cheerful little blaze. It was a cozy place, small and simple, but Jessie had given it many wonderful feminine touches.

"This is marvelous," Rosalyn said warmly, if somewhat wistfully.

"A poor player's lodgings. There's no kitchen, but at least I can make tea." Jessie set a kettle on a hook over the fire. "I do hope to have a proper flat someday."

"Will you continue in the theater, do you think?"

Jessie settled into a chair. "I expect so. After fourteen months in *Pinafore*, I am much more confident in my acting. My part in the new production will be much larger, and I'll have speaking lines in addition to the singing. Plus, they are giving me a pay rise for going with them to America."

"America!" Rosalyn exclaimed.

"Yes, isn't it exciting? The new opera will premiere in New York at the end of December, and I'll be in the cast. It seems almost unbelievable. I've always wanted to be a singer, but I never thought I'd be able to travel the world."

"I think you are very brave to leave England. And to face the dangers of ocean travel."

Jessie waved a hand in dismissal. "Oh, there's nothing to it nowadays. The steamships take you right across. A few days of lounging around—and, I hear, eating far too much elegant food—and you're there."

The teakettle began to whistle. As Jessie set about making the tea, she said, "Now, tell me about you. What has brought you to London, alone and in such dire straits?"

Rosalyn took a deep breath. How could she explain the terrible circumstances that had brought her here? And what would Jessie think of her? Perhaps she would regret having brought Rosalyn into her home.

Jessie handed a cup of tea to Rosalyn before serving herself and taking the chair next to the sofa. "I don't mean to be a busybody, but you are in my home, after all. And I confess I am genuinely curious."

She studied Rosalyn with a friendly expression, and Rosalyn felt her wariness relax a little. She *wanted* to tell her story. But how could she do that and still make Jessie understand that she was innocent in the whole affair?

"Where are you from?" Jessie prompted. "Do I hear a trace of Bristol in your accent?"

"I was actually born in Plymouth, but I grew up in Bristol. My sisters and I lost our parents when I was nine years old, and we were taken to an orphanage there."

"An orphanage!" Jessie looked horrified. "I suppose you were treated abominably."

"Like *Oliver Twist*?" Rosalyn answered with a smile. "I assure you it was not like that at all. The children were treated with kindness. We always had food to eat and adequate, if plain, clothes to wear. It was truly the best thing for me and my sisters, considering the circumstances."

"A *pleasant* orphanage? That sounds like a miracle."

"I think the real miracle is how it keeps going. There are hundreds of children to care for, and yet the founder, Mr. Müller, has never asked for donations or solicited financial help of any kind. Instead, he prays his petitions directly to God. And God has always answered. People have sent money, or clothes, or food, or other items as they have been moved to do so."

"How astonishing," Jessie murmured. Rosalyn could see she was genuinely intrigued.

"Of course, the young children don't realize this. We discovered it as we grew older. We were taught to rely on God to meet our needs."

Jessie leaned forward, her face lighting up. "That's rather like what happened today, isn't it? You didn't tell us you needed food or a place to stay. We offered it to you! I suppose you must have been praying?"

Rosalyn tried to recall exactly what she'd been thinking prior to the moment Mr. Gilbert had stuck his head out the window and begun yelling at her. "At that point, I don't know if I even had the presence of mind to pray," Rosalyn admitted. "And yet Mr. Müller is fond of quoting the Scripture that says, 'For your Father knoweth what things ye have need of, before ye ask him.'"

Jessie set down her teacup and focused intently on Rosalyn. "I still don't understand exactly how you came to be in our little back alley today."

Rosalyn sighed. She almost didn't want to speak of the situation, and yet she felt a need to unburden herself to someone. For whatever reason, Jessie was proving a willing and sympathetic listener. "At the orphanage, the girls stay until they are seventeen years old. At that time, suitable work is found for them. Most go into service, or they are trained as teachers or nurses. I was sent to work as a parlormaid for a wealthy widow who lived in the Wiltshire countryside. But we got on so well that within a year or so, I was serving as her companion rather than a maid."

Rosalyn went on to describe how things were going well, how she'd even learned to play the piano and taken a few voice lessons so that she and Mrs. Williams could entertain one another. "But Mrs. Williams was still fairly young, and she had a variety of suitors. Finally, last spring, she married."

"I see." Jessie nodded. "They tossed you out on your ear because you were no longer needed."

"No, Mrs. Williams—Mrs. Huffman, she is now—is too kind for that. She kept me on. But I was placed in rather an awkward position." Finding her hand was shaking, Rosalyn set down her teacup. "Unfortunately, Mrs. Huffman was so in love with her new husband that she couldn't see he was not an honorable man. More than once I came upon him with one of the servant girls backed into a corner. Finally, he tried for me, as well."

"I knew it!" Jessie said with feeling. "Didn't I ask you, when we met, if a man had caused your dilemma? So what did you do?"

"I resisted quite vigorously, of course. I slapped him so hard it left a red welt on his cheek. When he threatened to dismiss me, I boldly told him to go ahead, that I would be very glad to tell Mrs. Huffman exactly why I was being let go."

"Bravo!" Jessie cheered. "But I don't suppose that was the end of it."

"You're right. He found a way to blackmail me. Somehow, his gold watch went missing, and *somehow* two maids could attest to the fact that I'd been seen in his room."

"I can't believe your fellow servants would be so heartless. I should think you'd all want to stick together."

"It's possible he had blackmailed them, as well. Or perhaps they thought he would grant them something in return."

"Men always think that women are pliable, that they can be made to give in to their demands. But you did not."

"No. But I am ashamed to say that I ran away."

"Don't be ashamed! You ran for your life! And what better place to come to than London."

"Well, that part was not intentional."

Rosalyn explained how she'd ended up on the train to London, and related the things that had transpired after she had arrived—including Nate's intervention and how she had misunderstood his intentions.

When she began to speak of the brothel and the ugly events that followed, Jessie sat next to her on the couch and drew one of Rosalyn's arms into her own. "This is why I felt moved to befriend you this evening. I just know it."

This display of sympathy and affection startled Rosalyn. She realized she had not had a friendly embrace since the day she'd last seen her sisters.

"Now I understand why you were willing to go home with Nate Moran tonight. It seems he truly was just trying to help you."

"Do you know anything about this charity home for women that he spoke about?"

"I'm afraid I don't. The actors don't really have much interaction with the stagehands—not from snobbery, mind you! It's just that we are all so busy with our own jobs. But Patrick always struck me as a friendly and helpful sort. We all felt sorry for him when he got hurt. On the other hand, I don't know what to think about Nate. He is much quieter and keeps to himself. I suppose I've been viewing him as a dangerous sort of fellow."

"Dangerous! Surely not." But hadn't she initially seen Nate that way as well?

"He is a *battle-hardened* veteran," Jessie replied dramatically. "But it could be good to have such a man on your side."

"He does seem a friend now." In fact, Rosalyn still felt a bit guilty at turning down his offer to stay with his family. He'd seemed oddly disappointed. Had she somehow hurt him by refusing his help a second time?

"I'm your friend, too," Jessie reminded her. "And I've some grand ideas for helping you out of your tough situation. But let's sort everything out tomorrow, shall we? Even the worst of circumstances can look better after a good rest."

⁃⁃⁃

Nate let himself in quietly, replacing the latch with care.

"Is that you, Nate?" Patrick called in a low voice from the parlor.

"Aye." Nate shrugged out of his coat and hung it by the door. He removed his boots, too, for rain had come in the last hour, and the streets had turned to mud. He padded to the next room to find his brother seated in the best armchair, his splinted leg propped up on a stool and a small bundle close to his chest. The room was lit only with the glow from a small but cheerful fire. "You're up late."

"Tommy was giving his mum a hard time, so I thought I'd take him off her hands for a while. I was awake anyway."

Patrick was definitely the night owl in the family. Nate, on the other hand, never cared to see the back side of midnight unless he was on guard duty. He took a seat on the sofa and leaned back, exhaling a long sigh as he stretched his legs out in front of him.

"You look tired," Patrick observed. "More tired than normal, I mean. I can't thank you enough, you know. It means the world to me, what you've done." He gestured to the child in his arms. "To us."

Nate met his brother's gaze. "It's no more than you'd have done."

He meant it, too. Despite Patrick's carefree demeanor, he was a man of integrity. He'd taken on many responsibilities at an early age—even going to work as a messenger boy in a theater when he was twelve years old to earn money for the family. Nate couldn't ask for a better brother.

Patrick rocked his son gently and sang an old lullaby that Nate well remembered from their childhood. Although Patrick sang with great tenderness, he was also—as always—off-key.

"If you want him to sleep, I'd go easy on the singing."

This helpful admonition only brought a grin from Patrick. "How did things go tonight?"

"Fine, I guess. Except Sam has a cold. It gets him sneezing at inopportune times. I think they could hear him all the way up to the galleries."

"Sam always has a cold. Comes on in October and doesn't leave until spring." Patrick shifted slightly, wincing from the effort. "I'll be glad to get back. How I miss all the fellas."

Nate closed his eyes, enjoying the crackle of the fire and the play of firelight on his closed eyelids. The peacefulness of the room provided a welcome respite after a very long day. The clock on the mantelpiece ticked away several minutes. Nate ought to be going to bed, but his muscles felt too tired to move. His mind was, paradoxically, too awake. He scrubbed his fingers through his hair, as if that might calm the restlessness of this thoughts.

"Something on your mind?" Patrick asked.

Nate opened his eyes to see that his brother was eyeing him curiously. He sat up and blew out a breath. "I was thinking about something that happened at the theater tonight. Something rather extraordinary."

Patrick's eyebrows lifted. "I'm intrigued."

"Yesterday at the train station, I met a woman."

"So I heard. Ma told us all about it."

Nate shook his head. "I should have known."

"She wanted us to pray for the woman, which we dutifully did prior to saying grace before supper."

"Well, it worked. She walked into the theater this afternoon, safe and apparently unharmed."

"Praise God!"

This comment came not from Patrick, but from the direction of the parlor door. Nate turned to see his mother, a heavy shawl thrown over her nightgown. Nate couldn't resist a sly comment. "Is the whole household awake, then?"

She crossed the room and took a seat next to him on the sofa. "No, they're all asleep—now that he is." She indicated the baby in Patrick's arms. "But what is the news about the woman?"

Nate related to them how he'd spoken with Rosalyn when she'd arrived at the theater, and about what had happened after the show.

"That Jessie's a generous soul," said Patrick. "Wears her heart on her sleeve, especially for downtrodden women."

"That may be so, but she is still an *actress*," Ma said. Over the years, Ma had come to accept that Patrick had made a life in the theater. But she retained a certain distrust of actors and their Bohemian lifestyle. "Nate, I don't think it was right of you to let Rosalyn go with her."

"What did you expect me to do—grab her by the arm again? That worked really well last time."

The baby made a grunt of discomfort and shifted in his father's arms. Patrick readjusted the child and rocked him gently, whispering a few soothing words. He looked over at Nate. "If you get him crying and wake the rest of the family, you're liable to find *yourself* homeless."

Nate took a deep breath. "I'm sorry."

He couldn't say what had caused him to react so harshly. Nor was he particularly comfortable with the way his mother was looking at him. It signaled that more things were going on in her head than she was speaking aloud.

"You needn't worry, Ma," Patrick said. "I believe Jessie is about to leave for New York, so Rosalyn is not likely to stay with her long. She may well end up at the charity house after all."

"Well then, we'll just continue praying for her. She seems safe enough for the moment, and that's what's important, eh?"

She patted Nate's knee and rose from the sofa. Crossing the room, she touched the back of her finger, featherlight, to Tommy's cheek, her eyes filled with tender love for her grandson. "Sleep well, everyone," she murmured, and left the room.

"There is one thing you didn't tell us about this woman," Patrick said as the sound of their mother's tread on the stairs slowly receded.

Nate rubbed his eyes. "And what's that?"

"Is she pretty?"

Nate looked up sharply. "What does that have to do with anything?"

Even in the semidarkness, he could see a slow smile spread across his brother's countenance. Patrick knew him too well, understanding that a stern rebuke usually meant he had hit upon something.

Still, Nate wasn't going to give him any ground. He leaned forward, trying to meet his brother's eye. "Patrick, the sooner you stop trying to pair me off with women, the happier all of us will be."

"Oh, that's right, I forgot. You're not in the marriage market. You'd rather remain bitter over the loss of a woman you don't even love anymore."

Nate hated when his brother tried to broach that subject. "Patrick, I've told you time and again—I am going back in the army. I will *not* be taking a wife with me."

"And I've told you I don't understand your reasons for *either* decision," Patrick returned. "You know it will break Ma's heart to see you go away again. And what about your injury?"

"Ma is resilient. And she has you. And my hand—" Nate bit off what he'd been about to say: that it was the distraction of a woman that had led to his injury in the first place. "Yesterday at drills I was nearly able to load and fire in the acceptable time."

"Nearly."

"Patrick, you know my stay here in London is only temporary."

"Is it? I thought you were seriously considering becoming a policeman. They're always looking for good men—especially veterans who are decorated heroes."

Hero. Nate hated that word.

"No. My becoming a policeman was *your* idea." Nate spoke through gritted teeth, trying to put force behind his words without waking the baby.

Patrick gave an annoying, nonchalant shrug. "If you say so."

He wished his family could just accept his decision and let him be. As much as he loved his brother, Nate could not disclose the real reason he was returning to the army. It was better if they believed he was a hero returning to active duty, not a failure trying to make amends for his past mistakes. And if he was going to be successful, there could be no woman interfering with his heart and thinking. It was painful for Nate to keep that secret, but he still felt it was the right thing to do.

He stood up. "I'm going to bed. Good night."

As Nate left the room, he could hear Patrick's off-key crooning starting up again. Surprisingly, the baby seemed to enjoy his father's terrible singing. Nate paused for a moment as his heart did a weird, squeezing turn in his chest. There was a time when Nate, too, had looked forward to having a son and to forging such a special bond. He'd since resigned himself to the idea that it would never happen. It was only at odd, unexpected times like this that it seemed to hurt.

CHAPTER

8

SLOWLY, GROGGILY, Rosalyn became aware of footsteps and the rustle of a skirt near her ear. She gave a start as she gained consciousness, disoriented.

"It's only me," Jessie said gently. Rosalyn's eyes focused on Jessie, who stood next to the sofa, fully dressed and looking down at her. "How are you?"

Rosalyn sat up, feeling a stab of pain in her neck from her awkward sleeping position on the sofa. "I'm a little stiff," she admitted. "But I feel a thousand times better than yesterday."

Jessie smiled and placed a teacup in Rosalyn's hand. "My apologies for waking you, but I need to go out soon, and I'm afraid you'll have to go with me."

The tea was hot, the bergamot fragrance of Earl Grey wafting into the air. What luxury. She inhaled, savoring the scent. "Where are you going?"

"To St. Peter's Italian Church in Hatton Garden. Don't you

remember? Of course you don't, poor thing. You were exhausted last night."

"What time is it?" Judging by the sunlight and the noise of traffic piercing even the closed window, Rosalyn was sure the morning was pretty well advanced.

"It's nearly eleven."

"Eleven!" Rosalyn was dismayed to have slept so late. "Surely the service has already begun."

"It's not for the service but for an afternoon concert. We have plenty of time."

Rosalyn wasn't sure whether to be relieved or to feel guilty for missing a worship service. From the day she and her sisters had arrived at Müller's orphanage, Rosalyn had never missed a Sunday at church.

"It's a program of sacred music," Jessie explained. "I will be on the program with two other soloists."

"It sounds wonderful."

"I think you'll enjoy it," Jessie said, briefly lowering her gaze in a theatrical display of modesty. She winked and smiled. "The songs are lovely, and a Sunday concert is one way for a poor singer to keep the Sabbath holy and yet still earn something toward the rent."

"Thank you for inviting me to come along."

"To be honest, my actions are not entirely altruistic. I don't for a moment distrust you, for I believe I am an accurate judge of character. However, you must see why I need to take the cautious route and not leave you alone in my lodgings."

"Of course." The idea of disturbing Jessie's belongings, much less stealing anything, would never have occurred to Rosalyn. But this was London, and she'd already learned the hard way that people here must always be on their guard.

Jessie took her empty teacup and set it aside. "Let's see how we can get you dressed. I can loan you some fresh undergarments, but I'm afraid you'll have to wear your own gown. I would gladly give you one of mine, but I'm at least three inches shorter than you, and there isn't time to let out the hem." Her mouth quirked to a cheeky grin. "You'd likely cause a sensation in church if your ankles were on full display." She picked up Rosalyn's skirt from where it had been draped over a chair. With a frown, she gave it a shake and scrutinized it. "We can brush off the dried mud and give it a quick press with a flatiron. That will make you present-able, at least."

Within an hour, Rosalyn was dressed and had eaten a gener-ous breakfast of bread, cheese, and cold sliced beef. Jessie ate only bread and tea, explaining that she never ate anything else before a performance.

"But we shall have a nice supper afterward," Jessie assured her, although Rosalyn had not asked.

Once they had left the boardinghouse and were walking down the street, Jessie said, "I'm glad we did not see my landlady, Mrs. Kramer, on the way out. She watches the comings and goings of her boarders very carefully, and there isn't time to explain to her what you're doing here."

"Will she object to my staying with you?"

Jessie gave a dismissive shrug. "Not to worry. We'll get it all sorted out later."

⁓

She sat just four rows ahead of him. Nate could see her fine features in profile as she turned toward her husband to read the words from the hymnal he held.

Last night Nate had not acknowledged Patrick's statement that he no longer cared for Ada. He wasn't entirely sure that was true. He was resigned to it—after all, what choice did he have?

But try as he might, he still felt resentful when he saw the two of them together. Ada's letter telling Nate she'd fallen in love with someone else had arrived in India just in time to be the catalyst for disaster. How could he help but think of that with anger, especially when he saw her now, without a care in the world?

To avoid looking at her, Nate carefully studied the back of the older gentleman seated in front of him. Only to realize he was the police inspector Patrick kept trying to get Nate to speak to. Patrick would not let go of this idea that Nate should stay home and become a bobby. It was a course taken by many veterans, but it held no interest for Nate. The army was the life he had chosen, and one he was honor-bound to continue, even if no one else understood that.

Surrounded as he was on all sides, he felt the same agitation as last night. Even Patrick's question about Rosalyn still bothered him. *Is she pretty?* Yes, she was. Any man would have to be blind not to see that—not to notice her expressive brown eyes or her high cheekbones. But Nate disliked the insinuation that he'd been moved to help her for only that reason. Why shouldn't he want to help someone in need? Even now, the minister was preaching on the Christian's joy in service.

He did find himself wondering what Rosalyn was doing this morning. She'd likely follow whatever Jessie's plans were. Nate didn't think Jessie was the type to attend church regularly—most actors preferred to sleep late on Sunday morning after being at the theater so late on Saturday night. And yet he had to admit she had shown tremendous generosity by taking Rosalyn home with her. Or was Jessie motivated only by the idea that she was rescuing Rosalyn from Nate? Her actions could just as easily be ascribed to her distrust of men as to Christian charity.

It took the movement of the congregation rising to sing the final hymn to bring Nate's mind back to where he was. He joined in robustly, as though that might atone for the way his thoughts had been wandering, but it led only to an amused smile crossing the face of his mother, who stood next to him. Even Patrick, propped up on a stick for support of his splinted leg, sent a curious glance in his direction.

After the minister gave the benediction and dismissed the congregation, Nate joined his family as they walked down the center aisle toward the door. Nate knew without even having to look that Ada was not far behind, perhaps even hurrying to catch up to him. He deliberately kept his face forward, taking his mother's arm to help her navigate the uneven floor.

Of course, he should have known she would not be dissuaded that easily.

"Nate!" Ada called.

He would have kept right on walking, but his mother stopped, forcing him to stop, too. She turned, and Nate had no choice but to do the same. Ada was smiling, her arm firmly affixed to her husband's. Matthew Wilkins beamed at Nate pleasantly, the two of them acting as they had since he returned to London—as though by being nice to him they could easily repair the hurt and mortification they had caused him.

"Good afternoon." He didn't bother to keep the frost out of his voice.

Undaunted, Ada pressed her gloved hand into his. "How are you? You look tired."

He withdrew his hand. "I think I'm most tired of people telling me I look tired. It happens when a person works two jobs."

Immediately he regretted saying this. Not because of the pain his words brought to her cool blue eyes, but because Patrick had heard him. Never did he want his brother to think Nate begrudged the hard work he'd done on his behalf. This was the problem with trying to talk to Ada. It never did anything but fuel his frustration.

Matthew was the first to rally and break the awkward pause. He said jovially, "Thank heavens for the Sabbath, eh? A day of rest. I hope you've given some consideration to our invitation to come and dine with us today."

"I can't make it."

"Nate, don't be rude," his mother murmured.

"It's the truth," Nate insisted. "Please excuse us," he said to Ada and Matthew, and steered his mother toward the exit. He could sense the frosty disapproval of his family as they followed him.

"Next Sunday, then?" Ada called after them.

Nate hurried up to shake the minister's hand. It gave him an excuse for not answering.

Reverend Smith regarded him with kind eyes. "I want to thank you in advance for the work you'll be doing at the parsonage this afternoon. The missus and I regard your kindness as a gift from the Lord."

"It will be our pleasure, sir."

Nate had offered to assist another church member, who was a plasterer by trade, in repairing some of the walls in the parsonage. His mother was still holding on to his left arm, and he felt her stiffen. He realized he'd forgotten to tell her about this. Another lapse he would ascribe to being overworked and under-rested. No doubt she worried about his adding yet more work to his schedule, but at least it was proof that he'd not been lying when he told the Wilkinses he had other plans.

Due to Patrick's leg, they took a cab home. "You know I have to do it, Ma," he said as the carriage navigated the busy street. "The plaster is in terrible shape and threatening to fall down around Reverend Smith's ears."

She sighed. "Yes, I know. To be honest, son, I'm more troubled by the way you treat Ada and Matthew."

"The way *I* treat *them*!"

"I know you feel you have a right to be angry. But you cannot keep wallowing in your bitterness. They're trying to find a way to make peace with you. Won't you at least go and dine with them?"

"Don't ask me to do it, Ma."

It wasn't often that he rejected her advice, and it pained him to do it now. But on this subject, Nate was immovable.

He closed his eyes, knowing the weight of these cares was more to blame for his tiredness than any physical work.

※ ❧ ❧ ※

Jessie's performance was beautiful. The music, played on the church organ, filled the cathedral and provided the perfect accompaniment for her singing. She had a sweet mezzo-soprano voice and sang with an earnestness befitting the music. Several of the songs allowed her to show a range and level of skill that were not so much on display in her role as Cousin Hebe in *Pinafore*.

Rosalyn closed her eyes and bowed her head, saying a silent prayer of thanksgiving. It was restful here. The audience listened with rapt attention.

Afterward, Jessie greeted the well-wishers who stayed to give their compliments. Rosalyn remained in her seat, observing. Many people waited to speak to Jessie and give her rapturous praise. Even though Rosalyn couldn't hear their words, she could see it on their faces. Clearly Jessie was admired by many. She accepted the attention with unpretentious friendliness.

As the crowd thinned out, a young man wearing servant's livery approached Jessie and handed her a note. Rosalyn judged him to be a footman in a fine household. Jessie opened the note and read it, then spoke a few words to him. He tipped his head and left.

Jessie walked over to Rosalyn. "Well, my dear, it appears I will have to trust you in my lodgings after all. I've been invited to sing at an important soirée tonight. I could not refuse it, and I would

117

be an ogre to leave you out on the streets. But first we shall get something to eat, yes?"

Rosalyn's stomach rumbled in agreement. She had not sat down to a proper meal since the day before she'd left the Huffmans' house. That seemed an eternity now. But she said, "I thought you didn't eat before a performance?"

"That rule can only go so far—a girl has to eat sometime! And in any case, this particular soirée will not be a full-scale performance. It is something altogether different."

This intrigued Rosalyn, but before she could ask more, Jessie was leading her out to the street. "I know a cozy place with excellent lamb chops, and the prices are very good."

The mention of cost gave Rosalyn pause.

Sensing the drag in her step, Jessie said, "I shall be buying for the both of us."

"I hate to be a burden—"

"Never you worry. I'll have extra money in my pocket after tonight, and I am free to spend it any way I choose. Not that I'm a spendthrift, mind you! Which is why we are going to the Lamb and Bear rather than the Langham."

Jessie laughed. It was a joyful, infectious sound, and Rosalyn easily joined in. "At this moment I am quite sure the Lamb and Bear will seem every bit as luxurious as the Langham."

"I'm sure it will. Don't think I didn't hear that rumble of your belly a moment ago!"

Rosalyn put a hand over her stomach. "You couldn't have!"

Jessie grinned. "Aha! I caught you out. No, I didn't hear it, but the look on your face when I mentioned supper spoke loudly enough. Come on, then!"

To Rosalyn, London was an endless maze of jumbled streets going off in all directions. But Jessie walked with the clear confidence of someone who knew exactly where she was going. They took several shortcuts down narrow, crooked lanes between the thoroughfares, finally stopping in front of an old wood-beamed building with a colorful sign over the door. It was a whimsical painting of a bear tipping his hat to a lamb, who looked very uncertain about the whole thing.

"What is the origin of this name?" Rosalyn asked, pointing at the sign as they walked through the door.

"I have no idea," Jessie admitted. "But it's charming, isn't it? Just like this place."

It took a few moments for Rosalyn's eyes to adjust to the darker setting inside. The dining area was about half full, with the tables nearest a large stone fireplace already taken. People clustered in groups of three and four at various tables, chatting animatedly.

Several people smiled and waved at Jessie as she and Rosalyn seated themselves and removed their shawls. A few friendly, curious glances rested on Rosalyn, too. "Everyone seems to know you," Rosalyn observed.

Jessie tugged off her gloves. "Many of the patrons here are actors. Or singers. Or both, like me!"

Rosalyn immediately recognized Tony Hayes sitting at a table on the far side of the room with two other men from the chorus. He was in the middle of saying something to them when his gaze met hers and he paused. Rosalyn saw a slight lift of his eyebrows and a slow smile spread across his face. He brought his hand to his forehead and gave her a little sailor's salute. Rosalyn couldn't help but smile in return. After saying a few brief words to his companions, Tony rose from the table.

Jessie was seated with her back toward that end of the room, so she had not noticed this little interchange. She was not aware, as Rosalyn was, that Tony was sauntering toward their table. She said, "Now, I think we should talk more about your future plans.

I want to help you find your way in London as best I can. We'll need to work fast, since I leave so soon for America."

Tony reached their table and said, "Good afternoon, ladies."

Jessie looked up at him, her face reflecting vague irritation, but Tony's attention was fixed on Rosalyn.

"If it isn't the pretty flower-bearer! I see Jessie is introducing you to the most congenial pub in London. Are you new in town? Staying with Jessie?"

"Why, yes, I—"

"Don't be a busybody, Tony," Jessie reprimanded.

Tony laid a hand over his heart. "It's only a kindly interest in the newest member of our theatrical family. But I see Ruth is here to take your order," he said, as a stout, red-cheeked young woman approached their table. "I shall leave you to it."

With another smile and a wink at Rosalyn, he returned to his friends at the other table. Rosalyn watched him go, flattered at his interest.

Jessie immediately turned her full attention to the serving woman, ordering two plates of lamb and vegetables. "And two glasses of red wine, too," she finished.

"Oh, no, I couldn't," Rosalyn protested. She had no idea what wine cost in the city, but it couldn't be cheap.

"Nonsense," Jessie said. "It's good for the digestion." Giving Ruth a nod to confirm her request, she motioned the girl to be on her way. "Now, as I was saying, we must concern ourselves with you. I'd like to share a cautionary tale, if I might. Something about myself that is not generally known."

"Certainly," Rosalyn answered, intrigued.

"When I was seventeen, I had a singing master who was very enamored of my talents. He took an interest in me that was . . . well, unhealthy. He was much older than I, and far better acquainted with the ways of the world. On one particular day when

I was to give a performance, he met me at the door of the concert hall. Instead of walking me inside, he dragged me into his carriage. He took me—alone—to his house."

Rosalyn gasped. "That's terrible!"

"He kept me there all night. He did not touch me—not on that particular night, at any rate," she added darkly. "That would come later."

Jessie closed her eyes briefly, and her shoulders trembled as she gave a little shudder. Rosalyn sensed this was not mere stage drama, but Jessie's true reaction to the terrible memory. "What did you do?"

"What I felt I had to do, of course. He told me my reputation was now ruined—or at least, that it would be, unless I married him right away. I was young and naïve, and I didn't know any better, so I married him."

"But what about your parents? Did they agree to this?"

She shrugged and gave a sad nod. "Even they thought it was best at the time, although they quickly came to regret it as soon as they realized how my husband was treating me. When living with him became utterly unbearable, they welcomed me back with open arms."

She paused as Ruth came to the table and set down the wine. Once the serving girl was again out of earshot, Jessie continued. "Ultimately, I was able to obtain a divorce. It wasn't easy, but it is done. Marriage is in my past, and that is where it will stay."

"So this is why, when you first saw me in the alley, you asked if I was there because of some man?"

"Exactly. I've come out the other side of some very dark times. That is what I hope for you, as well. Be very careful about the company you keep, especially when it comes to men." Although Jessie's back was toward the table where Tony Hayes sat, she gave a slight sideways lift to her chin, which Rosalyn took to be an indication in his general direction.

"You can't think Tony is the sort of man who would take advantage of a woman!" Rosalyn couldn't picture Tony forcibly dragging her off in a carriage.

"I believe in *caution*," Jessie stressed. "There's no telling what any man might be capable of. The best way to survive in life is to never put yourself in a position of being controlled by a man. The only way to accomplish that is to stay single."

Rosalyn glanced toward Tony's table and was surprised to find that he was looking at her. When their eyes met, he did not look the least bit abashed, but rather smiled and tipped his chin in acknowledgment. It crossed Rosalyn's mind that perhaps Tony and the others had been talking about her. Immediately she dismissed the thought as foolish conjecture.

"It is all very wise advice," Rosalyn acknowledged. "I'm sure I'm just as likely to find unscrupulous men in Bristol as in London."

"Do you mean you still intend to go to your sister?"

"I think in the end it might be better. When we return to your lodgings, would you be able to loan me pen and paper? I would like to write to her and see if she can send me the money for train fare."

Jessie set down her glass. "I will gladly loan you pen and paper, but I urge you to think carefully before you write to her. Given what I have just told you about my past, I hope you will believe me when I say there are men vindictive enough to harm a woman who has scorned them. Some will stop at nothing in their desire to retaliate. Does this Mr. Huffman know you have a sister in Bristol? Suppose he sends police there to arrest you?"

"But I am innocent!"

"Can you prove it? How can you prove you did not pawn his watch once you got to London?"

122

A chill worked its way down Rosalyn's back. "I hadn't thought of that. Do you suppose he really would do such a thing?"

"I believe, from what you have told me, that it is possible. That's why I would counsel you to wait awhile. Allow time for his anger to dissipate and his mind to focus on something else. Or some*one* else."

Rosalyn knew what she meant. Mr. Huffman would likely seek out another victim. But that was beyond Rosalyn's control. As was so much about her life right now. "But I don't see how I can stay in London. I have nothing to live on. Nowhere to live."

"You can stay with me—at least until I leave for America. By then I'm sure we can find someplace suitable for you. And as for money, that part is easily solved. We'll talk to Miss Lenoir. She has to hire someone to replace Lilly. I don't see why it can't be you."

Rosalyn considered Jessie's words. Although she truly longed to see Julia, she couldn't deny the possible danger of Mr. Huffman tracking her down. And hadn't Rosalyn thought, as she watched the show last night, how marvelous it would be to work at such a place?

Jessie eyed her sympathetically. "I can see you are torn. How about this: You stay and work at the theater for the next two weeks. If at the end of that time you still feel you should go to Bristol, you will have the money you need to do so."

It seemed like the perfect compromise. Rosalyn smiled and nodded.

"Excellent!" Jessie clapped her hands in excitement.

Later, after a delicious meal, they left the pub to walk home. As she matched Jessie's pace, Rosalyn began to feel the rhythm of the city. Although the shops were closed because it was Sunday, the streets were busy with pedestrians and traffic. Rosalyn enjoyed glancing at the window displays as they walked. One shop in particular arrested her attention. She paused, staring through the window at a display of secondhand household items.

"See something interesting?" Jessie asked.

"I just remembered something I overheard at the brothel," Rosalyn said. "Mrs. Hurdle talked about being able to pawn stolen goods without being caught. Later, I was forced to give her my mother's watch. I thought I'd never see it again. But now . . ."

She pressed her face to the glass, trying to make out what else was in the shop. On the far wall she saw a case filled with watches and jewelry, but it was too far away to see any of the items distinctly.

"Ah, I understand," said Jessie. "You think perhaps the watch might show up at a pawnshop?"

"Yes!" Rosalyn smiled as this idea took hold. "Since I'll be in London for a while, perhaps I could find the watch." With a sigh she added, "It would be worth any price to have it back again."

"Did this woman say which pawnshop she frequented? There are dozens and dozens in London."

Rosalyn felt her initial excitement fade a little. "No. That is, not exactly. She did mention a man's name—Simon." She took a step back to read the shop name painted above the window: *Whitby and Son.*

"Simon could be either a first or last name," Jessie observed.

"I'll come back tomorrow. If the watch isn't here, perhaps I can ask the owner if he knows of a pawnbroker named Simon."

Rosalyn was happier than ever that she had decided to stay in London.

⚬⚬⚬

Nate helped load the plastering equipment and leftover supplies onto the wagon. He was tired but satisfied at the work he and two other men from his church had been able to accomplish at the parsonage. He paused for a moment to wipe his brow, still sweating from the afternoon's efforts despite the chill in the air. He happened to look down the street, and another kind of chill reached him. On the corner where the church's charity house stood, he saw the man who had troubled Rosalyn at the train station.

Actually, Nate couldn't be sure it was him, because the man was some distance off. His cap was pulled low and his coat collar turned high, almost obscuring his face. He gave no direct indication that he'd seen Nate, but he did begin to walk away with measured swiftness. In a moment he had turned the corner and was out of sight.

Nate ran to the corner, intending to catch him up, but it was impossible to see very far down the narrow, crooked lane the man had turned onto. Men and women stood at their doors, chatting with their neighbors, while ragged children played tag, darting in and out of dozens of lines of drying clothes and sheets. The man had disappeared.

Nate rapidly walked the length of the lane, but the other end opened onto a thoroughfare and there was no sign of the man. Still, the incident disturbed him. Nate had assumed the encounter he'd interrupted at Paddington had been the usual case of a ruffian trying to pick up a vulnerable woman. Once deterred, he would simply look for someone else. Rosalyn had clearly left with the old woman, so why would the man think he'd find her here? And why would he be following her? Nate couldn't make sense of it. Perhaps it had been a good thing Rosalyn had gone home with Jessie last night. At least it meant she was far from here.

~☙~

As soon as they returned to Jessie's lodgings, Jessie opened her wardrobe and began to sort through her gowns. "I really must prepare for tonight's event. It's important that I look my best."

"Can you tell me what it is?" Rosalyn asked.

Jessie pulled out a lovely gown of burgundy velvet and draped it on the bed. "I'm afraid I cannot. But I will tell you that some very important people will be there, and I shall be expected to be a sparkling member of the party."

"It sounds so exciting," Rosalyn said, envisioning a grand salon filled with elegantly dressed people and infused with music and laughter. "You lead such an interesting life!"

"Yes, London has been good to me. I am sure it will be good to you, too, in its own way." Jessie pulled out several hatboxes. Setting them next to the gown, she lifted the lids and began to look through them. "Which hat should I wear? I must decide quickly, for my hosts will be very put out if I keep them waiting." But she said this with a gleam in her eye that suggested she was half joking.

With Rosalyn's help, Jessie was quickly changed and ready to go. On her way to the door, she paused next to a table, upon which was a portable writing desk. "You will find pen, ink, and paper in here, everything you need to write a letter to your sister. *Au revoir!*"

She sailed out the door, closing it briskly behind her.

CHAPTER

9

N ATE'S FAMILY had been talking about him.
He could sense it the moment he came through the door. His mother and sisters, along with Patrick and his wife, Hannah, were all in the parlor. They paused what had apparently been, until his entrance, an animated discussion.

"Am I interrupting something?" he asked dryly as they all looked at him.

"Not at all," his sister Mary said. "You're just in time."

"For . . . ?" After everything that had happened today, Nate was in no mood for any new schemes his family wanted to undertake.

His mother answered. "We thought it would be nice to invite Rosalyn Bernay to join us for dinner tonight. You could go and ask her."

Mary pushed her glasses up her nose and peered at him. "Since we know you don't have any other plans."

This not-so-veiled reference to Ada's invitation instantly aroused his suspicions. He could easily guess his brother was behind this. "Patrick, I told you last night that I have no interest in Rosalyn."

Patrick tilted his head and gave him a knowing look. "On the contrary. You told me you are concerned about her welfare. What better way to show her we care than to ask her here for dinner?"

"We can find out more about her," added Ma. "If she's truly alone and homeless, with no family to turn to, perhaps we can help."

It was characteristic of his family to want to jump in and offer assistance if they perceived a need. It was also true that Nate had the very same questions about Rosalyn's circumstances— especially now, after seeing the man from the station lurking near the charity house. Still, he wasn't entirely comfortable with the idea of seeking her out—probably because of the way Patrick had quizzed him last night and the way they were all looking at him now.

There was also an obvious problem with their suggestion. "But I don't even know where Jessie Bond lives."

"I do," Patrick replied. "She lives at 98 Southampton Row, not too far from Russell Square."

Everyone turned to look at Patrick, but it was Hannah who said what they were all thinking. "And just how did you come by that particular bit of information?"

"Agnes Mitchell used to live next door. She and Jessie would share cabs sometimes." At this mention of Miss Mitchell, an actress for whom he had once carried a torch, Patrick threw a sheepish glance at his wife. "I may have walked Agnes home from the theater once or twice—long before I met you, of course."

Hannah pretended to scorch him with a harsh glare, but she couldn't hide the hint of amusement underneath it. Everyone, including Hannah, knew that from the moment Patrick had met his future wife, he'd never again had eyes for anyone else.

Even so, Ma couldn't resist giving a little sniff. "Thank the Lord you found our sweet Hannah before that other woman got you thoroughly in her clutches. Look at this beautiful family you have now. And this home."

She was referring to the fact that Hannah had unexpectedly inherited the very fine house they lived in from her great-aunt. It was a blessing no one had expected. While Nate was happy for their good fortune, he knew Ma was most relieved that Patrick had married a stable, "normal" woman outside the theater.

"Water long gone under the bridge, Ma," Patrick chided.

"It's all settled, then," said Mary firmly, her focus not swayed by this conversational detour. "Nate and I will go and fetch Rosalyn directly."

He raised his eyebrows. "You're coming, too?"

"Well, naturally. It wouldn't be proper for you to go there alone."

Nate could only shake his head in bemused acceptance. When Mary stared you down through her wire spectacles, there was no refusing whatever she was after.

"But what about Jessie? Won't it be rude not to invite her, as well?"

"The more the merrier," Patrick said. "Invite her, too."

Ma bristled at this but nodded in acquiescence.

And so, as soon as he'd had time to bathe off the dirt and plaster and make himself presentable, Nate found himself walking at a brisk clip with his sister toward Southampton Row.

◦⁓✧⁓◦

Rosalyn settled herself at Jessie's writing table, uncapping the ink and pulling a sheet of paper from a little drawer. Closing her eyes, she said a brief prayer, asking God for help. In the end, the letter was not so difficult to write after all.

Sunday, 12 October, 1879

My dearest Julia,

I hope and pray this letter reaches you before any other news about me. I must tell you that I was forced to leave my employment with the Huffmans quite suddenly. I can't give you more details in a letter. However, I want you to know that I am safe in London. Perhaps I should not even tell you my whereabouts, but I cannot bear the thought of losing contact with you. Please address any letters for me to Miss Jessie Bond, 98 Southampton Row, London. Do not put my name on the envelope.

Please burn this letter after reading it. If anyone should come to you accusing me of theft or any other wrongdoing, know that I am innocent of any charges against me. I'm guilty only of leaving my position with no advance notice. I was fleeing to protect my good character, not because I had thrown it away already.

I originally intended to come straight to you in Bristol, but circumstances hindered me. How close I came to disaster! But thank God, He protected me. Now I think it is good that I don't come to you. I want to be sure the Huffmans do not find me, and I think you would be the first person they'd seek out.

Will you write to Caroline and give her this news? Share as little of this information as you can and do not give her my address. For now, I must entrust that to you only. But be sure to tell her how dearly I love her, and that I long to see you both again soon.

All my love,
Rosalyn

Rosalyn set the pen in its stand and blotted the ink dry. She rose and stretched. Her eyes filled with tears, blurring the view as she looked out the window. How utterly strange it was to be cast adrift like this, with no home, no belongings, and no livelihood. Yet it was oddly freeing. She thought once more of everything she'd witnessed at the theater last night—the joy, the excitement, the energy, and yes, even the petty argument she'd overheard between two chorus ladies. She thought of that corner in the wings where she could watch not only the show but also the bustle of the men moving props and pulling ropes and operating the lights. Everything contributed to making the production run seamlessly.

Then there had been Nate, whom she'd spotted looking at her more than once from his station at the spotlights. He'd come to mind often today. She didn't dwell so much on their first meeting at the railway station, when she'd been apprehensive and even fearful of him. Instead, she kept recalling their subsequent encounters at the theater—his friendly expression, the warmth of his touch when he'd taken her hand, his genuine concern for her. Somehow, in his rough work clothes and with the dirt smudge across his cheek, he'd seemed more handsome than when he'd been wearing the crisp red coat of a soldier. Although she still knew little about him, she couldn't help but admire his willingness to take on extra work for his brother's sake. Despite Jessie's warnings, Rosalyn decided she could not judge all men based on the bad actions of a few.

The sun was fading behind the rooftops even though it was only midafternoon. At this time of year, the darkness came early. A lamplighter was busy at his task, moving his ladder from post to post and nimbly climbing it. As he lit the lamp closest to her building, another man stepped away from where he'd been leaning against the post. It was Tony Hayes.

Now standing in a pool of golden light, he peered up at Rosalyn's window. She took an involuntary step back, but she was sure he had seen her. What was he doing there? Perhaps it was coincidence. Over dinner, Jessie had mentioned that many actors lived in this vicinity. Whatever the reason, one thing was certain: Tony was now striding purposefully across the street toward the lodging house.

In a matter of moments, Rosalyn heard the clang of the front doorbell.

Surely he wasn't coming to pay a visit to *her*! When he saw her, he must have assumed Jessie was home, as well. Rosalyn hurried over to a small mirror on the wall. A good thing, too, as she had a blue smudge of ink on her chin. Hastily she wiped it off. Would he come directly up here? Rosalyn didn't know the protocol for rooming houses such as this, but she doubted it. But what if he did? Should she let him in? London had so many customs unknown to her.

While she considered these things, a knock sounded at the door. The knock was peremptory and resonated authority. Hesitantly, Rosalyn opened the door a few inches and was relieved to see not Tony, but an elderly woman. Her relief was quickly tempered, however, when the old woman glared at her. Jessie's unflattering description of Mrs. Kramer, the landlady, came immediately to mind.

Mrs. Kramer's eyes narrowed as she regarded Rosalyn. "Where is Miss Bond?"

Rosalyn swallowed. "Miss Bond has gone out for the evening."

"And who are you?"

"I am a friend of Miss Bond's."

"Your name?" Clearly, Mrs. Kramer was not the type to waste time on idle chitchat.

"Rosalyn Bernay."

"So says the *gentleman* downstairs." Mrs. Kramer put an odd emphasis on *gentleman*, as though she didn't quite believe its veracity. "He told me Miss Bond had a guest staying with her, and I said I didn't know anything about any such guest."

It was more of an accusation than a statement.

"I only just arrived last night," Rosalyn replied, giving the woman a polite smile. "This is a charming house. Quite a commodious location."

The landlady gave a brief nod to acknowledge the compliment, but it didn't seem to thaw her temperament. "Have you any references?"

Rosalyn stared at her in surprise. Who asked for references for a house guest? Was this a common practice of boardinghouses that she knew nothing about? If so, Rosalyn was in trouble. She knew very well, after what had happened with Mr. Huffman, that providing a good reference was out of the question.

She decided the best course of action was to exude the self-confidence of someone who had nothing to hide. "Surely references are not necessary for a guest staying but a few days?"

"If you stay longer than three days, I shall require a reference from the owner of your previous abode," Mrs. Kramer replied curtly. "This ain't no flophouse. I run a respectable establishment."

Rosalyn felt a blush rising to her cheeks at the insinuation that she might be a disreputable woman. She pushed aside the remembrance of what had nearly happened to her at "Aunt Mollie's" lodgings. "I had no doubt this was a proper boardinghouse before I arrived. My friend Miss Bond would only live where all is correct and aboveboard."

She was tempted to smile, feeling she'd done a good job imitating a well-bred young lady.

"So you're an actress, are you?"

Clearly Rosalyn had congratulated herself too soon. Perhaps

she had not done so well as she'd thought, if her "acting" was so obvious. "No, I'm not an actress. I assure you, I will not cause any trouble."

"You already have."

Although she was quickly becoming accustomed to Mrs. Kramer's sharp retorts, this one caught her off guard. "I beg your pardon?"

"The gentleman downstairs—a 'Mr. Hayes'—asked specifically for you." Her eyebrows rose suggestively.

"He did?" It was surprising, and not a little flattering, to think Tony was showing an interest in her. She stared at Mrs. Kramer, unsure what to do or say.

"That's why I asked if you was an actress. Miss Bond has trouble all the time with men who see her on the stage, then come here hoping to make an introduction."

Rosalyn decided there would be no profit in pointing out that Jessie thought of herself primarily as a singer. "Mr. Hayes works with Miss Bond. He's an acquaintance of mine, as well."

"Fine." Despite her nod, Mrs. Kramer did not look overly happy at the situation. "The boarders meet gentleman callers in the parlor. As I said, this is a respectable establishment. No men allowed in the rooms." She looked at Rosalyn as if daring her to object.

But Rosalyn was glad to know this strict guideline was in place. "Thank you. I shall go down and speak to him."

"As you like." Mrs. Kramer peered over Rosalyn's shoulder, her eyes taking in all aspects of the sitting room, almost as if she expected to see that Rosalyn was entertaining an entire cohort of men. Rosalyn was glad she had put the room in order and neatly folded the blankets she'd used while sleeping on the sofa.

Stepping out into the hallway, Rosalyn closed the door behind her. Mrs. Kramer motioned for Rosalyn to walk ahead of her. At the bottom of the stairs, Rosalyn hesitated.

"To your right."

"Thank you."

Rosalyn entered the parlor. Tony stood at the window, idly looking out into the street. He turned immediately upon her entrance, smiling as he approached her. In his coat, crisp white shirt, and expertly tied cravat—all well-cared-for though not new—Rosalyn thought he looked every inch a gentleman. Why Mrs. Kramer would have had any doubts on that score was incomprehensible.

Aware that the landlady was still observing them, Rosalyn reached out a hand and said politely, "Mr. Hayes, how nice to see you again."

He took it, holding it briefly in both of his own, his blue eyes holding her gaze. "The pleasure is all mine, I assure you."

"I will leave this door open," Mrs. Kramer said. With one last warning look, she left the room.

"The old dragon is gone—we are safe," Tony said in a stage whisper. He grinned. "Nearly bit my head off when I said I'd come to pay a call on Miss Bond and her friend."

"How did you know I was here?"

"A guess." He gave her a dazzling smile. "And what a lucky guess it turned out to be."

Rosalyn realized he was still holding her hand. She withdrew it slowly, not wanting to appear discourteous. "It's kind of you to take an interest in me. I'm only one of the backstage workers."

"Well, that's where you are now, but anything is possible in the theater." He went over to the upright piano in the corner of the room. "Do you sing?"

"I've had a few lessons."

He motioned toward the piano stool. "May I?"

Rosalyn realized he was asking permission to sit down. Etiquette required that a lady should be seated before the gentleman.

There was a sofa nearby, but as much as she enjoyed the idea of hearing him play, she said, "I don't know if we should. I wouldn't like for Mrs. Kramer to get put out again."

"What is the piano here for, if she doesn't intend for her boarders to use it? Besides, most people only object if one plays badly." When Rosalyn still looked doubtful, he added, "Fear not. I shall personally ensure that Mrs. Kramer does not toss you out on your ear."

She had no idea how he could promise that, but he spoke with such assurance that she believed him. She took a seat on the sofa, perching on the edge, ready to jump up in an instant if Mrs. Kramer should come storming into the room.

Tony settled himself and sorted through the sheet music on the piano. "Ah, here's a nice one," he said, and began to play.

It wasn't a tune Rosalyn recognized, but it was spritely and appealing. When there was no sign of Mrs. Kramer, Rosalyn began to relax. "You play very well. What is the name of that song?"

"Don't you know it?" He placed a hand over his heart. "It's called 'The Heart that Beats in the Tender Breast.' Here, allow me to sing you a few lines."

The lyrics were sweet and sentimental, filled with the overripe romanticism common to many popular ballads. Tony was a polished tenor, and to Rosalyn's untrained ear, he sounded every bit as good as the lead.

He finished with a flourish, and she applauded. "That was wonderful! How is it that you are only in the chorus?" The words had just spilled out. She put a hand to her mouth. "I beg your pardon. I don't mean to cause offense—"

He laughed. "Thank you! I am George Power's understudy, as it happens. If he were to become ill or incapacitated, I would sing the lead role of Ralph Rackstraw. Unfortunately, Mr. Power is disgustingly healthy. But I fully expect to be the lead tenor in a future production. Mr. Sullivan has his eye on me."

"Is that generally how it happens, that a person starts in the chorus and works their way up?" Rosalyn had never taken time to consider the hierarchy of the theater.

"It's one way."

"Well, I certainly wish you the best! Your singing is wonderful."

He looked genuinely pleased. "I enjoy duets, too. Would you care to join me, if I sing this song again?"

"But I don't know the words," she protested.

"Come stand by me, and you can read from the sheet music."

Hesitantly she approached the piano. He tugged her just a little closer to him before beginning to play.

Rosalyn felt a familiar exhilaration as their voices joined together in song. Nothing satisfied her as much as singing.

"Excellent!" Tony said when they finished. "Your voice floats on the air, light as a bird catching the summer breeze."

"I think you are indulging in hyperbole," she protested. Nevertheless, his compliment thrilled her.

He winked. "Shall we try another?"

꧁꧂

As Nate and Mary pressed the doorbell of the boardinghouse, they could hear singing and piano music.

"We must be at the right place," Mary said. "Do you suppose that's Miss Bond singing?"

"No, that's someone else." By now, Nate was familiar with each voice among the leads.

"Well, whoever she is, she sings beautifully."

"Yes." Nate was impressed by the light, smooth soprano.

"Do you suppose it's Miss Bernay? If so, Mr. Sullivan should hire her posthaste."

Before Nate could respond, the door opened and a dowdy, grey-haired woman stood frowning at them. "Yes?"

"We are looking for Miss Rosalyn Bernay. I believe she is staying with Miss Bond, one of your tenants."

The woman's frown deepened. "She must have put a notice of her whereabouts in *The Times*."

Nate shook his head. "I beg your pardon?"

The woman didn't clarify. Instead, she opened the door wider to allow them inside. "The lady you are looking for is in the parlor with another guest."

There was a tinge of disapproval in her words.

"Goodness, she's just the perfect sort of creature who should make a living hosting other people," Mary commented under her breath as they followed the landlady down the hall.

They reached the parlor doorway just in time to see Rosalyn singing the final note, which she rendered very sweetly.

She stood next to the piano, leaning in toward the man playing, her face flushed with joy and her eyes sparkling. Nate was astounded at how beautifully she sang. He would not have been surprised to learn she was a trained singer and that this was why she'd come to London. It would explain a lot about why she'd arrived alone and why she'd shown up later at the theater.

Nate's happiness at seeing her quickly soured when he saw that her expression of delight was directed at none other than Tony Hayes. After the conversation Nate had overheard last night, he found it especially provoking that Hayes was gazing up at Rosalyn as though she were the most beautiful person in the world. She was indeed lovely, and her singing had been exquisite, but over the past few weeks, Nate had seen Hayes use that same expression on women with far less claim to it.

Rosalyn's smile faded as soon as her gaze landed on Nate. She looked flustered. Was it merely surprise at seeing him, or was it irritation at having her singing party with Hayes interrupted? Nate couldn't tell.

On the other hand, it was easy to see how Hayes felt. He stood up, a flash of anger crossing his face. He switched it to something resembling a smile as he smoothed his cravat and straightened the coat sleeves that he'd pushed back for ease of playing. "Well, isn't this a pleasant surprise."

Nate's sister was, as usual, completely oblivious to the subtle mood change in the room. She clapped enthusiastically. "Bravo! That was wonderful!"

This was primarily directed toward Rosalyn, who seemed taken aback by the praise. "Thank you. I—I wasn't aware anyone else was listening."

"Never apologize for commendation—especially when it's well deserved," Hayes said, patting Rosalyn's hand in a way that Nate thought showed far too much familiarity. "Always sing as though thousands were listening. Perhaps someday they will be." He extended a hand toward Nate. "Good afternoon, Moran."

Despite his dislike of Hayes, Nate could not refuse a handshake. He prepared himself for any pain this gesture might bring to his wounded hand, but he needn't have worried. Hayes' grip was weak and perfunctory.

Hayes quickly turned his attention to Mary. "And who is this delightful creature, who has such an excellent ear for music?"

His flattering words raised all of Nate's brotherly protective instincts. It didn't help that Mary smiled back easily in response. He made stiff and cursory introductions. He knew Hayes had a pretentious surname, but he wasn't about to use it.

"*Enchanté*," Hayes said, shaking Mary's hand in the same delicate manner he'd done with Nate.

"Very pleased to meet you," Mary replied. She extended a hand to Rosalyn. "And you. I heard all about your terrible introduction to London! Certainly God blessed and protected you at a most difficult time."

Hayes cleared his throat. "Yes, we can thank fate for bringing Rosalyn to our doorstep."

It wasn't an outright contradiction of Mary's words, but to Nate it felt that way.

Mary said brightly, "Miss Bernay, we've come to ask you to join us for dinner this evening. Join our family, I mean. We are quite a large household—my mother, my sister, my brother Patrick and his wife, Hannah—and their adorable baby boy, Tommy—and, of course, Nate."

Being tacked on at the end of that long description only increased Nate's aggravation. Leave it to his sister to speak of him as an afterthought.

Hayes said, "So you would take her away before I'd had an opportunity to ask her to dinner myself?"

"Oh!" Rosalyn looked surprised and—Nate was perversely happy to note—wary. He was glad to know the actor's wily attentions hadn't peeled away all of her common sense.

"That hardly seems proper," Nate pointed out. "You could not expect her to go out with you unaccompanied."

"This is *London*," Hayes replied acerbically, as though that simple fact nullified all rules of propriety. "And in any case, I assure you she'd be quite safe. Several other cast members from *Pinafore* will be there."

Nate could see worry and embarrassment in Rosalyn's face now that she was presented with two competing offers.

"I do thank you all, but I'm afraid I will have to decline both invitations. Jessie won't be home for several hours, and I don't want to leave without consulting her first. I am, after all, her guest."

"Do you plan to stay with Jessie and continue on at the theater?"

Nate asked. Now that he'd come, he wasn't leaving until he at least garnered some facts about her future plans.

"Jessie has invited me to stay here until she leaves for America," Rosalyn affirmed. "As for working at the theater, I hope I shall. I'm going to ask Miss Lenoir about it tomorrow."

"That is great news!" Mary exclaimed.

Nate had to admit he was happy to hear this too, although he was less than enthused about the look of satisfaction that Rosalyn's answer gave to Hayes.

"You will come and visit us sometime, won't you?" Mary persisted. "Perhaps you would like to come to chapel with us? You would be most welcome there. And it's a fine congregation for singing."

Rosalyn's smile was large and genuine. "Thank you very much. I would like that."

Mary beamed at her response. "We will keep after you until you come."

"The afternoon is wearing on," Hayes said. "Perhaps we all ought to be going."

He spoke brusquely. Nate figured he was irked at no longer being the center of Rosalyn's attention.

When they had said their good-byes to Rosalyn and were back in the street, Hayes said, "Which way are you going?"

"South."

"Ah, what a pity. I'd love to walk with you, but I am going north." He tipped his hat. "Good afternoon." He turned on his heel and walked away.

Mary took Nate's arm as they began to walk in the opposite direction. It was all Nate could do not to look back.

"You don't think that was just a ruse to get us to leave, do you?" Mary said. "That Mr. Hayes seems to have developed a bit of a *tendresse* for Miss Bernay."

"The thought had crossed my mind," Nate admitted. Perhaps Mary wasn't as oblivious to these things as he'd thought, and he felt a stab of concern at her mention of a *tendresse*. She was only seventeen! Surely that was too young to know about such things.

"I'm not worried," Mary declared. "Rosalyn said she would not leave while Miss Bond was away. Even if Mr. Hayes should return, she will turn him down."

Nate wished he had the same confidence. It bothered him that Hayes was turning his oily charm on Rosalyn—and that she seemed to be enjoying it. Worry over this—and a vague annoyance at himself for caring so much about it—occupied his thoughts so completely that he heard not a word of his sister's animated chatter as they walked home.

CHAPTER

10

R OSALYN MUST HAVE been only half asleep, for she heard the door open and gently close again. She raised her head and peered over the back of the sofa. In the moonlight she could make out Jessie as she removed her shawl and tossed it over a chair.

"What time is it?" Rosalyn asked groggily.

"Past two. The soiree went longer than I anticipated. Thankfully, His Highness insisted on paying for the cab home."

"His Highness!" Rosalyn repeated in surprise. She was alert now.

"Oh, dear, I've let the cat out of the bag!" Jessie giggled, plopping into the chair. "I was at Mr. Sullivan's home, but the Duke of Edinburgh was there. He is such an admirer of Mr. Sullivan's work. But you mustn't tell anyone. It might lead to some resentment among the other cast members that I've been singled out. Not to mention that there is such a lot of bother these days about people having fun on Sundays. His Highness needs to preserve his reputation—even if he is only second in line to the throne."

"I won't tell anyone," Rosalyn assured her, but she was awed to know someone who could rub shoulders with royalty.

A knock, loud and harsh, sounded at the door, causing Rosalyn to nearly jump off the sofa.

Jessie merely frowned and said, "Oh, dear. That's the knock she usually reserves for people who are behind on their rent." Seeing Rosalyn's worried expression, she added, "Don't worry. I'm paid up through the end of the month. She owes *me* a day, if we're honest; I found out after I'd paid that our ship sails on October thirtieth instead of the thirty-first."

The knock sounded again, louder and more insistent. Jessie gave an exaggerated sigh, rose from the chair, and went to the door. Pulling the blanket around her, Rosalyn stood, too. A stab of dread went through her as she considered the possibility that Mrs. Kramer had found out about Rosalyn's history and thought she was a thief—or worse.

Mrs. Kramer looked even sterner than usual, if that were possible. "A word with you please, Miss Bond."

"Can't it wait until tomorrow? The hour is quite late."

"No, I have been waiting up specifically, and I am quite aware of the hour." Her withering glance showed exactly what she thought of Jessie's late arrival. She strode into the room and raised an accusing finger toward Rosalyn. "Who is this woman?"

"This is Miss Bernay."

Mrs. Kramer took in Rosalyn's disheveled appearance, and the blanket and pillows that were clear evidence of where she was sleeping. *At least she can see there are no men here,* Rosalyn thought.

"And where do you know her from?"

"She's a friend of mine from Wiltshire. She's only here for a few days."

"So she says."

"Why would you doubt her?"

"I have no basis to doubt—or to trust. I don't know her. But I do know that she has no references. And she has already entertained two male guests this evening."

Jessie turned a surprised—and somewhat amused—look toward Rosalyn.

"I haven't had a chance to tell you yet," Rosalyn said. "And to be fair, one of the gentlemen came with his sister."

"She *said* she was his sister." Apparently Mrs. Kramer didn't trust anyone about anything.

Jessie blew out a breath in exasperation. "Mrs. Kramer, you know I am leaving at the end of the month. Surely there can be no harm in Miss Bernay staying with me until that time?"

"Out of the question."

"But—"

"I'll give you a day or two, but then she must be gone."

"But I am the best boarder you have. I've never caused you trouble, and I always pay my rent on time."

"I don't like actresses. I made an exception for you, because you are in a respectable production and you are, as you have noted, *well behaved*." She sounded like a mother judging a child. "But I simply cannot allow this place to be given over to members of the theatrical profession. And she has no references. What is she hiding?"

"Don't you think you are blowing things a bit out of proportion?" Jessie asked. But her appeal to Mrs. Kramer's basic good sense had no effect.

For Rosalyn, it was galling to be treated with such suspicion and to face the prospect of being homeless yet again. But if she was going to end up on the street, she'd rather walk out than be pushed out.

The Captain's Daughter

"This works out just fine," she broke in. "Jessie, I already told you I'm leaving soon to visit my sister in Bristol."

She spoke earnestly, her expression silently appealing to Jessie to let the matter drop.

She could see Jessie's natural spunk and pride warring to continue this fight, but she must have decided further argument was futile. She said resignedly, "So you did."

Seeing she had won her point, Mrs. Kramer stalked to the door and opened it. "Just remember, I'll be watching you closely in the meantime."

There was a moment of silence after she was gone. Rosalyn expected Jessie to express regret at having taken Rosalyn in. Instead, she grinned. "And here I thought *I* had the more interesting evening." She put her hands on her hips. "What have you been up to? And who were these two gentlemen?"

"Tony Hayes and Nate Moran."

Jessie drew her head back in surprise. "That seems an unlikely pair."

"They didn't come together. Tony was here first, and then Nate came, accompanied by his sister."

"So he brought his sister!" Jessie's face lit up in amusement. "Because that is more proper than coming to visit a young lady alone. It seems our dangerous warrior is also quite the gentleman." Settling once more into her chair, she said, "I think you had better tell me all about it."

After Rosalyn filled her in, Jessie said, "I'm sorry Mrs. Kramer is determined to be unreasonable about your staying here. But you can't really be serious about going to Bristol? Not after what we discussed this afternoon?"

Rosalyn pulled the blanket tighter around her as she sank deeper into the sofa. "I don't know what to do, to be honest."

"Stay in London," Jessie urged. "We need you at the theater,

146

and I'm sure something will work out with your lodgings. After all, didn't you say you were raised to believe that God would always supply your need?"

It seemed odd to have Jessie state her words back to her. But it was a good reminder. Perhaps, Rosalyn reflected, the need was met already. She could ask Nate once more about the charity home.

Surprisingly, Jessie added, "Of course, if you stay, you will have your hands full, what with two men pursuing you."

"Surely neither of them thinks of me in that way," Rosalyn protested.

Jessie gave her a knowing look. "Just remember my advice about being careful around men."

Still not believing she could be the focus of two men's fancy, Rosalyn simply nodded. "I will."

⚜

"You can't keep avoiding Ada forever, you know. Sooner or later you have to make your peace."

Nate lifted his head over the withers of the horse he was grooming in order to scowl at his brother through the open door of the stall. "I *have* made my peace. We are all agreed that she is much happier as the wife of a prosperous draper than she would ever have been as a lowly sergeant's wife."

"So it's your *vanity* that's smarting. I knew as much."

Nate didn't answer but went back to brushing the mare with a vengeance.

"I had thought you a better man than that," Patrick continued. "It seems you don't mind hurting her in return."

Nate threw the brush into a nearby bucket and turned full force toward his brother. "Let me remind you of a few things. Ada broke our engagement and married another man—without even having the decency to tell me first. She left me hanging for months and finally wrote to me long after the fact. Explain to me again just how I am hurting *her*?"

Patrick was forced to take a step back as Nate led the horse from the stall, but he remained unrattled by Nate's attempt to cut short the conversation. "Nevertheless, the way you cut her in church yesterday was uncalled for."

Nate gritted his teeth. "All I did was tell her quite honestly that I was unable to accept her offer to dinner."

"You're fooling yourself if you truly think that's all you did," Patrick contradicted, stumping along with his crutch as Nate led the horse into the stable yard. "Perhaps you would not harbor such bad feelings if you allowed her to tell you her side of the story. There's more to it than you realize."

"Oh, I agree there's more to it," Nate shot back.

"I knew there was something you're not telling us," Patrick replied with an air of triumph. "What is it?"

Nate set about hitching the mare to a waiting hansom cab. The driver stood nearby, well within earshot, and Nate did not care to have his personal business aired in front of strangers. He hissed to his brother, "I don't want to discuss this right now."

"The trouble is, you won't discuss it at home, either. That's why I'm here. You should be ashamed that your brother had to haul himself all the way over here with his leg in a splint."

Nate did not answer, merely going back to getting the mare into harness. Patrick leaned against a feed barrel. With the weight off his injured leg, he seemed content to wait until Nate finished his task.

That was the trouble with Patrick. When he was convinced he was right, he was impossible to shake until he had won his point.

Nate knew he'd been unreasonable in his attitude toward Ada. He knew he was allowing his personal pain to overwhelm his Christian calling to forgive. The many trials his family had faced over the years and the grueling challenges he'd endured in the army had all been easier than admitting that, somehow, he'd come up short in proving his worth—both to Ada and as a soldier. He hadn't wanted to face either of those facts. But perhaps it was time.

Patrick did not speak again until the driver had mounted the cab and taken it away. "So you'll speak with her, right?" he said calmly as the dust settled in the stable yard.

Nate's mouth went dry, and he felt the sickening mix of restlessness and nausea that always ran through him before a battle. Even the onslaught of enemy soldiers would be more welcome than what he knew he had to do.

He gave a long, resigned sigh. "Yes."

⸙

Rosalyn stepped out the door of the boardinghouse and down the front steps to the sidewalk. It was her first time alone on these streets since she'd ended up at the Opera Comique. But the city did not seem so threatening now. Although the air was cold, the sky was clear and there was little wind.

She had two pennies Jessie had given her—Rosalyn had insisted it was only a loan—which was enough to post her letter to Julia and have change to spare. At the end of the street, the post office stood just where Jessie had described it. Rosalyn went inside and posted the letter. Things seemed brighter to her today than yesterday. She had written that letter before the unexpected visits from Tony and the Morans. But the letter was sealed, and she would just have to send it unchanged. She knew Julia would take the news in stride, odd and alarming as it was. No one was more unflappable than her sister.

Her next stop was the pawnshop she'd seen yesterday. She

stepped inside to find the place bustling with people. At least half a dozen women were holding nice gowns to be pawned. She attempted to move past them to get to a harried-looking woman writing pawn tickets at the front counter.

"You'll have to wait your turn," said the woman.

"I just want to look at your watches," Rosalyn answered. "I'm not here to pawn anything."

"Well, if that's the case, come have a look." She waved Rosalyn forward. "Mondays is our busiest day," she explained as Rosalyn began to examine the items in the glass case. "Everyone pawns their Sunday dresses."

Rosalyn had never set foot in a pawnshop, so she had little knowledge of their trade. "Is that normal?"

"Oh, yes. Gives them a few pennies for the week. They'll all be back on Saturday."

Rosalyn could see now that the women were waiting to speak to a man in the back room. He was visible through the half-open door, doling out coins to a customer.

It didn't take long for Rosalyn to determine that the watch she sought was not among the articles on display. The clerk gave her the names of several other shops in the area but didn't know of anyone named Simon.

Rosalyn thanked her and left the shop. She'd not really expected to find the watch so quickly, but at least she'd made a start.

❧

Nate walked along the busy thoroughfare, still out of sorts from his conversation with Patrick. He was so intent on his own thoughts that he barely paid heed to his steps. It didn't matter. He knew the way by heart. Day after day he took this walk to the theater, not wanting to spend money on the omnibus even when he was dead tired from working at the stable. He didn't know when he would meet with Ada. Now that he'd given his word, he knew he ought to do it soon, but working day and night left little time for anything else.

He was only a block or so from the theater when the steady beating of drums registered in his thoughts. When he became fully cognizant of the sound, he paused, listening. The drumbeats were growing louder, joined by the measured pace of men marching together. Nate hurried to the street corner just in time to see a regiment advancing down the thoroughfare.

It was a sight Nate knew well. These men were probably on their way to the train station, and from there to the ships that would take them to foreign lands. Just as Nate had done once— and would do again, he reminded himself.

People on the sidewalks paused to watch, and some shouted or cheered. In Nate's experience, the people of England did not think of their soldiers much, except at times like these or whenever the news of some battle reached them via the newspapers. This was a time for them to show their patriotism, and they heartily expressed it.

As the soldiers marched by, Nate saw that a few looked pensive, but many were smiling, appreciative of the attention of the crowd. One soldier briefly caught Nate's eye and gave a cheerful smile as he passed.

That will be me before long, Nate thought. In a few months he would be on the march, joining his regiment as they prepared to sail for India. As far as Nate was concerned, it couldn't come too soon.

≈◈≈

Jessie led Rosalyn down the hall to the business offices of the theater. "We should tread lightly, I think. I overheard that Mr.

151

Gilbert and Mr. Sullivan are meeting with Mr. Carte today. They're working out the last-minute details of our trip to America."

Sure enough, as they passed a door labeled *Mr. Richard D'Oyly Carte*, they heard men talking. The door was open a crack, enough for their voices to be heard.

"Don't worry, the libretto for *Pirates* will be done in plenty of time," Mr. Gilbert was saying. "I have broken the neck of act two, and it's all downhill from there."

"But you must give me time to score it," Mr. Sullivan answered. "I hardly think that qualifies as going *downhill*."

Jessie and Rosalyn both stifled giggles as they hurried down the hall.

When they reached a closed door marked *Miss Lenoir*, Jessie rapped soundly upon it.

"Come!" a female voice answered without hesitation.

Jessie opened the door and swept Rosalyn into the room before her. "Here is the answer to our problem," she announced without even offering a proper greeting.

The slight, neatly dressed woman seated behind a large desk had paused in the act of writing when Rosalyn and Jessie entered. She carefully set her pen aside, and after a brief, appraising glance at Rosalyn, turned a slightly ironic smile on Jessie. "I really must thank you for turning your attention to our pressing issues. It does make my work so much easier. Can you tell me what problem we have solved now?"

Her Scottish lilt instantly revealed her nationality, and the tartan colors woven as decoration on her gown confirmed it. She could not yet have reached her thirtieth birthday, yet she had the commanding presence of someone much older. The entire office was clean and orderly, with everything in its place. A reflection of its businesslike occupant, perhaps. But the gentle teasing in her tone hinted at a softer side, as well.

"And whose acquaintance do I have the honor of making?"

"This is Rosalyn Bernay. She's lately arrived in London and is looking for work. I'm recommending her for the position of dresser."

Miss Lenoir looked Rosalyn over, her gaze curious but polite. "Are you the waif who was found on our doorstep and filled in so admirably for Lilly on Saturday night?"

Rosalyn felt her eyes widen in surprise. Next to her, Jessie chuckled. "Nothing gets past you, does it, Miss Lenoir?"

"Well, I should hope not," she replied with a smile. "Mr. Giles and Millie keep me informed of the comings and goings around here."

Rosalyn would never have described herself as a waif—certainly not since she was ten. But she said only, "I'm glad to hear that others have spoken well of me. I always try my best with whatever task is set before me."

"Nicely said." Miss Lenoir continued to look her over. Rosalyn met her gaze without flinching, for it was not unfriendly, merely calm and appraising. "Do you have any experience in the theater, Miss Bernay?"

Rosalyn swallowed a lump in her throat. "No, ma'am."

"She was a lady's companion for five years," Jessie interposed. "A very fine lady."

"Let Miss Bernay speak, Jessie." Miss Lenoir turned back to Rosalyn. "Miss Bernay, what would you say makes you qualified to work here? In your own words," she added with an amused glance at Jessie.

"Perhaps at first glance there might not appear much to recommend me," Rosalyn answered honestly, "but I believe the work I did Saturday shows I can properly assist the ladies with whatever help they require. I can keep the rooms clean and organized. I'm good with a needle, too, so I can help if any of the costumes should need mending."

"So you see, she's perfect!" Jessie enthused.

Miss Lenoir nodded thoughtfully. "With Lilly gone, we certainly have an immediate need, which it appears you can fill." She took another moment to consider Rosalyn. "I do have to be honest with you, Miss Bernay, and I hope you will do me the same favor in return."

"Yes?"

"You seem to come from a respectable background, and yet you arrived at our theater jobless and hungry. Can you explain to me why that is? I do not make a habit of prying into other people's affairs, but everything that happens here is my affair. I have a responsibility to hire only workers who are trustworthy and reliable."

Rosalyn knew she was trustworthy and reliable—no matter what lies Mr. Huffman might spread about her. What if he should find her and his accusations become known to the management of this theater? Then she would appear to be a liar as well as a thief.

"She's here through no fault of her own," insisted Jessie.

"If that's true, you can be sure that whatever you tell me will not go beyond this room. But you understand why I need to know."

Rosalyn nodded. She realized that, after all, she had nothing to lose—except this temporary foothold that, tenuous as it was, she wished to retain. She told Miss Lenoir everything, laying out the details just as she had for Jessie.

Miss Lenoir did not interrupt but listened quietly, showing sympathy at Rosalyn's sudden need for flight, consternation at her deception by Mrs. Hurdle, and commiseration at the theft of her belongings. When Rosalyn reached the part where Mr. Gilbert saw her through the theater window, Jessie took over and finished the tale, relating breathlessly all that had happened since then.

"So you see why I say that her problems are not of her own making," Jessie finished.

Miss Lenoir leaned back in her chair and regarded them both. "I understand now why you decided to make Miss Bernay your personal project, Jessie."

"Yes. You know how I feel about men who force their attentions on women."

"I do. And I flatter myself that, after years of experience in the theater, I can tell the difference between truth and acting. Miss Bernay, I do not believe you are telling us some tall tale. But don't you think it would be better to face your accuser and state your case before an impartial judge?"

"What man could be impartial?" Jessie exclaimed. "You know he would take the man's side."

"*You* were able to find an impartial judge," Miss Lenoir returned, promptly but not unkindly.

She caught Jessie without an answer for that one. Jessie stared at her dumbly for several moments.

Miss Lenoir went on, "But that is not relevant to the topic at hand." She turned her attention Rosalyn. "You are looking for a job. I am willing to offer you one. We'll start you at five shillings per week."

For Rosalyn, this was a happy surprise. The salary was far less than she had received from her former employer but still more than she was expecting. Surely she could live on that amount if she were very careful?

Miss Lenoir extended her right hand across the desk. "Do we have a deal?"

Next to her, Rosalyn heard Jessie emit a tiny squeal of delight. Rosalyn reached out her hand and shook Miss Lenoir's. "It will be a pleasure to work here, I'm sure."

"You might revise that statement once you spend a week with the fussy ladies in the chorus." Once again, Rosalyn heard the teasing in Miss Lenoir's voice. "But I will accept it for now." She

155

opened a drawer and pulled out a small purse. "And here is six-pence for the work you did on Saturday."

Rosalyn accepted the money, grateful that her first night's work had been rewarded.

"Now, if you ladies will excuse me, there are some vendors' invoices that I must attend to."

Jessie and Rosalyn stood up. Rosalyn said, "Thank you so much, Miss Lenoir. I promise you will not regret hiring me."

"I'm sure you will work out fine. However, I do hope you will give some thought to my suggestion. It's a problem you may not want to leave hanging over your head."

Rosalyn nodded but could think of nothing to say. The specter of what Mr. Huffman might do seemed real only when she was forced to talk about it. Perhaps it was wrong of her, but she found it far easier to keep it pushed to the back of her mind, as though that alone could guarantee her safety.

Nate was heading backstage when he saw Rosalyn walking with Jessie down the adjoining hallway. He paused, waiting for them to reach him.

Rosalyn was looking a bit stunned, but Nate supposed she must be happy, as well, for Jessie was saying, "I told you Miss Lenoir would understand. She's a softhearted one deep down, even though she runs this place like the army."

Nate couldn't resist responding to that. "Like the army? This crew of coddled children?"

Jessie gave him an arch look. "We work very hard, I assure you."

"As does the crew," Rosalyn pointed out.

"And by 'crew,' are you now referring to yourself, as well?" Nate inquired, although he was sure he already knew the answer.

Pleasure lit up her face. "Yes, I suppose I am." She looked down at her hand, and Nate saw a sixpence coin in it. Returning her gaze to Nate, she said, "Would you have a moment for me to ask you about something?"

"Of course."

He wondered if Jessie would raise some objection, now that Rosalyn seemed to be her protégé, but she merely nodded and said, "Good luck. See you upstairs." She flashed a meaningful glance at Rosalyn and walked away. Some message had passed between them, but Nate could only guess at what it was.

"I'm sorry I couldn't accept your invitation yesterday," Rosalyn said, giving Nate an embarrassed smile. "I hope you understand. I wanted to accept, but I didn't feel right about leaving. And, of course, I didn't want to offend Tony, either."

Nate could have done without that last observation, but he let it pass. "What is it you wanted to speak to me about?"

"It's about that charity house. Do you think they will still take me in? I need someplace to live, and soon. Jessie's landlady seems to think I'm a shady character."

"Is it because of what happened yesterday?" As far as Nate was concerned, anything disparaging thrown on Rosalyn's character was more the fault of Hayes, for having the effrontery to visit her alone.

"There's more to it than that," she answered sadly.

Although Nate still didn't know what had brought her to London, he found it hard to believe she was the kind of woman who could be turned away from respectable lodgings. But he merely said, "I think that particular landlady suspects *everyone* of being a shady character."

She smiled at his joke, but the troubled look did not entirely leave her eyes.

"Why don't you come to my house tomorrow afternoon?" Nate said impulsively. "My mother and sister help out quite a bit with the charity house. They can give you all the details and advice you need."

"Thank you."

He had no idea how he was going to manage an afternoon away from the stable, but seeing the relief on Rosalyn's face, he knew he would find a way.

CHAPTER

11

ROSALYN WAS JUST about to mount the steps to the women's dressing rooms when she heard Tony call her name. She paused, waiting, as he bounded up to her.

"How lovely to see you again! Does this mean you've become a permanent member of our happy band?"

"Yes, although I confess I'm a little nervous. I know I have a lot to learn."

"Don't waste a moment worrying. This show is simple— although there is one rather tricky costume change toward the end, when Ralph and the captain exchange clothes. They have to have a *man* help them with that, of course. However, it does take place backstage rather than upstairs, so if you want some instruction on how a quick costume change is done, you might want to take a peek behind the set."

"Oh, I couldn't do that," Rosalyn protested.

Then she saw the glint in his eye. Yesterday he'd said a few risqué things, too. It seemed to be his nature.

159

She gave him her best disapproving look. "Mr. Hayes, that sounds rather too shocking."

"What a perfectly awful face!" Tony cried, laughing. "For a moment you looked exactly like my old Aunt Hilda. But only for a moment, for you are far more beautiful than she ever was."

"Thank you, I'm sure." Rosalyn could not say why she enjoyed this banter so much. It flirted on the edge of being scandalous, but she could see no real harm in it.

"I so enjoyed singing with you yesterday," Tony said. "Shall we do it again soon? How about tomorrow, say, an hour before call time? We can go up to the rehearsal room and sing there."

"Is that . . . allowed?"

"Why wouldn't it be?"

Rosalyn couldn't answer that.

"As I told you yesterday, I think you have real talent. You should consider a career on the stage."

"No, I surely couldn't," she objected. But inside, a small part of her thrilled at the thought.

He wrapped an arm through hers. "Never say never, my dear. For the moment, why don't we take an hour and enjoy singing together?"

"That does sound lovely," she admitted. "I can't do it tomorrow, though."

"All right then, how about Wednesday?" he pressed.

Rosalyn thought this over. If all went well, she would be moving to new lodgings on Wednesday. She would need time to get her bearings. "Would Friday be all right?" she countered.

"I see you've already learned the first rule of theater," Tony said. "Always build the audience's anticipation. Very well. Friday it shall be." He gave her shoulder a pat before releasing her and giving her a little bow. "Until we meet again—in about an hour, when Her Majesty's Ship *Pinafore* sets sail once more."

With a smile, he sauntered off.

Rosalyn was halfway up the stairs when Millie raced down to meet her. "Hurry!" she exclaimed, grabbing Rosalyn's hand.

Millie dragged her to the dressing room, where the ladies' chorus was in an uproar. Several were exclaiming in horror or anger. Elsie shook her finger at Helen. "Thoughtless fool! How could you not have known what would happen?"

"What's the matter?" Rosalyn asked.

Elsie jerked a thumb at Helen. "This one left food stashed behind the gowns. Now a mouse has eaten holes in the hems to get at the food."

"A dozen mice, I think," Sarah said. "Or rats."

Several of the ladies shivered in horror.

"Our beautiful gowns!" cried one of the other ladies. "They're ruined!"

Everyone was staring daggers at Helen.

"I'm sorry!" Helen said, in exasperation. "I put a bag there for safekeeping and forgot to take it home with me." She glared right back at them. "Draw and quarter me if you like. I didn't do it on purpose. My gown is ruined, too."

Rosalyn fell to her knees in front of the rack of gowns and began to inspect them. At first blush the damage did look pretty bad. But as she checked more closely, she saw that only half a dozen or so had actually been soiled or torn. "These can be mended," she said.

"How can they be mended?" Elsie asked. "They have one-inch holes in them!"

"We'll put on extra ribbon and flounces to cover the repairs. I saw some scraps in the costume shop that I think will work."

"You'll have to work fast," Millie pointed out. "There's just over an hour before they have to go down."

"We'll make it. Let's go up to the costume shop and collect those scraps."

Ten minutes later, Rosalyn and Millie returned, armed with plenty of pink thread, some bits of lace, and about a mile of ribbon.

Rosalyn marshaled the women like soldiers, showing them her trick for basting together torn garments. The gowns were already quite colorful, with the ribbon accents that were the current style. The additions only highlighted the effect.

"There!" Rosalyn said as they surveyed their efforts on the first gown, which was Elsie's. "The audience isn't going to notice the abundance of ribbons. If they do, they'll just ascribe it to the overall silliness of Sir Joseph's relatives."

"Well, I'd never wear it this way in real life," Elsie agreed, "but it should work."

Topsy-turvy. Rosalyn had read that was Mr. Gilbert's own description of the odd situations he created in his shows. It seemed an accurate assessment of backstage life, too.

By the time Millie was sent up to announce the ten-minute warning, all the women were dressed and ready to go.

"You saved my life, I think," Helen told her. "I don't know if Lilly would have thought of that."

Rosalyn beamed. She was pretty sure she'd just passed the first real test of her new job.

⁂

Mary walked between Nate and Rosalyn and kept the conversation lively as they made their way to the Morans' home. She never seemed to run out of things to say. She asked Rosalyn about her favorite books, pastimes, and other incidentals. Once or twice Nate admonished his sister for being a busybody, but Rosalyn didn't mind. Mary was, in some ways, a blend of Rosalyn's two sisters—clever and well-read like Julia, and friendly and talkative like Cara.

They turned onto a curved street lined with terraced homes.

Halfway down the street, they paused in front of a four-story house made of brick. The general feel of the neighborhood was of modest respectability. The Moran house, located halfway along the arched street like a keystone, solidified this impression.

"Here we are!" Mary exclaimed. "Home, sweet home."

After the gloomy chill outside, the large entryway radiated welcoming warmth. They entered the parlor, where a man sat on a large stuffed chair, playing with a baby on his lap. The child looked about six months old. He gave short bursts of laughter as his father lifted him up and down to make the child appear as if he were jumping.

Setting the child gently on his lap, the man extended a hand toward Rosalyn. "Please forgive my not standing." He pointed toward his splinted leg. "As you see, I am indisposed at the moment."

Mary said, "Rosalyn, this is my brother, Patrick, and his son, Tommy."

Tommy gave Rosalyn a toothless grin.

"Nate, is that you?" an older woman's voice called.

"Yes, Ma, we're here."

A plump, grey-haired woman bustled into the room, wiping her hands on her apron. She beamed at Rosalyn. "You must be Miss Bernay."

"You may call her by her Christian name," Mary announced.

Mrs. Moran gave her daughter an inquiring look. "Shouldn't that be for Miss Bernay to decide?"

But her deprecating tone had no effect on Mary. She said blithely, "Oh, it's all arranged. We decided on that earlier, didn't we, Rosalyn?"

Mrs. Moran gave Rosalyn an apologetic look. "I hope you don't mind my daughter's unorthodox ways. She's the youngest but seems to think she's the one who should direct things around here."

163

"Well, there's no point in being stuffy. The Bible says we are all children of God, so why shouldn't we address our fellow Christians as siblings?"

"Her logic is, of course, irrefutable," Nate remarked dryly.

Three other women had filtered into the room as they'd been talking, and Mary set herself to making the introductions.

The first was Patrick's wife, Hannah—a beautiful woman with blond hair and honey-brown eyes that matched her son's. Then came the two lodgers: the first was a surprisingly spry older woman who must have been in her seventies. She was introduced as Mrs. Fletcher, and Rosalyn surmised that Mary's avowal that everyone should use Christian names did not extend to the elderly, to whom she quite rightly wished to show respect. The second boarder was a pale slip of a girl named Liza Branson. She could not have been more than fourteen. Rosalyn was surprised to see a boarder so young.

"She lost her parents to a fever six months ago," Mary explained. "She had nowhere to go, so naturally we brought her here."

Liza cast her eyes down, and Rosalyn sensed the girl was uncomfortable having her life's story explained so matter-of-factly to a stranger. Despite Mary's good intentions, she was perhaps not as tactful as she might have been.

"I am an orphan, too," Rosalyn said. "I lost my parents when I was nine."

This information, along with the clear sympathy in Rosalyn's voice, seemed to set the girl at ease. Her thin shoulders relaxed, and her eyes, shining from a hint of tears, met Rosalyn's. "Then you understand."

"Indeed I do."

Mrs. Moran said, "Nate, not only is Miss Bernay as lovely as you said, but I can see she is kindhearted, as well."

"Wait a minute," Nate protested, "I never said she was lovely—"

He stopped and turned a highly embarrassed look to Rosalyn. "That is, not that you aren't, because you *are*—" He turned to his mother and glared. "Now look what you've made me do. I've insulted her."

"No, dear brother, you did that yourself," Mary interposed with a grin. "Go ahead, don't let us keep you from digging the hole deeper."

"Please, stop," Rosalyn said, but despite her words, she was laughing. She was enjoying this interplay between the siblings and seeing a more vulnerable side of Nate Moran. He gave her a sheepish look, and she found her breath catching. Did he really think she was beautiful? He might have been tricked into voicing the compliment, but from the expression on his face as their eyes met, Rosalyn was sure he'd meant it. She felt warmth wash over her and realized she was blushing.

Mrs. Moran ushered them into the dining room. What the Morans called tea was in fact a substantial meal. Liza brought out platters loaded with bread, meat, cheese, and sliced apples. Mrs. Moran explained that they had taken to eating this early meal in order to ensure that Patrick—and now Nate—was well-fed before leaving for work at the theater.

The only member of the household not present was Nate's sister Martha, who worked long hours at a dressmaker's shop.

Once everyone had been served, Mary said eagerly, "And now, Rosalyn, you must tell us all about yourself!"

All eyes fixed on her with kindly interest. When Rosalyn began her story by mentioning that she'd been raised in an orphanage in Bristol, Mary broke in, "Do you mean Mr. Müller's orphanage at Ashley Down? We know of it!"

"You do?"

"Our church sends a donation at least once a year," Patrick said. "Has for many years."

"How very kind." Rosalyn recalled how often such a donation might arrive unexpectedly at the orphanage, and nearly always it was just at a precise moment when it was desperately needed. God was never late—although Rosalyn remembered thinking many a time that He seemed to enjoy cutting it rather close. "And here I am, benefiting from your giving once again."

"God is the supplier of need," Mrs. Moran said. "We are simply blessed to be His agents sometimes."

"What did you do after leaving the orphanage?" Mary asked.

"And how did you come to be at that railway station on Friday?" Nate spoke calmly, but he was looking at her with the same intensity as when they'd first met.

Rosalyn gave a doubtful glance toward Liza, wondering if she was too young to hear about Mr. Huffman and the brothel. "Parts of my story do get . . . ugly." She couldn't think of any other way to say it.

"I've seen lots of things," Liza said. The words were simple but held far too much weight. Once more, Rosalyn's heart went out to the girl.

This was it, then. She took a deep breath and continued on.

❧

Nate didn't know what he'd been expecting, but it certainly wasn't this. Or perhaps, in some way, it had been. He'd heard similar tales of women in service who had been treated in such a criminal fashion by their employers. Rage flowed through him at the thought of what men could do so callously and without any reprisals. But he knew these crimes had not been committed only by rich gentlemen. He'd seen fellow soldiers behaving just as badly, and he'd been sickened by it.

"And now you know my story," Rosalyn said. "I felt I should tell you everything before presuming to ask for your help and advice."

"Our advice is simple, of course," Mary said. "You must come and live with us."

Nate nearly overturned his teacup as he moved in startled irritation. Mary had no right to make such an offer. Certainly not without consulting the family. But his dismay grew as he noticed that no one else at the table seemed the least surprised at her words.

Except for Rosalyn.

"But . . . I thought you were going to take me to the charity house."

"What's this about?" Nate demanded.

His question was directed at Patrick, who answered, "You know we've discussed taking on another boarder."

"After meeting Rosalyn, I knew she was the right person," Mary broke in eagerly. "We talked it over this morning, and we're all in agreement. You were already at the stable, but we were sure you wouldn't have any objections."

Nate had plenty of objections. Mostly he was indignant that his family had deliberately backed him into this corner. Everyone in the room was voicing their agreement that Rosalyn should come and live here. How could he be the one to say no? Especially after learning what she'd been through.

"We decided that, since Rosalyn will be working at the theater, this is the perfect place for her to lodge," Mary said. "Even though she must be out so late, she'll have you to see her home safely."

"And me, too," Patrick added. "Once I get the use of my leg back, I'll be returning to my job there. I promise to get you home safe, even if I'm not one of Her Majesty's soldiers."

Safe. Nate thought of the man from the train station—according to Rosalyn, his name was Mick. If it had been him at the charity house, it could have been a coincidence. Or perhaps he'd overheard Nate at the station calling out the address. Was the gang at the brothel looking for her? After hearing her story, he had to assume it was possible. Grudgingly, he had to admit that perhaps this was the best answer.

"Isn't it perfect?" Mary gushed. "It's as if God has brought you here."

Throughout this exchange, Rosalyn had been silent. But Nate had seen the play of emotions crossing her face. "I am grateful to you," she said at last. "I don't know how much money you would require, but—"

"We'll work it out," Ma assured her. "We live simply, and everyone pitches in with the work as they can."

"So you're moving in tomorrow, right?" Mary said eagerly.

Nate's heart twisted as Rosalyn leaned back in her chair and regarded them all with a misty smile.

"Yes," she said.

Nate still had some reservations about the arrangement, especially when it came to his family's expectations. They were eager to misconstrue his desire to help Rosalyn into something more than it was. He could tell even by their effusive comments as Nate and Rosalyn were leaving together for the theater. If this kept up, it could make things awkward for both of them, but he decided that Rosalyn's well-being was the most important thing.

And in any case, he was leaving in two months. He'd have to focus on that.

⁂

When they reached the theater, Nate left her to attend to his tasks. Rosalyn decided she would take a few minutes to explore and familiarize herself with the theater. At one point she came across Millie, who offered to walk with her. The theater was constructed rather oddly, with some hallways actually leading to rooms in the adjacent buildings. The place was as confusing as a maze.

They saw several chorus members on their way to a room at the end of one such hallway.

"What's happening now?" Rosalyn asked Millie.

"Vocal warm-ups."

"May we watch?"

Millie shrugged. "I suppose so."

Rosalyn followed them into the room, eager to learn how professional singers prepared for a performance. She stood against the wall, not wanting to interfere with the proceedings. A few people sent her curious glances, but no one seemed to mind her presence.

Everyone was there, from the chorus to the principals. Jessie was on the other side of the room, chatting gaily with George Grossmith and also with Rutland Barrington, the tall, hefty man who played Captain Corcoran.

"The three of them is together all the time, and usually laughing over something," Millie said. "Thick as thieves—that's what my father says."

Tony came their way as soon as he saw Rosalyn. "In the cast already, then?"

"No, no, I'm just watching," she told him. "I confess I'm curious to see what you do."

"It's pretty dry stuff, but it's the foundation of our craft. Here comes the conductor, Mr. Cellier. Enjoy!"

The chatter ceased as Mr. Cellier strode into the room. Everyone parted as he made his way to the center and pulled out a pitch pipe. "All right everyone, let's get started."

He led them in a series of vocal exercises. A few were familiar to Rosalyn from the singing lessons she'd been afforded by Mrs. Huffman. Rosalyn could only watch, although she was itching to join in. Then they did a challenging tongue twister. Rosalyn stumbled just trying to say the words in her head. She couldn't wait until she had a chance to try it out later.

"Enunciate!" Mr. Cellier directed. "You know how Mr. Gilbert feels when you muddle his lyrics!"

After about fifteen minutes, he pronounced them ready to go. Most people began to drift out the door, intent on getting to the dressing rooms.

"Well, what do you think?" Tony asked Rosalyn.

"It's very interesting! I think the tongue twister is going to stay with me awhile."

"We'll practice it when we get together on Friday, eh?" He grinned. "I know a few more that might even bring out that Aunt Hilda face."

Still grinning in amusement, Rosalyn practiced the tongue twister under her breath as she made her way down another hallway to collect towels and other items she'd need for her work. As she walked backstage, several of the stagehands greeted her by name. Seeing Nate on an upper platform preparing the limelights, she gave him a wave. He returned the gesture, smiling. Her heart did a little dance as she continued on. At this moment, Rosalyn couldn't imagine a better place to be.

CHAPTER

12

"Jessie, it's too much," Rosalyn protested as Jessie added another gown to the growing pile of clothes on the bed.

"Nonsense. You'll be doing me a favor by taking it. It would only end up in storage while I'm in America, and goodness knows what the fashions will be like when I return." She struck a coquettish pose. "Since I make my living on the stage, I must always be in the latest style."

Rosalyn fingered the material, a lovely blue tea gown that was finer than anything she'd ever owned.

"They will need alterations, of course," Jessie went on. "Particularly in length. You may need to get creative with those hems. Thank heaven ruffled flounces are all the rage right now."

"I'm sure I'll manage." It seemed a small price to pay for such extravagance. "I can't thank you enough for all you've done for me."

Jessie paused in the act of examining a petticoat she'd pulled from a drawer. "One is always better for having helped a fellow

171

creature in need, don't you think? 'Cast thy bread upon the waters,' as the Bible says."

"'For thou shalt find it after many days.'" Rosalyn finished the verse, nodding. "The good we do comes back to us. I've always felt that way, too."

"I think this petticoat will fit you." Jessie handed it to Rosalyn. "Don't you dare protest. This is the last thing I shall give you, you ungrateful creature."

Rosalyn relented and received the gift with a smile.

"Now, let's see how much we can fit into this trunk. I will need it back, though. Perhaps Nate can help you return it?"

"I'll arrange something," Rosalyn replied. She wasn't sure how comfortable she felt asking Nate for more favors. He had already done so much.

They began to place the clothing in the trunk.

"I'm sorry my landlady was so immovable on the subject of your staying here, but perhaps it's for the best, eh? You'll be able to have a proper bedchamber again. Your description of the Morans' house sounds very agreeable, too."

"So you're not concerned about me moving in with a man?" Rosalyn teased.

"Scandalous woman," Jessie returned. She sobered. "I know you'll be chaperoned by half a dozen people, yet I can't help noticing the very admiring looks he gives you. Please promise me you'll be careful."

Rosalyn wanted to protest that Nate couldn't possibly have that kind of interest in her, but she didn't think there would be any profit in arguing. So she said simply, "I'll be careful."

"Good." Jessie pulled Rosalyn into a hug. "I want only the best for you as you begin your new life in London."

My new life in London.

Those words echoed in Rosalyn's thoughts two hours later as

she unpacked her things in her new home. She paused and once more surveyed the room that was now hers. It was on the top floor and had originally been designed as servant's quarters. But the Morans had added homey touches to make it more cheerful and less spartan. The room held two narrow beds, but one was covered with a colorful quilt and pillows to give it the appearance of a sofa. Cheery curtains decorated the small window, and a jar of rose-scented cold cream—a gift from the Moran sisters—was set out with a comb and brush on the nightstand.

Rosalyn thought she could be quite content here.

A light tap on the open door startled her. She turned to see Nate leaning against the doorframe. "How are you getting along?" he asked.

He was watching her with a friendly expression, his lips turned up in a slight smile.

Jessie's words came back to her. *"I can't help but notice the very admiring looks he gives you."*

Was that what he was doing now? Suddenly self-conscious, Rosalyn pushed a stray bit of hair back into the bun at the base of her neck.

He was looking at her expectantly, and she realized she had not yet answered him. She also realized she was still holding one of the chemises Jessie had given her. Quickly she tucked the item into a drawer and closed it. "All moved in."

She spoke a tad too brightly to cover her embarrassment, but Nate didn't seem to notice. He stepped into the room to close the lid on the empty trunk. "Mary mentioned that you need to get this back to Jessie. We can borrow a dog cart from the ostler's where I work. Cheaper than hiring a cab."

"Thank you." She gave him a sheepish smile. "I seem to be wearing out that phrase here."

"It's no trouble." He was standing quite close to her now. He had to stoop a little, on account of the way the wall nearest him sloped downward. Even so, he filled the room with his presence.

It was strange standing there, the two of them alone. Suddenly, they both seemed at a loss for words. Only the pigeons cooing under the eaves prevented the room from falling completely silent. Perhaps the novelty of being with him like this would wear off as Rosalyn spent more time in the Morans' home. For the moment, she could not help feeling disconcerted.

Nate pulled the trunk to the doorway, where he could straighten to his full height. "There's no time to deliver it today, though. We need to leave for the theater soon."

Rosalyn found her voice as the distance between them widened. "That will be fine. I don't think Jessie expects it before tomorrow."

He reached down for the trunk handle. "Are you coming? Ma said to be sure to eat something before you go."

"I'll be down shortly." She met his gaze. "Thank you. For everything."

"There you go, wearing out that phrase again." He smiled, but Rosalyn thought she saw something else in his eyes. A touch of unease, perhaps.

He lifted the trunk as easily as if it were nothing. "I'll go ahead and set this downstairs for now."

⁂

After the show that night, when Rosalyn had finished her duties, she met Nate at a prearranged spot backstage. While she was staying with Jessie, they had taken a cab directly from the stage door. Nate, however, had told her that he generally preferred to walk home. She supposed it was because his family was doing all they could to save money.

Rosalyn felt a twinge of uneasiness as they stepped outside.

She found this area daunting enough in the daytime. The narrow street was a motley collection of old Tudor buildings that were rickety and down-at-heel. More recent structures of brick were interspersed here and there, but nothing looked newer than a hundred years old. The pub directly across from the stage door looked decidedly dodgy.

"Do any of the cast or crew ever go to that pub?" she asked.

Nate shrugged. "A few of the stagehands go there sometimes. Not Patrick, though. He has his wife and son to go home to. Why would he stay here?"

As if to punctuate Nate's point, there was a commotion at the pub as the barman hauled a customer outside and shoved him away from the door. "Go home, Harry," he said gruffly. "Your wife won't thank you for spending all your coin here."

The man took a few wobbly steps before leaning against the wall. "How do you stay in business if you keep chasin' people away?"

The barman only turned on his heel and went back inside.

"Come on," said Nate. "The streets get better after this."

The streets did get wider and better lit as they continued on. They met other pedestrians along the way, and Rosalyn was glad that most were more sober than the man they'd seen at the pub. Every block or so, a patrolling constable nodded a greeting to them as he passed. Rosalyn was surprised to see so many carriages and even work carts on the streets. Still, the volume was nowhere near as high as it was in the daytime.

Every sound seemed heightened and more distinct: their footsteps echoing on the pavement, the clop of horses' hooves, the church bell tolling the half hour.

They paused briefly to wait for a passing carriage before crossing the street. Nate took a deep breath of the crisp night air. "I enjoy this time of night. The city doesn't seem so suffocating."

175

He turned to look at her. "How are you doing? You seemed wary when we first left the theater."

"It feels strange, being out at this hour," she admitted. "I can't remember any time that I've been out on the streets past midnight." She wasn't going to count her flight from Mrs. Hurdle's house in the predawn.

"That's a good thing. I don't think it's proper for ladies to be out so late."

She looked at him. "What is your opinion of the singers, then?"

"They chose their profession. They do what they need to do. Just be careful around the men."

It seemed a humorous irony that this advice was coming from a man—and one Jessie had described as a *battle-hardened veteran* at that. "Jessie has already warned me to watch out for *all* men—not just the actors," she said. "I think that covers it."

"It's good counsel. I hope you heed it."

"I'm doing fairly well so far. Except for right now, of course. Although Mary assures me you're safe enough."

Her teasing tone must have taken him by surprise. He shot her a glance. "Don't be so sure. My sister isn't always right, even if she does like to think so." His face was in profile to her, but Rosalyn saw the corner of his mouth quirk in a smile. She liked seeing these little moments of levity in him.

When they reached the Moran home, Nate motioned for her to be very quiet as they stepped inside. They went silently down the hall, pausing at the open parlor door. In the dim glow of the banked fire, she could just make out Patrick, asleep in his chair with Tommy on his chest.

"They do this almost every night," Nate whispered. "It's Patrick's way of allowing the rest of the household to sleep."

Rosalyn studied the sleeping pair. "They are charming. What will the family do when Patrick goes back to work?"

"Suffer."

Even though they were still whispering, she heard the playful note in his voice.

She saw Nate stifle a yawn. After a very full day, Rosalyn ought to have been tired, too, but the walk with Nate in the bracing night air had left her unaccountably alert and refreshed. The prospect of more evenings like this filled her with pleasant anticipation.

❧

They took the stairs, pausing when they reached the landing on the second floor, where Nate's bedroom was located. Tired as he was, Nate found he was reluctant to see the evening end.

Rosalyn seemed in no hurry to continue to her room. "Looks like I made it home safely with you after all." She kept her voice low to avoid disturbing the sleeping household.

Nate didn't think to respond. His attention was focused on the way a smile played around her lips as she spoke. By long lashes framing eyes that glittered in the candlelight.

She peered up at him, perhaps thinking it odd that he couldn't answer. Couldn't move. "Good night," she said. "Sleep well."

He stood there for several moments after she'd gone. A delicate, floral scent lingered where she'd been standing. He breathed deeply, his eyes closed, drinking it in. He might well have stood there all night had not cold conscience brought him back to his senses.

What am I doing?

The question burst into his mind. He should know better than to spend any time at all dwelling on a woman's charms. Such thoughts were the first steps on the road to disaster. He turned and hastened to his room.

If anything could bring him back to reality, it was the sight of the note lying on his bed. He recognized the handwriting. It was from Ada.

With a heavy sigh, he sank onto the bed and slowly unfolded the letter. She was replying to the note he'd sent her, fixing the day he would go to their house. Friday.

Whether the meeting would change anything was doubtful, but Nate was resigned to going through with it. Especially if it meant his family would finally let the matter rest.

A thought struck him out of the blue. He'd never once thought of Ada whenever Rosalyn was in his presence. As he mulled over the implications of that, it took him a very long time to get to sleep.

❧

It was midmorning by the time Rosalyn made her way downstairs. She found Mrs. Moran and Hannah in the kitchen. Mrs. Moran immediately offered her breakfast. While Rosalyn ate at the plain block table, Mrs. Moran busied herself preparing food for the rest of the day's meals. Hannah sat in a narrow wooden chair near the fireplace, nursing Tommy.

By that hour, Nate and Martha had already gone to work. Mrs. Moran told Rosalyn that Liza and Mary were out delivering laundry. They did washing for several large households to bring in extra money. Rosalyn also discovered that she wasn't likely to see much of Mrs. Fletcher, who spent most of her days working at various charitable organizations, including the charity house run by the church. As a widow able to support herself with a small pension, she said she felt most useful when she was able to use her time to help others.

"Everyone seems to have such a sense of purpose," Rosalyn observed. "I feel as though I should be helping out, too."

"You have plenty of work to do, with your long hours at the

theater," Mrs. Moran pointed out. "But we will be glad of your help once you've settled in."

"There is something I need to attend to as soon as I can," Rosalyn said. She told Mrs. Moran about the clothing Jessie had given her.

"Oh, I can help you with the alterations," Hannah said. "This little fellow will be asleep soon. I'll go upstairs with you so you can try on the clothes, and we'll see what's needed."

By midafternoon, Rosalyn and Hannah were at work in the parlor, sewing the hems on two skirts they'd agreed would be simplest to alter and most useful for Rosalyn. Mary had joined them, too, though she was proving to be less skilled with a needle. She kept them entertained by reading aloud from the newspaper.

Mrs. Moran came into the room. "Patrick, you're shirking your duties," she said to her son, who was in his usual chair by the large fireplace. "It's too cold in here."

"Right you are."

Rosalyn was surprised at how mobile Patrick could be, even with his leg in a splint. Using his crutch, he was able to get out of his chair and tend to the fire.

Still absorbed in the newspaper, Mary turned a page and made a *tsk* sound. "More action in Afghanistan. I think it's only going to get worse. It says here—"

"I don't think you need to read that to us right now," Patrick broke in, speaking with uncharacteristic sharpness. Rosalyn saw him send a worried glance at his mother.

Mrs. Moran sank into a chair. "I am very much aware of what is going on overseas. Why do you think I'm so dead set against his leaving?"

"I think we all know why he's re-enlisting," Patrick said.

No one answered, but they all seemed to silently agree, understanding the meaning of Patrick's words.

Re-enlisting! Rosalyn pricked her finger with her needle in her surprise. *Why?*

Mary caught Rosalyn's questioning gaze. "Jilted. We tried to tell him he's better off, but he won't believe us."

Nate had been jilted? This was even harder for her mind to grasp. It was something she never would have considered. Not now that she was getting to know him. He was a good man. And handsome, too, if she was honest. Immediately she found herself—like Mary—offended on Nate's behalf. Who would turn away from such a man?

"Mary, let's not speak ill of anyone," Mrs. Moran admonished. "What's done is done. Nate ought to put the past behind him. And I *don't* mean by going to India."

"He's not gone yet," Patrick pointed out. "There's still hope. I did finally get him to agree to see Ada."

"Good" was Mrs. Moran's crisp reply. "That's one answer to prayer, at least."

Rosalyn could see that Mary was brimming with eagerness to discuss the matter further, but Mrs. Moran apparently considered the subject closed. With great effort, she rose from her chair. Motioning to Mary, she said, "Come help Liza and me prepare tea."

"Yes, ma'am." Mary reluctantly followed her mother out of the room.

Rosalyn's mind filled with questions. Was a broken heart truly driving Nate back into the army? Surely there had to be more to the story than that. Whatever his reasons were, she found herself fervently sharing the Morans' hope that he would change his mind.

ↂ

"We'd like to take this up to Miss Bond's room—with your permission?"

Mrs. Kramer eyed Nate and Rosalyn with her characteristic

suspicion. But he figured even this irascible old woman would have to admit there wasn't any other practical way to get the trunk up the stairs.

She heaved a dramatic sigh. "Follow me."

Jessie met them at the door and opened it wide for them to enter. Once inside, Nate took a moment to look around. He was curious to see just how one of the leading players of London's most popular show lived. Mary was curious, too, apparently, as Nate could think of no other reason why she had tagged along on this trip.

Jessie lived quite simply, as it turned out. Or perhaps it seemed so because the mantelpiece and shelves were bare of any personal items. They were presumably packed away in the boxes and trunks scattered about the sitting room.

She directed Nate to the small bedchamber, and he set the trunk down next to the bed. Behind him he heard Jessie tell Rosalyn, "Good news! A letter has come for you from Bristol!"

He turned to see Rosalyn's face light with joy as she took the letter from Jessie. She tore open the envelope and eagerly read the note inside. Her brows drew together as she read, then lifted in surprise. "My sister says she is coming to London!"

"That's wonderful!" Jessie exclaimed. "When?"

"On Sunday. She says she has business here on Monday morning. I haven't any idea what business she should have! But she does ask if she can stay with me on Sunday night."

"She's welcome at our home, of course," Nate said. "We're a bit more flexible than Mrs. Kramer in that regard."

Rosalyn laughed. "Imagine! Julia said that I should stay in London, and she will come *here* to visit *me*."

Mary clapped her hands in glee. "When does her train arrive?"

"Two o'clock."

"I'll go with you to the station," Nate offered. He groaned, suddenly remembering his other commitment. "No, I'm sorry. I won't be able to go. I have to work at the stable on Sunday."

Mary stared at him in astonishment. "You're working on Sunday?"

"It couldn't be avoided. I had to switch with Charlie in order to have Tuesday afternoon off."

He saw Rosalyn assimilating this information, realizing he'd done it on her account. He could see her preparing to thank him yet again. He was growing uncomfortable with the thought that she might feel increasingly beholden to him, but still he said, "I don't like the idea of you going to the station alone. Not after what happened last time."

"It will be the middle of the day," Jessie pointed out. "I'm sure she'll be fine."

Rosalyn nodded, but Nate thought he still saw some trepidation.

"Martha and I can go with her," Mary suggested.

"That will work out splendidly, I'm sure," Nate replied. "If any man accosts her, Martha will pinch his arm, and you'll give him a stern tongue-lashing."

His remark only brought a laugh from Rosalyn. "Once Julia arrives, the rogue will be done for sure. My sister is a force to be reckoned with."

"Hoorah!" Mary cried. "I can't wait to meet her!"

Nate wasn't willing to let this go. "Maybe we could get Patrick to accompany you."

"Mary and Liza go places all the time," Rosalyn pointed out.

"That's different. They know the city."

"And I am *learning.*" She spoke with emphasis. "I can't be dependent on you for everything."

Jessie looked pleased at these words. So did Mary, for that matter. But then, she was always an independent one. In ordinary circumstances, Nate supposed he might have been glad to hear this, too. After all, Rosalyn was correct that she would have to learn to navigate the city by herself. But once again he thought of the man he'd seen skulking around the charity house. Nate had since made a point of passing by there every day, but he hadn't seen the man again. He didn't even know for sure if it had been the henchman from the brothel. Even so, he couldn't help but be worried.

There wasn't time to sort it out now, however. Evening was fast approaching, and they had to get to the theater. "Let's go," he said. "I've got to return the cart to the stable."

That night, Rosalyn found the walk home from the theater less daunting than it had been the night before. Already the streets and the facades of the businesses, shops, and pubs were beginning to look familiar. The night sounds seemed friendlier, too: their echoing footsteps, the tolling bells from the church clock.

"I see now why you enjoy this walk," she said.

Nate slanted a look at her. "Really?"

"As you said, it seems easier to breathe somehow."

He nodded but didn't say anything. Tonight he seemed immersed in his thoughts. Their conversation languished, and they walked several blocks without speaking.

At length he said, "Are you sure you want to go alone to the station on Sunday?"

"Is that what's bothering you? I thought that was settled." The damp fog made the night unusually cold, stealing her breath as they walked, and her words came out harsher that she'd intended. She tried to amend her statement. "I mean, I understand your concern—"

"I saw Mick at the charity house last Sunday."

Rosalyn stopped dead in her tracks. "What? Why didn't you tell me?"

"I'm not entirely sure it was him. I didn't get a clear look." He briefly described what had happened. "Can you see now why I'm worried about you going to the station?"

Rosalyn could see. She took a long moment to consider the situation. "You say you're not sure, and that you haven't seen him since. Do you think that one incident is reason enough for me to be fearful wherever I go?"

"Not fearful," he insisted. "Just careful."

What was the definition of *careful* in London? Standing in the middle of a crowded railway station hadn't stopped bad people from waylaying her. She was just going to have to look out for herself. Rosalyn was learning that it was possible for women to travel around the city without any problems, provided they took some basic precautions. Helen had given her advice about the safest ways to ride an omnibus or tram, or even the Underground. She didn't feel brave enough for that yet, but she would get there.

"I believe I'll go on my own to the station," she declared. "Although I was tricked by Mick and Mollie, I went with them willingly. They cannot drag me somewhere I don't want to go. Not in broad daylight."

She spoke with all the bravado she could muster, refusing to cower in fear.

"While we are on the subject," she continued, "tomorrow I'll be leaving early for the theater."

"Why? What for?"

"Oh, there are some things I need to attend to." She purposefully kept her words vague. He didn't seem to like Tony, and there was no point making this conversation even more sour by bringing up the fact she would be seeing him. "I'll need to leave the house before you get back from the stables, but I know the way."

184

"I see." His voice was hard, as though he was affronted that she'd turned away his offer of help.

Rosalyn came to an abrupt halt, determined to find some way to smooth his ruffled feathers. She placed a hand on his arm. "I don't want you to think I'm ungrateful. I *am* grateful—more so than I could ever express. Is that what's bothering you, or is there something else?"

He looked at her for several long moments. Any number of thoughts might have been going through his mind, but his expression was unreadable. She offered him an encouraging smile. The last thing she wanted was friction between them.

Her hand was still on his arm, and she could feel as well as see the moment when he relaxed and let out a breath. "I apologize. What's bothering me . . . well, it's not your fault."

That was something, anyway.

"It's just as well you're going to work on your own tomorrow. I have some business to attend to myself."

"Oh?" She looked at him hopefully, trying to show she was ready to listen if he wanted to say more.

But that was apparently all he was willing to divulge. They spoke no more as they walked the rest of the way home, but she could feel that his silence was due to introspection, not anger.

CHAPTER

13

R OSALYN HEARD the music before she made it to the top of the stairs. Someone was playing a lively tune, undoubtedly on the same piano whose music had led her toward this building.

She reached the top of the stairs and followed the sound to the rehearsal room.

It looked much as Rosalyn had envisioned. A piano sat along the shorter wall. At the far end of the room, the floor was raised about a foot. It was clearly a rehearsal area. As she expected, Tony sat at the piano.

He stopped playing and stood up when he saw Rosalyn. "Are you ready for your lesson, my dear?"

"Lesson!"

"Don't look so surprised. You have a great deal of natural talent. Wouldn't you like to hone it to a skill that will bring envy and applause from all?"

"But . . . you want to give me *lessons?*" She was still having a difficult time believing this. "Why would you do that?"

He laughed. "Oh, Rosalyn, you are such a delight. You speak your mind with absolute honesty. Let me explain."

He took her hand and led her to a row of chairs lining the wall. She noticed he still held her hand once they were seated. He leaned toward her, speaking earnestly. "Being in the chorus of this production has been a tremendous opportunity for me. But it's only a stepping-stone to greater things."

He sent a glance toward the door, as though to ensure they were alone. He lowered his voice. "I'm not one to spread backstage gossip, but I have heard that George Power was offered a good deal of money to take the lead in a production at the Gaiety."

"Really?" Rosalyn wondered whether London theater owners made a habit of trying to steal each other's cast members. She supposed it was possible.

Tony put a finger to his lips. "Don't tell anyone I told you."

"I won't. But what does this have to do with you giving me lessons?"

"If Power leaves, I will take on the lead tenor role of Ralph Rackstraw. You can chart the same course: establish yourself in the chorus and rise from there. You have the talent. All you need to do is develop it. Although, in my opinion, you are already good enough for the chorus. Singing these light operettas is not so difficult as mastering the grand operas from the continent."

Rosalyn had to admit the idea of being on stage was appealing. The performers clearly loved their work, and the excitement coming from the audience each night was palpable even though *Pinafore* had been playing for over a year and was nearing the end of its run. Who wouldn't want to be on the receiving end of such approbation?

"All right," she said. "What can you teach me?"

"Excellent!" He pulled her to a standing position. "Let's begin with vocal exercises."

To Rosalyn's surprise, he led her through half an hour of various warm-ups. It was taxing and exhilarating at the same time.

"Now you are ready to sing a proper song," he announced, and took a seat at the piano.

They sang several duets, and then Tony sang a solo, pausing to explain certain breathing techniques that Rosalyn could use, as well.

"Now it's your turn."

Once more he began playing, and Rosalyn recognized Josephine's aria toward the beginning of *Pinafore*. "Oh, I couldn't sing that," she protested. "The higher notes would be quite beyond me."

"Just do your best," Tony urged. "After all the practicing we've done, I think you'll be surprised at your range. It's like flexing a muscle."

The idea was daunting, but she decided to try. With nervous determination, she launched into the song. She reached the lovely, poignant final line:

> Heavy the sorrow that bows the head,
> When love is alive . . . and hope is dead.

Her voice wobbled on the last few high notes—Emma Howson's job was certainly safe from her—but it did sound better than any time she'd previously attempted to reach such high notes.

Tony bolted up from the piano stool, took hold of her forearms, and gave her a kiss on both cheeks. "That was splendid!"

Excitement surged through her. "Can we try that again?"

He grinned. "We most certainly can."

Rosalyn sang the aria again, feeling strength coming to her as she applied the techniques Tony had taught her. At the end of the song, she closed her eyes and reached deep within herself, trying to imagine how it must feel to love so deeply but in vain. Strangely, a picture came to her mind of Nate. His family had said he was suffering from unrequited love. Could such pain really drive a man from the country and from his family? Her own heart went out to him at the thought of what he was going through. She gathered all this emotion into her singing, and this time when she hit those final high notes, they came out very sweetly indeed.

Rosalyn opened her eyes and was startled to see Tony standing mere inches from her. His eyes were alight with admiration.

She was aware of her heartbeat, light and shallow as though she'd run a far distance. She seemed unable to refill her expended lungs. Uncertain, she wanted to withdraw, to put space between them. But part of her did not want to break this moment of triumph, this vision of what her future could be—to feel and sing with such passion.

From the doorway came the sound of a throat clearing.

Rosalyn jumped. Tony turned toward the door and said smoothly, "Good afternoon, Mr. Cellier."

Mr. Cellier was indeed standing there. So was Miss Lenoir. They were staring at Rosalyn and Tony with expressions she could not decipher.

Immediately she felt a rush of guilt—and not just because she'd been found alone with Tony. Perhaps she wasn't allowed up here at all.

"Taken to giving lessons, Hayes?" Mr. Cellier said dryly.

"Rosalyn was helping me rehearse," Tony answered. "Isn't she wonderful?"

"She does seem to have some talent," Miss Lenoir said.

"It's passable." Apparently Mr. Cellier was not one to give out easy praise.

Rosalyn smiled tremulously at Miss Lenoir. "I hope I'm not out of order being here."

Miss Lenoir shrugged. "It's only a practice room. You are not yet on duty, so I see no harm."

Rosalyn felt her shoulders relax.

"It certainly doesn't hurt Hayes to get more practice," Mr. Cellier added.

Tony stiffened, his casual attitude falling away. "You gave me quite generous praise last week during the after-show notes, as I recall."

Mr. Cellier's eyes glinted in amusement. "Don't be so thin-skinned, Hayes. Nobody doubts your ability."

"Carry on." Miss Lenoir pulled a watch from her lapel. "You still have a few minutes to call time."

She gave Rosalyn a thoughtful look, and then she and Mr. Cellier left the room.

Tony went to the door to give a quick glance down the hall. Then he bounded back to Rosalyn. "What did I tell you! They were quite impressed!"

"How can you be so sure?"

"If they hadn't, I have no doubt one or the other—or both—would have sternly told you to mind your business with the costumes and stay away from the practice room." He took her hands again and swung her around lightly. "You just passed your first audition, and you didn't even know it!"

Rosalyn could only laugh in return.

⚬⚭⚬

Nate pressed the doorbell to the Wilkinses' home.

He felt out of place on the polished marble steps of their townhome, and not just because he was wearing working clothes for the theater. At one time he'd sworn that he would never cross this threshold. But now, here he was. And again he had the sensations that always came to him before a battle, where anything could happen and all careful preparations could turn out to be utterly useless.

A maid opened the door, invited him in, and offered to take his coat and hat. He'd heard from Hannah that the Wilkinses had half a dozen servants. That was precisely six more than he would have been able to afford.

Such a very fine house, too, he thought, as the maid led him into a large parlor that was elaborately decorated and filled with expensive furniture. But he felt no bitterness or envy on that account. It came to him suddenly that such a place would never make him happy—no matter who shared it with him.

Ada was already waiting in the parlor. "I'm so glad you came!" she cried, and actually threw her arms around his neck in a hug.

Nate heard the door close behind him as the maid withdrew. He stood there, not moving, and certainly not returning the embrace. "Is this proper?" he asked, trying to speak with an ironic air to cover the pain this was causing him.

She let him go, taking a step back. "Matthew is here. He's in his study. He knows we need time alone to talk."

"A very understanding husband you have."

"Please, let's sit down." She motioned him toward a plush green sofa large enough to seat them both and still leave comfortable space between them.

Now that Nate was forcing himself to sit and talk to her, to look at her without turning away, he found to his surprise that he could study her dispassionately. He saw vulnerability and uncertainty in her eyes despite her smile. She was still beautiful, but it wasn't the girlish beauty she'd had when he fell in love with her. Seven years had matured her.

"There doesn't seem to be any good way to begin." Her pale

cheeks tinged in a blush—from the awkwardness of the situation, he supposed.

"Start wherever you like."

"All right." She took a deep breath. "Even though I believe I did the right thing in marrying Matthew, I'm sorry the news came to you in a letter. But we had no idea when you might return home. I felt it was better to tell you as soon as possible. It took me days to write that letter. I tried so hard to put into words what I was feeling. I wanted to explain my actions in a way that might cause you the least amount of pain possible, and—"

"Yes, it was quite a letter."

"—and apologize," she finished, undeterred by his interruption.

So many words were on the tip of Nate's tongue, so many caustic things he could say about how deeply she'd hurt him. About how her letter had nearly gotten a man killed. Perhaps one of the reasons he'd been avoiding her was the fear that he *would* say those things. His shame over his own actions that day were so great, he hadn't even been able to tell the truth to Patrick, who was not only his brother but also his dearest friend. He wasn't about to share it with the woman who had jilted him. Even if he could, deep down he knew that both of them would only be worse off for it.

He remembered how Rosalyn had placed her hand on his arm the other night. That simple gesture, plus her kind words, had arrested his attention. It was a call for him to stop and consider the ruts he'd allowed his bitter thoughts to form in his mind. He'd thought on it all the way home and late into the night. His dereliction of duty that day was solely his responsibility. He alone could atone for it, which was precisely why he was returning to the colors. Right now, he needed to resolve his disappointment over losing the woman he once thought was the love of his life.

"Just tell me why you decided not to marry me." He waved a hand to indicate the room they were sitting in. "Looking around, one can get a pretty good idea . . ."

"It isn't that," she replied, her voice earnest and appealing. "We were very young when we got engaged. While you were away, I believe I matured. Certainly I changed. Something very important happened that made me realize I should not marry you."

Nate shook his head. "I don't understand."

"I was with my sister when she went through a very difficult childbirth. She came so close to death. All that saved her was the fact that a good doctor was close by. I began to grow scared at the idea of leaving England. Scared about living in a strange land. I am not as strong or as fearless as you."

"I would have protected you. I would have done anything to help you."

"But so many things are out of your control! Shipwrecks, storms, deadly diseases . . ."

"We can look to God in those situations. He watches over us."

She sighed. "I admire your faith, but I always felt weak in comparison. At times when I tried to express a concern, you would simply dismiss my fears as irrelevant—as, in a way, you did just now. I don't feel you ever really heard me."

Nate wanted to protest but realized he couldn't deny the truth of what she was saying. Had he truly run roughshod over her feelings? "I don't think my example has been so very admirable. Certainly not lately."

"You're here listening to me and, I hope, ready to forgive. I find that very admirable." Nate saw a glimmer of a tear as she spoke. "I think we have both gotten wiser over the years. We would not have been happy together, though you may not believe me when I say so."

"Actually, I think I do." It might pain him to admit it, but he and Ada had never truly been right for each other. "Patrick's been telling me for weeks that my problem wasn't a broken heart, it was wounded pride."

"Because of the husband I chose?" She smiled. "He's no dashing soldier, but he is a solid, feet-firmly-on-the-ground kind of person, and he's perfect for me. You, on the other hand, need someone who has your wanderlust, your fearlessness, and your faith."

"Now that we've narrowed down the qualifications, perhaps I'll take out an advertisement."

They both smiled at the joke. But in truth, Nate wasn't going to look for someone else. His course was set another way now. He was going back to India.

And he was going alone.

❧

Rosalyn stood at the platform, her whole being alight with anticipation as the train screeched to a halt. Never one to waste a moment's time, Julia was one of the first people to step off the train.

She was at the far end of the platform, but Rosalyn saw her instantly. To Rosalyn's eye, her sister's confident step and the alert way she took in everything around her set her apart from the crowd. Julia paused for a moment to get her bearings, then began to walk in Rosalyn's direction, joining smoothly in the flow of her fellow passengers spilling out of all the carriages. She strode up the platform as if she owned the entire station.

"Julia!" Rosalyn cried, walking swiftly toward her sister.

Julia's expressive face lit up with a wide smile, and she ran forward, threading her way through the crowd. The moment they reached each other, Julia enveloped Rosalyn in a hearty embrace despite the carpetbag she was carrying. "Oh, my dear Roz, how I've missed you!"

"I can't believe you came all the way to London," Rosalyn breathed. "But I'm so glad."

Julia gave her another fierce hug before pushing her to arm's length to get a good look at her. "How old you look," she pronounced.

Rosalyn cocked an eyebrow. "I hope you mean 'mature,' not 'aged.'"

"Well, of course, dear sister." She gave a light tweak to Rosalyn's chin. "However, you seem none the worse for wear, despite your recent adventures—which you only hinted at in your letter." She scrutinized Rosalyn's face. "How are you really?"

"I am well." Rosalyn blinked against stinging tears. *I am so much better now that you are here*, she wanted to add, but she kept those words to herself, remembering how easily Julia's sisterly compassion could evaporate if they veered into maudlin territory. "I have so much to tell you. And I'm curious to know what the *business* you spoke of in your letter is—"

"Time enough for all that." Julia took Rosalyn's arm. "For now, you must direct me to the ladies' lounge, for I've some personal business that needs immediate attention. I drank too much tea this morning, and I thought I might burst on the train."

Rosalyn had to grin. Her sister never hesitated to speak of matters that would leave others blushing. Perhaps it was because she was a nurse and discussions of bodily functions were part of her daily routine.

While Julia busied herself in the ladies' retiring room, Rosalyn waited in the seating area reserved for ladies and kept watch over Julia's carpetbag. Thinking of Nate's warning about Mick, Rosalyn looked warily around her. Today, as sunlight poured through the arched glass ceiling of the station, she saw only people who had a legitimate reason for being there: clerks, businessmen, passengers, and well-wishers who had come to send them off. There was nothing of the sinister mood that had pervaded the place the last time she was here. Rosalyn was glad she had opted to come on her own. She could not allow fear to dictate her actions.

"All done!" Julia announced, striding up to her. "My, but this is a very nice railway station. Of course, I expected nothing less of London." She picked up her carpetbag. "Shall we find a good place to chat and share our stories? According to this map I brought with me, Hyde Park is nearby. I would love to see it! And we must find something to eat, too. I'm positively famished."

It didn't take long to reach Hyde Park. Along the way, they stopped at a baker for meat pies and bottles of lemonade. They ate their impromptu picnic while seated on a bench near Kensington Gardens. The air was cold, but the sun shone brightly, and both sisters felt comfortable enough. Nor were they the only ones in the park. Plenty of people from all walks of life strolled along the pathways. In the area designated for riders, men and women in stylish riding costumes trotted their fine horses.

"Cara would love to paint this scene," Rosalyn observed. "Have you told her about my coming to London?"

"Not yet. I wanted to hear everything from you first. She is easily distressed, and I wanted to ensure you were safe and happy before I gave her any information."

"That's wise," Rosalyn agreed.

"Did you know she has taken a new position?"

"No, I didn't!" Cara's inability to stay at one place was becoming a pattern. This would be her third position in as many years. "She's no longer in Barnstaple?"

"No, she is now a nursery maid for a family near Exeter. They have just one child, two years old. Apparently he is a rambunctious chap, but he amuses her, and she enjoys the work."

"Perhaps she has finally found her métier then," Rosalyn said.

"Heaven knows she wasn't a good housemaid and even worse as kitchen help. Let us hope she remains happy there."

"Amen to that," Julia agreed.

"How long has she been there?" Rosalyn hated to think Cara might have stopped telling her of these changes out of embarrassment at having lost yet another position.

"Only a few weeks. She probably did write to you, but the letter might have arrived after you left."

"I suppose I won't get that letter now," Rosalyn said ruefully. She loved receiving letters from Cara, who always seemed to have very colorful and unique ways of describing any situation. "Oh!" Her hands flew to her face. "I did receive it! It came the last afternoon I was at the Huffmans'."

Rosalyn hadn't even had time to read it. She'd merely stuffed it into her carpetbag as she prepared for her hasty departure. Now it was lost, along with her other belongings. She'd had several letters from Julia in there, too. As precious links to her sister, she hadn't had the heart to burn them or leave them behind.

"And now *she* has them!" A new dread took hold of her, knowing that the names and addresses of where Rosalyn had lived, and those who were closest to her, had wound up in Mollie Hurdle's hands.

Her outburst had Julia looking genuinely alarmed. "Rosalyn, what has happened? You must start at the beginning."

Rosalyn told her everything.

Julia was understandably appalled and did not hesitate to state her opinion of Mr. Huffman in vehement terms.

"But what about the letters?" Rosalyn asked. "What if Mrs. Hurdle or Mick should somehow misuse them? They know Mr. Huffman is looking for me! And now they have his address! And yours, as well!"

Julia took several moments to consider this. "No," she said

at last, shaking her head firmly. "Petty thieves aren't likely to go tearing off to Bristol with no guarantee of getting anything for it. They only want cash or valuable items. I imagine they never even read the letters, just threw them into the fire as worthless paper. But if they *were* to come after me—" She waved her lemonade bottle like a sword. "I'll happily put up a fight! Or turn them in to the police."

Rosalyn took comfort from Julia's words. Perhaps she had nothing to fear after all.

Julia took a last swallow from her bottle. "Still, something might have to be done. I'll think on it some more."

"Such as?" Rosalyn asked, eager for her advice.

"Well, for one thing, I might not leave a forwarding address when I move to London. Just to be on the safe side."

Rosalyn's mouth dropped open in astonishment. "You're moving *here*?"

"As soon as I can arrange it."

"But why? I thought you loved your work at the hospital."

"Yes, but it's not enough. I am bound for bigger things. God has opened the door for me to attend the London School of Medicine for Women. I have an appointment tomorrow with Mrs. Isabel Thorne, the dean of the school. She's agreed to meet with me and discuss what will be required. I am going to become a real, licensed physician!"

This announcement gave Rosalyn such a shock that she nearly forgot any worries about her own situation. She stared at her sister incredulously. "I thought only men could practice medicine."

Julia gave her the look she often used when they were children and she'd felt compelled to point out one of Rosalyn's serious shortcomings. "Rosalyn, haven't you been paying attention to the national news? Parliament passed a law three years ago granting all medical authorities the right to license women. I've wanted to come to London ever since. I began saving every penny I could, and I also followed our dear Mr. Müller's example and lifted my need to God in prayer—without telling a single soul about it. My answer came by way of one of the orphanage's most generous donors. Do you remember the Stauntons?"

Still flabbergasted at this turn of events, Rosalyn struggled to keep up with her sister's rapid speech. "The family who live in that beautiful mansion in Clifton?"

"That's the one. Last winter I nursed their youngest child through a terrible bout of influenza, and Mrs. Staunton became convinced I am a miracle worker."

"Well, aren't you?" Rosalyn teased.

Julia responded with a pleased grin. "Anyway, a week or so ago we happened to cross paths in the street. She asked me what I was up to, and I said I was preparing to go to the London School of Medicine for Women. Naturally, I said nothing about money. I merely answered her question—just as Mr. Müller showed us so many times. Well, right then and there she said to come 'round to her house the following day, and she would write me a check to cover my first year's expenses. Can you imagine?"

"That is amazing," Rosalyn agreed.

"I received your letter a few days later. I'm sorry for the terrible things you went through, but now I see that God has been putting everything in place—for both of us." She turned her face toward the sun, still just visible above the high elms. "Oh, Rosalyn, I know we shall both love living here."

"So this interview with Mrs. Thorne—that is the business that brings you to London?"

"Yes—aside from the important business of seeing you, of course. I am not a typical student. Many come from university backgrounds, not practical nursing like me. She wants to interview me about my qualifications and knowledge. Of course, I believe I am the perfect candidate because I already have so much experience. I have set those curmudgeonly old doctors straight a time or two."

"I don't doubt that for a minute," Rosalyn said dryly.

"Well, they might have killed somebody if I hadn't!" Julia replied passionately.

Rosalyn could only shake her head in wonder. She found it hard to believe that any woman—even her intrepid sister—would want to be a doctor. "Does that mean you'll be doing things like dissections and surgery?" She couldn't keep the horror from her voice.

"Rosalyn, you are such a squeamish thing. Just think how thrilling it would be to delve into the mysteries of the human body. You know the verse in Psalms that says we are 'fearfully and wonderfully made.'"

Rosalyn could not deny that.

"Will you be able to come with me to the school tomorrow morning? I'd love for you to see it with me."

"That should work out fine. I don't need to be at the theater until late afternoon."

"Excellent! The school is on Henrietta Street—do you know where that is?"

"I'm afraid not. There is so much about the city I still don't know."

"No matter. I have the map."

That was Julia. Ever the resourceful one. And Rosalyn was so glad she was here.

CHAPTER

14

Nate spent the money on the omnibus to get home from the stable. Although fatigue seemed to be part of his life these days, he couldn't recall feeling as absolutely bone weary as he did right now. Even his one day of rest had been denied him. Without it, the week ahead loomed ominously long.

It didn't help that several of the horses had been particularly ornery. It was a good thing for those horses that Nate had been working today. He knew Charlie would not have been as effective at calming them. They might even have done harm to themselves or to someone else. But this knowledge did nothing to ease his weariness.

He had just gotten off the omnibus when he saw Rosalyn walking with a woman who must be her sister. His first thought was relief that she'd returned from her trip to the railway station unmolested. On top of everything else, he'd spent far too much of the afternoon worrying about her.

He hurried to catch up to them, calling out Rosalyn's name. Both women paused, turning in unison. He could see a similarity in their resemblance, although Rosalyn's hair was a lighter shade of brown. Her features seemed softer, too. Maybe that was a reflection of their temperaments, given what Rosalyn had said about Julia being a "force to be reckoned with."

She was studying him now with alert, expressive eyes. She extended her hand. "I'm Julia Bernay. You are Nate, of course. I could tell from the way Rosalyn described you."

Her directness startled him. She was definitely a bolder sort than her sister. Another stray thought crossed his mind, wondering exactly how Rosalyn had described him. Whatever she'd said, it probably didn't include clothes that reeked due to hours of grooming horses and mucking out stalls. He took a step back. "Please excuse me for not shaking hands. I'm rather dirty. But I am very pleased to meet you." He did extend a hand toward her bag, however. "May I carry that for you?"

"Please don't trouble yourself. I am quite able to carry it."

This woman definitely had an independent streak in her. But if his time in the army had taught him one thing, it was that even self-sufficient ladies enjoyed a touch of chivalry now and then. Holding himself as though he were wearing a full dress uniform and not filthy stable hand's clothes, he said, "Dear lady, I insist."

Gently but firmly, he pried the bag from her hand and was treated to an approving smile. Turning to her sister, Julia remarked, "Rosalyn, this man is every bit as polite and handsome as you told me."

"I never said he was—" Rosalyn began, then put a hand to her mouth in chagrin.

Nate laughed outright, remembering how his family had put him in the same predicament. Now that the shoe was on the other foot, he took a perverse delight in seeing her embarrassment.

Rosalyn remained silent the last few blocks to the Morans' home. Not that her sister gave her much room to speak. Julia hit Nate with a volley of questions about the neighborhood and how far they were from Henrietta Street. As he answered, he kept throwing sidelong glances at Rosalyn. Her blush had faded, and now a simple, beautiful smile played around her lips. He attributed it to pride in her sister and the joy of having her here.

There was no doubt in Nate's mind that Rosalyn was the prettier of the two. He also found her warm gentleness more appealing. Julia seemed all starchy crispness and energy. He said, "My sister Mary will enjoy meeting you, I think."

Rosalyn laughed. "That's exactly what I was thinking."

It did him good to hear her laugh. Perhaps he was not so tired after all.

<hr/>

Mrs. Moran met them with a hearty greeting as soon as they came through the door. She even drew Julia into a welcoming hug, which Julia accepted with an amused smile.

"Don't leave them in the hallway all day, Ma," Patrick called from the parlor.

They crossed the hall to the parlor. Patrick was seated in his chair near the fire. Martha was playing with Tommy on the carpet. He lay on his stomach, propped up on his little arms, his gaze following Martha's hands as she played with four brightly painted wooden blocks in his line of vision. Hannah watched them from the sofa, where she and Mrs. Fletcher were both engaged in sewing tasks. Mary had been writing at the small desk, but she immediately set her pen aside and joined the others in greeting the newcomer.

What a genial picture they make, Rosalyn thought, seeing them all gathered there in the large, welcoming room. As she introduced her sister to everyone, she was brimming with thankfulness at living with such a wonderful family.

Nate hung back at the parlor door and soon excused himself to go upstairs and clean up.

"Why don't you take Julia to your room and get her settled?" Mrs. Moran suggested. "Dinner will be ready soon."

After assuring Mary they would be down again as soon as possible, Rosalyn led Julia upstairs.

"Why, this is delightful!" Julia said, setting her carpetbag on the extra bed. "I do believe it's larger than the dank little room I share at the boardinghouse in Bristol. And that window is perfectly placed to give light, even on winter days. That will be helpful for all the reading I'll have to do for my course work."

As Rosalyn began to help her sister unpack, she said, "Just think how happy Cara will be to know we are together again!"

Julia's brows knit together. "Perhaps we should be cautious in how and when we tell her. Knowing Cara, she'll immediately want to move here, too."

It was true their little sister could act impulsively. But Rosalyn also knew Cara's greatest dream was that they should all be together again. "Would it be so terrible if she did come here?"

"She ought not uproot herself again, not after she has finally found employment that suits her. There are no guarantees she'd find the same in London. And besides, there isn't room for her here." Julia indicated the small room.

"We could always find another place." But even as she spoke, Rosalyn knew she would hate to leave the Morans' household.

Julia shook her head. "Don't be so quick to give up what God has clearly provided."

Everything Julia said made perfect sense, of course. Yet Rosalyn knew that Julia might well be saying these things because she was not keen to live with Cara again. The two had such

JENNIFER DELAMERE

different temperaments that they were often at odds with one another. Reluctantly, she decided it was better for now to drop the subject.

As they were heading back down to the parlor, Nate caught up with them on the last set of stairs. His face had the sheen of having been freshly scrubbed, and his hair was still damp around the edges. He wore a pressed shirt and trousers that were nicer than anything Rosalyn had seen him in before.

Julia looked him over approvingly. "No qualms about shaking hands now, I suppose?" she said with a smile.

He obliged. Rosalyn couldn't help but think back to that moment in the theater when he'd first shaken her hand, and how his touch had warmed her.

It didn't seem to affect Julia that way, however. Instead, she took his hand in both of hers and raised it toward the light in the wall sconce, scrutinizing it. "My, but that is an interesting scar. How did you get it?"

Rosalyn was mortified at Julia's directness. Nate seemed to take it in stride, however. "Enemy fire," he said evenly. "A skirmish at an outpost near Peshawar."

"I see," murmured Julia, tracing the scar from its starting point near Nate's knuckles up to where it disappeared into his cuff. "It's a long scar, like a graze, only deeper."

"That's right. It hit at an odd angle. I'm lucky it didn't lodge. Or blow my hand off."

The matter-of-fact way he said this startled Rosalyn. It reminded her that he was a toughened man of war, even if he didn't always show that side of himself.

Julia merely nodded as she continued to inspect his hand. "But it disrupted the extensor tendons, yes?"

Nate looked impressed. "Rosalyn told us you were a nurse. You seem to be a very knowledgeable one."

205

Mary was watching them from the foot of the stairs. "He was wounded while rescuing two men taken captive in a surprise attack. One of the men almost died, but Nate saved his life!"

Something flickered in Nate's eyes. He cleared his throat and gently extracted his hand from Julia's hold. For the first time since she had begun to examine the scar, he looked uncomfortable. "Perhaps you might want to take a look at Patrick's leg, too? I'd be very interested in learning when he'll be well enough to take his job back from me."

If his plan was to shift the attention away from himself, Nate succeeded. Turning once more down the stairs, Julia said, "I would love to examine it. Of course, if it has been weeks since the break, there's little I could do to fix a bad splint. . . ."

"Nate doesn't like to talk about his heroism," Mary whispered to Rosalyn as they all went to join Patrick in the parlor. "He's humble as well as brave."

From all she'd seen of Nate so far, Rosalyn wasn't surprised to learn this.

After several minutes of scrutiny, Julia decided that the doctors had done an adequate job on Patrick's splint. "I'd say you should be able to walk on it in two to three weeks," she pronounced.

"Hallelujah," Nate murmured as everyone else also voiced their happiness at this prognosis.

Rosalyn smiled at him. "Won't you miss the theater, even just a bit?"

"I miss my pillow more."

She shook her head. "You jest, yet whenever I see you up on the lighting platform, you always look like you're enjoying your work with the limelights."

Nate's eyes rested on her for several moments, as though her words had arrested his attention. She noticed Julia looking at her, as well, one eyebrow slightly cocked, and that especially made her uncomfortable. It wasn't as though she spent all her time watching Nate. Perhaps that was how it sounded.

She was glad when Mrs. Moran came into the parlor to call them all into dinner.

As they ate, Julia kept the conversation lively, sharing several humorous anecdotes from the Bernay sisters' years at the orphanage. Rosalyn had never thought of their childhood as a rosy one by any means. But they had been kindly treated at the orphanage, and now as Julia shared these stories, Rosalyn realized they had much to be thankful for. Nothing would ever erase the pain of losing their parents, that was certain, but Julia made her see there were plenty of happy things to recollect, as well.

"How did you end up at the orphanage?" Mary asked.

Martha poked her in the ribs.

"You don't have to tell us if it's too painful to talk about," Mary amended.

"I don't mind," Rosalyn answered. This was true, for despite the sorrow she felt at losing her parents, she loved to talk about them. It was a way of keeping them alive in her memory. "Our father was the captain of a merchant ship. He made frequent trips to America and the Caribbean. We missed him so much while he was away, but we loved the little presents he brought back to us. Then on one voyage, his ship disappeared in the Atlantic without a trace."

"Disappeared?" Mary repeated. "Sank, you mean?"

"That's the most logical answer. But I don't suppose we'll ever know for sure."

"Many facts about the situation are murky," Julia said. "The ship's owners quickly concluded the ship had been lost in a hurricane—probably to make an insurance claim and reduce their losses. A hurricane had been reported at that time, but unless my father's ship was way off course, it would have been well to the south of it."

"It took months for my mother to accept that he was truly gone," Rosalyn said. "Until that time, she just kept telling us Papa's return had been 'delayed.'"

"Oh, how sad," Martha said.

"She was already ill, and I don't think she could bear the idea that she would be leaving us orphans. She died of consumption about two years later. Even at the end, she wouldn't talk about my father except to repeat that he loved us very much and we should always remember that."

Rosalyn reached instinctively for her mother's pocket watch, feeling a fresh round of regret at having given it to Mrs. Hurdle. "After our mother's death, we were taken to the orphanage, since we had no other family."

"No other family willing to take us in," Julia corrected sternly.

"I think 'able' is a more charitable way to put it," Rosalyn countered. She explained, "Our father had two cousins. One was a widower who was also in the merchant marines. He was en route to India when my mother died. The other cousin had left with his family for America shortly before my father's death."

"Our mother sent a letter to him before she died, begging for his help, but he never replied."

"The letter could easily have gotten lost," Rosalyn pointed out. "The civil war going on in America at the time disrupted many communications."

"Well, it's a mystery that won't be solved today," Julia stated. "I believe it is more important to look to the future, don't you?"

"So what are your future plans?" Mary asked eagerly. She'd been hanging on Julia's every word.

When Julia informed them of her intention to go to the medical college for women, everyone was visibly surprised.

"Oh, my heavens!" Mrs. Moran exclaimed. "Why would you want to do that?"

"Because I want to help people."

"But you are a nurse. You already help people."

"Yes, but when I get to Africa, I will need every bit of knowledge I can glean. Who knows what medical crises may arise?"

"Africa!" Rosalyn repeated, horrified. "You never mentioned going to Africa."

"Well, I can't tell you everything all at once, can I? We've had so many things to discuss."

Although this was true, Rosalyn suspected that Julia had another reason for delaying. She was waiting for the moment when her announcement would have the greatest impact.

Mary was staring at Julia with wide eyes and an almost worshipful expression. "How very adventurous of you! What will you do there? Open a clinic?"

"The primary thing will be the saving of souls—but yes, there is a clinic, too. I plan to join the missionary society that is already at Lake Nyassa in southeast Africa."

"How long will you be there?" Mary asked.

"Years, I expect," Julia answered breezily. "There will be lots to do."

Mrs. Moran frowned. "Your intent is admirable, but I must say that Africa hardly seems a place for a young lady."

"Oh, there are lots of young women there," Julia said.

The blank look on Mrs. Moran's face showed she was not following Julia's meaning.

Mary gave her mother a little nudge. "I believe she means the *native* women, Ma."

Mrs. Moran pursed her lips. "Well, that is quite a different thing."

"The Bible says that God has 'made of one blood all nations,'" Julia said. "Dr. Robert Laws has begun a successful work there, and I intend to join his staff."

For Rosalyn, this entire conversation boiled down to just one thing. "You can't mean you would leave England—leave me and Cara!" No wonder Julia had not wanted to encourage Cara to come to London. She wasn't planning to stay here. "How can you break us up like that? You know the dread Cara has of any of us going overseas." Rosalyn had the same fear, too, although she didn't say so.

Julia set down her fork with an air of exasperation, leaning forward so she could look Rosalyn in the eye. "We all must do what God has called us to do. My calling will take me overseas, and that's all there is to it. I cannot live my life simply to satisfy our little sister's whims."

"*Whims!* You know the poor girl feels our parents' loss the greatest because she remembers them the least. We are all she has. She craves our companionship and longs to be together again. It's her *heart's cry*, not a *whim*."

After this outburst, an uncomfortable silence ensued. Julia sat back in her chair, crossing her arms. Rosalyn expected some kind of retort, but Julia was silent. To her credit, she seemed to be considering Rosalyn's words. Rosalyn almost thought she saw a flicker of doubt cross her sister's features. But Julia quickly averted her gaze to her plate, so it was difficult to tell.

Rosalyn saw the others trading glances. For some reason, she was especially embarrassed by the curious way Nate was looking at her. She thought she could read disappointment on his features.

"I apologize," she said to the table at large. "We should not have ruined your lovely dinner with our quarreling."

Mrs. Moran reached over to pat Rosalyn's hand. "You were only expressing your concerns. Disagreements can happen, even in the best of families."

"Excepting ours, of course," Patrick interjected. This remark brought him a swat on the arm from Martha, but it was enough to ease the tension.

"Perhaps I might offer a suggestion," Mrs. Moran said. "If Julia's first aim is to finish her medical studies, it seems like the other decisions are quite a ways down the road. Perhaps they should be held in abeyance for now. Often God's purposes become most clear when we are truly ready."

Rosalyn noticed that Mrs. Moran sent a meaningful glance toward Nate as she said this. She sensed that her hostess's advice was directed at him as well as Julia. Nate's only response was to focus on carefully arranging the silverware on his plate.

"Thank you," Julia said to Mrs. Moran. "That is good counsel."

Rosalyn was still unsettled, knowing that once Julia's mind was made up on something, it was unlikely to change with time. Still, she appreciated the way Mrs. Moran had provided a gracious way to recover the geniality of the conversation. She sighed, knowing this truce was the best she could expect for now.

When everyone had finished the excellent trifle that Liza had made, Patrick pushed back his chair and said, "Time for some entertainments, don't you think?"

Mary walked between Rosalyn and Julia, taking their arms as they made their way to the parlor. "We enjoy singing together on Sunday evenings," she informed them. Cutting a glance at Patrick, she added, "Even if not everyone is exactly on key."

"I take comfort in the fact that the psalmist simply said, 'Make a joyful noise unto the Lord,'" Patrick replied. "It says nothing about being on key."

Turning to Julia, Mary said, "We already know that Rosalyn sings beautifully. Do you sing, as well?"

"I wouldn't say it's my best talent, but I can hold my own."

"Let's not *talk* about singing," Martha directed, seating herself at the piano. "Let's *sing*."

211

Although still deeply troubled by Julia's announcement of her plans, Rosalyn found comfort for the next hour, losing herself in the joy of singing. The Morans and their boarders certainly had a wide repertoire. They sang hymns, mostly, many of which Rosalyn knew, but Hannah and Martha's preferences seemed to lean toward the popular ballads.

Rosalyn noticed that Nate sang with visible pleasure. She enjoyed the way his expression eased while he was singing. He had a reasonably good baritone, rich and full. Unlike Patrick, who kept trying to imitate the tenors but who did not—as Mary had forewarned—hit the correct notes. Patrick seemed to purposefully solicit the disapproving scowls from his siblings and his wife, which only increased his clowning all the more. Several times Rosalyn had to stop singing because she was laughing so hard at his antics.

"But enough of Martha's banging about," Patrick said finally. This rough dismissal of his sister's adept playing brought a shove from his wife, but he continued, "Nate has promised us he'll play, and I intend to make sure he keeps that promise."

"My hand is not yet where it needs to be," Nate protested. "I don't know if we should subject others to my playing just yet."

"It's not your fingering hand," Mary argued. "You sounded fine to me when you played last week."

Rosalyn was mystified by this interchange. It became clear when finally, after much cajoling, Nate pulled a small case from a cupboard in the corner of the room. He opened it and removed a fiddle that looked like it had seen plenty of use.

"You play the fiddle?" she gasped.

"This is actually a violin made eighty years ago by one of the best luthiers in France," Nate said. "But yes, I play the fiddle."

It was another flash of his dry humor that always seemed to show itself at odd moments.

"And how did you come to possess such an instrument?" Julia asked.

Mrs. Moran answered. "My father—Nate's grandfather—brought it home from the Napoleonic wars. It was a gift from a grateful officer whose life he had saved."

"He taught me to play when I was ten," Nate added. "When he was too feeble to play anymore, he gave the fiddle to me." Holding the violin to his ear, he plucked the strings and adjusted their tautness. When he was satisfied, he picked up a small block of rosin and ran his bow over it in several smooth strokes.

Rosalyn watched this process with fascination. It intrigued her to think this man who had made a living as a soldier had musical leanings, as well. "Can you play the songs from *Pinafore?*"

Nate gave a little grimace.

"He expressly refuses to play anything from the show," Patrick said.

"I hear it every night at the theater," Nate pointed out. "Besides, classical music is not exactly my forte."

"Give us something from home," his mother said.

Nate thought for a moment. "Let's start with Grandad's favorite." He lifted his bow and began a lively reel.

Never would Rosalyn have guessed that Nate had this particular talent. His entire demeanor changed as he played. He seemed less stiff, more flexible, bending and moving with each note, his entire body keeping tempo with the music. The transformation surprised and riveted her. As she took pleasure watching and listening to him, Rosalyn could see a measure of the same lightheartedness that was so evident in his brother.

Her thoughts were echoed by Mrs. Moran, who leaned over and said to her, "I think playing the fiddle is how Nate finds joy—or at least, the way he expresses it."

Despite Nate's earlier protestations, he played very well. As

Rosalyn watched him, she tried to discern what impact his injury was having on his ability. There was none that she could see. If his hand or wrist were still stiff, perhaps he made up for it by the fluid movements of his upper arm and elbow.

Nate finished with a flourish, and everyone applauded enthusiastically.

"I'm glad you haven't forgotten those songs, son," Mrs. Moran said, dabbing a handkerchief to her eye. "They're part of your heritage."

"Play one of those lovely ballads," Martha urged him. "Something sweet and sentimental."

"So you can get all misty-eyed and dream of your beau?" Mary teased. "It seems to me we've had enough of those songs this evening."

"It always sounds better on the fiddle," Martha insisted.

Nate plucked a few strings absently, as though weighing both of his sisters' comments. "All right," he said at last. "Here's an ancient Irish ballad. Most know it either as 'Slane' or"—he sent a glance at Martha—"'With My Love on the Road.'"

He lifted the fiddle once more to his chin. He paused, bow poised, allowing several moments of silence before striking the first note.

The tune was warm and tender, soft as a caress. Nate took his time, letting the melody unfold at its own pace. His expression showed deep concentration but joy, as well. The player was being uplifted by his music. Even without words, the ballad conveyed a yearning that was bittersweet, perhaps, but infused with hopefulness.

Martha sighed, a dreamy expression on her face. Rosalyn, too, felt a soothing peacefulness as she listened. *This ought to be a hymn*, she thought. It made her soul feel lighter just to listen to it. She always believed that, whether singing or playing, a person's innermost essence was often revealed in their performance. She was astounded by this glimpse into Nate's soul.

After he drew down the bow on the last, sweet note, there was another moment of quiet stillness. Everyone in the room seemed moved. Nate's eyes met Rosalyn's, and she saw a tenderness there that touched something deep within her. It occurred to her that through his playing, Nate could express not only joy, but many other emotions, as well.

CHAPTER
15

THE NEXT MORNING, Rosalyn and Julia made their way
to 30 Henrietta Street and found themselves standing in
front of a large, four-story redbrick building. The sign carved
over the doorway clearly proclaimed this was the London School
of Medicine for Women.

Three women, chatting intently among themselves, passed
them as they entered the main hall. They gave brief smiles to
Julia and Rosalyn before continuing on their way.

"Isn't it exciting?" Julia exclaimed. "Soon I will be one of them."

An older woman seated behind a large desk inquired what
their business was. Upon hearing that Julia had an appointment
with Mrs. Thorne, she led the two of them down a short hall and
into the antechamber of another office.

Rosalyn took a chair as Julia was escorted into Mrs. Thorne's
office. To pass the time, Rosalyn picked up a journal she saw
lying on the table next to her chair called *The Lancet*. She quickly
replaced it, however, after a brief glance through it revealed it was

filled with precisely the sort of detailed medical information she would prefer not knowing. She shuddered at her sister's choice of occupation.

After half an hour, Julia emerged from her interview. Mrs. Thorne walked out of the office with her. The director of this school looked younger than Rosalyn had anticipated. She'd expected the overseer of a medical school to be an older, stolid kind of woman. Mrs. Thorne was in her early forties, with a pleasant face and wearing a gown that managed to be both practical and feminine at the same time.

She was speaking to Julia as they came out. "It was a pleasure to meet you, Miss Bernay. I look forward to seeing you again in a few months, and we shall see how you are getting on."

Julia thanked her with an expression that, while not exactly ecstatic, was not crestfallen, either. Rosalyn had seen that look before—generally when Julia had a difficult task set before her.

When they were back out on the street, Rosalyn asked, "How did it go?"

"She worries that my rudimentary knowledge of Latin will be a hindrance. I shall have to find a way to become conversant in it before I sit the matriculation exam."

"Can you find a tutor?"

"I expect so. It will cost money, of course. But God will provide. He has brought me this far. He won't let me down now."

To get to the railway station, they followed Julia's map. The area between the medical college and the station was one Rosalyn had not been to before. As they walked, she noticed a pawnshop.

"Do we have time to go in?" she asked.

"I believe so. My train doesn't leave for another two hours."

A short, portly man stood behind the counter where the best jewelry and watches were located. "Good afternoon, ladies. Might I help you with something special?"

"We are looking for a particular watch," Rosalyn explained. As she began describing it, her eye roved over the items beneath the glass in front of her. She could tell, almost at a glance, that the watch she sought wasn't there, and the shopkeeper confirmed that he hadn't seen a watch of that description.

"Might I interest you in one of these others?" he said. "I've an excellent selection—"

"Oh, my heavens!" Rosalyn blurted as her gaze snagged on a pair of emerald pendant earrings. They were set in fine gold, in a delicate, distinctive pattern. "Those belong to Mrs. Huffman."

Julia lowered her face to the glass for a better look. "Are you sure?"

"I'd know them anywhere." She lifted her eyes to the shop-keeper. "Can you tell me who pawned these?"

He shook his head, resting his hands on his wide girth. "Information about my clients is strictly confidential."

"Can you at least tell us if it was a man or a woman?" Julia asked.

But the shopkeeper was adamant about giving out no details. When Rosalyn questioned him about whether he knew of any pawnbroker named Simon, he answered that in the negative, as well. By then, Rosalyn was sure he wouldn't answer any of their questions, no matter how benign. Realizing that the more they pressed, the more suspicious he got, Julia and Rosalyn finally left.

Rosalyn threw a last dejected look at the shop before they continued on. "That's so disappointing. If I could find out who really stole the jewelry I was accused of taking, then I could re-store my good name."

"That would be wonderful," Julia agreed.

"I suppose there was a thief among the servants after all."

"Perhaps," said Julia thoughtfully. "Whoever it was, they seemed content to allow you to take the blame for it."

When they reached the railway station, they stood together

at the platform, Julia poised to board the train only when it was absolutely necessary.

"You will be careful, won't you?" Rosalyn was still worried about having left her sister's address in the hands of Mollie Hurdle.

"I'll be fine," Julia assured her. "In the meantime, I suggest you take your soldier back to that pawnshop and see if he can, well, *persuade* the owner to give you more information."

"He's not *my* soldier," Rosalyn protested.

Julia lifted her eyebrows. "No? There's something between you, I think. Something more than mere friendship, perhaps."

Rosalyn couldn't believe her serious-minded sister would express such a fanciful idea. "He's going back into the army—and to India."

"That may be his plan now," Julia conceded. "However, life doesn't always go according to plan. I think you have seen that these past two weeks."

"Perhaps you would do well to remember that, too," Rosalyn pointed out. She had not forgotten—nor accepted—Julia's determination to leave England.

The train began to pull away, leaving them no time for anything more except hasty farewells.

Rosalyn pondered her sister's words as she hurried toward the theater. Perhaps she would ask for Nate's help in the matter of those earrings. But she could never think of him as *her soldier*. He was leaving England and she wasn't. That was something she was absolutely sure of.

⚬⚬⚬

During their walk home from the theater that night, Nate listened intently as Rosalyn told him about finding Mrs. Huffman's earrings in the pawnshop.

When she was finished, he said, "What does Julia want me to do? Go in and strong-arm the man? That doesn't seem right."

"I'm not advocating violence at all," Rosalyn answered. "But surely there must be some way to discover how the earrings got there."

"Do you really need to know?" He stopped, turning to face her. "Perhaps it would be better to stay far away from that place and leave well enough alone. If Huffman should ever decide to come after you, it would look very bad that you know the location of the earrings. It might even be taken as proof that you placed them there."

"But—but—" she sputtered. She placed her hands on her hips and looked at him askance. "How do you know about such devious things?"

"Seven years in the army," he reminded her. "I've seen men do a lot of things to get themselves out of a bad situation—or to get others into it."

In the glow of the streetlamps, he watched as she considered his words.

"Perhaps you're right," she conceded. "But do you think I should stay away from *all* pawnshops?"

This was a more difficult question. He could see how much her mother's watch meant to her. "Perhaps I can accompany you?" he suggested.

He was gratified to see the pleased expression on her face. "I'd like that," she said.

◦◦◦◦◦

Rosalyn's life soon fell into a satisfying routine. Every night the show ran on the same precise plan, until one evening when Miss Lenoir came into the dressing room and announced, "There's some bad news. Joan and Mariah are out sick tonight."

"What! Oh no!" several of the ladies cried out.

"Taken down by influenza. I just received separate notes from each of them. You're going to have to sing extra loud tonight. Especially the barcarolle in act one."

"It's difficult for the audience to hear us even when we're at full strength," Helen pointed out.

"Can't we just sing it onstage?" one of the other ladies asked.

Helen snorted. "And change Mr. Gilbert's blocking? Only if you promise to pay the half crown fine we'll each get for doing so."

"Just do your best," Miss Lenoir said. She hurried out of the room, evidently with other emergencies to handle.

Helen snapped her fingers. "I have an idea! And it's brilliant."

"As usual," Elsie said wryly.

"Rosalyn can join us!"

"What?" The disbelieving murmur of the ladies exactly matched what Rosalyn was feeling.

"I couldn't do that," she protested. Indicating her simple blouse and skirt, she added, "I'm hardly dressed to pass myself off as a relative of 'our admiralty's first lord.'"

"So it's only your gown you're concerned about, Cinderella?" Helen teased. "You don't doubt your singing abilities, do you?"

To answer that question, it seemed Rosalyn's only choices were either to sound overly boastful or hypocritically modest. By now, Helen knew of Rosalyn's desire to develop herself as a singer. Rosalyn had already had several more learning sessions with Tony, and she was beginning to feel confident that she could sing as well as any of the chorus ladies.

"Now who's trying to change Mr. Gilbert's blocking?" Elsie said. "If she went out onstage, she'd be bound to trip us all up. I can't afford a fine—my rent is due this week."

Several others began to voice similar sentiments, but Helen waved a hand to quiet them. "I'm only speaking of the barcarolle.

221

She's watched us do it every night—stood right next to us. I daresay she knows the song by heart."

"I don't know," Sarah said. "What if she makes a mistake? Mr. Barker will fine the whole lot of us!"

"Then we'll stop it out of Joan and Mariah's wages—they're the ones who got us into this predicament."

"Well, they could hardly avoid coming down with the flu—"

"Oh yes, they could. Those two never dress properly for the weather. You've seen the low-cut gowns they wear. They're too interested in catching men to worry about catching cold."

This brought a round of snickers and a few knowing nods.

"That's neither here nor there," Sarah said primly. "But if you insist on this mad scheme, we'll have to try it out first to ensure she can sing it." She eyed Rosalyn. "Do you think you can follow my hand motions as I transmit the direction from Mr. Cellier?"

"Yes. I know I can," Rosalyn said.

"All right, ladies, let's try it." Sarah motioned everyone into the formation they used when standing stage left and singing the song.

Rosalyn chose a spot at the rear of the group, in the corner nearest to where she usually stood and where she'd most likely escape the notice of the stage manager and the prompter.

Sarah began counting out the beats of the introductory music. "Two, three, and—"

"*Over the bright blue sea comes Sir Joseph Porter, K.C.B. . . .*"

Rosalyn joined in. This was her moment, and if she wanted to give a proper "audition," she might as well sing with the same strength she'd need to use onstage. She could not see Sarah's face but saw her head do an approving nod as she continued leading the song. Helen turned around briefly to send Rosalyn an encouraging smile.

Rosalyn knew exactly how the ladies would move when the song ended and easily stepped out of the way.

"That was excellent!" Helen said.

"It did sound fine," Sarah agreed. "Just remember the dynamic—forte."

Rosalyn nodded but could hardly speak. She was going to sing in the show!

"Don't get all choked up now," Elsie joked. "My landlord is counting on you."

Millie appeared at the door. "Ten minutes!"

As they hurried down the stairs, Rosalyn took deep breaths to stay calm. Elsie was right—she couldn't freeze up now.

Quietly they took their places in the wings. Helen squeezed her hand and whispered, "I know you can do this."

There was their cue. Sarah lifted her hand and struck the downbeat for their first notes.

Rosalyn's throat constricted from nervousness, and she missed the first few bars. Closing her eyes, she breathed in. By focusing solely on the music, she was able to ease her voice into the others'. Once she found her place, she opened her eyes again.

She was happy to see that Mr. Barker was not in evidence. He must be watching from the audience, in which case he wouldn't know what she was doing. Her heart lurched when she saw Mr. Giles give her a curious glance, but she kept singing. After several more bars, he shrugged. He knew it would be more disruptive to try to stop her. Exuberant, Rosalyn finished exactly on key and on cue.

And just as she had done upstairs, she gracefully stepped away, back into the deep shadows as the ladies traipsed onto the stage.

For the briefest moment, her eye caught Tony's. He'd been watching her! The sailors were supposed to be looking in their direction anyway, but somehow he'd noticed her singing along with the ladies. His face still in profile to the audience, he gave her a secret wink with his upstage eye before returning to his choreographed movements as the sailors greeted the approaching ladies.

Suddenly drained from the excitement ebbing away, Rosalyn sank down on a stool. Miss Bella immediately jumped up on the table next to her. Rosalyn gave the cat a hug and a scratch behind the ears.

"Bravo!" whispered Jessie, who had quietly appeared at her elbow.

"You heard me?" Rosalyn had been so intent on singing that she hadn't noticed Jessie's arrival backstage.

"Indeed I did. I had no idea you could sing like that. Perhaps you should audition for the new show next spring. I bet you could at least get a part in the chorus. Of course, that will leave us in the lurch for a dresser again." She heaved a dramatic sigh, but Rosalyn knew she was only teasing.

Jessie hurried off to join George Grossmith, since their cue to go onstage was approaching.

Rosalyn watched their entrance and the comic actions that followed. She was grinning widely—not from the show, but because a world of possibilities had opened up to her imagination.

❧

A few nights later, Helen and Tony approached Rosalyn after the curtain calls.

Helen said, "We wanted to let you know about a little impromptu going-away party we are throwing for Jessie tonight. The entire cast wants to give her a good-luck send-off before she goes to New York. We actually got her to agree to come out to dinner! Will you join us?"

"I will miss her," Rosalyn confessed. "It would be nice to go and join in the good wishes for her. I'll discuss it with Nate."

"He is neither your sweetheart, husband, nor keeper, last time I checked," Tony said. "Isn't that true?"

"True, but he is a *friend*," she pointed out, finding herself annoyed by his caustic attitude. "And since we walk home together every night, I need to let him know I'll be doing something else."

He looked ready to retort, but Helen said, "We won't get there at all unless we get out of these costumes."

"Right you are," Tony said, his face brightening once more. "I'll meet you both here later."

As Rosalyn hurried upstairs with Helen, her excitement at attending the party grew. Truly it was an honor just to have been invited. Tony was correct that Rosalyn had the right to do as she wished. It still seemed strange, having this kind of freedom, but she was starting to relish it.

❦

At the stage door after the show, Nate listened with apprehension as Rosalyn told him she'd been invited to a special cast party for Jessie Bond that evening.

"Are you sure you want to go? It's bound to be boisterous, and you know there will be plenty of drinking."

"Not by me," Rosalyn said. "I couldn't afford it."

"That's worse. If someone buys for you, you'll be beholden to them. And if it's a man—"

"No one is going to seduce me with drink," Rosalyn said firmly. "This is just a chance to have a good time and give Jessie the send-off she deserves."

Nate could see it would be futile to try to stop her, and she wouldn't thank him for the attempt. "Tell me again how you plan to get home."

"Helen and I will share a cab."

"Is that practical? Where does she live?"

"I don't really know," Rosalyn admitted. "But I have money for my own cab fare if necessary."

"That's good," he agreed. "It's best to be prepared for the unexpected."

Or the expected, he added to himself as he looked over her shoulder and saw Hayes approaching. At least Hayes had two of the chorus girls with him. She was bound to be safer in a group.

Nevertheless, a prickly sensation stole close to the edges of his heart that, had he not known better, he might have labeled as jealousy. But no, surely it could only be wariness on her account. Unfortunately, that wasn't any less troubling. It was an indication of just how quickly Rosalyn had become a significant part of his life. But she was also becoming enmeshed in the world of the theater. If all went as she hoped, this would be her life—long after Nate had left for India.

It was hard to watch her go off with them. Nate might offer warning or advice, but in the end, Rosalyn was free to make her own decisions. He accepted this fact. Told himself it was for the best for her and for him.

Even so, the walk home felt strangely different.

CHAPTER

16

T HE FIGHT BROKE OUT right onstage!"

"Surely you're joking," Rosalyn said.

They'd been at the restaurant for about an hour, cheerfully eating and drinking. Everyone had regaled her with stories of the odd or downright funny things that had happened at the performances of *Pinafore* over the past year and a half. Far from feeling like an outsider, Rosalyn found most of these stories were told for her benefit, since she was the only person in the group who did not know them.

At the moment, George Grossmith was describing the night a rival production company, who thought they had the rights to produce *Pinafore*, came to the theater and tried to take away the set—right in the middle of a performance. "I assure you, it actually happened," George said. "It made all the papers next day."

"What did you do?" Rosalyn asked, still astonished at this tale.

"We had to bring the curtain down right away, of course,"

Richard Temple said. "And blasted inconvenient it was, too—right before I was to do my song with Barrington!"

"That's when Temple decided to enter the fray," Tony said. "He can stand anything except having his performance interrupted!"

George said, "Naturally, it fell to me to go out in front of the curtain and calm the audience with a speech, assuring them that there was no fire and that they were in no danger."

"Naturally," Jessie repeated, smiling.

"Well, who else could have done it? Not Mr. Barker—one of the interlopers had knocked him down the stairs, and he was unconscious!"

"Oh, my heavens." Rosalyn could scarcely imagine people coming to blows over a theatrical piece.

"But we got rid of 'em," Mr. Temple said, a satisfied grin on his face. "And you can believe they never tried that again." Rosalyn saw a bit of his Dick Deadeye character as he said these words with villainous gusto.

There was a buzz of laughter and chatter, as the cast members talked amongst themselves, sharing what they had been doing during this bizarre altercation with the would-be scene stealers.

Rutland Barrington stood up, raising his glass of beer. "Ladies and gentlemen, it's time for a toast," he boomed. "To our own lovely and immensely talented Miss Jessie Bond."

"Hear, hear!" several people cried as everyone raised their glasses.

George Grossmith rose, too, and added, "We are all going to miss you, dear Jessie. I hope you go on to find great success in America, for the show here is liable to close as soon as you are gone. The rest of us will be languishing in sadness at your absence and will be completely unable to perform."

Jessie gave him a skeptical look. "What you really mean is that you will miss having me around to tease mercilessly."

"Well, of course! What else have we to live for?"

"Hear, hear!" shouted more people among much laughter, lifting their glasses to the toast.

Jessie opened her arms to them all and smiled. "I cannot express how much it means to me that you would throw this little party in my honor. *Pinafore* has truly changed my life. To think that at one time I was sure I would be a mere concert singer all my days! But somehow Mr. Sullivan saw in me the ability to be an actress, too!"

"He also thought Grossmith could sing opera," Barrington broke in. "Can't be right all the time, I guess!"

At some point during the evening, Tony had placed his arm along the back of Rosalyn's chair. When had this happened? She hadn't noticed. He seemed very close to her now.

"Last call!" the tavern keeper bellowed from behind the bar.

Everyone began to pull out money for the food and drink. Rosalyn began to do the same, but Tony's warm hand came down on hers. "Allow me to pay for yours."

"Oh, but I couldn't!"

"I insist. I'm sure you need every penny of the miserable pittance Miss Lenoir doles out to you."

"I've already paid for Rosalyn's meal," Jessie said, hearing this exchange although she was at the other end of the long table. She began to push back her chair as though to stand, and Grossmith quickly rose to help her. Jessie motioned for Rosalyn to come over to her.

Tony removed his arm from Rosalyn's chair and helped her up.

"I'll be right back," she told him and hurried over to her friend. "Jessie, I can't thank you enough for all you've done." She could not help the tears forming in her eyes, and she was sure she saw the same in Jessie's.

Jessie pulled her into a warm embrace. "'Cast thy bread upon the waters,'" she murmured, recalling one of their earlier conversations. "I will miss you, Rosalyn." As they separated, Jessie asked, "How are you getting home?"

"I plan to share a cab with Helen."

"Good." Then she added with a stern, motherly tone, "Don't allow any of these men to take advantage."

"I won't," Rosalyn assured her.

Jessie squeezed both of Rosalyn's hands. "Good-bye. God bless you. And if you ever get a chance to sing onstage, I hope you take it. Grab onto the opportunities that open to you."

Rosalyn nodded, too choked up to say more.

After more hugs and good-byes from all the cast members, Jessie was escorted by George to a cab outside.

Rosalyn returned to her chair in order to collect her shawl. Helen was dabbing a handkerchief to her eye. "I'm going to miss her. Such a firebrand she is! How friendly and kind she was, even to us chorus ladies."

"Cheer up," Elsie said. "You still have me."

She rose unsteadily from her chair, and Helen took her arm. Tony offered his arm to Rosalyn. "May I escort you home?"

Elsie looked as though Tony had just offered to murder everyone in the pub. It wasn't the first time tonight that she'd sent malevolent glances toward him, and now the look spilled over to Rosalyn as well.

"I have a better idea," Helen said. "Let's all go together. I'm pretty sure we can find one of those old growlers at the cabstand. Could be cheaper if we all share a cab."

"What's a growler?" Rosalyn asked Tony as they walked outside.

"It's a large old carriage. Most have been replaced by hansom cabs, which are nimbler but of course only fit two people."

At the cabstand on the next block they found a few carriages, all waiting for their final fares as the pubs began to empty. But there were none large enough for the four of them.

"This makes more sense, anyway," Tony insisted. "Helen and Elsie, you two should share a cab since you live in the same neighborhood. I'll make sure Rosalyn gets home safely."

"I'm sure you will," Elsie said, but her tone was laced with acid.

Helen pulled Rosalyn aside and said quietly, "Rosalyn, are you comfortable with this arrangement?"

"Should I not be?"

"I think we may have no other choice. Elsie positively detests Tony—did you know she was sweet on him once? But he jilted her for someone else."

"I have noticed their animosity."

Helen gave a dry laugh. "That's putting it mildly. Anyway, I know she won't ride with him alone. And if I go with Tony, that leaves you and Elsie to fend for yourselves, and I don't think that's a good option, either."

Elsie was clearly feeling the effects of all the wine she'd had that evening. Without Helen to lean on, she hugged herself and wobbled dangerously. Rosalyn could see she needed to get home as soon as possible.

"I'm sure I'll be fine with Tony," she said, although Jessie's earlier warning placed a whisper of doubt in her mind.

Elsie began to moan. She leaned over, looking as though she was about to be sick. Helen propelled her toward the nearest cab. After helping Elsie in, she turned back and wagged a finger at Tony. "Just remember, a big burly soldier will come after you with no mercy if you don't remain a perfect gentleman."

"Trust me, I have not forgotten."

He spoke in a jesting tone, but there was no mirth in it. Rosalyn put it down to the fact that he was likely as tired as the rest of them.

Tony helped Rosalyn into one of the other cabs. The driver gave them a blanket to put on their laps.

"It is a chilly night, isn't it?" Tony said, taking hold of her hands as though to warm them.

He was seated so close to her that she could feel the heat emanating from his body. The very design of the hansom cab, which had only the one narrow bench, made any other seating arrangement impossible. Still, Rosalyn found herself embarrassingly tongue-tied.

Seeing her distress, Tony gave her one of his most disarming smiles. "You mustn't listen to people who would impugn my reputation. I would never press myself on an unwilling lady. You do believe me, don't you?"

"Yes," she said. "I believe you would not act in any way that was less than honorable."

His eye twitched. "Very good." He gave her hands a caressing pat. "Now, let me tell you what I have in mind for your next singing lesson. I believe you're ready for a new challenge."

Rosalyn found her tension slipping away as they began to discuss music again. By the time they had pulled up to the Morans' home, she was even feeling comfortable at Tony's nearness. He'd continued to hold her hands throughout the ride, so when he helped her down from the carriage, his touch felt quite natural. His arm slipped easily around her waist when she stumbled on the uneven pavement, and remained there as they walked up the wide steps to the house. Rosalyn tested the door and found it was unlocked. She was glad for this, as she did not have a key and would have hated to knock and rouse the others at such a late hour.

She turned back to Tony. "Thank you again," she whispered. "Good night."

He placed a hand on hers to keep her from opening the door

further. Drawing her close, he murmured, "Good night, sweet Rosalyn." His mouth brushed her cheek. "Sweet dreams. And I will see you at the rehearsal room tomorrow for another lesson?"

She smiled as his breath tickled her ear. "Of course."

"Splendid." He kissed her cheek again, lingering a little longer this time.

Although the sensation was pleasant, Rosalyn felt a prickle of uneasiness at the same time. "I—I'd better go in."

She reached again for the doorknob, opening the door wider this time. A faint light was visible down the hall, indicating that someone was in the parlor. Tony saw it, too. Once more he bid her good-night, although his manner was cooler than it had been a moment before.

Stepping inside, Rosalyn quietly closed the door behind her. She crossed the hallway, treading carefully so as to make no noise, and paused at the entrance to the parlor.

By the dim light of the low lamp, she saw Patrick. He smiled and nodded a greeting, though he did not remove his hands from the sleeping boy on his chest.

"So you are the one keeping watch for me," Rosalyn whispered as she approached his chair.

"Not the only one," Patrick replied with a grin, "but the other two are asleep on the job."

"Two?"

Patrick nodded toward the far corner of the room. There, asleep on the sofa, was Nate. He was only half-reclined, one foot still on the floor. Clearly he had dozed off without meaning to.

"Poor man," Rosalyn said. "He gets so little sleep as it is, and I'm sorry he felt obliged to try to wait up for me."

"He was concerned about you. I believe he cares for you a great deal."

Rosalyn sat down on the footstool next to Patrick's chair. "You have *all* been so good to me."

"These are my usual hours," he said, minimizing the compliment she'd aimed toward him. "First because I worked at the theater, and now because of this little fellow." He touched the head of his sleeping son in a loving, tender gesture. Addressing the child, he added, "Your mum is going to be sad to see me return to work. She's been rather enjoying a bit of extra sleep at night."

How fortunate that boy is, Rosalyn thought. *He will have his father nearby as he grows up.* Not like Rosalyn and her sisters, whose hearts always ached for their absent father.

"And I've been enjoying having a wife who is not so tired and out of sorts," Patrick continued. "So everyone benefits. But I do look forward to getting back on the job."

"How long have you been working in the theater?" Rosalyn asked.

"Started when I was around twelve. At first I was an errand boy. I've worked just about every other backstage job since then, but lighting is my specialty now."

"I'm sure that's made for an interesting career."

"It has. I've been at perhaps half a dozen different theaters over the years, but now that I work for Mr. D'Oyly Carte, I plan to stick with him. He's the best impresario in the business. He has big plans. He's going to build a new theater not too far from the Opera Comique. Everything will be the best—with all the most advanced equipment and modern furnishings."

"It sounds wonderful!" said Rosalyn.

"Everyone thinks the life of a stagehand isn't as much fun as actually being on the stage, but I like it. It enables me to take care of my family, and that's what's most important."

He tilted his head toward Nate. "He's a good man, you know, although you may have seen his gruffer side now and then. He's been going through a hard time. However, I think your presence here has helped him a great deal."

"Me? I don't see how."

"When Nate first came back to England, he told me he'd sworn off women and marriage forever. But it's pretty clear you've been in his thoughts from the first day he met you. I believe it's quite possible he could change his mind about marrying."

He made this observation with discernable pleasure, but Rosalyn's feelings were more conflicted. "Why, Patrick Moran, are you playing matchmaker?"

"I admit it, and I am not ashamed."

First Julia, and now Patrick. Perhaps everyone saw a special connection between her and Nate. The trouble was, they were right. She was growing too fond of him. But she could not allow her attraction to develop into anything deeper. "Patrick, he'll be rejoining his regiment and going to India. I could never leave England. And I couldn't bear to have a husband who left me to go overseas." She bit her lip, twisting her hands in her lap. "That's what my father did, you see. And he never came back. I wouldn't have the strength to go through that kind of heartbreak again."

Why had she said all those things? There was something so open and generous about Patrick's personality that simply invited a person to share their heart. But what if Nate should wake and overhear them talking about him? She sent an uneasy glance in his direction. He did not appear to have moved. His breathing was quiet, but it seemed regular. He was still asleep.

"Is the theater perhaps taking hold of your affections, as well?"

"I love it there," Rosalyn admitted. "It's a fascinating place, as you know."

"It is," Patrick agreed. "Once the excitement of working there gets into one's system, it never really leaves."

"It's late." She rose from the footstool. "Thank you for waiting up for me."

"I shall pass your thanks along to the other two watchmen, as well," Patrick said.

She couldn't help looking at Nate once more. It seemed almost too intimate, seeing him lying there asleep, a lock of hair falling over one eye. Perhaps, if things had been different . . .

But she would never know. His commitments were taking him far away, and she wouldn't dream of keeping him from the life he wanted to live.

❧

"She's gone," Patrick said quietly.

Nate cocked open one eye. "How did you know?"

"I can always tell when you're truly asleep. I also knew the exact moment you woke up. Whenever you're awake, your forehead gets an unhealthy-looking wrinkle. You worry too much, my brother."

"You should not have told her I had an interest in her."

Patrick feigned an air of innocence. "Well, don't you?"

"No!"

Patrick gave a disbelieving smirk.

"In any case, that's not the point," Nate said. "The point is you had no right to speak on my behalf, to imply that I had feelings for her—"

"What I'm curious about," said Patrick mildly, "is why you did not interrupt our conversation. For some reason, you kept on pretending to be asleep. Was it because you wanted to know what her reaction would be?"

"You are far too clever for your own good," Nate said crossly. "I don't need you or anyone else in the family meddling in my life."

"Well, in a few months' time you will be off to India, and you won't have us to bother you anymore."

"Exactly. And you heard what Rosalyn said. She's not about to marry a soldier. Not under any circumstances."

"So you *would* be interested in marrying her if she agreed?"

Nate stood up. His brother could wear down a saint. "I'm going to bed."

"What I mean is, why are you so intensely determined to return to the army?"

"I've explained this before."

"So you have. But something still doesn't add up. Nate, what aren't you telling me?"

Nate fought back a retort. He could deny it endlessly, but he could never truly fool his brother. The urge to unburden himself, to tell the truth, nearly overcame his determination to stay silent. He reminded himself, as he had countless times, that there would be time enough to tell Patrick everything—*after* he'd returned to India and made good his intentions. After he'd regained his own self-respect. In the meantime, he had to stick to his guns.

"I can't help it if you won't believe me when I say that the army is my occupation, my calling. Just as you love your work in the theater."

"It's true that I wouldn't want to work anywhere else. And yet, if my occupation had ever stood between me and marriage to my Hannah, I would have left it in a heartbeat."

Patrick was free to say that, of course. Nate wasn't. Having no answer to give him, Nate headed for the parlor door.

He stopped short when he saw Hannah standing in the doorway. How long she had been there, he didn't know, but clearly she'd heard this last remark of Patrick's. She regarded her husband tenderly. "You're a good man, my love."

With her mother's instinct, Hannah had arrived just in time. Tommy had awoken and was beginning to fidget, on the verge of crying for his next meal. Nate excused himself as Hannah crossed the room to take the baby in her arms.

Although he had cut the conversation with his brother short, he did not stop thinking of it as he mounted the stairs to his room.

He sat on his bed and pulled off his boots. There was no point changing out of his clothes, as he had less than two hours before he had to leave for the stables. He was pretty sure he was going to spend that time thinking about Rosalyn.

Hearing her speak about how much she loved the theater only confirmed his belief that he was doing the right thing. Even if Nate could stay in England—which he couldn't—she had her own dreams to pursue, and they wouldn't include him.

He knew full well by now that when a woman got her heart set on anything, he hadn't a chance in all eternity of changing her mind.

CHAPTER

17

F OR ROSALYN, the next several weeks flew by in a haze of activity. The theater was gearing up for the Christmas season, including a special children's production of *Pinafore* to run in the afternoons. Rosalyn had been tapped to help with that, too, and found it immensely fun. She marveled at how well the children could sing and act at such a young age. They ranged from perhaps six to twelve or thirteen years old. Watching them rehearse, she imagined what it might have been like if they'd put on plays at Ashley Down. Maybe someday she would go back and see if they were interested in arranging such a production. They would put it on just for themselves, of course, but she guessed that the children would love it.

One evening just before the show, Miss Lenoir surprised them by entering the dressing room. Next to Rosalyn, Helen muttered under her breath, "Oh no."

By now, Rosalyn knew the reason for Helen's disgruntlement.

Miss Lenoir typically didn't come upstairs unless there was something important—and usually bad—to announce.

"Everyone will please remain onstage after the show tonight," Miss Lenoir announced. To the chorus of groans, she replied, "This is not for notes. I have some information about an exciting opportunity for you all."

Several people called out questions, but Miss Lenoir simply said, "I'll tell you all about it after the show," and left the room.

"I wonder what that was about?" Helen said once the door had closed.

Elsie said anxiously, "You don't suppose they're closing the show?"

This brought another chorus of groans, this time of fear.

"Don't be ridiculous," Helen scolded. "You see how full the house is every night. They wouldn't close it down while they're still making so much money."

Sarah said, "Maybe it's that lawsuit from the company that tried to steal *Pinafore*. Do you suppose they prevailed after all?"

For a brief moment, Helen had no answer. It was the first time Rosalyn had ever seen uncertainty cross her usually unflappable countenance.

But then Helen made a gesture as if to swat away the suggestion. "No. She said it was an 'exciting opportunity.' Not even Miss Lenoir would use that phrase if they were going to tell us we were out of a job."

Still talking over the matter amongst themselves, the ladies descended the steps to the stage. Rosalyn followed, her mind filled with the same questions. Once the ladies' barcarolle was underway, however, she forgot anything but the singing. The chorus was back to full strength, but no one had suggested that Rosalyn stop joining in on this song. She added a good voice and made their singing easier for the audience to hear.

After the ladies had made their entrance, Rosalyn went looking for Nate. Seeing him at his usual perch in the spotlight gallery, she waved up at him. He signaled back that he had seen her, and a moment later she saw him descending the ladder along the back wall.

He led her into the crossover hallway, where they could talk without causing any interruptions backstage. "Is something the matter?" he asked.

"Miss Lenoir has told the cast to stay onstage after the show tonight for an announcement. That will delay my being able to finish up in the dressing room."

"I've been asked to stay behind, too, as it happens. The whole crew has, actually."

"Do you know what this is about?"

"I have an idea." He held up a hand to stop Rosalyn from asking more. "I think it would be better to wait and allow Miss Lenoir to explain everything. Anything else is conjecture."

"Yes, there is plenty of conjecture among the ladies' chorus, I can tell you that!" Rosalyn joked.

"Backstage gossip. Moves faster than an express train." He gave her a grin and went back to work.

Instead of waiting upstairs during the curtain call in order to be ready to help the ladies, Rosalyn stayed in her usual spot in the wings. Marion Johnson had taken over the part of Cousin Hebe with reasonable skill, but Rosalyn missed seeing Jessie perform it.

Marion didn't have the same persistent admirer, either—which made the curtain calls less interesting. Seeing Mrs. Hill standing nearby, Rosalyn whispered, "You don't get to take your bows anymore, Mrs. Hill."

The charwoman gave a dramatic sigh, but there was an unmistakable twinkle in her eye. "It *is* a shame. But it was fun while it lasted."

It had been a good show with an enthusiastic audience, but Rosalyn wished for the bows to end so that the meeting could begin. Finally, after the third curtain call, the curtain came down for good.

Tony came over to Rosalyn and pulled her onstage to join the others. "Are you on pins and needles? I am completely eaten up by curiosity."

"That sounds terrible!" Rosalyn teased.

"Fortunately, I'm about to be saved from further harm. Here comes Miss Lenoir."

"Who's that with her?" Rosalyn asked, seeing Miss Lenoir accompanied by an unfamiliar gentleman.

"That's Mr. Gunn. He oversees the two touring productions of *Pinafore* going around England right now. I wonder what he has to do with this announcement." He rubbed his chin. "Hmm, 'curiouser and curiouser,' as they say."

The stage was crowded with the cast in the center and the stagehands standing at the edges. Everyone, it appeared, planned to be in on this conversation.

Miss Lenoir stood at the front center of the stage and held up her arms to get everyone's attention. When the murmuring had ceased, she said, "It's late, and I know you are eager to get home, so I shall get right to the point."

"You ain't closin' the show, are you?" This came from one of the lighting men, who clearly had no qualms about voicing what everyone was thinking.

"Nothing like that, I assure you," Miss Lenoir answered. "I want to talk about the next show, which as you know will be called *The Pirates of Penzance*. The official opening won't be until April. However, in order to secure copyright on both sides of the Atlantic, our lawyers have advised us that the show must be presented publicly in England at least once at the same time it opens in America."

"But that's in three weeks," Helen pointed out.

"Correct. The show opens in New York on December thirty-first. Therefore, we will be doing one performance here in England on the thirtieth."

This brought a whole new round of questions from both cast and crew.

"Here at the theater?"

"But how can we do that? We haven't even seen the music!"

"What about the set?"

Miss Lenoir waved her hands to quiet everyone down. "It won't be in London. We don't want anything to mar the grand opening in April. We're going to put on the show in Paignton."

Several people looked surprised, and with good reason. Paignton was a small coastal resort town in Devon.

"Why so far away?" someone called out.

"You won't get much of a house," added another.

"That is precisely the point. The show won't be fancy or polished or even very well-rehearsed. It simply needs to be presented. I have been tasked with producing this show. Again, I want to emphasize that this won't be the proper debut. Its only purpose is to give us legal recourse against anyone who would try to steal the show the moment the music becomes public."

"So you're protecting *Pirates* from the pirates?" said Mr. Giles.

Miss Lenoir smiled. "Precisely. We've been able to locate some actors already in the area of Paignton and Torquay to play the principal roles."

"That saves the traveling expenses, I expect," Helen whispered to Rosalyn.

"We still need six men and six women from the chorus to complete the cast. For those of you who are interested, you will enjoy the unique opportunity of presenting this exciting new opera for the very first time."

A round of comments and murmurs began as people discussed their reactions and how this event would impact them. This time Miss Lenoir made no effort to stop it. She waited patiently for a minute or two until it took its course.

Rosalyn was brimming with excitement. Before she could stop to wonder at her own boldness, she blurted out, "What about the crew? Will they be going?"

Miss Lenoir looked pleased at Rosalyn's eagerness, but she gave a regretful shake of her head. "For this one night, the ladies will have to make do without a dresser."

"That saves money, too, of course," Helen whispered. She gave Rosalyn a pat on the back. "That's too bad. I wish you could go with us."

"You're going, then?" Rosalyn said.

"Sure. I think it will be a lark."

"You're not worried one of the fill-ins will try to steal your place here?" Elsie whispered.

"Let 'em try," Helen replied with a snort.

"We are taking one of our stagehands, however," Miss Lenoir said. "Since Patrick Moran is expected back to work after Christmas, I have asked Nate Moran if he would serve as the properties overseer for the show in Paignton."

Everyone, including Rosalyn, looked at Nate in astonishment. He stood there looking modest but with a hint of a smile.

"Bravo, Nate!" one of the men called.

Miss Lenoir said, "Some of you may know that Nate was a supply sergeant in the army. I can't think of a more capable person for organizing the move of the costumes and the basic props and scenery. He also knows the lighting, so he'll work with the crew there to get us what we need."

"If we go, will our expenses be paid?" one of the chorus men asked anxiously.

"Train fare and hotel will be provided. We leave the morning of the show and return to London next day. Mr. Gunn will be the stage manager. Please see him if you wish to go. Thank you, that is all."

"Wait!" someone called out. "When will we rehearse?"

Miss Lenoir gave an ironic smile. "As soon as the music arrives from America. It's still being written."

"This really will be a bare-bones production," Tony said to Rosalyn. "But even so, every other singer in London will be jealous that we know the new show before anyone else."

"I wish I could go," Rosalyn said with a sigh. It sounded like a true adventure.

"There's no reason why you shouldn't," Tony said. "Come on."

He took her hand and led her over to Miss Lenoir and Mr. Gunn. "I would like to respectfully submit that Miss Bernay here be considered for one of the cast members."

"What?" Rosalyn cried in embarrassed surprise. She would never have been bold enough to ask for that.

"She's very good," Tony continued. "Miss Lenoir, you've heard her sing. If she goes, you lose one less member of your London chorus, plus you'll have a singer and dresser all in one."

Mr. Gunn looked understandably puzzled. "You want the dresser to perform in the show?"

Miss Lenoir said, "She is a competent singer, but she doesn't have any acting experience."

"You said yourself that the production doesn't have to be very good," Tony pointed out.

Rosalyn poked him. "Thank you very much."

He grinned.

Miss Lenoir studied Rosalyn with interest. "Do you really want this chance to ride in a second-class carriage to a cheap hotel and perform in an under-rehearsed show that probably only fifty people will attend?"

"Yes!" said Rosalyn without hesitation.

Miss Lenoir laughed. "You have been a good and loyal member of our staff. We'll have a tough time doing without your services for two days, but we'll manage."

"Does that mean I can go?" said Rosalyn.

"Yes."

"Thank you! I promise you won't regret it!"

"Let's hope not," Mr. Gunn said, looking doubtful even as he accepted Miss Lenoir's decision.

Rosalyn and Tony stepped back as others began approaching to add their names to the cast list.

"What fun we'll have!" Tony exclaimed, taking her arm. "We should work extra hard on those lessons and make sure you're fully prepared."

Wanting to share her joy, Rosalyn looked around for Nate. But he'd already been called over by Mr. Turner, the head of the stage crew, to attend to other business.

There was no further time to talk or even to think on the matter. Everyone hurried off to their dressing rooms, and Rosalyn went along with them. She knew that as soon as she finished her tasks upstairs, she and Nate could discuss the show in Paignton during their walk home.

◈◈◈

Nate and Rosalyn said good-night to the custodian and went out the stage door. Since they were leaving later than usual, the street was quiet, with only a few people still out and about. The cold fog was bitter enough to send people scurrying home, but at least tonight it was not thick enough to overpower the street lamps. The visibility was good enough for Nate and Rosalyn to make their way easily along the streets.

Nate could see that Rosalyn was brimming with excitement.

She playfully slapped his arm. "You knew exactly what this was about and didn't tell me."

He made a show of pretending to fend her off. "Easy, now. You're starting to take entirely too much after my sister."

She grinned.

Nate loved bringing out her smile. The feeling of ease that he so often felt when he was with her was like a balm to his soul—so long as he didn't dwell on the fact that it would all be ending soon.

They were about halfway home when they came upon a policeman. "Good evening," the constable said in a deep, authoritative voice. "Might I ask why you are out so late?"

Nate felt Rosalyn's grip tighten on his arm. It wasn't the first time he had seen her freeze in fear when the police were nearby. He could tell she still hadn't shaken her dread of them after her experience on her first day in London.

"Good evening, constable," Nate said. "We're just walking home from the Opera Comique. We work backstage there."

"The Opera Comique?" The policeman's stern countenance immediately softened. "That's where *HMS Pinafore* is playing! Took the missus there just last week. Fine show."

"Yes, sir, it is." Nate could sense Rosalyn's tension easing at the policeman's genial tone.

"So many of those operas at the other theaters are unwatchable, you know," the constable went on. "Scandalous stuff. But *Pinafore*, well, that's completely different. It's got real *English* characters for a change, despite the Frenchy name of the theater. And there's nothing lewd or distasteful—not even when the captain says 'the big, big D!'" He guffawed. "I hope we see lots more such shows."

"Perhaps Mr. Gilbert will include a policeman or two in the next show," Nate said, even though it was akin to revealing government secrets. When Miss Lenoir had filled him in on his duties for *The Pirates of Penzance* in Paignton, the props and costume list had included policemen uniforms, lamps, and night-sticks. He knew this man would be pleasantly surprised come April.

The policeman laughed again, this time in disbelief. "A bobby! In an opera! That'll be the day. Well, you two had best hurry on home. There's lots of unsavory types out and about at this hour."

It wasn't until they'd made it to the next block that Rosalyn loosened her grip on his arm.

"You really have nothing to worry about," he assured her.

"I know. Not while you are with me, at any rate."

Her guileless and matter-of-fact answer warmed him in ways he craved, despite his better judgment.

She gave a little laugh. "You know there are policemen in *Penzance*, don't you?"

"Aha! So you, too, have been privy to some of Mr. Gilbert's secrets."

She pretended to look abashed. "Jessie told me the storyline before she left. She'd wheedled it out of Mr. Gilbert."

Once more they shared a smile—this time as co-conspirators in an important but very secret endeavor. For most of these weeks, Nate had been concentrating on living one day at a time. His day of departure was fast approaching, yet he carefully relegated that awareness to a back corner of his mind. He had a premonition that every hour he spent with Rosalyn would only make the pain of leaving greater. Nevertheless, he did not regret accepting the job in Paignton. Whatever future pain might come, the way she looked at him just now made it absolutely worth it.

On the Sunday before Christmas, Rosalyn and Mary chatted as they followed the rest of the family out of church after the service. After several weeks of attending services there, Rosalyn felt quite comfortable.

Patrick was walking now, his leg out of the splint. He was still using a cane, but soon he would not need that, either. As the family walked home together, Rosalyn found she was still keeping a wary eye out as they approached the intersection where the charity house stood. She could see Nate doing the same, and she knew that he, too, had not forgotten his glimpse of Mick, the man who'd been in league with Mollie Hurdle.

Today Rosalyn saw nothing amiss. A group of women who lived at the charity house and had also come from the church were filing in the front door. Everyone else on the sidewalk was moving along, intent on their destinations.

There was, however, a carriage parked at the curb. It was an open barouche, for the day was fine despite the cold. As Rosalyn and the others approached it, the woman sitting inside signaled for her footman to help her down.

Rosalyn pulled up short, watching in stunned disbelief as the woman walked straight toward her.

"Hello, Rosalyn," Mrs. Huffman said.

Rosalyn darted a nervous glance around, looking for any sign of Mr. Huffman—or the police.

"Don't worry, I came alone," Mrs. Huffman said. "I wonder if we might have a word together—just the two of us?" She offered a small smile as she spoke. It was not at all the sort of expression Rosalyn would have expected from her. Not after all that had happened.

"You are not here to accuse me of stealing or . . ." She stopped, unable to finish the sentence.

Pointing toward the carriage, Mrs. Huffman replied, "Perhaps we might talk there?"

"Is everything all right?" Nate asked. He moved to Rosalyn's side, looking poised to offer protection as much as assistance. The whole family looked on with mystified expressions, but Rosalyn felt this was not the time to explain. "I will see you all back at the house," she told them.

"Are you sure?" Nate looked worried.

"Yes."

After five years as Mrs. Huffman's companion, she knew her well enough to see that she wasn't lying. It seemed she truly meant only to talk. If so, it would be a great relief. Rosalyn had always regretted that she'd been forced to leave Mrs. Huffman without explanation.

After a few last assurances to the Morans, Rosalyn followed Mrs. Huffman into the carriage.

"Shall we ride as we talk?" Mrs. Huffman suggested. "It might make the conversation easier." She signaled to the driver to set the carriage in motion.

It occurred to Rosalyn that perhaps she ought to be worried. Was this a ruse to take her to the police after all? But no, she could not believe it. Still, she said warily, "Does Mr. Huffman know where I am?"

"Rosalyn, you have nothing to fear from him. I know the whole story now."

"But how? And how did you find me?"

"A few weeks ago, I got a very interesting visit from a remarkable young lady. Your sister, in fact."

"Julia came to see you?" Rosalyn's initial reaction to this news was horror—what if Julia had miscalculated the Huffmans' response? She might well have gotten Rosalyn sent to prison. "She should not have done that. If Mr. Huffman had been there—"

"Oh, she didn't come to the house. Somehow she knew I was fond of attending the Tuesday lecture series at the town hall. She came and introduced herself to me there."

Rosalyn had mentioned the lectures in her letters. How astounding that Julia had remembered.

"Don't be upset with your sister," Mrs. Huffman urged. "I'm glad she came. I was distressed at your sudden disappearance and confounded by the news that you had stolen valuable items. I just could not believe you were guilty. It was so completely at odds with what I knew of your character." She paused, sighing. "I wish I'd had as accurate an understanding of my husband's character."

The pain with which she said those last words brought a lump to Rosalyn's throat. "I'm so sorry."

The carriage pulled into Hyde Park and moved along the lovely carriageway bordered by grass and elms. Mrs. Huffman turned away, as though watching the passing scenery. But Rosalyn could see she was collecting herself and her emotions.

Rosalyn could hardly believe she was driving through Hyde Park on a Sunday afternoon, just like the upper-crust folk she and Julia had watched from their park bench. She looked around at the passing carriages, wondering what joys—or perhaps sorrows—were in their minds right now.

After a few moments, Mrs. Huffman spoke again. "When Julia told me your story—which was quite different from what I'd heard from my husband and the entire household staff—I felt at once that it must be true. Not only did it fit with what I knew in my heart, but your sister can be quite a persuasive speaker."

"Bossy, you mean," Rosalyn answered reflexively. She gasped, surprised at herself for trying to make a joke at this time.

Perhaps it was exactly what Mrs. Huffman needed. She actually laughed. "Oh, the bonds of sisterly love."

They shared a smile, and Rosalyn saw again the woman she'd first met six years ago—beautiful, carefree, self-possessed. Before she'd been hoodwinked into falling in love with a man who didn't deserve her.

"I will tell you exactly what happened. When Julia said she'd seen my emerald earrings in a pawnshop, I was naturally flabbergasted. Those were not among the items you had purportedly stolen. In fact, I was not even aware they were gone. I only bring them out for special occasions. But I went home, and sure enough, they were missing. I knew who must have taken them, because they are kept in a locked cabinet and only one other person knows where the key is."

"Are you saying Mr. Huffman pawned your earrings?"

"Yes."

"Did you confront him about it?"

"No. In light of what Julia had told me, I decided I would do better to track them down myself. I went to London and got a police inspector involved. Mr. Huffman was in Liverpool on business, so he never knew. By the time he returned, I knew the whole story. The jewelry you had supposedly stolen was sold outright to cover gambling debts. The earrings he'd pawned for ready cash to make an investment. He intended to redeem them back before I missed them." Another look of pain crossed her features. "My husband's actions have gotten us into some financial straits. There are more issues than what I have just shared, but now that my eyes are open to the situation, we will get it sorted out. Rosalyn, I know I can never properly make amends. I can only give you my sincerest apologies and tell you how relieved I am that you are safe and sound."

The carriage moved out of the park, rolling into the fine neighborhoods that bordered it. Rosalyn was elated to be cleared of any wrongdoing. At the same time, she felt sorry for Mrs. Huffman, who would have to live with the consequences of being married to such a terrible man.

Rosalyn knew full well the apology ought to have come from Mr. Huffman, but she wasn't going to press the issue. It was enough just to know she was free.

CHAPTER

18

"Two shows? On Christmas Day?" Ma shook her head. "That's not right. Think of all the actors and crew who won't be able to spend the day with their families."

Rosalyn had been sharing news from a letter she'd received from Jessie. The company in New York had spent the past several weeks performing *Pinafore* even as they prepared for the official American debut of *The Pirates of Penzance*.

Although in England the theaters were closed today, in New York the customs were quite different. According to Jessie's letter, they were to present both a matinee and an evening performance.

"Good thing we are more civilized than our American cousins," Patrick quipped. "When do they have time to eat their plum pudding?"

"Agreed," said Nate, finishing off the last bite of his pudding with satisfaction. His family was nowhere near as destitute as the Cratchits in *A Christmas Carol*, but he still marveled at how his mother could pull together such a holiday feast on so modest a budget. "I can tell you I'm thankful we have time to savor this." He was also grateful for some time off in the middle of the week. It was a rare treat.

"We do have much to be thankful for," his mother agreed.

"And much to celebrate!" Patrick added.

"Do you mean because you will be out of our hair as of tomorrow?" Hannah teased.

"Exactly." Patrick gave a little flourish with his fork before setting it down on his now-empty plate. "It will be good to get back to work. But I was thinking of Rosalyn's good news, as well."

Nate turned his gaze to Rosalyn. He'd been hard-pressed not to look at her during the meal. She wore a very becoming pink gown, one of the many frocks she had received from Jessie. The low neckline revealed her lovely throat and a hint of her soft white shoulders.

Rosalyn's expression added to her beauty. She was beaming with happiness. Her situation with the Huffmans had been resolved, and the worry of retribution or arrest no longer hung over her head.

"I still say Mr. Huffman ought to be drawn and quartered," Mary stated roundly. "Although even that would be too kind."

"Christmas is a good day to offer forgiveness," Rosalyn said. "The best day, perhaps."

"Well spoken, my dear," Ma said. She sent her gaze around the table. "What a joy it is to have the entire family gathered for Christmas." Her gaze settled on Nate. "Families should always be together on Christmas."

He felt a pang of remorse. He knew his imminent departure for India was weighing on her mind, but he'd been hoping to get through the day without the subject clouding everyone's thoughts.

So far, the day had gone well. The morning had been cold but bright, the sunshine sparkling on fresh snow as they'd made their way to church. Everyone had taken pleasure in the service. Afterward, they'd returned home to enjoy this feast. But now the afternoon was waning, and this was when his mother often grew overly sentimental.

Patrick wasn't having any of that, however. He picked up the Christmas cracker next to his plate and gave it a sharp tug. It burst open with a substantial pop. "That's a celebratory sound if ever I heard one," he announced. He rummaged through the remains of brightly colored paper and pulled out a little tin whistle. "At last, an instrument I can play."

"Oh no," Mary groaned. "Someone get that away from him, quick."

Everyone else followed Patrick's example, pulling open their crackers and examining their little gifts. Nate watched Rosalyn unfold a delicate blue fan. It was no bigger than her hand, but she made a coquettish little motion with it, her eyes finding his as she did so. He swallowed, feeling his chest tighten.

"What did you get, Nate?" Mary asked, displaying a pretty bracelet of fine, multicolored thread.

Nate sifted through the paper and pulled out a tiny wooden boat. He held it up, examining it. It was just two inches long but nicely painted with blue sides and three white sails. He saw Rosalyn's eyes flicker with a troubled look. His mother, too, gave a thoughtful frown. They were perhaps thinking of the boats that had taken loved ones away from them.

"It's the HMS *Pinafore*!" Patrick said brightly. "A souvenir to remind you of your brief time on our humble little ship—that is also the bestselling show worldwide," he finished, not so humbly.

"And *The Pirates of Penzance*—Rosalyn's singing debut!" Mary added proudly.

256

JENNIFER DELAMERE

Nate saw his mother's frown deepen. She alone of the household had not been completely thrilled at the news that Rosalyn would be trying her hand at performing. He understood her concern—being an actress was far more precarious than holding a steady job backstage. But like his brother, Nate was determined to keep this day joyful.

He pushed his chair back from the table. "Shall we enjoy some Christmas carols?"

It was the right suggestion. Soon they were assembled in the parlor, with Martha and Nate taking turns providing the music as they sang their favorite songs. Everyone's voices blended well together, so long as Patrick didn't sing too loudly.

Nate played when they sang "The First Noel." Rosalyn's fine soprano seemed especially lovely on this graceful hymn. It put him in mind of another carol they hadn't sung yet. As he began to play it, the others seemed inclined merely to listen and enjoy the music rather than sing along.

He paused after the first chorus.

"That's such a beautiful song," Rosalyn said.

"Why don't you sing it?" Martha suggested. "It's perfect for you and Nate to do together."

Rosalyn tried to demur, but Mary said, "You can't act shy now, Rosalyn! You'll be singing before a much larger audience soon."

"All right, you win," she said, turning eyes bright with laughter toward Nate.

She was so beautiful. A lovely face to match her lovely voice. Nate drank in the sight of her, painfully aware that after a few weeks he might never see her again.

Everyone was looking at him, perhaps wondering why he didn't start playing. Collecting himself, he once more raised his bow. He played a short introduction, and Rosalyn gleaned exactly when to begin singing.

What sweeter music can we bring,
Than a carol, for to sing
The birth of this our heavenly King?
Awake the voice! Awake the string!

Although the carol had some irregular timing, Rosalyn followed his lead flawlessly. It gave him such pleasure to hear her voice meeting and flowing with his music.

The Darling of the world is come,
And fit it is we find a room to welcome Him.
The nobler part of all the house, here is the heart
Which we will give him. . . .

Nate was sure he'd never heard finer singing. Was he simply biased because he knew the person behind the voice? No. She understood the music and felt it deeply. It was a rare joy to come across. Possibly one of the best Christmas gifts he'd ever been given, and one he would remember for a very long time.

Perhaps she felt the same way. When they'd finished and everyone was clapping enthusiastically, she wiped a tear from her eye as she gazed at Nate. "Thank you."

Given the freedom to follow his own inclination, Nate could have spent hours basking in the way she was looking at him. But he became uncomfortably aware that the clapping had stopped and his family was watching the two of them with particular interest. When he saw Mary and Martha exchange knowing nods, he knew their imaginations were running in directions that could never mirror reality.

Even though it pained him, he was glad for an excuse to leave. The stable owner had given him the morning off, but in exchange, he'd required Nate to work that evening.

Wiping down his fiddle, he said, "I've got to leave. I have to get the horses bedded down for the night."

This brought a murmur of discontent. No one could deny he had to go, but it was the disappointment he saw on Rosalyn's face that nearly did him in. Feeling a lump rising in his throat, he bid everyone good-night and walked swiftly out the parlor door.

He went to his room to change into clothes suitable for the stable. When he came back downstairs, he found Patrick dressed for the outdoors and waiting for him in the front hallway.

"I'll walk with you a ways," Patrick offered.

"Are you sure you want to go out in the cold?"

Patrick gave his stomach a pat. "A bit of a walk will do me good after that dinner."

It was a plausible answer, but Nate guessed his brother had another motive for joining him.

Patrick walked stiffly down the front steps, but once they were on the sidewalk, he moved easily. Their feet crunched on the snow as they made their way down the street.

"Rosalyn looks very fetching today, doesn't she?" Patrick began. "I don't think I've seen her in that frock before."

Here it came, just as Nate had suspected. "So you want to torture me about leaving, just like Ma."

"You ought not give up on Rosalyn, you know. Women will do amazing things for love."

"Well, they *won't* go to India," Nate retorted. "I think we've already proven that."

Patrick was not to be swayed. "I saw what happened in there just now. In fact, there's something special in *all* your interactions with Rosalyn. I can't recall ever seeing it between you and Ada. I think you were simply enamored with Ada because of her beauty. Not that Rosalyn isn't beautiful—indeed, I would say she is more so."

"I don't think a married man should be speaking of the attractiveness of another woman."

"Don't change the subject," Patrick admonished.

"I think of her like a sister," Nate said.

This was patently absurd, and Patrick's expression confirmed that he knew it. "Really? Let's think on that. Stop and get a good picture in your mind of Mary and Martha." Patrick did indeed pause for emphasis—although the fact that they had reached a busy intersection could have caused that. "Now tell me you think of Rosalyn just as you do of them."

It was impossible to even attempt Patrick's suggestion. Nate said nothing, just stared out at the street.

Patrick studied his face. "No, I'm thinking not like a sister."

Seeing a break in the traffic, Nate strode swiftly ahead. "I'm going to India. She will not leave England. That's the end of it."

"If you ask her, and she turns you down *only* because she won't leave the country, then it seems to me you should set aside this mad idea of chasing a commission."

Not knowing the full story, Patrick was blithely recommending the one choice Nate could *not* make. Sick with frustration, he picked up a clump of snow and threw it at a tree.

"You know the police force would accept you in a trice." Patrick's voice was mild behind him. "Inspector Browne at church has told you the same thing. He thinks you could even become an inspector, once you've gained enough experience."

"I've got a profession. I don't need to seek another."

"Nathan Stuart Moran." Patrick spoke each word with distinct emphasis, laying on an Irish accent as thick as their mother's. "If you are a soldier, why don't you act like one? Soldiers are brave. They fight for the victory. So are you a soldier, or aren't you?"

"This isn't a skirmish we're talking about."

"No. It's a fight for love—which is far more dangerous."

"Don't I know it," Nate rejoined harshly.

Patrick surprised him by responding with a hearty laugh. It was so infectious that Nate had to crack a tiny smile.

Nate shook his head. "How can you irritate me and make me want to laugh at the same time?"

"It's my personal specialty." Patrick eyed his brother. "Will you at least consider what I said?"

Nate sighed. "Yes, I will."

But even as Nate continued on alone to the stable, he knew his answer couldn't change. He *was* a soldier, and that was the crux of the problem. He had a greater responsibility to fulfill that had to come first. Even if he might wish otherwise.

‹•◦✦◦•›

For the Boxing Day performance, the house had been full to bursting, and the audience had been loud and appreciative. Four curtain calls, an indication that the Christmas revels were at their peak.

Pleasantly exhausted, Rosalyn sat on a crate near the stage door after the show, waiting for Patrick. She was absently petting Miss Bella, who had jumped into her lap, but she was thinking of Nate.

Yesterday had been a Christmas unlike any she could remember. To spend the holiday with a close-knit family like the Morans was a dream Rosalyn had nurtured since she was a child. She'd spent the whole day immensely thankful for the love and laughter.

But the music had made it most special of all.

There was something in the way Nate played his violin that stirred her soul. She could think of no better way to describe it. Every night at the theater she was surrounded by first-rate singers and musicians, but none had touched her as deeply as Nate had. He had an innate gift, that was sure. Over the past few weeks, he'd seemed distant in his interactions with her, as though keeping her at arm's length, but yesterday, as she had sung to his accompaniment, she felt so close to him. She would treasure that feeling.

A hand lightly touched her shoulder. "Still here?"

She looked up to see Tony. Although she returned his smile, she felt perturbed at having her reverie interrupted.

"Need an escort home? I'll happily go your way." He gave her shoulder a gentle squeeze before taking a seat next to her on the crate. His knee bumped hers as he sat down, causing Miss Bella to jump from her lap and stroll off into the shadows.

"Thank you, but I'm waiting for Patrick."

"Ah, of course. One brother is gone, but the other is here. It's like the changing of the guard. Why don't I wait with you until he gets here?" He slipped an arm through hers. "Are you excited about the rehearsal?"

"Yes!" Rosalyn answered. Tony's reminder pushed aside her other thoughts. Tomorrow they would have their first run-through of *The Pirates of Penzance*. Rosalyn still could hardly believe she would be among the first singers ever to hear the new show.

"Shall we meet here early? I'll run you through some warm-ups so you can be at your best."

"That would be lovely!" Rosalyn answered.

"Excellent!" He gave her an exuberant kiss on the cheek. "I feel like you are my very own protégé, and this is your big moment. You will outshine all of the others."

Rosalyn was about to admonish him for being too flattering, but seeing Patrick coming toward them, she stood up instead. Tony rose with her, his arm still looped through hers.

"My apologies for keeping you waiting," Patrick said, putting on his coat as he talked. "Everyone wanted to welcome me back to work. I think I may have gotten a few too many slaps on the back tonight." He spoke casually enough, but his expression was grave as his gaze took in Tony and Rosalyn's intertwined arms. "Are you ready to go?"

She gently worked her arm free. "We were just talking about the rehearsal tomorrow for *Penzance*. Tony has been helping me so much."

Tony lifted her hand and kissed it. "My dear, the pleasure of your company makes all my efforts worthwhile."

As he released her hand, she saw Tony's and Patrick's eyes meet. Neither one looked particularly happy with the other. It seemed Patrick was as wary of Tony as Nate was.

They all walked out the stage door together, and Tony bid them good-night, placing another kiss on Rosalyn's cheek before sauntering off.

Patrick watched him go. "Hayes seems very friendly toward you."

Hearing the concern in his words, Rosalyn said, "That's just how theater people are—as you know."

"Hmm, yes," he said. But he didn't sound entirely convinced.

A cold breeze blew up the street, sending a chill down Rosalyn's neck.

Patrick turned up his collar to ward against the cold. "Let's get home, shall we? I wonder if my son is keeping everyone awake."

As they made their way home, Rosalyn was struck by how different this was from all the nights she'd walked with Nate. Patrick walked briskly, intent on getting home as swiftly as possible. Nate had moved at a slower pace, taking time to enjoy the sights and sounds along the way. Being outside late was something Rosalyn had done little of before coming to London, but Nate had taught her to appreciate the intriguing character of the city at night.

Patrick kept up the chatter to match his stride. His stories were entertaining, but once or twice Rosalyn thought of the times she and Nate had walked for blocks in companionable silence.

When they entered the house, all was quiet. Rosalyn half-hoped to find Nate waiting for them in the parlor, as she hadn't seen him today. He'd gone to the stables before dawn and had not returned before she and Patrick left for the theater.

The parlor was dark and empty, the banked coals providing only the faintest light. The room seemed lonely. Rosalyn supposed this was how things would be from now on. The thought carried a breath of sadness with it.

"How strange," Patrick murmured.

"What do you mean?"

He shook his head, replacing his frown with a little smile. "Even Tommy seems to be asleep."

But Rosalyn had the feeling Patrick had been thinking about something else.

❦

Nate sat by the window in his darkened room, watching until Rosalyn and Patrick rounded the corner and came into view. They were well illuminated by the street lamps and the full moon, and he drank in the sight of her. He loved how confidently she moved, her manner alert, but not with fear. She took in her surroundings for the enjoyment of it, a change he'd seen happen gradually during the nights they'd walked home together.

He moved away from the window, lest either of them should look up and see him watching. He padded to his door, opening it a crack. His room was nearest the staircase, so he could hear them as they came inside even though they were being careful to move as quietly as possible.

He'd been sorely tempted to wait up for them in the parlor, but he had deliberately come up to bed instead. The fact that he wanted so badly to see Rosalyn was precisely why he'd argued with himself until reason prevailed. He would be leaving England soon, and it would be better to get used to the separation now. He was certain that the more time he spent with her, the more it would hurt when he left.

He could hear Rosalyn and Patrick murmuring softly, and before long they were coming up the stairs. When they reached the second floor, where Nate's room was, he fancied he heard a slight pause before they continued on. Patrick and Hannah's room was one flight up, and Rosalyn's was above that. As he gently closed his door, Nate pictured her taking that last set of stairs, candle in hand, moving through the shadows. He returned to his bed.

As he lay there, he heard footsteps coming back down the stairs. It had to be Patrick, for although he was walking softly, the tread was unmistakably a man's. The footsteps paused outside Nate's door. Did his brother expect to talk to him? Nate fervently hoped not. At the moment, he didn't even have the strength to try to fool his brother.

He held his breath, waiting. Long moments passed. But then, the steps moved away. Patrick was going upstairs.

Nate sighed and stared up at the darkness.

CHAPTER

19

M R. CELLIER WALKED into the rehearsal room with his assistant, Mr. Benson, following and carrying a large sheaf of papers. The energy of expectation in the room was palpable. Everyone wanted to know what Mr. Sullivan and Mr. Gilbert had come up with this time.

Mr. Cellier clapped his hands. "All right, everyone! Let's get to it. We've only had time to copy out the parts relevant to each role, as the music arrived on the ship yesterday. When we are done, you will return each and every sheet to Mr. Benson. Do you understand?"

"Yes, sir!" they said in unison. No one was going to argue with the terms of the agreement.

Mr. Benson began distributing the papers, starting with the men. "You will play Frederic tonight," he told Tony, who looked immensely pleased with himself and not the least bit surprised to be given the lead tenor role.

He approached Rosalyn and the other ladies from the chorus

standing with her. As he handed them their music, he said, "You will play the daughters of the major general."

Mr. Cellier's gaze focused on Rosalyn. "Aren't you the dresser?"

"Yes, sir. But Miss Lenoir has asked me to fill one of the chorus roles."

He looked at her silently for a few moments—was he perhaps recalling the time he had heard her and Tony singing together in this very room? At that time, he'd said her singing was "passable."

He gave a curt nod. "We'll give you the part of Isabel. She doesn't sing any solo parts. However, she does speak a few lines of dialogue. Do you think you can do that?"

"Yes, sir!" she replied, feeling almost as bold as her tone implied.

He moved to the other end of the room and held a hand to his ear. "What's that?"

Rosalyn took a deep breath. "Yes, sir, I surely can!" She spoke loudly and distinctly, proving she could be heard, even in the back rows.

He nodded, then returned to her. "No chance of *le trac?*"

Rosalyn looked at him blankly.

"He means stage fright," Helen whispered. More loudly, she said, "Sir, if you saw the way she orders us around in the ladies' dressing room, you'd know she is well able to handle a rowdy audience."

He laughed. "Fine, fine. All right, let's get started. It opens with the pirates all gathered on the shore by their ship. . . ."

What followed over the next few hours was more fascinating, intense, and thrilling than Rosalyn ever could have imagined. Many times she was rendered breathless, and it wasn't just from the singing. It was from the wonderful, sprightly music and the clever lyrics that never failed to amuse and enthrall.

When Helen, who for rehearsal purposes was singing Mabel,

began "Poor, Wandering One," Rosalyn got a little misty-eyed. But it was the parting duet when Mabel and her beloved Frederic were forced apart by circumstances that captivated her most of all. The main words in the chorus were simple enough: *"He loves you . . . he is gone . . ."* And yet they were rendered with such intense yearning and sorrow that Rosalyn could feel her heart break for the pair. She sighed, thinking of Nate.

Mabel and Frederic did ultimately get their happy-ever-after, thanks to a few clever plot twists. Rosalyn wished the same could be true of real life.

⁘

"I wonder why they're putting on the performance in Paignton instead of Penzance. That would have been even more amusing, don't you think?"

Helen made this remark as she settled into the seat next to Rosalyn. They had all boarded the train together. Mr. Gunn had met them at the station with tickets in hand for everyone.

Another of the chorus ladies in the seat in front of them turned around. "Maybe it would have frightened the audience members into keeping a close watch on their daughters as they left the theater. They could get attacked by pirates at any moment!"

Elsie said, "Thank goodness we're not going to Penzance. It's far enough just to get to Paignton."

"How long will the journey take?" Rosalyn asked.

"Four or five hours, I should think. I heard Mr. Gunn say we have to change trains at Exeter. There might be a bit of a wait there."

"We're going through Exeter?" Rosalyn said with a touch of excitement, thinking of her sister Cara.

Elsie looked at her like she was daft. "You haven't traveled much in the west, have you?"

"I haven't traveled much at all," Rosalyn admitted.

"You'd better get used to it, if you want to be a singer. I've spent half my life in railway stations, it seems."

Several of the others expressed similar opinions of the drudgeries of touring. But to Rosalyn the idea sounded exciting. She would enjoy seeing new places.

The train was still traveling through the outskirts of the city, passing houses, shops, and factories. But soon they would be in the country, and Rosalyn looked forward to this. Two months in the crowded streets of London had made her long to see open fields again. The freedom she felt, being on this train with these people, was an experience she would welcome many times over. As the vista outside the window changed, Rosalyn thought she could understand at least one reason Nate wanted to return to the army. The few times he'd spoken of it, he'd always emphasized that the frequent change of location required in foreign service suited him. Perhaps he would never be truly happy doing the same work in the same place year after year. She couldn't deny him that. She only wished he wasn't compelled to leave the country to find such a life.

⁓✥⁓

Nate stood in the shipping office at the railway station, still unable to accept what the goods manager on the other side of the counter was telling him.

"All of the goods wagons are booked until Thursday," the man repeated. "Do you want to schedule the shipment then?"

"So there's absolutely no way to get it on the train today?"

"Well, that's what I've been telling you, ain't it?" the man said impatiently. "Do you want to schedule for Thursday or not?"

"That's too late. I must get this to Paignton by end of day."

"You might have thought of that before this morning, then."

"What other options are available?" Nate pressed. "Are there other railway lines I can use?"

The man's look hardened. "My job is the Great Western, sir. We run a busy operation here, and our trains are always booked well in advance. It's all I can do to look after our own scheduling. I haven't time to do other people's work for them."

Seeing it was futile to try to get anything more from this man, Nate stepped away from the counter as the goods manager motioned another customer forward. He considered what other options might be available to transport the scenery and boxes of supplies for the show in Paignton. Moving everything by wagon would be far too slow, and sifting through the complications of getting it all onto a steamer would likely take even more time.

It wasn't surprising that he should run into these obstacles, given the last-minute nature of the task. But surely there had to be some way. While overseas in the army, he had successfully moved plenty of supplies with far fewer options available to him. He wasn't going to allow a surly clerk at a railway station to keep him from his objective. But where was he going to find more comprehensive information on his options?

While he stood there, thinking, a woman came out of the door that accessed the area behind the counters. She approached Nate. "Excuse me, sir, I might be able to help you."

He looked at her in surprise. "Yes?"

She was tall and wore a crisp white shirtwaist and plain brown skirt. Nate would have placed her at about twenty-five years old. "I'm a clerk here at the Great Western. I overheard your conversation with our goods manager."

It was odd to see a woman in that role, but times were changing. He had noticed her at a small desk set back from the counters but hadn't considered what she was doing there.

"Any help you can give me would be greatly appreciated."

"He didn't want to tell you about the London and South Western Railway because they are our competitors. However, it seems to me that if we're full, we can't lose any money by referring you to someone else."

"Thank you. That's a very commonsense approach."

"Their terminal for freight trains is at Nine Elms, near Waterloo station. If you want to telegraph them, here is the name of their goods manager." She handed Nate a piece of paper with a name written in a neat, legible hand.

Nate took the paper. "I see you take some pride in extending your knowledge beyond the immediate scope of this company. And in working a little harder to give your employer a helpful reputation."

"I have to work harder, sir." She gave a brief motion toward herself, and Nate understood what she meant. It would undoubtedly be more difficult for a woman to make her way in this occupation. She would have to put forth extra effort. "Just don't tell our goods manager that I sent you to our competition."

"I wouldn't dream of it," Nate said. "In fact, the next time I have goods to ship, I'll be sure to seek out this railway company—provided *you* can be the person I work with, Miss . . . er. . . ."

She gave a little smile and pushed her glasses up on her nose. "Jones. Annabelle Jones."

Nate didn't know why he was saying such a thing. This was a one-time event. But he wanted to give her the compliment and let her know how much he appreciated her help. With her prim clothes and wire-framed glasses, she reminded him very much of Mary. It wasn't difficult to visualize her in the same occupation someday. The salary was likely to be small, but surely it was more than Mary earned taking in laundry. It was something to think about—but for now, he had to get the goods on a train.

After thanking Miss Jones again, he went across the street to

271

the telegraph office. Within fifteen minutes he had his answer: there was room on a goods car if he could get everything there in two hours. Nine Elms was on the opposite side of the city, but Nate accepted the challenge. If there was one thing he knew from his work at the ostler's, it was how to quickly find wagons and horses to move cargo through London.

❧

When the train pulled into Paignton, the cast was met by a Mrs. Boyle, who informed them she worked for the theater and would also be their guide to the hotel.

"Our *guard*, more like," Elsie complained, as everyone followed her out of the station. "She's probably been sent by Mr. Gilbert to watch over all the ladies."

"Oh, I hope not," said Helen. "This is our chance to be free of all that nonsense for a while."

The Gerston Hotel turned out to be close to the station. The walk there was easily accomplished despite muddy streets from a recent rain. The hotel was not luxurious by any means, but it was clean and looked well kept.

"The theater is adjacent to this hotel," Helen said. "This will be very convenient."

They waited in the lobby while Mrs. Boyle collected their keys from the front desk, and a hotel porter approached them with a letter in his hand. "Is anyone here named Rosalyn Bernay?"

"Yes, that's me!" Rosalyn said eagerly, stepping forward.

The porter handed her the letter. "This was sent to you in care of the hotel."

Julia's familiar scrawl confirmed Rosalyn's first guess about who would have sent her a letter here. She was so excited to read it that she barely noticed as the porter tipped his hat and walked away.

"A letter!" Tony exclaimed. "Have you an admirer here already?"

Rosalyn was surprised that he actually looked alarmed at the prospect. "Nothing like that," she replied. "It's from Julia."

"Julia?"

"My sister."

"Oh, that's right. I had forgotten you had a sister."

It seemed odd that he would have forgotten. Rosalyn had mentioned Julia to him several times.

She opened the letter, savoring each word as she read it all the way through. Leave it to her ever-resourceful sister to think of sending her a letter here. She couldn't keep a smile from her face.

"You seem to be enjoying it," Helen said. "Is it good news?"

Rosalyn looked up to see everyone looking at her with interest. "It's actually very entertaining. Would you like to hear it?" Ordinarily she'd never share a private letter from a family member, but in this case, she thought they'd enjoy the contents as much as she did.

"We'd love to," Helen said, and everyone else nodded in agreement.

"All right." Rosalyn took a breath and began reading the salutation. "'My dearest and most talented sister—'"

"Such a shame when siblings don't get on," one of the men joked.

"Quiet!" Helen said to him and nudged Rosalyn to keep reading.

"'Since there is no time for a letter to reach you before you leave London, I'm taking a chance that this will find you at the hotel in Paignton. I dearly wish I could be there!'"

"So do we," said another man from the chorus. "Is she as pretty as you?"

"Don't be disrespectful," Tony chided with a smile.

Rosalyn gave a little sigh. How lovely it would have been if Julia could have come. She'd written to her sister in haste as soon as she knew she'd be part of this show. She knew it was unlikely that Julia would have the time or the means to get here, but Rosalyn had thought she should at least know about it.

"Go on, Rosalyn," said Tony. "We are beside ourselves to hear the rest."

"I *am* just getting to the good part," she agreed, and continued reading. "'I'm so excited for you! Even though the acting profession is generally considered to be a hazardous and unreliable way of earning a living—'"

"Ain't that the truth," Elsie chimed in. Everyone gave knowing nods.

"'—I applaud you for having the boldness to step out on the stage. Perhaps we ought not tell Cara's employer, though. From the way she has described them, I surmise they are very old-fashioned about these things. They might not be happy to know their nursery maid has a sister in such a scandalous occupation.'"

"Your secret is safe with us," Helen assured her.

"'I must end this letter now and post it before I rush off to work. But please know I will be cheering you on in spirit. God bless you, and good luck!'"

Rosalyn tucked the letter back in its envelope. It was nice to have Julia's approbation, even if given in such a teasing manner.

"That's such a sweet letter!" Helen exclaimed. "I wish I had a sister."

"Aren't we all like sisters?" Elsie wrapped her arm through Helen's. "After all, we have to stick together. Just like one big family."

It was heartening to hear Elsie's comment. She'd noticeably cooled toward Rosalyn since the night of Jessie's party, undoubtedly due to Rosalyn's continued friendship with Tony. Rosalyn kept seeking ways to lessen the friction, but it seemed a doomed cause.

Perhaps this was like one big, boisterous family, Rosalyn thought, as Mrs. Boyle returned and led them to their rooms. Even with its disagreements. And even a brother who seemed a tad forgetful at times, she added to herself, as Tony took her arm to walk with her up the stairs.

❧ ⚬❀⚬ ❧

It was pouring down rain when Nate's train pulled into Paignton, but he'd seen worse. He was immensely satisfied just to have arrived on time with his cargo.

The Bijou Theatre was close to the railway station, so that was one thing in his favor. He hired two wagons at the station and got everything to the theater in reasonable time.

The rain slacked off as Nate began to oversee the unloading of the wagons. Even so, the process took some time. Several of the stagehands from the theater carried the crates and boxes into a side door. Once inside, the backstage manager at the Bijou showed Nate around the theater to help him get his bearings. Since the Opera Comique was the only theater Nate had ever seen the back of, he found himself intrigued by how the Bijou was laid out. It seemed better designed than the Opera Comique.

He returned to the stage area to find the stagehands in the process of hanging the backdrop, the canvas that Patrick had damaged in his fall. The stagehands quickly hung it in place, working with rapid efficiency. Now repaired, this canvas didn't look too bad, even though it was crumpled in a few places from being shipped. It was now meant to represent Penzance rather than Plymouth, but Nate supposed the audience wasn't likely to be particular about the details.

275

He set two of the stagehands to the task of unloading and arranging the props, giving them a list of all the items in the order they would be needed.

The first man gave a low whistle when he pulled the lid off a crate and saw a dozen policemen helmets. "There are bobbies in this show? I'm sure I never saw *that* in an opera before!"

The other stagehand scratched his head. "I thought it was about pirates?"

"There are pirates, too." Nate pulled a black flag with skull and crossbones from another crate.

"Ha! This should be a good show!" the first man said.

Nate was about to leave them to their task when he saw Mr. Gunn walking toward him.

"I'm happy to see you here," he told Nate. "Last I heard, you were making a frantic dash across London with our cargo. I wasn't laying odds in your favor."

"It was close," Nate admitted, "but I know a few shortcuts."

Mr. Gunn gave him a friendly slap on the back. "Well done. I don't know if anyone else could have made it."

"Thank you, sir." Nate was genuinely proud to have come through this successfully. "I trust you and the crew had a less eventful trip?" Even throughout this busy day, he had found himself often thinking of Rosalyn, picturing her on the train with the rest of the cast.

Mr. Gunn gave a snorting laugh. "If you call being trapped in a railway car with overly energetic actors 'less eventful,' then yes, I suppose we did. They're getting settled at the hotel but will be here shortly. Are their costumes in place?"

"Just getting to that now, sir."

"Good. Well, I've got to go chat with the box office manager. I'll leave everything here in your capable hands."

"Thank you, sir. You can count on me."

"I know that," he replied with an appreciative nod. "Glad to have you on this trip."

Still happy from this praise, Nate located some other stage-hands to haul the crates of clothing upstairs to the dressing rooms. He was surprised to see the dressing rooms for the ladies and the men along adjoining hallways. Nothing at all like the Opera Comique, where they were split between two completely separate parts of the building.

None of the cast had yet arrived, so the men had no qualms about carrying crates into the ladies' dressing room. Nate lifted the lid on one of the crates to discover it held frilly lace nightcaps and the kind of thick woolen shawls worn for keeping warm at night. He wondered what kind of scene required the ladies to use these items.

The other men went back downstairs to fetch the crates designated for the men's dressing room. Nate lingered for a moment, curious. A row of tables and chairs was set against a wall, with a large mirror at each table. Nate tried to envision Rosalyn sitting at one of those tables, dabbing rouge on her cheeks and lips. But truly, she didn't need any embellishment.

He heard steps and the excited chatter of the ladies. He headed toward the door and had almost reached it when he was met by Helen and Elsie.

"Well, well, well!" Helen exclaimed, managing to smile and smirk at the same time. "Look who I found sneakin' around the ladies' dressing room!"

Nate stepped aside as the other ladies poured in, carrying satchels and small makeup cases. They made a beeline for the tables and began to lay out their supplies, each intent on securing their own bit of territory. Most gave him a mildly flirtatious look as they passed.

Rosalyn was the last to arrive. "You made it," she said, looking genuinely pleased to see him. "Mr. Gunn warned us there was some trouble with the shipping and we might have to perform the entire show in our street clothes."

Elsie went over to the open crate and pulled out a nightcap. "Nate, have you been inspecting our nightclothes?"

"Shame! Shame!" several of ladies said, saying the words in high-pitched unison exactly as they did during *Pinafore* when recoiling from the villain.

He held up his hands in a gesture of innocence. "Just delivering the supplies."

"And I'm sure you're *very* good at your job," Elsie said salaciously, waving the nightcap and giving him a wink.

"Actually, I've never been in a theatrical dressing room before."

"What, *never?*" Helen intoned, recalling one of the more famous lines from *Pinafore*.

Everyone groaned gleefully and then dissolved into giggles.

Nate knew that for these ladies, the jesting was only in good fun. Still, he hoped Rosalyn never became as garish in her talk as they were.

"It's a night of firsts for all of us!" Rosalyn exclaimed. There was a sparkle in her eye, and her cheeks were flushed.

Yes, she was beautiful without the aid of any gaudy stage makeup. But this knowledge only put a knot in his stomach. "I have to go," he said tersely. "Good luck."

Her smile faded a little as she looked at him in surprise.

Nate quickly walked out the door and into the hallway. Behind him, he heard Helen say, "Rosalyn, come over here! Take this chair beside me."

He might have worried that he'd hurt her, but he was quite sure she was already lost in this world and had forgotten him the moment he left.

CHAPTER

20

I DON'T KNOW WHAT I'm going to do with my hair," Elsie moaned. "This damp weather has made it so limp."

"The perils of being by the seaside, dearie," Helen said. "Still, this nice theater makes up for the inconveniences of travel. I've worked here a few times in touring productions. There's even a real greenroom."

"Thank heaven for that," Elsie said. "It's such an irritation to be kept away from *the men* while we're off stage. I mean, where's the camaraderie in that?"

"Exactly!" Sarah agreed.

Rosalyn barely heard them. She toyed idly with her comb, her mind more on Nate than her hair. Why had he turned so cold earlier? Perhaps he'd only been reacting to the teasing from the other women. She couldn't quite make out how he felt about the theater and about her involvement in it. She'd thought he was happy for her, but tonight all she'd sensed was disapproval.

"That Nate Moran seems an awfully fine fellow," Helen remarked, catching Rosalyn's gaze in the mirror. "I hope he didn't get put out by our foolish talk."

"I think he's just concerned about me," Rosalyn said.

Elsie pulled a hairpin from her mouth and set it in her hair. "Is it because you have joined a—how did your sister put it—'hazardous and unreliable profession'?"

"Something like that."

"He's a fine one to think so," Elsie scoffed. "Isn't he going back to the army? What's more hazardous and unreliable than that? I have a brother who came home from the army minus a leg."

"My cousin didn't come back at all," Sarah said. "Died of dysentery in one of those miserable camps they have to live in while marching to a new location. Left behind a widow and four children. Very sad."

Rosalyn felt a spasm of worry at the picture these women were painting. Nate had already been wounded once; suppose he never came back from this next tour of duty? She couldn't bear the thought of a wonderful man like Nate being lost. And what would it do to his family? No wonder his mother had been so adamantly trying to persuade him not to go back. Rosalyn blinked back tears as all these worries stockpiled in her heart.

"Ladies, ladies. This is no time for moroseness." Helen gave a brief, comforting squeeze to Rosalyn's shoulders. "We've got a show to put on, and we've got to be ready to spread some happiness!"

Helen was right. Rosalyn inhaled deeply and looked in the mirror, testing out a smile. It would do no good to worry about Nate just now.

"Let's look through the greasepaint," Helen suggested, opening up her supply case to reveal an array of choices. "We need to decide which shade will look best on you."

⚜

"I like the layout of these lights very much," Nate remarked. "This is so much better than the Opera Comique."

With everything delivered and unpacked, Nate had asked Joe, the head lighting man, if he would show him around. Joe seemed pleased to do this, evidently proud of the theater. At the moment, they were on a catwalk that ran above the stage, and Joe was showing Nate the battens, the rows of gaslights that lit the stage from above. He'd also shown Nate the gas table, which was a central board that controlled the batten lights with minimal effort.

Joe looked pleased at the compliment, as if he owned the lights himself. "Let me show you our calcium lights, too."

The calcium lights, or limelights, were in excellent condition. Nate was about to ask if he could test them, but they were interrupted by Mr. Gunn, who asked Joe to bring the lighting crew together so they could discuss what would be needed tonight.

"May I join you, sir?" Nate asked. "I'd love to see what you're planning. That was my job at the Opera Comique." It seemed odd to use the past tense like that. Working with the lights had turned out to be more intriguing than he'd ever expected, and Nate pushed back a surge of regret that this would be his last chance to do so. He decided to make the most of it while he could, before the army life reclaimed him and this would all be in the past.

Mr. Gunn looked pleased at his request. "Absolutely."

After introducing himself to the crew, Mr. Gunn began to discuss what he envisioned for the lighting scheme. "You've had productions of *Pinafore* at this theater before."

It wasn't a question, but Joe answered, "We have! Twice! A popular show, that is."

Mr. Gunn nodded. "This show will be set up a lot like *Pinafore* in terms of the lights. Act one takes place in the afternoon; act two takes place at night. We can set it up the same way: for act one, we'll have everything full up at every available point throughout. For act two, the white lights are down for rise of curtain. Have blue medium on everything possible. Raise the white floats slightly at the general's entrance. Battens raised slightly at ladies' entrance.

"Near the end, when the constable says to the pirates, 'Stop! In Queen Victoria's name!' we want the blue medium off everything and white lights full up until fall of curtain. So the minute he says this, everything changes dramatically."

"Quite right," one of the men said. "Always give honor to Her Majesty." Nate smiled. The other man had no idea of the specifics of the show, but Nate was amused to see his patriotism was on display nonetheless.

"Exactly," said Mr. Gunn. "Now, let's discuss the calcium lights."

Joe looked surprised at this announcement. "We're doing follow spots? We had the idea that wasn't going to be necessary."

Mr. Gunn frowned. "Why did you think that?"

Joe shrugged. "We heard it was going to be more like a simple run-through. And we're not expecting much of a crowd."

"Even so, why not give the audience their money's worth?"

"It's just that we have a smaller crew tonight, as you can see."

Nate said immediately, "I'd love to run one of the calcium lights. They are the finest I've seen." Admittedly, he hadn't seen very many limelights, but he knew these were better than the ones he'd used in London.

Joe said proudly, "They're the latest design."

"Excellent," said Mr. Gunn, taking this as the affirmative. "Here's the plan."

Nate knew there was never any doubt that Mr. Gunn would prevail. While working with him over the past few days, Nate had come to appreciate his forthright attitude and to admire his organizational abilities. It was no wonder he was responsible for coordinating the touring productions.

"For the calcium, we want the white open from right to left, all strength on act one," Mr. Gunn explained. "During most of act two, they'll be blue medium from right and left. Be sure to carefully follow the principals throughout, since the lighting will be lower. And then, once again, we switch to full white at—"

"Queen Victoria's name!" Joe finished with a grin, and everyone laughed.

The men were dismissed to begin setting the lights. As Nate worked with the crew, he once more thought about Rosalyn. He was glad he had this opportunity to run the spotlight. He would be sure she was well-illuminated during her time onstage. Mr. Gunn might notice and quiz him about it afterward, but since this was Nate's last two days working for the opera company, he didn't see that the touring manager could do anything about it.

He still harbored concerns about Rosalyn vying for a stage career, but there was no denying she had a gift for music worth sharing. If this was his only chance to see her on stage, he would give her the best send-off possible.

※

Rosalyn and the others had been pleasantly surprised when Mrs. Boyle introduced them to Betsy, the dressing room attendant. "She will help you with whatever you need," Mrs. Boyle had told them.

Their first task had been to get the gowns and other costumes out of the crates. There was a stove set up for a flatiron, and Betsy worked diligently to get the gowns wrinkle-free and looking their best.

They sorted through the nightcaps and shawls, each picking the one they preferred. "So this is all we have to simulate being in our nightclothes?" Rosalyn said. "The audience will be able to tell we still have our gowns on under the shawls."

"No money wasted on costumes," Helen said dryly.

Mrs. Boyle popped her head in the door. "Ladies, we need you downstairs for the run-through in ten minutes."

"This is it!" Helen said to Rosalyn. "Are you excited?"

Rosalyn nodded as she placed the cap and shawl she'd use that night at her dressing area. "I almost can't believe it's happening."

"Enjoy it while it's new and exciting," said Elsie. "That first blush of excitement will wear off."

"Well, aren't you a ray of sunshine," Helen teased.

Rosalyn knew Elsie might be right, but at the moment she couldn't imagine not being thrilled before going onstage.

In the hallway they met up with several of the men. Tony immediately came to Rosalyn's side as the group went downstairs. "How are you liking it? This is a nice theater, isn't it?" He winked. "Certainly much friendlier backstage."

They reached the wings and saw that Mr. Gunn was already calling the actors into position. "Onstage, please! We have time for one run-through." When everyone was in place, Mr. Gunn said, "This is our preliminary rehearsal, technical rehearsal, and dress rehearsal rolled into one. We won't stop to discuss lighting; the men have their instructions and will work independently as we concentrate on getting some basic blocking and hitting the singing cues."

At the mention of the lights, Rosalyn looked up almost reflexively and was surprised to see Nate in the same place behind a spotlight that he occupied while working on *Pinafore*. Catching his eye, she smiled and waved. He gave a brief wave in return.

Seeing this, Tony gave Nate a mock salute. Nate frowned and

looked away, turning to speak to another lighting man in the perch with him.

"All right, everyone, let's have a quick warm-up," Mr. Cellier said. "And then we'll begin."

⁓◌⁓

It was tough for Nate, watching the run-through.

Not because the singers were less than perfect as they worked to learn their music and memorize some basic blocking at the same time. They were more fluid at doing both of those things simultaneously than he would have expected. He supposed most of the actors had spent a good deal of time touring and must be used to learning things quickly. Rosalyn was proving to be a quick study, too. She held her own against the others. Once or twice when she stumbled on a note or a movement, she quickly recovered and caught up.

He wasn't even too bothered when the actor playing the major general came out and sang about how he had every kind of knowledge *except* how to run a modern-day army. It was the same kind of satire Mr. Gilbert had done with the head of the navy in *Pinafore*. Nate had personally known a few commanders who were not as thoroughly vetted on tactics as they ought to have been.

No, what was most difficult for Nate was seeing how much time Hayes was managing to spend with Rosalyn on the stage. He was playing one of the pirates, and when they all swooped in on the ladies, each intent on carrying one off as a bride, he attached himself to Rosalyn. It troubled Nate to see the way his hands moved so familiarly around her waist. At one point Hayes even lifted her off her feet and twirled her around, though to be fair, many of the others were doing the same. The ladies all shrieked in dismay, but their characters were secretly enamored at the idea

285

of being carried off. He told himself Rosalyn was only playacting, but it certainly looked like genuine delight.

At the moment, Patrick's suggestion that Nate stay in London and become a policeman sounded mighty good. Sometimes it seemed criminal what those men could get away with on the stage.

He was glad he had the lighting issues to keep him occupied. He was also, along with the rest of the crew, seeing this show for the first time.

When the constable arrived with his police force—which for this production consisted of five men—Nate was surprised at how they were portrayed. In *Pinafore*, Mr. Gilbert had portrayed the sailors as "noble men and true," in a generally positive light—even if the idea that sailors never swore was completely unbelievable. From what Nate had seen, appreciation for England's navy men had soared, thanks to *Pinafore's* popularity. But in this show, the constable and the bobbies were cowardly buffoons who shook down to their boots at the thought of having to go after the pirates.

Nate thought of the policeman he and Rosalyn had spoken to one night and how pleased the man had been at the thought of seeing his profession portrayed in an opera. Nate could just imagine the policeman's consternation next spring when he took his "missus" to see *Penzance*.

"Isn't this a funny show?" Joe said, laughing at the antics of the bobbies. "It looks like Mr. Gilbert and Mr. Sullivan have done it again."

"Doesn't it bother you that the policemen are portrayed so negatively?"

"What?" Joe scratched his chin. "Nah. It's all in good fun. Everyone knows real policemen ain't like that. Real bobbies also ain't as short as some of them actors there. There's a minimum height requirement for them, you know. Got to be able to keep criminals in line." He chuckled. "Or pirates."

They reached the point where the constable called out to the pirates, "Stop! In Queen Victoria's name!" Nate and the rest of the lighting crew immediately brought up the white lights. It was a good effect, he thought.

The pirates complied at once, because after all, who could deny the authority of the Queen?

Joe was nearly crying with laughter. "Such clever fellows who wrote this show. When Her Majesty sees it, she'll be so delighted she'll knight them both on the spot."

But the show wasn't over yet. After a few final twists and turns, the pirates won the women anyway. Just about everyone was paired with someone at the end.

"Yeah, it's always the rogues them ladies go for, ain't it?" said Joe, laughing as though he'd just told a joke.

That hadn't been the case with the women Nate had known. But looking at Rosalyn wrapped in Hayes's arms and smiling, he figured there must be times when that was so.

≈❧≈

Rosalyn eagerly sat down at one of the mirrors. After weeks of watching the women apply makeup on themselves, she was thrilled to try it herself.

"First we spread this Vaseline on your face to fill in the pores," Helen instructed. "That way the greasepaint will go on nice and smooth."

Once that was done, Helen showed her how to apply the greasepaint. It was definitely an odd feeling, having the heavy stuff cover her face. "I look so different already!" she exclaimed.

"Like a little china doll," Helen said. "Time to get some color there. I'll apply rouge to my face, and you follow what I do. We'll start with the cheeks."

She applied and spread the rouge, and Rosalyn did the same. They touched a small amount to the chin, as well.

Helen looked her over and nodded. "That looks very good. Now we'll put just a tiny bit up under the eyebrows, to give brightness to the eye. Like so . . ."

Over the next few minutes, Helen showed her where to add white highlights so her features would not be washed out by the bright stage lights. Last of all, they put red coloring on her lips. When they were done, Rosalyn stared at herself in the mirror. She had been utterly transformed.

"You are beautiful," Helen said proudly, as though Rosalyn were a product of her own creation.

"It's amazing!" Rosalyn could hardly believe she was looking at herself.

"Don't stare at yourself too long, Narcissa," Helen teased. "We've got to finish getting dressed."

By the time Mrs. Boyle told them they were wanted in the greenroom for warm-ups, Rosalyn was almost giddy with anticipation. The run-through they'd done earlier had been her first chance to stand on a stage and actually perform. It had given her an exciting taste of what was to come.

"A proper greenroom," Elsie said with satisfaction as they entered.

The room was large and liberally furnished with comfortable sofas and chairs. Most of the men were already there. Everyone had their music and notes for act one in their hands.

Rosalyn's eye sought—and immediately found—Tony.

He grinned as she walked over to him. "What is this vision of loveliness that approaches? You are perfect, absolutely perfect." He leaned in, placing his lips very close to her ear, and murmured, "I'd kiss that lovely cheek, but I don't want to spoil the makeup."

It was an even greater boost to Rosalyn's confidence, having his approbation.

"Do you know the Greek myth about Pygmalion, the god who falls in love with a statue he created? That is how I feel about you when I think of how far you've come since the day you wandered into the theater."

"It is only for one night, though," Rosalyn said. "My story may end up being more like Cinderella's."

"But she had a triumphant ending, too, did she not? After all, she lived happily ever after." He took her hands, drawing her close. "Your happy ending may well be to bring joy to others by performing on the stage."

"It is an appealing thought," Rosalyn admitted.

"Keep that vision right there, in the center of your heart." He tapped her chest, ever so lightly.

Just a few short weeks ago, she might have been taken aback by a man touching her so casually. But by now she'd grown comfortable with the way Tony and the other actors showed their affection in a physical way. It was, in fact, rather freeing. She had never realized how bound-in her life had been before she'd come to London.

She took a moment to breathe in, savoring the happy feeling. Tony always smelled good, too. Whatever shaving lotion he used, it was immensely appealing.

"What are you thinking, my dear?"

"You always smell so good," she confessed.

His eyebrows lifted. "So forthright you are. I'm glad it appeals to you. Listen, tonight after the show, everyone is going to dinner at the hotel. You're going to sit with me, right?"

"All right."

Mr. Cellier strode into the room. "Time to get started!" he announced, pulling out his pitch pipe.

Rosalyn quickly found her attention fully focused on the task at hand. Even so, she enjoyed having Tony next to her as they went through the warm-ups. He'd believed in her from the beginning and had fought to get her here tonight. At one point they turned and shared a smile, and Rosalyn's heart soared with excitement for the evening ahead.

CHAPTER

21

N ATE STOOD IN THE LOBBY, watching the audience
straggle into the theater. Mr. Gunn was right in saying there wouldn't be much of a crowd. The show had
barely been advertised, and performing it on a Tuesday in this
little coastal resort in winter all but guaranteed a small turnout.

Still, he could see that those who'd come were excited to be
here. He overheard snippets of their jovial conversation as they
passed. "What a lark!" one man exclaimed. "We get to be the
first to see the new show."

"Have you seen *Pinafore?*" another asked.

"I've seen *Pinafore* at least a dozen times! Never tire of it. Can't
wait to see what they've come up with next."

Nate could understand their excitement. He, too, had been
curious to see what the new show was about. While the plot had
been full of silliness, the music had been excellent—even hearing it with only a piano. He could imagine how good it would be
with a full orchestra.

Mostly, though, Nate anticipated tonight's show on account of Rosalyn. How would she perform? He had no doubt about her voice, but he hoped she would not be distracted or make mistakes now that she was performing in front of an audience. If she did poorly, would she be hurt or disappointed? If she did well, then what? What if she decided to take on the life of a vagabond actress? He found the thought troubling, knowing that she was still largely unproven in the ways of the world. Right now she only spent time with the actors during defined working hours. But traveling together would put them on a much more intimate basis. It did no good to tell himself that she was free to make her own way in the world. He could make no claim on her, nor would he even be near enough to offer help. He was bound to a different life.

One of the posters for the show caught his eye, and he noticed something he hadn't seen before. The subtitle for this show was "The Slave of Duty."

It was nearly time for curtain. Still grimacing from the poster, Nate made his way to the back of the theater and joined Joe and the other stagehands in the final preparations.

In his perch next to the limelight, Nate was ready when the curtain lifted. As act one progressed, he trained his light on the principal actors playing the pirate crew as they sang their songs. But he was waiting for their exit, which would signal the entrance of the ladies' chorus.

At last they entered, singing. They were all dressed in white muslin frocks suitable for strolling along the beach in summer. Nate immediately spotted Rosalyn, even though with her face in full stage makeup, she almost looked like a completely different person. But her smile and the light in her eyes as she sang were unmistakable.

The ladies traipsed around the stage in a circular motion, a very simple pattern that was all they'd had time to learn. Like the actors in the first scene, they held their music and prompt sheets in their hands. He wondered what the audience was making of that.

He couldn't take his eyes off Rosalyn. He trained the spotlight on her as the song ended and she and two other ladies began their dialogue. She was enchanting as she said the two lines allotted to her character.

The only thing that marred his enjoyment of the first act was when the pirates swooped in to steal the ladies for their brides, and he had to suffer through seeing Rosalyn clutched in Hayes's arms once again.

During the second act, as the policemen sang, Nate recalled Joe's words and realized they weren't quite as bad as he'd first thought. Everything in Mr. Gilbert's shows had an element of the ridiculous. Just looking at the motley collection of characters on the stage right now confirmed that. There were ladies wearing nightcaps and holding candles, trembling policemen, and improbably sympathetic pirates.

Nate kept his eyes on Rosalyn whenever she was on stage. The entire production was woefully unpolished, yet she performed beautifully. Certainly as well as anyone else in the cast. As the show ended with a final joyous chorus, he suffered mixed emotions once more. He was proud of what she'd accomplished tonight but concerned about where this success might take her.

Although meager in size, the audience applauded so enthusiastically that the sound filled the modest theater. The cast beamed with happiness as they took their bows. Nate swept his spotlight over each individual as he or she stepped forward, lingering when he got to Rosalyn. She deserved this much tonight. She looked up at him and waved, just managing to send him a bright smile before she was pulled into another group bow.

After two more curtain calls, Mr. Gunn called the show over, and the curtain came down for good. Nate hurried down to the stage, wanting to catch Rosalyn before she went off to the dressing rooms. The stage was filled with people in motion. Actors cheered and hugged one another. A few tossed their music into the air. Stagehands began to crisscross the stage, collecting props and smaller bits of scenery. But Rosalyn still stood center-right, exactly where she'd been when the curtain had come down. She was looking around at all that was happening, as though trying to memorize every detail.

When she saw Nate, she gave him a smile of such sweet happiness that it did something very particular to his insides. To his surprise, she ran toward him, throwing her arms around his neck in an effusive hug. "Did you enjoy it?" she asked enthusiastically.

"Yes." There was so much more he should be saying, so many compliments to give her. Her impulsive gesture undoubtedly stemmed from the pure joy she was feeling. All around her, others were doing the same thing. But as his arms wrapped reflexively around her, he found that her nearness had stolen his ability to speak.

Nate didn't move. He wasn't even sure he breathed. For a brief moment it felt as though Rosalyn stilled as well, relaxing into his embrace. Nate had the impression that the ground beneath him was shifting. He closed his eyes, hoping that might help him regain his bearings, but it only heightened his awareness of her, of how she felt in his arms. He caught mingled scents of soap and face cream and makeup. He remained only vaguely aware they were standing in the middle of dozens of people. It took all his strength not to pull her closer to him.

She gave a little start and stepped back. "Oh dear, I must be careful not to get greasepaint on your clothes!" There was a breathless tremor in her voice.

He thought he saw a glimmer of tears in her eyes, as well. The stage makeup looked garish up close. It was smearing in places, the result of performing so energetically for nearly three hours under the hot lights. There was a sheen of perspiration on her brow, and her hair was tousled from the moment when she and all the ladies removed their sleeping caps to take their final bows. And with all of this, she was still beautiful.

"I don't mind a little greasepaint," he said. He couldn't resist reaching up with his thumb to gently remove a smudge near her eyes. Warm, lovely brown eyes that were regarding him intently. "Not nearly as bad as the stuff that gets on me at the stables."

It was a foolish thing to say, but at least it eased some of the intense emotion battle-ramming him.

She said with a teasing lilt, "I think you might have placed the limelight on me more times than was strictly directed by Mr. Gunn's prompt book."

"I felt the performance merited it."

She beamed at him. "I could *feel* when the light was on me. It was an extraordinary sensation. I can understand why actors begin to crave it."

She lifted her face and inhaled deeply, as though gleefully recalling the experience. Nate realized what he'd done. While he'd been worrying about her going into acting tonight, his actions had spurred her desire to do just that.

"It isn't real," he said sharply. "It only feeds vanity."

Her expression sobered. "Do you think I'm a vain person?"

"No," he said quickly, "that's not what I meant." Frustrated at his clumsy words, he tried again. "Rosalyn, be careful. You've had good experiences with the theater so far, but it isn't always going to be this way. There are very real dangers to that life."

She wiped a strand of hair from her forehead, perhaps intending it to be a defiant gesture, but he saw a slight tremble in her hand. "Why are *you* telling me to take the safe route? Is that what you're doing by returning to the army?"

Her voice held an edge of recrimination, the same kind of accusation laced with worry that he'd gotten from his family. His nerves felt raw and taut, knowing he could not truly explain to her why he was leaving.

"I know it will be hard work, and I've a lot to learn," Rosalyn continued. "But tonight on this stage, I felt something very real, very rewarding. It's a chance to use this gift I've been given. I have to pursue it."

She spoke with absolute conviction. He loved that fire in her, but now it was scorching his heart. How ironic that he could wish for her to be happy and yet be so pained to see it. He reminded himself—yet again—that he was in no position to object to her decisions.

"I won't try to stop you," Nate said. "You have every right to live your life as you see fit."

She blinked, as though unsure what to make of his words, whether he was agreeing with her or still fighting. "Thank you," she said, evidently striving for neutral ground.

The activity around them was winding down as most of the actors filtered off stage, bound for their dressing rooms. Nate noticed Hayes was still there, though, on the opposite side of the stage. He was speaking with one of the other actors, but his gaze kept flitting back to Rosalyn.

"Are you coming to the party?" Rosalyn asked, referring to the supper Mr. Gunn had arranged for them.

The hopefulness in her voice, despite the things he'd just said, twisted something inside him. Never in his life had Nate thought it possible to run through such a range of emotions in one day. And considering what he'd gone through in India, that was saying quite a lot. "No. I'll be working to get everything packed up and to the station. The morning freight train leaves at six."

Rosalyn gave him a tremulous smile. "I'll see you in London, then."

She placed her hand on his arm as she spoke. It was the same placating gesture she'd used the night they'd argued about her going to the railway station alone. This woman had so much kindness in her. He prayed it wouldn't be wrung out of her by her associations with the theater.

Her touch reminded him that just a few short minutes ago, he'd held her in his arms. He would give anything to relive that moment, but it had passed, never to return.

❦

"Three cheers to Messrs. Gilbert and Sullivan for providing this wonderful feast!"

The actor who had played the pirate king lifted his glass as he spoke. Although he was three tables away from Rosalyn, she heard his resounding voice easily above the clamor.

"Don't forget Mr. Carte and Miss Lenoir!" someone called out. "I think, if left to make the decision, Mr. Gilbert would have sent us all home with nothing more than a 'well done' and maybe an apple."

"Do you think he'd have been that generous?" Tony quipped.

The pirate king said, "Let us all raise our glasses once again to honor the venerable impresario Mr. D'Oyly Carte and his redoubtable assistant, Miss Lenoir, who, I believe, also has the title of this show's producer."

Rosalyn joined in the toasts, but her happiness was tempered. The exaltation she'd experienced during the show had been muted by the unsettling discussion she'd had with Nate afterward. Why had he gone out of his way to give her the spotlight, and then roundly criticized her for liking it? It made no sense.

Had she somehow offended him with her impulsive hug? She'd

done it without thinking, carried away by the excitement of the moment. And he had not rejected her. Quite the opposite. He'd held her carefully—gingerly, even—as though she were made of glass. Yet it had felt surprisingly tender, too. For those few moments when she'd felt his breathing against hers, his warm arms around her waist, she'd been intensely happy. Even now as she recalled it, the sensations it aroused in her were impossible to define.

From his seat beside her, Tony gave her shoulder a little nudge. "Rosalyn, are you there? I think we've lost you down the deep well of thought."

She gave him an apologetic smile. "It has been quite the trip. There is a lot to think about."

"I saw you talking with Moran after the show. Did he say something to upset you?"

Rosalyn shook her head, not wanting to bring Tony into this particular problem. "It's nothing."

"Is there something—anything *particular*—between you two?"

Tony was asking, as he'd done once or twice before, whether Nate was her sweetheart. Unfortunately, the answer was far from straightforward. That there was something between them was undeniable. That nothing could come of it was equally true. That was what she must focus on.

"He's a good friend. Friends disagree sometimes, that's all."

"I see." Tony took her hand and caressed it, his bright blue eyes smiling into hers. "You were splendid out there tonight. You know that, don't you? This is your moment to dream and to follow your heart. Don't let anyone stop you."

"Thank you," she said. "You're right."

Tony pointed to her empty wine glass. "Let me refill that for you."

When the meal was over, Mr. Gunn announced, "London crew,

don't forget you are needed at the theater tomorrow night. Therefore I expect to see everyone in the hotel lobby, ready to leave for the station, at nine-fifteen tomorrow."

Elsie had been sitting at another table with some of the actors from Torquay, whom she knew from a previous touring production. "How can he expect us to be anywhere at nine in the morning?" Rosalyn heard her say woefully as she passed them on the way to the door. "I need my beauty sleep." She stumbled over a chair that had been pushed back from one of the tables.

Tony looked at her askance. "With the quantities of wine you've consumed, I should think you'd be able to sleep quite well tonight."

Elsie glared at Tony. "I don't know how people the likes of you get any sleep at all."

She actually moved to slap him, but Tony stepped nimbly away. Caught off balance, Elsie wobbled dangerously.

Sarah took her arm. "Let's go," she urged, and guided Elsie from the room.

Rosalyn hated to see the ugliness that kept cropping up between Elsie and Tony. This was the first time she'd seen Elsie try to strike him, though.

Tony seemed to have immediately dismissed the matter from his thoughts. He settled his attention on Rosalyn, offering her his arm. "May I walk you back to your room?"

She nodded. "Thank you."

But when they reached the third floor, Tony paused long before they reached the room Rosalyn was sharing with Helen and Elsie. He drew her closer. "There's something I'd like to say to you tonight, if I may."

She looked at him expectantly. "Yes?"

"It's too important to say out here in the hallway where anyone might interrupt us." He reached out and opened the door next to them. "Wait here."

299

Rosalyn stood alone, looking around uneasily. After a moment, Tony slipped back into the hallway. "My roommates haven't come back yet. We can talk in here."

"But—"

"Shhh," Tony said, tugging her through the doorway.

By the dim glow of the lamp, which had been set very low, she could see men's clothes and other personal items scattered about. "I don't think I should stay here," she said. "It doesn't seem right."

"Just for a moment," Tony assured her. "Surely there can be no harm in that?"

Before she could answer, he quickly cleared off the bed closest to them and led Rosalyn over to it. Slipping his arm around her waist, he gently coaxed her to sit down. "I've always been a perfect gentleman, haven't I?"

She had to admit that was true. Still, she swallowed nervously as she sat perched on the edge of the bed.

"Rosalyn." He said her name tenderly, his mouth very close to her ear. "I believe I have loved you from the first moment I laid eyes on you."

Rosalyn stiffened in surprise, her eyes opening wide. Tony had been flirting with her for weeks, ever since she'd come to the theater. But she never thought he would declare himself to her like this. The roomed seemed very small and far too warm. The rich food and the wine she'd consumed began to feel heavy in her stomach. She sent another glance at the door. Tony's roommates might come through it any moment. How would it look to be found here?

"My beautiful, sweet, charming Rosalyn," Tony continued, still in that caressing tone. "The hours we've spent together have been among the happiest I can remember."

"I care for you, too, Tony," she said, flattered and astonished at his words. "But surely this isn't the time or place—"

"You *do* care for me! I knew it. I could tell by the way we meshed so well today at rehearsal and during the show." His hold tightened around her waist. "How I should love to take you away, just like one of those pirates, and make you my bride!"

"Tony!" In her surprise, the word came out nearly as a shriek.

"Shh!" he cautioned. "These are thin walls."

She twisted toward him, trying to look into his eyes, still unable to believe what she was hearing. "Are you . . . proposing to me?"

"Dearest," he murmured, his free hand gently grasping her chin. "We could be like the great stage couples—the Bancrofts or the Kendals—starring together in the best shows."

He leaned forward, placing a caressing kiss on her cheek, just to the side of her mouth. She had the feeling he was testing her. He must sense that she was poised to bolt. In truth, she was too bewildered to move. Tony had been kind to her over these past weeks, but in all the time they'd spent together, he'd shared almost nothing about his personal life. They discussed very little outside of matters relating to the theater. Why was he suddenly talking about marriage?

Once more the appealing scent of his shaving lotion reached her, confusing her senses even more. It *had* been fun to dance with him, to sing together, their voices harmonizing so well. She had enjoyed pretending to be chased and caught by him, being held in his arms. But that had been only acting, hadn't it? Hadn't the other actors, also paired together as happy couples at the end of the opera, seen it that way? It had all been music and laughter, and she'd let her guard down, perhaps. She'd become too casual about allowing him to be so near her, and he'd taken it the wrong way. Or had he? Did she perhaps love him and not fully realize it?

He placed a hand behind her head, gently drawing her toward him—not for a kiss, but for a hug, pressing her against him. "Just feel how right we are together," he murmured.

Rosalyn allowed herself to remain settled against him, trying to sort out the tangle of emotions. As Tony's hands caressed her arms, a hollow uneasiness crept over her. This was no longer playacting, and despite what Tony said, it did *not* feel right.

She'd been in another man's arms that day. For those few, brief moments after she'd impulsively hugged Nate, he'd stood there, holding her. She recalled the way she'd found herself relaxing into his embrace, surprised by how warm and solid and comfortable it felt to be in his arms. That moment came back to her in a powerful flash, even as Tony tilted her chin upward, clearly intent on kissing her.

She leaped from the bed, stumbling over a chair in the process and knocking it over. It hit the floor with a loud thump.

"Rosalyn!" Tony quickly stood and took hold of her arm to steady her. "Dearest, what's wrong?"

"I have to go," she said breathlessly. The heaviness in her stomach felt dangerously like nausea. She pulled open the door, though Tony still held one hand.

"Don't leave," he begged, his voice low but insistent.

"Let go of me, Tony." There was no way she could have explained what she was feeling, even if she'd wanted to.

A man came up the stairs just in time to see the two of them standing at Tony's door. It was another member of the men's chorus. He took one look at them and smiled a lazy, knowing smile.

Now Rosalyn was sure she was going to be sick. She ran down the hallway, not stopping until she was in her room and had locked the door behind her.

◦⁓◉⁓◦

Helen turned, startled, from the vanity table as Rosalyn slammed the door behind her. "What on earth?" she cried.

Elsie lay stretched out on the bed, only half undressed. She made a sound of protest at the door closing with such force. "Don't do that," she moaned, crooking one elbow over her eyes to block out the light. "My head hurts."

Helen came immediately to Rosalyn's side. "Are you all right? What's happened? I saw you leave with Tony. Did he mistreat you?"

Rosalyn couldn't answer. She leaned against the door, trying to regain her normal breathing, willing her stomach not to revolt.

"Why don't you sit down?" Helen said, coaxing her over to a chair.

Rosalyn sank down onto it. Her stomach seemed back in place for the moment, but now tears were flowing.

Helen handed her a handkerchief, studying Rosalyn with worry. "Tony can be a rogue sometimes, but I never thought he would . . . He didn't . . . *force* you to do anything, did he?"

"No," Rosalyn breathed.

He had been trying to seduce her, though. That was obvious enough. His weeks of compliments and casual forwardness that subtly tested the bounds of propriety, all the time he'd spent giving her singing lessons—these were things she'd ascribed to his interest in her as a fellow artist and the unconventional gregariousness of theater people. And yet, tonight he'd talked of love, as well. . . .

"He proposed to me," she blurted.

"What?" Helen said in surprise. "In so many words?"

"He said we could be like the great acting couples."

From the bed, Elsie made a sound of derision and hauled herself up to a sitting position. "That's not a proposal, dearie. At least, not a proposal of *marriage*. You forget, this is the theater. Regular rules don't apply."

"Speak for yourself," Helen said sharply.

This rebuke rolled off of Elsie. "Oh, you can trust me on this one. I learned a piece of interesting information tonight from Emilie Petrelli," she said, referring to the soprano who had come from Torquay to sing the part of Mabel. "Mr. Hollingsworth Hayes is married already."

"No," Rosalyn protested, looking at her in shock.

Elsie nodded. "Apparently he keeps the wife squirreled away up in Lincolnshire. She's not in the theater. She's a milkmaid or something. I shouldn't be surprised if there are children, too."

"Married!" Rosalyn repeated in disbelief. She squeezed her eyes shut, overcome with powerful humiliation. "How perfectly willing he was to lead me into ruin."

Helen took her hands, giving them a little shake to grab her attention. "Rosalyn, listen to me. If you want a life in the theater, you have to accept that these things happen. It's not a reflection on you. Not if you take the high road." She glanced at Elsie.

Rosalyn expected one of Elsie's characteristic retorts. Instead, a raw, unguarded pain stole into Elsie's eyes. "At least you found out *before* the damage was done."

In all the time she'd known Elsie, Rosalyn had never seen her display anything but hard-edged bravado. She ought to have guessed, perhaps, that it was a mask to cover deeper hurts.

"Oh, Elsie, I'm so sorry."

Helen went to the bed and gave Elsie a hug. "That's all right, dear. We all stick together, don't we?"

Rosalyn wiped the tears from her cheeks. Tonight she had learned a hard lesson—and she was determined not to forget it.

CHAPTER

22

THE FOLLOWING MORNING, Rosalyn was armed with steely resolve as she walked toward the railway station in Paignton. She'd left early so as to avoid the possibility of seeing Tony at the hotel. She hoped she could get on the train without having to speak with him at all.

The street was quiet. It seemed this seaside resort slept late during the off-season. Rosalyn savored the salty breeze as she walked, regretting that there had been no time to take in the little town or stroll along the seaside.

She paused at a notice board that still had a poster advertising *The Pirates of Penzance*. "For one night only!" it proclaimed. "The first production seen in any country!"

Rosalyn carefully dislodged the notice from the board. It had water stains and one edge was tattered, but it was a memento worth keeping. Perhaps this would be her only chance to perform publicly. Perhaps last night was the first of many to come. Looking at the notice, the thrill of having been part of such an important occasion ran through her again. She *wanted* to perform again, of that she was sure. It might take time, and it would unquestionably take hard work to bring herself to the level of skill required. Last night's debacle with Tony had left her sorely discouraged, but this morning, with the sun breaking through the coastal mists, Rosalyn understood she had no reason to let it keep her from pursuing this new dream.

Carefully she rolled up the notice and placed it in her carpet-bag, then continued up the street.

In the end, keeping her distance from Tony was easily accomplished—if not without discomfort. He arrived flanked by several men from the chorus, including the man who'd seen her leaving Tony's room. They seated themselves at the far end of the carriage. Once or twice she saw them looking in her direction, and she knew they were talking about her. She was aware how easy it would be for Tony to spread lies about her—even by saying nothing. The other man had surely seen enough to draw his own conclusions.

Although the long train ride afforded her plenty of time to mull over all that had happened, by the time they arrived in London, there were still many unresolved issues in her mind. She would have liked nothing more than to go straight home, suddenly anxious to be away from the world of the theater for a few hours. She wanted to see Nate again, too. Tomorrow he'd leave for Aldershot, and who knew when she might see him again?

But there was no time to go home. It was nearly call time, and everyone rushed to find cabs to the theater. Rosalyn ended up sharing a hansom cab with Sarah.

"I'm glad we have a chance to talk," Sarah said. "I wonder if tonight you might be able to cajole Mrs. Hill into giving us more towels in the dressing room. It's scandalous how penny-pinching this theater is at times."

"Of course," Rosalyn replied.

It was a timely reminder that she was going back to her job as a dresser, not an actress. Was this intentional on Sarah's part, to put Rosalyn in her place? Sarah went on to speak of other needs in the dressing room, such as the leaky water tap. As far as Sarah was concerned, Rosalyn's brief foray onto the stage had been just that.

London was a dreary place today, covered in snow filthy from soot. Clouds were thick overhead. The cab's pace was slowed as the horse struggled on the icy streets. But at last they arrived, and the inside of the theater, while cold from the inadequate heating system, was already bustling with actors and crew preparing for the evening show.

Rosalyn quickly deposited her bag in a corner of the dressing room and set about work. There was plenty to do. Last night's production, which consisted of the cast who had remained behind plus a few temporary fill-ins, must have been a slipshod affair. Certainly the cleanup had been. The clothing racks and shelves for accessories were in complete disarray. Rosalyn did what she could to restore order. This was no easy task, as the other women were arriving and adding to the general confusion.

As she worked, she heard Sarah say to one of her friends, "Have you heard the big news? Mr. Power is out with pneumonia. Tony Hayes goes on for him tonight. Possibly for the whole week."

"That's good news for Tony, isn't it?" said the other woman. "He's been looking for this chance to prove he can carry a show."

So here was Tony's big moment. His career was likely to keep its upward trajectory, just as he'd been telling Rosalyn all these weeks. What kind of man he was when not on the stage made no difference at all. It was another hard rule of the theater.

Elsie was already seated at her usual spot at the makeup tables. Her eyes caught Rosalyn's in the mirror, and Rosalyn knew they were both thinking the same thing.

Scooping up a pile of dirty towels that had been left in a heap the night before, Rosalyn left the room. She heaved a sigh as she carried her load down the stairs. If she felt just a little bit sorry for herself, could she be blamed?

At the bottom of the stairs, she nearly tripped over Miss Bella. The cat looked up at her and meowed. It felt like a welcome. Dropping the towels to one side, Rosalyn sat on the bottom step and scooped the cat into her arms. "Hello, Miss Bella," she murmured, holding her close. "Did you miss me?"

The cat purred, its warmth comforting. Rosalyn stroked it affectionately. Its soft fur felt good against her cheek as she continued to speak endearments. "There was no cat in the Paignton theater. Can you imagine? However do they manage?"

Hearing footsteps, she looked up to see Millie approaching.

"Miss Lenoir has asked if you could come to her office straightaway," the girl announced. She pointed to the pile of towels. "Do you want me to take those to the washing room?"

"Thank you," Rosalyn replied, setting the cat down gently and standing up. She wondered at this unusual summons. As she hurried toward the business offices, she worried that some negative gossip about her had reached Miss Lenoir's ears already.

"Come!" said Miss Lenoir's businesslike voice in response to Rosalyn's knock.

Miss Lenoir was not alone. Seated in a chair by the desk was a young woman Rosalyn hadn't seen before. She was slender and pretty, and neatly if somewhat shabbily dressed. She met Rosalyn's gaze squarely.

"Rosalyn, this is Lilly," Miss Lenoir said. "She's just come to ask for her old job back."

For several seconds, Rosalyn could only stare. Finally, she regained enough presence of mind to close her mouth, which seemed to have fallen open in shock. Did Lilly's return signal the end of Rosalyn's time here?

"Please take a seat so we can discuss the situation," Miss Lenoir directed. She motioned toward the door as she spoke, and Rosalyn realized she was still holding on to the handle. Closing the door behind her, she took a seat in the chair next to Lilly.

"This is an unusual situation, to be sure," Miss Lenoir began. "I've already informed Lilly that she was highly remiss in leaving without notice. But when she explained the circumstances surrounding her departure, I began to understand. She has also given me permission to share this information with you—provided you agree to hold it in confidence."

Lilly was watching Rosalyn. Her expression did not reveal much about what she was thinking, but her hands, twisting a pair of very worn leather gloves in her lap, indicated a degree of nervousness.

Rosalyn nodded, but her heart began a slow, heavy thud. If Miss Lenoir intended to turn Lilly away, it was unlikely she would have called Rosalyn into the office. Was she about to get the sack?

"Lilly has been with us for several years," Miss Lenoir said. "She has proven herself to be a good worker. Unfortunately, a few months ago she fell in love with someone in our theater and was led to make some unwise decisions. When she found herself in trouble, she knew—for reasons which she chooses not to divulge—that she could not apprise the man of her situation."

"Who was the man?" Rosalyn demanded. It was no doubt rude to ask, but she couldn't help it. Not with so much at stake, and knowing the men in this theater as she did now.

"Does it matter?" Lilly burst out. "It's over now. I never had the baby, anyway. I miscarried while trying to reach my parents' home in Hounslow. It's hard to walk ten miles in such condition."

As she spoke, Lilly's face displayed a poignant combination of pain and defiance.

Rosalyn's heart went out to her for this terrible tragedy. But it fueled her anger, too. "Surely the man must be confronted and punished!"

"Everyone is responsible for their own actions," Miss Lenoir replied calmly. "Mr. Gilbert can set as many rules for conduct in this theater as he likes, but he has no jurisdiction over what happens when working hours are over. I'm afraid we must acknowledge that Lilly has a share of the fault in this, as well. She has sworn to me that she was not forced or coerced to do what she did."

"It's true," Lilly affirmed, her voice laden with regret. "Only stupid."

Once more, Rosalyn seethed at the injustice of these things. "Why is it always the woman who pays so dearly?"

"That is a topic ripe for endless and important discussion," Miss Lenoir agreed. "Unfortunately, it's not something we are able to spend time on today." She rose from her desk, coming around to the front of it so that she was nearer to both women, placing a brief, reassuring pat on Lilly's shoulder. "Lilly has come to me, asking for work—or at the very least, a good reference to enable her to find a new job elsewhere."

"And—?" Rosalyn prompted, holding her breath for the answer.

"I have offered her both things," Miss Lenoir replied, "because I do not wish for her to pay for her actions more dearly than she already has." Rosalyn heard the deliberate echo of her words. "Our children's production of *Pinafore* has been so successful that we are extending it through March. Lilly will work with them. Some of the little tykes are especially hard on their costumes, and the woman we hired to help simply cannot keep up. It's driving Madame Dupree to distraction."

"So I'm not losing my job?" Rosalyn felt almost guilty for asking, in light of what Lilly had been through. And yet she walked a fine line right now. She might dream of one day performing, but for the moment she still had to earn a living.

"It would be a shame to let go of two such valuable workers," Miss Lenoir responded. "So, ladies, are we happy with this arrangement?"

"Yes!" said both women without hesitation.

"In truth, I will be glad not to have to work late at night—at least for now," Lilly admitted.

Rosalyn thought she could understand the woman's sentiment. "I think it took a lot of bravery for you to return here," she told her.

Lilly's expression warmed with a tiny smile. "Thank you."

"Rosalyn, I won't keep you any longer from your duties," Miss Lenoir said. "Lilly and I have one or two more things to discuss privately."

Rosalyn nodded and stood up, thanking Miss Lenoir and offering a few words to Lilly before leaving the room.

She was making her way down the hall when she saw Tony. He was just about to mount the stairs that led to the men's dressing rooms, but he paused when he noticed her. She would have preferred he just kept going. She braced herself as she approached.

He gave her one of his bright, self-assured smiles. "I've been wanting to talk to you. I want to apologize if I overstepped my bounds last night. I hope there are no hard feelings?"

Rosalyn stared him down coldly. "How can you have the audacity to speak to me like that, after all the lies you've told me? You wanted me to think you were proposing to me, but you are married already!"

Instantly his expression cooled. "Who told you that?"

"It doesn't matter. But it's true, isn't it?"

He made an impatient gesture. "Rosalyn, this is *business*. I

311

meant what I said about us being a fantastic duo, about how well we perform together. There are opportunities out there for the taking! Don't allow personal matters to interfere with your chance to make a name for yourself."

He reached out to her, but Rosalyn withdrew sharply, taking a step back. "If I ever make it onstage again, I hope I will not have to perform with you," she hissed. "But if I should be forced to do so, rest assured I will not allow these mere *personal* matters to interfere. In the meantime, I'll thank you to stay away from me."

He actually had the effrontery to look insulted. "Is this really the thanks I get for all I've done for you?"

Rosalyn could only stare at him, astonished at his brazen arrogance. It was true he had given her valuable help. Her voice and her confidence were better for it. But she reminded herself that he had only been using it as bait to lure her toward a corrupt path.

Out of the corner of her eye, Rosalyn caught a movement. She turned, as Tony did, to see Lilly standing at the far end of the hall. Lilly gave them a brief, troubled look before turning away to disappear down another hallway.

"So it's like that, is it?" Tony said, returning his gaze to Rosalyn. "Very well." He turned away crisply and began to mount the stairs. After a few steps, he paused, turning back just long enough to add, "I do hope you enjoy my performance tonight. I know how much you like watching the real actors from your little corner in the wings."

His sudden verbal assault hit Rosalyn like a slap in the face. Suppressing a gasp, she turned and walked quickly away, her heart bruised but proud.

❧

"So it seems Lilly has returned," said Patrick as he and Rosalyn rode home together from the theater. A light snow was falling, but the blustery wind sent it stinging into their eyes and faces, so they'd decided to splurge on a cab.

"Yes. How did you know?"

"I saw her briefly in the hallway. Is that why you are so quiet tonight? You haven't said three words so far. What is the news? Is she coming back to work?"

"Yes, but on the children's production."

"So your job is safe, then."

"At least for the present. That gives me time to plan."

"Plan for . . . ?" Patrick queried.

"Helen showed me an announcement in *The Era* about an audition next week. It's for a traveling production of a comic opera by Offenbach. I'm going to try out for it. I have little real chance of getting a part, but I've got to start somewhere."

"I see," said Patrick thoughtfully.

The cab pulled to a stop. Rosalyn sighed. "I can't believe how happy I am to be home."

Patrick gave her a smile as he helped her down from the carriage. "I'm glad you think of this as home."

A light shone in the parlor window, and Rosalyn's heart leapt. Was Nate waiting up for her? She hurried up the steps. To her surprise, they were met at the door by Mary.

"Welcome back!" Mary spoke in an excited whisper, no doubt to keep from waking up the others in the house, and gave Rosalyn a warm hug.

"What are you doing up so late?" Rosalyn asked.

"Well, I couldn't go to bed before welcoming you back from your important trip to Paignton, could I?" As soon as Rosalyn had shed her coat and hat, Mary tugged her toward the parlor. "I want to hear all about it."

"Surely Nate has already told you everything," Rosalyn protested.

She came to a halt at the door of the parlor when she saw Nate standing by the sofa. Her heart made staccato leaps in a way that she now fully understood. Here was a man who had never been anything but honest with her. Although his directness had felt sharp at times, she now recognized that his genuine concern for her had always underlay it. And wisdom, too. His worries had not always been unwarranted.

As he looked at her now, his whole bearing was reserved, deferential. Rosalyn suddenly felt reticent, as well. It was brought on, paradoxically, by the unexpected rush of emotion she felt at seeing him. There would be no running into his arms tonight. She could only stand there and stare at him.

Patrick gently dislodged Mary's grasp on Rosalyn's arm. "Mary, don't forget that Rosalyn has had a very long day. I'm sure she will be glad to tell you all about it tomorrow."

"But—"

"Come along," Patrick admonished. "Don't argue, or we may wake the rest of the family."

Still put out, Mary looked as though she might resist further. But then her gaze traveled between Nate and Rosalyn, and a tiny smile curved her lips. "You're right," she said to Patrick. She gave Rosalyn another hug. "Good night. I look forward to hearing everything tomorrow."

It *had* been a very long day. Rosalyn ought to be following Patrick and Mary up the stairs, turning in for the night. Yet neither one had suggested it. Instead, they had left Rosalyn and Nate alone in the parlor.

"I'm sure you are tired," Nate said. "If you wish to go to bed, I understand."

"No, I'm glad you waited up." She walked toward him, closing the distance in order to make it easier to speak quietly. "I've been thinking a lot about what happened last night."

He frowned. "So have I. I apologize if I said anything to hurt you. It was not my intention."

She shook her head. "There's no need to apologize. You've been right about many things—most especially in your warning that the theater can be a dangerous place."

"Did something happen? Did anyone hurt you?" His fists clenched. "If Tony—"

"I'm fine," she assured him. But she could see from his reaction that it would be better not to tell him what had happened. "I just want you to know that I will always cherish the memory of what you did for me in Paignton—with the lights, I mean—and all your . . . kindnesses to me over these weeks."

Her words felt woefully inadequate. Rosalyn could only hope that somehow she had conveyed the depth of their meaning.

He was looking at her intently. She couldn't begin to guess what his thoughts were. "It is *you* who are the kind one. Last night I should not have berated you. I should have told you how impressive you were on that stage. How talented, and . . ." He swallowed. "And beautiful."

It cost him something to say those words. She could see it in his expression. He looked both pained and nervous. But it was the unvarnished honesty of it that drew her heart the most. It must have drawn in all of her, for she realized they were now standing very close.

"Thank you," she breathed.

He reached out to gently take her hands in his. "Rosalyn, I have to leave tomorrow."

"Yes, I know. For your two-week reserve duty." Like the rest of his family, she fervently clung to the hope that he would change his mind about his plans after that, about returning to the colors. She was heartsick at the thought of him leaving forever.

His eyes continued to search hers. Perhaps he was trying to

decipher her innermost thoughts, as she had been doing with him. "But after that, I will be leaving for India. It's something I *must* do."

She heard the resolve in his words. Disappointment settled on her, heavy and unwelcome.

"If I thought there was any chance you would come with me . . ."

The question hung in the air. Rosalyn's heart began to thud unsteadily as she realized what he was asking. To be married to this man was what she yearned for. But although she believed this love they were tentatively admitting to one another was real, she knew with anguish what choice she must make.

He was watching her, his whole body tense, waiting for her response. Perhaps he had a foreboding of what her answer would be.

"Please don't ask it of me," she begged. "I cannot do it."

Slowly he released a long breath, wincing in disappointment. He let go of her hands, taking a step back. "I understand."

He spoke with calm acceptance. She might even have called it stoicism. He loved her, but the words she wished to hear above all else, him offering to stay, were not forthcoming. There were so many facets to this man, and yet he was first and foremost a soldier. How could she ask him to give that up?

Rosalyn felt betrayed by her own heart. If she loved a man, shouldn't she want to do anything to be with him? But the idea of leaving England was as bitterly painful as the prospect of never seeing him again. How could she abandon her sisters? And how could she abandon this new life that, despite its challenges, made her feel for the first time as though she were living as the person she was meant to be? Above all, her ever-constant dread of the sea, very real and ever-present, held her captive to this island.

CHAPTER

23

I T WAS COLD in the barracks.

Nate had forgotten how easily the wind could find its way through the cracks in these buildings. They had not been the best design to begin with, and this one was clearly showing its age.

He sat on a low stool near the heating stove, cleaning his rifle. His hand ached from the cold, but Nate figured that wouldn't be an issue once he got to India.

The drills had gone well enough. Slippery frost on the ground had made some maneuvers a challenge, but the men in his company had shown admirable proficiency in marching and presenting arms. Nate had had no problems keeping up with the others in all aspects, including loading and firing. In a few days, Colonel Gwynn would come to observe their drills. Nate had no doubt the colonel would find him fit enough to resume his army career. He told himself it was better for them both that Rosalyn had turned down his inept and admittedly foolish proposal. She would never have been happy with such a life, and he ought to know by now that he could not allow his mind to be wrapped up in a woman. That path had already led to disaster once before.

The door to the barracks opened and a man entered, bringing a gust of cold air with him. This brought howls of complaint from the other men. Nate looked up and was surprised to see Jim Danvers. He had not expected to see his old comrade-in-arms until he'd rejoined his regiment.

Shoving the door shut against the bitter January wind, Danvers crossed the room and joined Nate by the stove. He was a tall man, with alarmingly red hair, who always stood out in a crowd.

Nate rose to shake his hand. Danvers somehow looked a lot older than the last time Nate had seen him. Had it really been just a year? His face was lined and dry, a result of years of sun scorching, although the tan had faded now in the British winter. Hints of grey were working their way into his temples, too.

Danvers' ready smile hadn't changed, though. "So you did come back! I thought for sure the easy life of a civilian would have tempted you to stay out."

To be given such a warm welcome after all that had happened began to ease the gloominess that had been plaguing him. He gave Danvers a wry smile. "Who could pass up these first-class accommodations?"

Danvers gave a grunt of amusement. "Looks like it's healed nicely," he remarked, observing Nate's hand as the two men released their grasp. "My scar's not so visible, of course." He patted his right side, just below his rib cage. "But after six weeks or so, they told me I was good as new. Since that was in the army's official report, it must be true."

"I'm glad to hear it. You didn't look so good the last time I saw you." Nate matched his friend's lighthearted tone, but in truth he spoke in all seriousness. He hadn't seen Danvers since the attack, after which his friend had been sent to a surgical hospital located in a nearby garrison. There weren't too many men Nate would count as friends, but Danvers was one. It was both ironic and painful to think Nate had once saved his life, when he was the one who'd put that life in jeopardy to begin with. Now that Danvers was here, Nate had an opportunity to come clean and set things right.

"I'm not as easy to dispatch as all that," Danvers returned. "Unless the cause of death be bad army food. Come over to the sergeant's mess, and I'll get you a proper meal."

"I haven't officially reenlisted yet," Nate protested. During these weeks of reserve drills, the men ate in a temporary messing hall that was indifferently run, to say the least.

"You're still a sergeant, aren't you?" Danvers insisted. "I'll see you get in the door. Besides, if you bring your fiddle, I guarantee no one will deny you entry."

Nate felt his mood lightening another notch. "Done."

◦◦◦◦◦

"I apologize for not seeking you out before today," Danvers said as they sat down to a meal of roast beef and potatoes that was, as he had promised, far better than what was offered in the general mess hall. "I just got back from a short leave and was of course immediately posted to guard duty. Isn't that always the way it works?"

Nate knew what he meant. Guard duty—a generally monotonous task taken in twenty-four-hour shifts—came around with irritating regularity. It was the bane of every soldier.

Nate sobered at Danvers' mention of guard duty. He frowned, forcefully spreading a slab of butter on his bread. His gaze focused more on the scar running the length of his hand than on the bread.

"Of course, guard duty isn't nearly as *interesting* here as it is in

Peshawar," Danvers continued. "But perhaps that kind of excitement is something one can do without, eh?"

Nate was astounded that Danvers could speak so cheerfully about the event that had nearly ended his life. He still had a vivid memory of Danvers' unconscious form, of the deathly pallor on his friend's face as Nate worked desperately to staunch the flow of blood until the medical men could arrive.

"I never had a chance to tell you what happened that night," Nate said.

"You don't have to. I got all the details later, after I was well enough to speak with the commander."

"I'm sure you got the official version."

The meaning of his words wasn't lost on Danvers. His eyebrows lifted. "So you did not dispatch three attackers while simultaneously managing to sound the alarm for reinforcements?"

"It was my fault they got into the guard house to begin with."

Danvers took a quick glance around and said quietly, "Perhaps we should discuss this after supper, when we can find a private corner?" The long table where they sat was rapidly filling with other diners. Many were throwing curious glances at Nate, no doubt wondering what he was doing there. Danvers probably didn't want them to overhear anything that could put Nate in a bad light.

Nate had to admit this was a good plan. Much as he wanted to unburden himself to his friend, he knew he could not publicly contradict what the army had decreed.

Danvers set about introducing him to the other men at the table. Aldershot was headquarters for a number of regiments, so few of the men here were known to him.

"Tell us, what have you been doing since returning to England?" Danvers asked. "What's out there for a veteran of Her Majesty's service? It will be a long time before I need that information, of course, but it's good knowledge to have."

Several of the men nodded at this. Perhaps they were nearing the end of their enlistment. Nate was glad that Danvers' injury wasn't going to keep him from continuing to serve in the army. He knew Danvers had never wanted to do anything else.

Nate told them about working at the ostler's, but it was when he spoke about his weeks filling in for his brother at the Opera Comique that he garnered their unqualified attention. Several of the men who were attached to engineering regiments were fascinated to hear his detailed description of how the limelights worked through the careful manipulation of oxygen and carbon gases. Others simply wanted to know what it was like to work backstage at a theater—especially for such a famous show. Nate spent the rest of the meal answering their questions. It surprised him to find he was looking back on his time in the theater with great satisfaction.

When he told them about the problems he'd faced moving supplies to Paignton, nearly everyone at the table had a comment. As seasoned soldiers, most had experienced the kind of logistical problems that arose with the need to meet unusual demands with limited resources.

The one thing Nate didn't talk about was Rosalyn. Every moment he'd spent with her—both joyful and painful—was a memory for him only.

"Nate is also an excellent fiddle player," Danvers informed them.

"Can you play the music from *HMS Pinafore?*" one of the men asked eagerly. He was a stout, round-faced man with short black hair that seemed to stand straight up on his head.

"Bayne is a fine tenor," another man explained, indicating the sergeant who had just spoken. "But despite that, he's still a first-rate soldier."

"In truth, I've never played anything from *Pinafore,*" Nate admitted. "But I'm sure I can find plenty of other music."

Much later, after Nate had played everything from jigs to marches, the room finally began to clear out as men made their way back to their sleeping quarters. By the time Nate set about wiping down his fiddle to put it away, he and Danvers were virtually alone. The remaining four men were busy at a game of cards in the opposite corner of the room.

Although it was late, Nate was reluctant to leave. There was still so much he wanted to get off his chest.

Danvers seemed in no hurry to go, either. He leaned back in his chair and lit a pipe, puffing on it for a few moments. When he spoke, it was to move the conversation in a direction that took Nate by surprise. "Tell me, Moran, will your sweetheart be joining you on this latest excursion to India?"

"No," said Nate. "She won't." He shut his fiddle case with a sharp snap. He paused, realizing that when Danvers had said "sweetheart," his thoughts had immediately turned to Rosalyn. "Ada broke off the engagement," he added, knowing that was who Danvers had been referring to.

"Tough luck," Danvers commiserated. "I suspected something like that. Tonight you talked about your life in London in great detail and yet said not one word about Ada."

"Women and the army don't mix," Nate declared bitterly.

Danvers raised his bushy red brows. "That's an interesting claim. Can you explain your reasoning?"

Nate met his eye. "I need to tell you what really happened the night we were attacked."

Danvers took another puff from his pipe. "I'm all ears."

"Just before we reported to the guard shack, the post from England arrived. There was a letter from Ada. It had been three months since I'd heard from her, and I was desperate to know what had caused the silence. Was she ill? Had some accident occurred?"

"It might just as well have been the vagaries of the mail service," Danvers said.

"That's true, but I was inclined to think the worst." Even now, it galled Nate to think of the hours—days, even—he'd spent worrying over her. "At any rate, I put the letter in my coat pocket, intending to read it at the guard shack. But Taylor and I were the first two posted on patrol. When we separated for our rounds, I took a quick scan of my area and determined all was quiet before taking myself to a place where I could finally tear open the letter and read it." He looked Danvers squarely in the eye. "It was the first time I was derelict in my duty, and it was because of a woman. Just the sort of thing you used to warn us against."

Danvers murmured something that might have been assent, but offered no criticism. He merely looked at Nate thoughtfully. "Care to tell me what was in the letter?"

"She told me she'd decided to marry someone else. It came completely out of the blue. I was so thunderstruck that I just stood there for who knows how long. When the attack came, I wasn't at my post. As you well know, we were caught flat-footed."

"But we rallied and eventually got the upper hand," Danvers pointed out. "You were instrumental in the victory."

Nate grimaced and shook his head, the overwhelming weight of his guilt as real as any physical pain. "By then the damage had been done—to you, especially."

"They did not achieve their aim, though."

"If you had died—"

"But I didn't." Danvers leaned forward, nearly poking Nate in the chest with his pipe as he brandished it for emphasis. "Moran, this is the army. We accept that there are risks. We know—all too well—that fatal errors will occur. It's a hard truth we live with every day."

This gravity and unflinching candor was unlike Danvers' usual buoyant demeanor. But Nate knew it was the underpinnings of his friend's soul. There was no better man in the army.

Nate swallowed. There was nothing he could say. Danvers was right, but it still did not assuage his guilt.

Danvers gave him a comforting slap on the arm. "Don't worry—you'll have plenty of opportunities to prove yourself on guard duty in the future."

"That's what I'm counting on," Nate replied grimly.

"Wait a moment." Danvers' eyes narrowed as he inspected Nate. "That's not the sole reason you're re-enlisting, surely?"

"I couldn't live with myself otherwise. It's a black mark on my life that I must erase."

"Moran, we all got medals! As far as the army is concerned, we're heroes!"

"But I know the truth," Nate insisted.

"So it's not enough to tell you I forgive you?"

"All I know is, I can never forgive *myself.*"

Danvers shook his head. He settled back in his chair and tamped down the tobacco in the bowl of the pipe, but it was clear he was considering Nate's words. "Moran, I don't think I mentioned what I was doing on leave this week. I was in Somerset making arrangements for my wedding."

"Congratulations," Nate said, his astonishment temporarily overriding his worries. "This seems unexpected." He'd never known Danvers to express any particular interest in getting married. In fact, he used to mercilessly ridicule some of the men—Nate included—about mooning too much over women.

"It's true that I never considered myself the marrying kind,"

Danvers acknowledged. "But that has changed. And I have *you* to thank for it."

Nate stared at him in surprise. "How so?"

"When I was at the hospital recovering, the chaplain's daughter came to visit me every day. It was her habit to extend help and comfort to all the patients. But somehow, she ended up taking a special interest in me. And eventually . . ." The twinkle returned to his eye. "Well, I took an interest in *her*, too. If I hadn't been forced to stay behind with the 89th, I never would have met her. On the long voyage home, as we were returning with the regiment to England, we became engaged."

Still dumbfounded at this news, Nate could say nothing.

Danvers gave him a sympathetic eye. "My friend, it would appear you've been castigating yourself for no reason. If you return to the colors because you believe it's your calling, that's all well and good. But if you do it solely out of guilt, you will only be compounding the error."

"No," said Nate. "I'm happy—amazed, even—at how things have turned out. But that still doesn't absolve me for what happened."

"Perhaps not. But then, absolution doesn't come through what *we* can do, does it? It comes from another source. One greater than ourselves."

This was perhaps the most surprising thing to come out of Danvers' mouth all evening. He was not the kind of man who spoke of spiritual matters, either directly or indirectly. It may have been a novel way to receive such a godly reminder, but Nate knew his friend was right. Never once had Nate gone to God to ask for forgiveness. He'd been too intent on earning it.

"You have changed." Nate was too choked up to say anything more. As the weight of self-reproach that he'd been carrying all these months began to lift from his shoulders, he realized just how heavy the burden had been.

For the briefest moment, it looked as though Danvers would succumb to emotion, as well. He blinked and turned aside, ostensibly to set down his pipe, which he did with overly deliberate care. By the time he turned back to Nate, he was able to shrug and give him a sly grin. "If I've changed, I suppose we can blame it on spending too much time with the daughter of a chaplain."

Rosalyn didn't have time to dawdle. Her errands had taken longer than she expected, and she needed to be at the theater soon. But still she paused at the window of a pawnshop. After weeks of searching, she knew full well it was like looking for a needle in a haystack. Still, it was a dream she clung to.

She stood at the door, telling herself there really was no time to go in. While she lingered in indecision, a woman half-walked, half-stumbled out of the shop. She had no coat, and Rosalyn saw her flinch as the bitter wind hit her. She bumped into Rosalyn, offering no apology as she walked past. But Rosalyn had gotten a look at her face and immediately recognized Penny, the woman who had taunted her at the brothel. It seemed a lifetime ago.

"Penny!" she called.

The woman stopped, turned. "Who's askin'?" she said crossly.

Rosalyn approached her. "Do you recognize me?"

Penny hugged herself in a vain effort to ward off the cold. She met Rosalyn's eye blankly. "Now how would I know someone like you?" she replied, taking in Rosalyn's appearance. Rosalyn was dressed simply enough, in sturdy leather boots and a warm woolen coat she'd recently purchased secondhand. But it was a far cry from the rags Penny had on.

"A few months ago, I met you at . . . Mollie Hurdle's." Rosalyn didn't even want to say the name out loud, but she forced herself to do it.

Penny approached her, scrutinizing her face. Then remembrance dawned. "Miss I'm-from-Bristol! Oh, what a lot of bother you caused." Her words were punctuated with a rattling shiver as a blast of cold air hit them.

"Where's your coat?" Rosalyn asked, genuinely concerned.

"Well, I had to pawn it, didn't I? The old woman finally kicked me out—and on Christmas Day, too! But a person's got to eat. So away the coat goes." She sniffled, wiping her nose with her hand as she looked Rosalyn over once more. "You're doin' well for yourself."

The truth was, Rosalyn had spent the past two weeks in a kind of daze. She exerted herself wholeheartedly at the theater, working at the job she was grateful she still had. She'd also followed up on a few leads Helen had given her for reputable singing coaches—although she wasn't sure how she was going to afford them.

But so often, especially when she was at home, she felt nearly overcome by an aching sense of loss. She missed Nate. Her mind still turned over in regret.

Now, as she beheld Penny, her troubles seemed dim indeed. Rosalyn had so much to be thankful for. Perhaps she hadn't been thankful enough for all the ways God had watched—and would continue to watch—over her. "Come with me," Rosalyn offered. "I know a place you can get warm and get something to eat."

It would make her late for work, but she had to do it. She couldn't leave Penny here on the street. She would take her to the charity house, where they would offer Penny warmth and food and a chance to recover her life—if she was willing.

Penny looked at her in surprise. "You want to help me?"

"Yes. But we'll have to go quickly."

She took Penny to the charity house, leaving her in the care of Mrs. Fletcher. By the time Rosalyn had raced off to work,

Penny was seated by the fire with a warm shawl around her, eating a hearty bowl of soup. She had accepted all these things with reluctance, distrust being well-ingrained into her about the motives of others, even those offering kindness. Whether Penny would stay at the house or leave because she felt too chafed by the strictures of living there was anyone's guess. But at least Rosalyn knew she was safe and warm for tonight.

When she arrived at the theater, she was surprised to find herself approached by Mr. Cellier. "Miss Bernay, have you a moment?"

"Yes, of course," she replied, astounded not only that he would want to talk to her, but at his formal address.

"I don't think I ever got a chance to tell you what a fine job you did in Paignton."

Her eyes widened. "Thank you."

"It takes a special and, I would say, very flexible kind of person to be able to perform well under such less-than-ideal conditions. You seem to be such a person. I hope you will continue to seek out opportunities on the stage. I thought you would like to know that Mr. Carte is planning another touring production of *Pinafore*. We'll be holding auditions in the near future. I believe there could be a place for you in the chorus, should you choose to try out for it."

Rosalyn could barely believe what she was hearing. "Thank you, sir!" she exclaimed, barely able to suppress her excitement. Her chance to return to the stage might be happening faster than she'd anticipated.

⁂

Nate left Colonel Gwynn's office and walked along the rows of plain buildings, deep in thought. As expected, the colonel had recommended him for a return to duty. He'd been surprised when Nate asked for a few days to think it over.

Nate paused at the end of the street, looking out at the large drill grounds beyond. Ever since his conversation with Danvers, his mind and heart had been in turmoil. An enormous burden had been lifted from his soul, and yet so many questions remained. From his childhood, Nate had wanted only to be a soldier. He'd been living with this plan for so long, it seemed unbelievable that he should now be considering giving it up.

Even if he returned to London, what then? Rosalyn would continue to chase her dreams of the theater. He'd received a letter yesterday from Mary, telling him Rosalyn already had hopes of joining a new traveling production. He could not conceive of simply returning to the life he'd led before he met her. He might do better to stay with the army after all.

He returned to the barracks to find a letter waiting for him on his bed. The camp messenger must have left it. Nate quickly tore open the envelope to see who it was from and stared down at the letter in surprise. It was from Mr. Gunn.

Five minutes later, Nate knew he had his answer.

CHAPTER

24

ROSALYN ARRIVED at the theater early. She'd just had her first lesson with a singing master whose studio was nearby. She was still thinking over some of the particulars of the lesson as she walked in the stage door. So intent was she on her thoughts that she nearly bumped into Patrick.

"What are you doing here?" Rosalyn exclaimed.

"Good afternoon to you, too," Patrick replied jovially. "There were a few things that needed my attention, so I thought I'd get here early. I'm heading backstage now. I'll walk with you."

"All right." She was going to ask what specifically had brought him here, but when they reached the wings of the stage, her attention was arrested by the sound of a violin. "That's odd," she said. "Is someone still here from the children's matinee?"

"Could be," Patrick said with a shrug.

Rosalyn followed the sound, which she could tell was coming from the orchestra pit. She recognized the slow, tender ballad immediately and heard the lyrics in her head.

A maiden fair to see, the pearl of minstrelsy,
A bud of blushing beauty . . .

It was the ballad sung by Ralph Rackstraw, pining for the woman who could never be his. Rosalyn could feel the yearning and tenderness like a physical embrace. She recognized not just the melody but the hand of the man playing it. She walked to the front of the stage, knowing even before she peered over the edge who she would see there.

Nate stood alone in the orchestra pit, playing the music he'd steadfastly refused to play before. He kept playing as though unaware anyone else was there, pouring his soul into the music. He reached the last stanza, and Rosalyn could still hear the words as well as the music.

O pity, pity me!
A captain's daughter she,
And I, that lowly suitor!

Nate brought the final notes to a long, lingering close. He had just shown his love for her in the boldest, clearest way he could.

Rosalyn made her way down the short steps into the orchestra pit as Nate lowered the violin, carefully setting it aside. When his loving gaze met hers, Rosalyn did not hesitate. Once more, just as she had in Paignton, she raced over and threw her arms around him. This time, it wasn't merely an impulsive gesture. This time, she knew this was the right place to be. She held on to that one thought despite the multitude of questions crowding her mind.

Nate gently pried her from his neck just long enough to bring his hands to her face and pull her into a kiss. She was nearly undone by the pleasure of it. Never could she have imagined a kiss could be so beautiful, so powerful and tender. She kissed him unreservedly, with all of her being, and he answered back. A finer duet than she could ever have dreamed of.

After a time, his arms enfolded her, drawing her close to his chest. She could feel his heart beating as wildly as hers as he caressed her hair.

"I should like to remain just like this forever, I think," Rosalyn murmured.

"I was thinking the same thing." He paused. "I was also thinking what excellent payment the musicians here get. Perhaps I ought to apply."

She smiled against his chest. Then the meaning of what he'd said found its way into her happily muddled thoughts. She pulled back to look at him. "Are you not going back to the army?"

"No. But the truth is, I already have another job. Mr. Gunn has asked me to join the upcoming tour as a stage manager."

"You . . . you're . . ." she stammered. Her mind could barely take it all in.

"I just finished meeting with him. It will be similar to the job I did in Paignton, but there are other duties, as well. It sounds like just the kind of challenge I would like; however, I told him I could only accept if there is time for us to get married first."

"Married!"

"You don't think I'm going to risk having any man think he can win you away from me, do you?"

Rosalyn's heart longed to say yes. But so many questions remained. "This is only a six-month tour. What happens after that? I know how important your army career has been to you. If, somewhere down the road, you should decide to return—"

"No," Nate replied firmly. "Believe me, I've had plenty of time to think this over. I won't be going back." He took her hands in his. "One day soon I will tell you the whole story. But that part of my life is done now."

"I believe you. But I can hardly believe this change." Her words came out rather breathlessly due to her awareness of the warmth of Nate's touch.

"Patrick has been badgering me about becoming a policeman. He insists I'd rise through the ranks just as quickly as I did in the army and could maybe even become a detective. That might happen someday, perhaps. We will have to take each day as it comes."

He kissed her again. This time it was long and lingering, filled with the promise of a lifetime together.

She took a step back, placing her hands on her hips, doing her best to look and sound stern. "You seem to be counting on quite a lot of things, Mr. Moran."

He shook his head and *tsked*, giving a very creditable imitation of Mr. Barker. "You'll have to work hard to become a better actor than that."

She swatted at him playfully but did not resist when he took hold of her and once more drew her close. Caressing his cheek, she murmured, "Here is one thing that I guarantee is not an act."

He accepted her invitation without hesitation, kissing her and wrapping her in his arms. She melted into his warmth, his solid frame. Here was a man to hold on to, someone to walk with together—wherever life should take them.

Author's Note

IN THIS BOOK, I was able to merge three of my longtime interests and passions: the operettas of Gilbert and Sullivan, life and times in Victorian England, and the work of George Müller.

When I was about twelve years old, my parents took me to see my first Gilbert and Sullivan production. That was the first of many. The operettas are funny, with wildly unbelievable plots, and the music is gorgeous. Many companies, both amateur and professional, still perform these operettas today. They are endlessly adaptable and highly enjoyable. If you ever have an opportunity to attend a show, I highly recommend it.

The Captain's Daughter is set during the time of the original production of *HMS Pinafore*. Many of the characters in this book are based on real people: Jessie Bond, Helen Lenoir, George Grossmith, and others of the lead players and the theater management. The single show in Paignton to protect the copyright for *The Pirates of Penzance* actually happened. The Bernay sisters, the Morans, and all of the chorus members are fictional. I have veered from the actual historical record in a few minor ways, but I have done my best to remain true to the spirit of the time and to the people who presented these wonderful shows.

My love for Gilbert and Sullivan was probably the beginning of my fascination with Victorian England. As an admitted history geek, I love reading books about that era, as well as novels written during the time. The nineteenth century was one of rapid change, with huge strides in science and invention. Railways, telegraph, and photography began to turn their world into one we'd recognize today. New avenues opened up for women to support themselves independently. The London School of Medicine for Women was established in 1874, making it possible for women like Julia Bernay to pursue a career in medicine. More and more women were taking to the stage, too, although that profession was as precarious then as it is today.

Religious and spiritual inquiry was a very real part of most Victorians' lives, both in the intellectual approach via biblical research, and in the practical application of everyday life. The life of George Müller is one example.

In the 1840s, Müller opened a small home for orphans in Bristol, England. He determined from the start never to solicit donations or money; he was a man of fervent prayer and believed that God would always provide. In time his work grew, along with the buildings, until by the end of the century, the orphanage was caring for over two thousand children! They were a very tangible example of God's faithfulness in answering prayers. Several good biographies of Müller have been written, including *Delighted in God!* by Roger Steer.

Müller's story is an inspiring example to Christians. A few years ago, I began to wonder what a person who had been raised in this atmosphere of trusting God to meet every need would be like. When they went out into the world as adults, how would they respond to life's challenges? That's when the idea for this series was born.

Acknowledgments

MY HEARTFELT THANKS to the many people who helped make this book possible:

David Long, for bringing me on board to Bethany House, and Jessica Barnes, my fabulous editor, for your enthusiasm, patience, and excellent guidance. Thanks to you both and to everyone at Bethany House for believing in this series.

Jessica Alvarez, my wonderful agent.

Elaine Luddy Klonicki, beta reader and now critique partner extraordinaire, for giving me the vital insights into my characters that I so desperately needed, and for saving this book when I was pretty sure it was not salvageable.

Karen Anders, for mentoring me over the years and specifically for helping me brainstorm the initial draft.

Sonja Foust and all of the Durham Savoyards cast and crew, who allowed me to spend time backstage at their production of *HMS Pinafore* and steal ideas for this book. The operetta may be well over a hundred years old, but it is evergreen.

Alan Jessopp at the George Müller Charitable Trust in Bristol, England, for an enlightening and inspiring two hours kindly answering my questions about daily life at Müller's orphanage and the Trust's continuing work today.

Georgette Nicolaides, for the violin demonstration, answering some admittedly strange questions about violin playing, and being brave enough to let me try my hand at it.

Everyone in the North Raleigh Fellowship, for their love and prayers, and for believing in me and cheering me on.

And, as always, my husband, Jim, for unfailing support and love.

To God, the Author and Source of all good things, who has provided so many amazing opportunities for me to write, and whose blessings I see daily.

Jennifer Delamere's debut Victorian romance, *An Heiress at Heart*, was a 2013 RITA award finalist in the inspirational category. Her follow-up novel, *A Lady Most Lovely*, received a starred review from *Publishers Weekly* and the Maggie Award for Excellence from Georgia Romance Writers. Jennifer earned a BA in English from McGill University in Montreal, where she became fluent in French and developed an abiding passion for winter sports. She's been an editor of nonfiction and educational materials for nearly two decades, and lives in North Carolina with her husband.

Sign Up for Jennifer's newsletter!

Keep up to date with Jennifer's news on book releases and events by signing up for her email list at jenniferdelamere.com.

If you enjoyed *The Captain's Daughter*, you may also like...

Growing up on the streets of London, Rosemary and her friends have had to steal to survive. But as a rule, they only take from those who can afford the loss. They've all learned how to blend into high society for jobs. When, on the eve of WWI, a client contracts Rosemary to determine whether a friend of the king is loyal to Britain or Germany, she's in for the challenge of a lifetime.

A Name Unknown by Roseanna M. White
SHADOWS OVER ENGLAND
roseannawhite.com

More Historical Fiction

In 1917, British nurse and war widow Evelyn Marche is trapped in German-occupied Brussels. She works at the hospital by day and as a waitress by night. But she also has a secret: She's a spy for the resistance. When a British plane crashes in the park, Evelyn must act quickly to protect the injured soldier who has top-secret orders and a target on his back.

High as the Heavens by Kate Breslin
katebreslin.com

Lady Georgina Hawthorne has kept a secret her entire life. She must marry during her debut season or she could lose everything—and Colin McCrae is not her idea of eligible. But as their paths cross, their ongoing clash of wits has both Georgina and Colin questioning their priorities.

An Elegant Façade by Kristi Ann Hunter
HAWTHORNE HOUSE
kristiannhunter.com

◊BETHANYHOUSE

Stay up to date on your favorite books and authors with our free e-newsletters. Sign up today at bethanyhouse.com.

Find us on Facebook. facebook.com/bethanyhousepublishers

Free exclusive resources for your book group! bethanyhouse.com/anopenbook